MEAN STREETS

By the time Theo Warner finally stepped out from his drugstore it was ten after eight and Tommy, Jo and Manford White were inside the tavern. They had gone in after Jo saw Theo's brother leave more than an hour earlier, Jo figuring Theo would now probably be the one to stay and lock up and if they weren't going to freeze to death they had better wait somewhere else than in the car. She decided she could keep watch through the window of the tavern, something that made Tommy happy.

As Theo walked to the corner and then headed east on Belmont, Tommy and White grabbed their coats and started out after him. Jo waited until they had turned the corner too and then walked out to the car.

The two stayed on the opposite side of the street from Theo and about thirty feet behind him. The snow and cold that they had been complaining about over the previous two hours had turned into their friend. Only two people passed them on the street, both with heads lowered. Theo walked east to Broadway and then headed south. When two blocks later he turned onto Barry Street, nearing home, they began to close on him.

STATE STREET

RICHARD WHITTINGHAM

BANTAM BOOKS

– NEW YORK –
– TORONTO – LONDON –
– SYDNEY – AUCKLAND

STATE STREET

A Bantam Crime Line Book / published by arrangement with
Donald I. Fine, Inc.

PUBLISHING HISTORY
Donald I. Fine edition published 1991
Bantam edition / January 1993

CRIME LINE and the portrayal of a boxed "cl" are trademarks of Bantam Books, a division of Bantam Doubleday Dell Publishing Group, Inc.

Library of Congress Catalog Card Number 90-56049.

ISBN 0-553-29827-5

Published simultaneously in the United States and Canada

Bantam Books are published by Bantam Books, a division of Bantam Doubleday Dell Publishing Group, Inc. Its trademark, consisting of the words "Bantam Books" and the portrayal of a rooster, is Registered in U.S. Patent and Trademark Office and in other countries. Marca Registrada. Bantam Books, 666 Fifth Avenue, New York, New York 10103.

PRINTED IN THE UNITED STATES OF AMERICA

RAD 0 9 8 7 6 5 4 3 2 1

To the memory of
Jim Ertel,
Editor and Friend

ACKNOWLEDGMENTS

I would like to thank the following for their special help during the creation of *State Street*: former acting Police Superintendent of Chicago and onetime Chief of Homicide Joe DiLeonardi, Homicide detectives Gary Bulava and Bobby Brown, Burglary detective Mike Herbert, and former police investigator Bill Ryan.

In addition, I owe a great debt of gratitude to Knox Burger for his support and editorial guidance.

Chicago, Chicago,
That toddlin' town
Chicago, Chicago,
I'll show you around . . .

On State Street,
That great street,
I just want to say,
They do things,
They don't do
On Broadway . . .

1

HE FELT the rush of hot, oily air when he pushed open the door and stepped out into the crazyquilt glitter of nighttime Chicago.

He paused there just outside the lounge whose name pulsated from a window in lime green script—Palm Gardens . . . Palm Gardens . . . Palm Gardens—standing underneath a large green-and-gold palm tree sculpted of neon tubing that hung out over the sidewalk and flickered down on him . . .

Liars . . . liars—the word kept ringing in his head without meaning. He stepped into the clutter of people swarming the sidewalk this sultry summer night, a shuffling obstacle course surging back and forth between him and the unmarked Plymouth out at the curb parked beneath a No Parking/Tow Away Zone sign. He could feel himself dissolving into the glitz of the night, enveloped by the hypnotic blinking lights with their throbbing colors cascading over everything and orchestrated by the clatter of dissonant street sounds. It gave the people, the cars, the movement and noise a flapping staccato effect like a fast-forward movie. He made his way through it to the car, thinking of Times Square and other nightmares. Liars . . . liars . . . so many of them.

He loosened his tie, the perspiration was already flow-

ing, he could taste its saltiness. From his inside coat pocket he took a slender spiral notebook and began scribbling in it. When he finished he said to himself, "Next stop, Queerborn and Perversion." One of his people would be waiting for him there.

When he turned at Dearborn onto Division Street he saw the place, The Super Fly.

"My lady of the night, my old friend." He buttoned his collar, used the rearview mirror to be sure his tie was straight. He could feel a clammy wetness inside his clothes. She was sitting there at a table by herself, toying with the swizzle stick in an Old Fitz–and–ginger ale and looking bored. Tina, that was the name she went by on the street, didn't dress like a hooker, liked to think of herself as a call girl. He doubted she'd even held hands for less than a double sawbuck since she was sixteen, and he knew she only worked the street. He nodded toward her and she cocked her head, sending him a give-me-a-break look, but got up and followed him out into the street.

"I got your message, Joey," she said. "Meeting Joey Morrison like this doesn't do great things for my reputation on the street, you know. Plus it's prime time. The housewares convention's in town."

"I'm thinking maybe you might've run across a little street talk that might help me. C'mon, I'll buy you a cup of coffee."

He watched her strike her hooker's pose, hand on hip, three-inch spike heel dug into the sidewalk, toe moving back and forth. "At least when I return a favor to you I don't have to do it by copping your joint, if you'll pardon the pun. Not like the rest of your buddies."

Sitting across from her, using a handkerchief to blot the perspiration from his forehead, temples, neck, he wondered why she wasn't sweating, her skin in fact looked cold, marbleized. Suddenly his beeper went off and he knew he had to be someplace else.

Sliding out of the booth, he reached over and gave his whore's chin a little chuck, "It's been short . . . but sweet."

"Hey, Morrison, you're not the only quickie in the world," she said.

And he was up, walking toward the door, back out into the oppressive night . . .

In front of the three-story apartment house the street was alive with the curious and morbid, milling about in the sweltering heat. A paddy wagon and two squad cars were already there, the beacons on top of the cars sending beams of light sweeping across the faces of the neighboring apartment buildings. A fat uniformed cop who had logged more than thirty years on the job was at the doorway, sweating. He went on past, flashing the badge, and climbed the stairs.

Inside the apartment he nodded to the two uniformed cops in the living room but didn't recognize them. Then things began to register . . . cheap furniture, thrift shop specials, the place dirty, stains on the carpet remnant, old wallpaper with a veneer of grime, a couple of empty beer bottles next to a large ashtray overflowing with cigarette butts, a bra and sweater on the floor next to the sofa, two highball glasses with a little water left at the bottom of each from melted ice cubes, lipstick on one of the glasses, a stale odor hanging in the air.

"Crime lab's not here yet," one of the cops was saying. "Pretty ugly one. Little girl, maybe thirteen, fourteen, looks like a rape, strangulation, the body's in the bedroom . . ." The words seemed to run together, coming from the mouth of this unrecognizable cop who seemed to know him. "The mother's out in the kitchen, came home with her boyfriend and found the kid, been to a bingo game, she said, and didn't get home till about nine-thirty. The sergeant, Kornhoffer, he's talkin' to her out there. She's half in the bag, didn't know they served booze at bingo games . . ."

On into the short hall that led to the kitchen, the sound of garbled voices coming from down there, he felt like he was gliding now. He looked into the bedroom. The body was on the floor, small and still. He could smell death in the room. There was an odor to it, singular and gagging. For ten years he had smelled it now, like working in the stockyards, only the slaughtered weren't cattle.

He walked over to the body. Thirteen was about right. Long brown hair splayed out behind her head. Eyes open and protruding. Caked blood around nose and mouth, one cheek swollen and an ugly purple color. Had she been pretty? No telling now. Bruises on her forearms and shoulders from trying to hold off whoever was beating her. Jeans and panties on the floor. Blouse torn open and the bra still on but pushed up above her small breasts. There was a pool of blood on the floor between her thighs, more of it in her pubic hairs. He felt sick at the sight of it. The blue and red discoloration on her throat defined where life had been squeezed from her young body. He looked around the room for the instrument of death—a rope, pantyhose, telephone cord—but nothing sent him a signal.

When he looked back at the girl, her eyes were closed. Weren't they open before? Oh, Christ. What was that coming from one of the eyes? He dropped to a knee beside her. A tear, weaving its wet path down her face. And then her eyes were open, terror-filled, and her spine-chilling scream tore through him as she grabbed him by the coat sleeves, pulling him toward her, shrieking louder and louder in horror—

MORRISON BOLTED up in bed, the sound of the scream still hanging in the air; no, in his head. It was silent in the room. He was drenched in sweat and breathing heavily.

He swung over to sit on the edge of the bed, listening for movement elsewhere in the house. Had he scared the kids awake again? A month ago he had cried out from another grisly dream and both of his frightened little girls had run from their bedroom out to the kitchen, screaming themselves, until he got there to calm them down.

But there was no other noise, just the echo of the screaming in his mind, and the sound of his heart pounding. Suddenly he realized he was very cold, the soaked top of his pajamas was stuck to his body. He took it off and tried to dry himself with it but it was too damp. He went to the bathroom to get a towel. When he came back he grabbed a T-shirt from the chest of drawers, put it on, then went to the closet and took out the bottle of schnapps he kept there these days, filled a water glass halfway full and went back to bed, wide-awake. The red numerals on the digital clock radio told him it was 4:48. The schnapps helped. At least he was getting warmer.

Thank God he'd gotten out of Homicide, Morrison thought as he sat propped up in bed, feeling the sting of the liquor in the lining of his empty stomach. Out more than a year now, but it still kept coming back, the bodies, the gore, the smell. The last of the schnapps was soothing. Another glass, he decided, getting up and going to the closet, one more and maybe he might get back to sleep.

2

VINNY WAS sitting at a little Formica-topped table by the window in a hashhouse on Wilson Avenue. In the condensation-frosted window pane he caught his reflection and smiled back at it. Vinny was convinced he looked like Tony Bennett. A couple of years ago in an article about old crooners in *People* magazine he'd seen him in a photo with Frank Sinatra when Sinatra was skinny and Bennett was making a bundle singing about leaving his heart in San Francisco. He didn't look like Bennett though. He had the same kind of narrow face and hawk-nose maybe, that was about all. But then that was Vinny. When he was really skinny, he always thought of himself as wiry, and when he started to get puffy about a year ago from all the drinking and drugs, he told himself he was finally filling out . . . nicely. Vinny sometimes pictured himself playing Vegas and palling around with Sinatra.

He crumpled up a handful of paper napkins and started to rub clear a panel in the window so he could see what was going on in the street. When he finished he stared absently through the watery trickles on the window at the whirling snow out there and the people walking through it bent against the piercing Chicago wind, especially punishing here so close to the lake. Most were headed toward the el station a block away.

The snow had begun in the early morning, a heavy fall with mothball-size flakes, the wet kind that floated to the pavement and clung there, accumulating in deep, slushy layers. A radio behind the counter was on and some guy with a too-friendly voice was talking about the weather, saying that things were not going to get any better, perhaps as much as six inches of new snow before it would end late that night. He sounded like he was happy about it, Vinny thought.

Vinny had no worry about getting to work in the snowstorm because he didn't have a job, in fact he had not held a job for more than a month or two since he dropped out of high school when he was sixteen, eight years earlier. So he just sat there sipping his coffee, feeling now a kind of numbness setting in and thinking he probably ought to go home and get some sleep.

It had been a good night. He had made a decent score, dealt the stuff away within an hour after he had lifted it for an even three hundred less, of course, the twenty-five percent "street tax" that the Outfit assessed and he religiously paid so that he could continue his career without being kneecapped or worse. Then he had picked up another yard and a half, as Vinny called it, a hundred-fifty in monetary translation, in a poker game in a basement over on Winthrop, one he had joined with particular pleasure because three firewater-guzzling Apaches from the neighborhood had been lured into it. Not just them, but there was a bonus thrown in too, the hillbilly from West Virginia. He was known around Uptown as Coalman because he'd worked in a coal mine just outside Wheeling until it closed down before coming to Chicago. According to Vinny, Coalman was just as stupid as the Apaches and just as much a born loser.

Leroy Tolliver, a black, known to be a pimp and whose ladies sometimes lowered themselves to work Uptown, had gotten the game going. Tolliver was not from the neighborhood, just wandered into Uptown routinelessly from somewhere else in the city. He was probably from the west side, Vinny figured, because for some reason or other the south-side blacks seldom came into the neighborhood. They rode the els to the north side to roll drunks or do a quick hit on somebody on a station platform, but they almost never made it to street level in Uptown. Maybe they had better taste than the west-side blacks. Wherever Tolliver was from, no one really cared. When he came he always got a game going. And he always won. Vinny won some of the time.

Thank God somebody, sometime decided to let the Apaches wander off their reservations, Vinny thought as he fiddled with his coffee cup. Most of them who made it to Chicago ended up in Uptown, Uptown Redskins they were known as around the neighborhood, like they were some kind of football team. They fitted right into the milieu, which had a kind of special squalor to it, peopled by alcoholic Indians, hillbillies from Appalachia and the Ozarks, smalltime crooks, dopers and pushers, halfway-house denizens, runaways turned kid prostitutes and others who one way or another were on the flip side of life's rich pageant. The streets were dirty and dangerous, the taverns worse. Vinny Salerno had lived on the edge of it for three years now.

Vinny loved it when they got some Indians in a game. The Apaches would end up drunk after about ten hands, start losing their ass and get drunker. But he had to play the scene right, or they might get into the other game they liked to play when they were sloshed, which usually involved pounding somebody's face into something that resembled a head of cauliflower. Vinny always marveled at how one of them could be lurching across the room grunting and mumbling like he had a couple of golf balls in his mouth one minute, and fighting just as ferociously as if he was rock-cold sober the next.

The one waitress in the place finally came by to refill his coffee cup. He flashed her a little Tony Bennett smile from the corner of his mouth as she poured. "Anything new in the neighborhood?" Vinny asked.

Her eyes moved from the coffee cup to him. "It's snowing."

"No shit."

She shrugged and took the coffee pot back behind the counter.

Vinny knew her from the neighborhood, a boozer who had the sad, watery eyes and the tremble in her hands to prove it. But she made it to the greasehouse every morning at six and worked until two in the afternoon. He knew her only as Clare and that she hung out mostly at J.J.'s, a bar down the street on Wilson Avenue whose habitués were mostly hillbillies who liked to fight just as much as the Apaches, but more often than not did it with knives or broken beer bottles. Vinny had seen her in there a couple of times but never talked to her, never bothered to. She was not old, maybe thirty, but was known as a dead fuck around the neighborhood because whoever went home with her after she was sufficiently blotto ordinarily ended up working out on a lifeless body that had passed into oblivion as soon as her butt hit the mattress. He mopped up the coffee that had spilled over into the saucer with some more napkins, laced it with sugar and powdered cream, and went back to looking out the window.

As he watched the snow, the recollection drifted into Vinny's mind as chillingly as if it was coming in straight off Lake Michigan; it had been the goddamn snow that had almost done him in . . . forever. What was he, seventeen, eighteen maybe, then? Down where he grew up, around Grand and Racine, a corridor section known as the Patch, because that's what it was, a patch of pure Italian turf where everyone had a special territorial pride, a snow just like this mess had started falling during the night. It was about five in the morning, very dark under the cloud-shrouded sky when he kicked in the basement window at Fryar's Appliance Store.

It seemed so easy, he had thought back then, because he was quick, he was the cat. It was a snap, just go up and spring the door to the first floor with a crowbar, even though it set off a burglar alarm, run into the showroom and grab a couple of portable color TVs, then back down to the basement and shove them out the window. And he was gone, catlike quick. God they were heavy, he remembered.

He got down the alley a block and a half with them, turned onto Sangamon Street, another block, then past a few row houses to the right one and trudged down a gangway to the back of Al Scarpano's house. Breathing heavily he pounded on the back door until Al looked out and saw the skinny, panting kid with the silly smile on his face standing there with a television set sitting in the snow on each side of him. Scarpano recognized him, having dealt a few things for Vinny in the last couple of months, so he unlatched the door and let him in. The kid brought the sets in one at a time and put them on the kitchen table.

By the time Al Scarpano got back from the bedroom where he'd gone to get the eighty dollars he said he would pay for the two sets, two uniformed cops were not only at the door but through it, having followed Vinny's footprints in the freshly fallen snow from the basement window of Fryar's to Al Scarpano's backdoor. A few minutes later it was like a police retirement party, there were so many cops in Scarpano's kitchen. Burglary detectives not only grabbed the two TV sets from Fryar's, their price tags still dangling from them, but elsewhere in the house found about eight thousand dollars' worth of similar merchandise and some necklaces, bracelets, earrings and other jewelry they felt safely sure were not part of Al Scarpano's hope chest. They confiscated all of it. And with a sudden burst of police benevolence let Al, who had been standing there in pajama bottoms and an undershirt, glowering through it all, put on some clothes before taking him and Vinny over to the Chicago Avenue precinct station for booking.

Scarpano was back on the street that afternoon, his little brother Joey making bail for him, which had required more than a little pocket change. But it was no surprise because the Scarpanos, even though they were somewhat smalltime, were well connected with the Outfit.

Vinny was not so fortunate in his connections. All he could do was call his older sister, who lived with their mother. In a little trouble, is what Vinny told her, and he didn't want their ma to know, not to upset her. He told his sister where he currently was, and she told him flat out to go screw himself and that he was nothing more than a piss-ass punk who could rot in jail for the rest of his life as far as she was concerned.

But his mother heard her and got on the phone and so Vinny told her he had been in the wrong place at the wrong time and had been wrongly arrested along with this jerk who was a crook although he hadn't known the guy was a crook until the cops got there and told him. It seems, he said, that they thought he might have swiped two TV sets. Vinny hadn't, of course, he assured his ma, but they were holding him on $5,000 bail anyway, which meant he needed $500 to get out of jail. He was still at the precinct lockup on Chicago Avenue, but God knows what would happen to him if he got sent over to Cook County jail with all the gangbangers and hopheads and other assorted creeps there, he told her.

It took his mother until the next day to get the $500 because the bank was already closed by the time they had gotten around to letting Vinny make his one telephone call, but she withdrew the money and sent her unsympathetic daughter unhappily down to the stationhouse to bail Vinny out.

Vinny, however, would probably have been safer in a cell with a couple of members of the Black Insane Disciples whom he'd just called chicken-niggers than he was on the street. Which is where he was just after having dinner at his ma's house when Al and Joey Scarpano found him about eight o'clock. Needless to say, they had not been looking for Vinny with the intention of buying him an Italian ice for dessert. The brothers Scarpano dragged him into an alleyway between the Scioto Fruit and Nut Company and the Allied Tool and Dye factory and proceeded to show him just what they thought of the predicament in which he had got Al. First, Joey held him as Al whaled on him, starting with the stomach, working his way up the chest, the punches fast and shattering. Al was wearing gloves but there was something in them besides fingers and knuckles, Vinny quickly realized, something hard, probably little pyramids of brass, which became even more terrifyingly evident after Al worked his way up to Vinny's face. Just as Vinny was losing consciousness, Joey dropped him and he sunk to his knees in the snow, bent over like a Moslem in prayer. Then Joey walked around in front of him, lifted Vinny's now-swollen, distorted face up by the chin, although Vinny could not tell who it was through his puffed-closed eyes, and said, "You little motherfuckin' weasel, if you're still fucking breathing when we're done with you, you remember one thing, you never deal with the Scarpanos again, never." Then with the practiced motion of a Notre Dame placekicker drove his foot into Vinny's crotch, catapulting the skinny kid onto his back in the snow. The sudden excruciating pain and shock of it scorched Vinny back to consciousness and he screamed, then whimpered. The Scarpanos just stared absently down at him as he curled into a fetal position, clutching his pulpified balls. Joey added a few kicks to the ribs for good measure and Al did a José Greco on him even though Vinny was now unconscious.

Someone found him groaning in the snow about a half hour later and called the police, who radioed for an ambulance to take him to Cook County Hospital. Besides the multiple contusions and cuts and a case of hypothermia, he had three broken ribs, one of which had punctured a lung, a ruptured spleen, a cracked pelvis, and a groin injury of sickening proportion although one testicle, the doctor felt, could be saved. It was the same doctor who had asked the paramedics when they brought him in if the kid had fallen off the John Hancock Building.

All because of the whitefucking snow, Vinny thought.

He finished the last of his coffee and picked up the check, left a dollar tip because it had been a good night and he felt the boozer Clare would put it to good use, paid the cashier and then turned up his collar and walked out into the falling snow.

3

MORRISON'S STOMACH felt raw, like somebody'd sandpapered it while he was sleeping. Noticing the empty glass on the table next to his bed, he knew why. What a day this is going to be, he said to himself, picking up the glass and gazing out through the blinds at the whirling snow. He felt loggy too. Goddamn dreams, goddamn booze. Got to get something in the stomach before going out in that crap, he thought, putting the glass back in the closet next to the schnaaps.

It was quiet in the kitchen, nobody else awake yet. He boiled a pair of eggs and ate them along with a piece of toast and drank some instant coffee.

The door to the bedroom across the tiny hall from his was slightly ajar when Morrison went back to get dressed and the movement inside caught his eye. She was sitting on the edge of the bed rolling on a pair of pantyhose, then after getting her second leg in stood to slide them over pale yellow panties. The hips were a little wide now, but the rest of the body was lithe. No cellulite or handles there, Morrison thought as he stood watching. Damn, she still looks good. Thirty-three and two kids neutralized by Jane Fonda's workout tape and a diet of salads and assorted birdfood, as he called it. Her breasts, bare at the moment, familiar now only in a *déjà vu* sort of way, were full and nicely shaped although they sort of lolled on her chest, settled, so to speak, from the way they were when he had married her twelve years earlier. The sight of them bouncing a little as she put on her bra backwards, hooking it and then twisting it around the right way, caused a stirring somewhere in the vicinity of Morrison's prostate. It was once so good, he remembered. But the feeling fled abruptly when she looked over her shoulder and saw him in the hall, their eyes meeting for just a moment before she turned, picked a slip from a bureau drawer and, her back to him, shimmied into it.

He turned and went back into his bedroom, feeling a little like a voyeur who just got caught and thinking that was probably the first time in at least a year he had seen Joanne's bare breasts. He had been sleeping alone for about six months now, since the night Joanne finally told him she wanted the divorce. The day after that he moved the two girls into one bedroom and took the other for himself. It was odd, Morrison often thought later, that when she, usually so self-assured, an opinion about everything, sat across the kitchen table and, nervous as a little kid, laid it out for him. Odd not so much because she had such an uncharacteristically shaky voice and twitching hands, but when the words came out, zilch, he felt nothing one way or another. Reached that point. Thinking about it, maybe one feeling—relief. So Morrison just said okay, got up from the table and went to a bar over near Area Six where a lot of the dicks hung out.

It had not been a great marriage in the first place, and they had been drifting apart for some time. She had never really liked his friends on the force or their wives when they got together at the cop parties in the earlier days, and the different shifts he had to work, and his hanging out in cop bars, and especially the locker room slap-ass buddy system, as she called it, which seemed so natural to him. All that had changed for him in the intervening years. With the burn-out, he had withdrawn from most of that, become, so to say, a seeker of complacency.

On the other side, and he didn't know for certain, he thought she was having an affair with somebody in the office where she worked or maybe with some salesman who called on them. The clues were there, all too obvious, the detective in him told him that, but he never tried to find out because purely and simply he did not want to know. Whatever had been there in the marriage had dissipated and there was no desire on either part now to try to repair it. They agreed he would stay in the bungalow they owned until the divorce was final so they would not have a mortgage payment as well as rent on an apartment to face each month. Burned out in Homicide, now burned out at home, he told himself, that was life. No, it wasn't, Christ, he was too young for that, he kept telling himself.

Back in his room, Morrison got dressed. He always prided himself in the clothes he wore. They weren't Brooks Brothers—who could afford that on a detective's pay?—but they were, he knew, a giant step above the polyester most of the plainclothes dicks wore and which he hated. But that went back to Homicide. You did things with a lot more class there. Elitist, maybe. He enjoyed nice clothes, enjoyed not looking like a dick. Since he took off the uniform for good twelve years ago, he had made it a point to keep himself trim, never above 180 on his six-foot-two frame, and to spend more on clothes than he really ought to have. "Michigan Avenue" was a nickname he'd carried in his earlier days in Homicide. He checked himself in the mirror, adjusted his tie, a paisley he'd gotten on sale at Lord and Taylor just after Christmas, then threaded the holster onto his belt so it hung just above his right cheek. The snubnose, five-shot Smith&Wesson was made of aluminum and was much lighter than the regulation four-inch-barrel Smith&Wesson he had worn when he first came on the force. He couldn't hit a Mack truck with the snubnose at fifty feet, he knew, but deskbound most of the time now in Organized Crime, he felt it was unlikely he would ever have to draw it much less put a bullet into somebody's body. He tucked one loop of the cuffs inside the back of his pants so the other hung over his left cheek.

In the hall he noticed her door was closed now. She preferred to avoid him in the mornings, in fact the only time they spoke was at dinner, on the few occasions they had it together, and that was always brief and stilted these days.

"Will you drive the kids to school this morning," he said through the door. "I've gotta get going. It's snowing like hell out there."

There was no answer. "Did you hear me," shifting his weight to the other foot, peeved. "Can you take them?"

"Of course I'll take them." Silence again.

Well, it would only be another month, he thought as he stepped into the girls' room, that's what the lawyer told him. They were still asleep. Peggy was ten now, still blond, but her little sister, Sandy, eight, had gone from a blond to a true brunette. "Better get up or you'll be late for school," he said. They stirred, almost in unison, but did not get out of their beds. "C'mon, c'mon. I'm not leaving until four little feet hit the floor." They climbed out of their beds. "Gimme a kiss," he said. "It's awful out there. Be sure your mom makes you a good breakfast before you go out."

It was normally about a half-hour drive for Morrison to central police headquarters, but it was going to take a helluva lot longer this morning. Scraping the snow and ice from his windshield, he decided he had been a real asshole when he told his wife a month or two back that she should use their one-car garage and he would just keep his car, the beater, in the space next to it in the alley. When he finally got into the car, he was cold and covered with snow and very aware that the heater in the six-year-old Chevy took at least ten minutes before issuing anything resembling warm air. As his car slipped and slid through the snowstorm down the Edens Expressway, with the semis heaving huge slops of slush at him as they sped past in adjoining lanes, Morrison told himself this truly had to be the week's low point.

He was wrong.

When he saw the snow from his bedroom window that morning, Morrison thought he would spend the day shuffling papers in the office, maybe a few phone calls, cozy; maybe go out at noon with his partner to Diamond's and cadge a discounted butt steak, one of the perks, and maybe a couple of poppers too to ward off the cold and snow.

Wrong again.

POLICE HEADQUARTERS in Chicago, a sprawling eleven-story building situated on State Street, that great street, as it is known in song, is on the near-south side of the city, at the corner of 11th Street, to be exact. The six blocks from headquarters north to the Loop, the garland of elevated train track that has defined Chicago's downtown for almost a century, has since World War II been nothing more than a swath lined with penny arcades, strip shows, dingy bars, flophouses, pawnshops, and more recently adult bookstores and peep shows. Over the years many of its feckless visitors had left that section of the street as new owners of tattoos, gonorrhea, or crabs—or all three.

In the Loop, State Street is an odd mixture of upscale and tawdry—Marshall Field's, Louis Sullivan's classic Carson, Pirie, Scott building, the Palmer House Hotel, interstitched with stores that specialize in bras with nipple holes and G-strings or drug paraphernalia, and movie houses showing the latest kung fu or black exploitation movies. North of the Loop, State Street takes on a certain bland tackiness for a mile or so and then suddenly narrows into a tree-shaded avenue of million-dollar townhouses, posh hotels, and doorman-posted condominiums, a major thoroughfare through Chicago's Gold Coast, before it ends abruptly at the southern boundary of Lincoln Park.

To the south of police headquarters, State Street cuts its way through what was once known as Bronzeville before Negroes were properly called blacks. That section, once riddled by dilapidated tenements with broken-out windows and collapsing back porches, has since become a city unto itself, dark and dangerous in the sprawling, decaying, gang-ruled housing projects.

And there in the middle of this boulevard of incongruity sits the core and cadre of law enforcement in Chicago.

Organized Crime is on the third floor, consisting of four desks in two cubicles, occupied at varying times by the twelve detectives assigned to the unit. It is in an area at the front of the building whose windows look down on State Street and out across a new housing development to the beginning of industrial Chicago.

Joe Morrison had been transferred to OC more than a year ago after ten years in Homicide had turned him into a near-classic case of aggravated burn-out. He had wanted Homicide from the time he was a raw recruit, a twenty-one-year-old with dreams of solving murders and finding his name in the newspapers, and with the girls fawning all over him as a result, and his father implying—not saying, he would never say it—that he was proud of him. Joe had been a good street cop for three years running, made detective then and landed in Homicide. But it did not turn out the way he had imagined it. There were the murders, of course, grisly and gruesomely varied: the juice–loan shark who had offended his superiors in enough ways to earn for himself a little hideous torture before having his skull crushed in a vise on a basement workshelf bench; the pretty brunette or blond or black-Afroed girl whose rapists wanted to be sure they were not later identified; the husband stabbed through the heart by his long-suffering wife; the wife with the fractured skull who fell down the stairs trying to get away from her abusive, drunken husband; the homosexual who picked up the wrong boy and brought him home; the victims of the street gangs' swift vengeance, and on and on.

He and his partners had solved a lot of them, most with his next-to-last partner, a black man named Sam Pickens. They had been together from his fourth year in the department until his ninth, a year before Morrison chucked it all for anything else. They were considered to be one of the very best teams in the department, broken up by a grimly ironic turn of events when Sam, off-duty, was killed trying to stop the holdup of a Popeye's Fried Chicken store where he had gone to get a bucket of the stuff for his wife and three kids one night. Joe went down to the county morgue to identify the body so Sam's wife would not have to see the carnage that several shots from a Saturday night special could do to her man's head.

It had all come apart after that. He had long before realized that his name was not regularly appearing in the paper and the girls were not hanging all over him, at least as a result of his being a homicide dick, and his father had gone to the nursing home with Alzheimer's disease and then died, neglecting to have implied any pride in his son's career. The first two hardly mattered after a while, the last bothered him more than he cared to admit to himself because he and his father had been close, did a lot of things together, although his father, introspectively Irish and coldly English, never revealed his inner feelings to anyone, Joe included. Sam's murder had devastated Joe and suddenly Homicide was a painful, draining experience, no longer a job but a morbid, inexorable hell, like memories of the holocaust. He had gotten so he loathed going to work and at night he could not sleep well, spent most of those dark, lonely hours dozing, waking, too often just lying there trying to put the pictures of corpses out of his mind but rarely succeeding. Finally he filled out a PAR form, Personal Actions Request, asking to be transferred to a different department, any department, and his request was granted.

Now Joe Morrison spent his days serving as a liaison to the FBI, the Illinois Crime Commission and the various departments in the Chicago Police Department that might be handling cases involving organized crime and that included just about all of them except Traffic Control. He still dealt with his old unit, Homicide, when some mobster bobbed to the surface of Lake Michigan or stunk up the trunk of some abandoned car, as well as Narcotics, Vice, Gambling, Burglary—the job offered a nice diversity, Morrison thought, and he did not have to look at dead bodies anymore, not real ones anyway, maybe just snapshots of them.

WHEN MORRISON finally got to his desk in OC, his partner Norbert Castor, a Croatian-American, as he liked to refer to himself, was already there. Castor had been in Organized Crime now the better part of twenty years and knew more about the Mafia than just about anybody below the level of *consigliore* in the Outfit itself. And he had stories to tell, so many one would have thought he was Irish. The walking, talking encyclopedia of bent-noses, Morrison called him. He came up with that his first day on the job downtown after Castor told him several tales, capping the session with the one about Mo Mo Giancana's little peculiarity. Castor explained he was one of the few people in the world who knew Mo Mo always unzipped his fly with his left hand while he did just about everything else with his right hand. Mo Mo, of course, wasn't unzipping any flies anymore, not since he got blown away frying eggs and sausage in his house one morning by somebody he thought was a brother—Cain, it turned out.

Castor was a big man, had been an all-city tackle when he played football in high school at St. Rita's back in the

1950s, but he had given up exercise years ago while satisfying his lust for beer, kielbasa, mountainous Italian beef sandwiches, pizza and Snickers bars.

"You drive today?" Castor asked as he watched Morrison shake the melting snow from his coat.

Morrison nodded. "It took me almost an hour."

Castor held up a manila folder. "Before you get too settled take a look at this. You're not going to believe it."

Morrison opened the folder, read the first line of the Responding Officer's report. "Holy shit."

"There are a lot of lames out there, Joe, but I think maybe we might just've run into the lamest of them all."

"Somebody really raped Rudy Facia's daughter? Christ, he must have a death wish bigger than one of those third-world cab drivers out there," Morrison said, gesturing toward the window that looked down on State Street.

"Two of 'em, not one. One black, the other light-skinned or maybe white."

"You mean she talked about it?" Morrison looked surprised.

"Until her old man and his lawyer got to the hospital."

"That's incredible."

"The kid's naive, what can I tell you. Actually, according to what I hear, she's a little slow upstairs, you know, the lights are a little dim in the balcony. She didn't think she was doing anything wrong, I gather, telling about the bad guys who did the bad things to her. But she no doubt got the message when Tulips got there. You know how Facia got that name?" Morrison shook his head. "He got it because one time in his salad days he left some wiseguy who got too wise for his own good with a tulip stuck in his mouth, the stem all the way down his throat, another tulip the stem was up his ass, and another sticking outa the hole in his chest. It was springtime, as I remember it. Maybe he just came back from the Holland, Michigan, festival . . . filled with spirit."

"This isn't the season for tulips."

"I think when he gets his hands on these guys, he'll forget the flowers. For starters maybe he'll thread a piece of barbed wire up their assholes and out their mouths and turn them into a monorail. Then I think he's going to get nasty. Bring the folder along and let's go across the street and get some decent coffee. The case is ours. I begged for it. We're on it along with Violent Crimes. This one's gonna be a classic, they're gonna be talking about it around here twenty years from now."

"For shitsake, Norb, I just got my coat off. You know it's a blizzard out there."

"Well, we're gonna be on the street all day, it looks like, so you might as well adapt early. C'mon."

4

After Vinny shivered his way through the snow to the one-room kitchenette apartment above an army surplus store on Broadway where he had lived for the past year, he stripped to his shorts and T-shirt, opened a can of Stroh's, and half-sat and half-laid on the couch without bothering to pull out the sofa bed. With a blanket thrown over him, he sipped on the beer and stared at the grayish ceiling with its paint curls clinging like the last leaves of autumn. The numbness was gone now and in place of it was a feeling of creeping anxiety, nervous legs, a little inner panic, and it was cold in spite of the blanket. The dexedrine he'd taken around three that morning for an edge in the card game had gotten its second wind, he thought, that and the goddamn coffee; between them he was not going to fall asleep, he knew, even though he'd been up for about twenty-four hours now.

He began thinking about Jo and that got his mind off the chills and the other nagging feelings. He had met her there in Uptown three months ago and they had got it together one night about a month after that when she was stoned and soaring and it was the greatest thing that had ever happened to him. Nobody had ever been quite like her, all motion and moans, and she did it all to him, sucking, playing with his nipples, which he'd never known could excite him, her on top, underneath, a tongue that wouldn't stop; he came three times, still couldn't believe he had but he did. But that had been it, a one-night, three-swack stand.

He had tried to get it on with her again, dropped over to her apartment a number of times—she only lived four blocks away—and he made it a point to hit some of the bars where she usually hung out. But nothing had come of it since. When he ran into her, she treated him with pretty much the same depth of feeling she imparted to the bar stool he normally found her perched on.

Jo had been known as Jo Jo Kane in Mound City, the town near the Illinois-Kentucky border where she grew up, but she'd dropped the second Jo after running away when she was fifteen. She hadn't totally run away, she had lived with her aunt in Chicago for almost two years and even tried to stay in high school for a while before moving in with a thirty-year-old dopehead in Old Town. That was six years earlier. The doper OD'd after a year and Jo had managed to survive on the meaner streets by her well-tempered animal instincts and with her body. She passed through several neighborhoods with several different companions on her way down the ladder to Uptown. But she still visited her aunt at least once a month, usually to do some errands for her because the woman could not get out of her apartment anymore, her arthritis had gotten so bad.

The girl wasn't all that good-looking, Vinny admitted: average face; short brown hair that was kind of ratty; hard, sharp features that made her look older than twenty-three; but her body was something else, Playboy-caliber breasts, nipples that seemed to be trying to look to the sky, wavering curves and knockout legs. Vinny could not get her out of his mind. And he kept hearing her voice. She talked with a southern Illinois mixture of drawl and twang that he found mesmerizing, although to most everybody else it sounded like just another hillbilly dialect. It drove him crazy to think she could be the way she was one night and so indifferent every time he saw her afterward. She would come around, though; he had told himself that at least twenty times over the past two months.

She would probably be up by now, Vinny thought as he started to put on the same clothes he had dropped in a heap two hours earlier. And sure as hell she wouldn't be going out in this shit. Maybe he'd pick up a bottle of Southern Comfort, her favorite, and go see her. It had been more than a week since he ran into her over at Carmen's, a combination liquor store and bar that was to its reputation grubbier than most of the dumps on Lawrence Avenue, but she hadn't been around any of her ordinary haunts since.

It was still snowing but not as heavily when he left for her apartment, which was in the Tudor Arms, a four-story, U-shaped building embracing a large courtyard that had a cracked and chipped concrete fountain in the middle that had not worked in twenty-five years. It was on a narrow, decaying one-way street that bore the inappropriate name of Sunnyside, and was flanked by rundown four-flats and six-flats built flush against each other. The sidewalks and gutters along the street were ordinarily full of garbage and litter, although on this day most of it was covered over with snow. The Tudor was the largest building on the block and was now a complex of small apartments, broken up from bigger ones by some slumlord sometime in the past. The building was granite, a dull, dirty gray, but with handsome moldings around the doorways and windows and a mosaic tile hall in each of the six entrances to the building that bore witness to it once being a much grander residence in the days several decades earlier when Uptown was a tony place to live, an age before the Appalachians, the Indians, the badasses, the derelicts and other destitutes began their invasion of the area.

Jo's apartment was on the second floor of the entrance closest to the street. The doorbells in the entryway rarely worked so Vinny just opened the inner door, whose lock never worked either, and started for the stairs. The door to the first apartment on ground level, the janitor's apartment, was open, and he glanced in when he heard voices.

Manford White, who had his own apartment upstairs, was sitting inside talking with the janitor, a youngish black man with a rust-colored Afro. They both looked out at Vinny in the hall. ''Look who's here,'' White said, ''Butter Cookie. And he's trackin' snow all over your clean hall. Where you been lately, little fella?''

Vinny looked down at the dirty floor and the slush that he had just added to it. ''Around.''

Manford White was black, Haitian black, although he had never been south of Ninety-third Street in Chicago except for the three years when he resided downstate in the joint at Pontiac and the other year at Stateville in Joliet. He conducted a lot of his business out of the janitor's apartment, and Vinny was a sometime customer. But as far as Vinny was concerned, White was one of the most detestable creatures ever to have wandered into Uptown, a ''one hundred percent smartass nigger,'' in Vinny's estimation. He was also big, six-two, maybe 210, a hard body, and reputed to be a savage street fighter.

''We been missin' you, haven't we, Head,'' White said. The janitor, whose real name was Tyrone Hawkins, nodded, his face taking on a kind of empty grin. He had gotten the nickname from White—Outdoor Head because the tight-curled rusty Afro reminded Manford of the basketballs the young boppers dribbled all over the park district court up the street and down the sidewalks and even tucked under their arms when they stopped in sometimes to make a buy, but over time it had gotten shortened simply to Head. Tyrone kind of liked the name.

Vinny turned toward the stairs, ignoring him, but White yelled after him. ''Don't bother, little man, she ain't there. Already gone out. Jokin''—his personal name for her—

"probably had a breakfast trick to turn." White laughed loudly and so did the janitor.

"Maybe I'll just go look for myself," Vinny said.

"Be our guest."

Fucking nigger, Vinny said to himself as he mounted the worn stairs.

White turned back to the janitor. "The Salerno Butter Cookie's love-struck, Head."

After several raps at Jo's door, Vinny knew the man had not put him on and went back down the stairs.

"Wops do not listen, do they?" Manford shouted through a big denigrating smile when Vinny reached the doorway. "Or maybe they don't dig things right away, have to think about 'em for a while before they understand what a man's saying."

"Fuck you, White."

"She done gone out with her new boyfriend, Butter Cookie, and he's a big one." Vinny stared coldly at White, but it was clear he was interested. "A very, very big red-necked motherfucker, a real live street animal. I believe he comes from Joe-ja. And I believe his hobby is beating dudes to death. I think he likes that a real lot." Manford White was enjoying this. "When he finds you slobberin' around the hillbilly, he gonna treat you like a little bit a bad Eye-talian sausage on his pizza, chew you up and spit you out. Ptooey."

"You know, I thought once you got outa the joint youda stopped bein' a buttfucker, but I guess once you guys get a taste of it you never change—"

"Better watch your mouth, little man," White said, the grin he had worn quickly disappearing. "Or maybe I'll have Head here do a little dance on your white little Eye-talian ass."

"You don't got the balls to do anything to me. Or to sick that looney Brillohead on me—" Vinny shot a glance at the front door just in case he had to bolt out of there—

"because, my man, you know fucking well I'm connected."

White's laugh was more like a roar this time. "Connected, my asshole."

"You know it. You fat fucking know it. And like I told you before, *they* know, *they* know anything happens to me *they* know just where to come. And when they do they'll cut off that foot-long dork you got, stuff it in your mouth and stuff you into the trunk of that pimpmobile you got."

White laughed again and then started to say something but Vinny was already out the door.

"You think maybe he be connected?" Head asked.

"Shit, man, you think every greaseball's connected? Some of 'em are popes, you know, some of 'em are barbers. Besides I know Salerno a couple years now. He ain't nothing more than a little errand boy, a little shitass gofer, and he's a snitch. They don't like him any more than I do. He tells 'em if he hears something on the street, some book cheatin' a little, a drug deal that just might go down, halfass stuff." Manford sat back and smiled suddenly. "Hey, Head, I wonder how he knew I got a foot-long dick."

A moment later Vinny was back in the doorway, only this time he stepped inside. He fidgeted for a second, then said, "Hey, White, you, ah, got any Ludes? I can't get down today. I don't know what the fuck's the matter but I gotta get some sleep."

"Oh, shit, that's what brought you back. I thought maybe you went for your connections and brung 'em back to do me a number. You sure they not out there in the hall waitin' to beat up on a poor black boy?"

"Knock it off. I mean, come on, you got any or not?"

"You got any money?"

"Yeah, I always got money."

"Head, go see what you can dig up for the man." The janitor got up and walked down the hall to the bedroom in the back. Vinny stood there thankful that Manford White was now ignoring him. Head returned carrying a plastic baggie containing four large white Quaalude tablets. White looked at the pills, then at Vinny. "Be forty, little fella," he said. Vinny dug out two twenty-dollar bills, took the Ludes and disappeared out the door.

5

SO MUCH for Diamond's discounted butt steak, Morrison thought as he walked with Castor to the elevator bank.

"We gotta go over to Cook County Hospital, the nurse lives in one of those apartment complexes next to it. Nurse Fralick, she was on duty in the emergency room when they brought Facia's little baby in last night. I called already, woke her up. Told her we'd be by this morning."

"I take it the Facia kid's above statutory."

"Oh, hell, yes, twenty-two in fact and according to this," Castor said, shaking the folder, which contained the Responding Officer's report and the Emergency Room report, "cherry, or should I say was cherry up until dessert last night."

They walked out of police headquarters through the First District squad room onto 11th Street. "You'd think they'd shovel the sidewalks here," Castor said as they headed east to Wabash Avenue. "After all, we are the goddamn police department, headquarters for shitsake."

"Well, we could've stayed upstairs. It's warm, dry, the coffee's for shit, but what the hell."

"You know, Joe, the snow fucks up everything in this city, even City Hall."

"It's screwed up without snow."

"I can't wait, three more years and all you'll see of me is taillights. I'm out of here, southland here I come. And it don't snow in Florida, Joe."

Dottie's was just around the corner on Wabash, and had been a cop hangout ever since it opened its doors back in the 1960s. Huge triple-glazed donuts, oozing bismarcks, ham and eggs and hashbrowns, enormous lunches, hot coffee, a lot of banter, a lot of respect for those on the job, open twenty-four hours straight—no discounts, but cheap prices. At any given time there were eight or ten, maybe fifteen detectives from headquarters in the place.

Castor always liked to tell the story of the two Mexican kids who dropped by one early spring night around ten o'clock, maybe five years ago, and hit on Dottie's son, Morty, who was working the cash register. One of them flashed a big piece of steel, looked like a machete. "All the money or I cut your fucking throat," he said, or something to that effect. There was a kind of big collective gulp from all the dicks in the place, nobody at first believing what was going down. Then the next thing the two punks see is an arsenal, enough barrels popping out from under coats to have carried off the invasion of Grenada and the St. Valentine's Day massacre at the same time.

The guy without the blade froze, looking at all the guns pointed at him. They just grabbed him and kicked him across the street to the First District lockup. The other guy—Castor loved to remember because he was there at the time—actually took a slash at one of the gunbearers. Unlike his buddy, he did not go directly to the lockup across the street, but instead went there via a patrol-wagon ride to the emergency room of Cook County Hospital. It seems he had to be treated for some injuries sustained when he took a nasty tumble tripping over the threshold of Dottie's as he was being escorted out—that was the explanation on the police report of the arresting officers. The public defender later questioned just how the young man managed to incur such a unique variety of contusions on both sides of his body, the loss of several front teeth, a broken wrist and a mild concussion by a simple topple to the pavement, but in the end it didn't matter because he went to the slammer with his buddy anyway, three-to-five for armed robbery.

They sat at the counter now, only a seat or two away from where Castor was the night the two would-be robbers came by. "A glazed and coffee, Alma," Castor said to the waitress. "Cream, of course, Norbert," she said back flirtatiously, and he smiled at the buxom fifty-year-old with her platinum-dyed hair wound into a beehive that had gone out of style a decade earlier. "Of course," he said.

"I'll have the same," Morrison said. No reaction from Alma, just scribbling on her check pad.

Castor looked over at him. "Not feeding you at home?"

"You know damn well no one's feeding me there."

"Too bad, how much longer?"

"The lawyer says maybe a month, then it's final."

"You got a place?"

"A possibility."

A shadow loomed behind the two, a large one. Morrison looked around first. "Well, if it isn't Six's biggest reprobate," he said, and stuck out his hand. "How you doin', Whitey?"

"Maybe not so good," Whitey Fortas said. "Got a call for a command performance this morning down here. I think I might have a bit of a problem. But we'll see."

Sitting down on the stool next to Morrison, he asked, "You heard about Blake?"

"Timmy Blake?" Morrison asked.

"Got himself shot."

"What happened? Timmy and I came on the job together," Castor said.

"Well, maybe I should put it this way, he sort of shot himself." Sergeant Fortas adjusted himself on the seat, his audience in tow. "You remember Sally," he said, nodding to Morrison, "when you were over in Six, in Homicide." Fortas looked at Morrison's momentary puzzlement. "The groupie, you know, Sally Spermatozoa, we called her."

Morrison nodded. "Oh, the one with the, ah, hangups."

"That's the one." Looking across Morrison, Fortas spoke directly to Norbert Castor. "I don't think you know her, Norbie, because you been down here on your ass for so long, but anyway she just liked cops. Right, Joey?"

"She did. So what happened to Blake?"

Fortas, ignoring Morrison, leaned across him again. "She was the one, Norbie, who used to like it handcuffed. Ever hear about that? Take her out in the car, put her in the backseat, cuff her hands behind her back and pump away. It was her thing. You remember her?"

"I think I heard about her," Castor said.

"Well, now she's got a new trick. In the backseat again, but now she likes giving head, only she wants the weapon against *her* head while she's doing it. A couple of guys did it that way. She thinks it's really hot stuff, then she gets this new twist and wants to try it out with Timmy. Just when he's about to come, she wants him to cock it, stuck right there against her temple he's supposed to cock it like he's going to blow her brains out, because when she hears the click, she knows she's going to have an instant orgasm, she tells him. Well, Blake tried it and I guess it was so good, or he was so wrapped up in coming himself that something happened, and he pulled the trigger."

"Jesus," Morrison said.

"Lucky for old Sally he pulled it away first—the gun, that is. Not a scratch, in fact she probably had multiple orgasms when she heard the shot. But poor Blake put a bullet right through his foot, straight through and out the old rubber soles. And when he fired off another round, God knows why, that went through the front windshield. It happened last night around eleven before the snow started.

He's at Weiss Memorial and a couple of the guys are over there trying to help him write up the report as to why there's a bullet lodged in the backdoor of his squad car and his blood's all over the floor back there and there's a hole in his foot and that the front window's blown away. I personally think they could use that guy who wrote 'The Twilight Zone' to write the report on this one.'' Fortas got up from the stool. ''Well, I gotta get my ass across the street. Internal Affairs. They got a beef with me.''

NURSE FRALICK did not look old enough to be a nurse, Morrison thought when she answered the door of her apartment. An eighteen-year-old maybe, little wispy-haired blond with a zit on the forehead of her otherwise porcelain skin, 110 pounds at most, probably pretty legs under the Levis. Every straight bartender in the city would card her. But of course, she was not eighteen—twenty-three, graduate of the University of Illinois School of Nursing—and in working County and especially the emergency room for the past year had seen more blood, guts and human carnage than most Vietnam field doctors.

''Sorry to get you outa bed when I called,'' Castor said as they stepped into the apartment.

''It's all right, I thrive on five hours' sleep.'' She nodded toward the couch. ''Go ahead and sit down. I suppose you want me to make coffee for you too.''

''No, that's okay,'' Morrison said. ''Don't bother.''

She smiled. ''Cut the bull, none of you guys are nice guys. Besides I already made a pot but it's decaf, better for you.''

When she returned with three mugs of coffee, she said, ''So the girl was a Mafia princess, huh?''

''She was the daughter of a man alleged to be a member of organized crime,'' Castor said. ''Her daddy had served some time in his younger days and is known lately to hang around with persons of questionable character, maybe for the last thirty years or so." He forced a grin. "That's why we wanted to talk to you, Nurse Fralick."

"Call me Judy. But I don't know why. I told the other cops everything I knew last night, everything she told me. They took it all down."

"I know, but we're from a different division," Castor said. "We maybe approach it from a different angle. That's why we'd like it firsthand, Judy."

She shrugged. "Okay. I was on the six-to-two shift, they brought her in about nine-thirty. Typical rape case. She was sort of hysterical at first, crying, more like whimpering. Really a nice person. She talked to me while we were waiting for the doctor, seemed to want to tell about it, get it off her chest. That's not all that normal, by the way, wanting to talk about it. Anyway, she said she had dinner with these two girlfriends and a guy at a restaurant, Mat-a-something down on Taylor Street."

"Mategrano's?" Morrison asked.

"That's the place. Well, she left before the others because she was tired, she said. Somebody from the restaurant called a cab for her and she went outside to wait for it. This was all before the snow started. Anyway, she was standing on the corner outside when this guy, a white guy, she thought, came up and said something about his buddy being hurt and could she help him. The guy said he's just over here and took her by the arm and kept saying he really needs help and led her a little way down the street off Taylor, I forget which one she said, and she didn't quite know what was happening."

"She just went with him?" Morrison asked.

"It all happened pretty fast, I guess. And, well, it seems she's a little retarded. It probably never dawned on her what was happening until it happened, really happened, you know what I mean."

Morrison nodded. "And?"

"Then he pulled her into this building, abandoned

building, and down some steps. Down there, there was another guy, a black guy. Anyway, they had her in this room in the basement and the black guy, she said, knocked her down. Then she said the first guy had his cock out and made her give him a b.j. He kind of knelt over her and grabbed her by the hair and so she did it because she was scared to death, she said. And while he was doing that the other guy was pulling down her pantyhose and panties. When the first guy was through the other one did it to her on the floor. Then he slapped her around and threatened her, took her wallet and said they now knew where she lived and if she said anything to the cops or anybody else they'd be back and next time they'd kill her. That was it. They took off. And she wandered outside, dazed, sort of, and bumped into some couple and they called the police. She was such a nice little thing, I couldn't believe she was a Mafia kid.''

''She isn't in the Outfit,'' Castor said. ''Her old man is.''

''I know, but just the same.'' The nurse shrugged. ''She wasn't physically hurt all that bad, though—swollen cheek, split lip, that was about all. You should see some of them they bring in.''

''Did she say whether she would recognize them—from pictures, say?'' Morrison asked.

''She said she'd never forget them, never. I'm sure she could identify them. She was describing one of them to the doctor when her father got there. You want some more coffee?''

''No,'' Morrison said. ''What kind of description did she give?''

''Well, as I said, she just started when her father came in and then kind of all hell broke loose. He was in a rage, screamed at the doctor, yelled at her. There were like three other men with him. One of them was a lawyer and he was running around talking to everyone and the next thing we all knew she was bundled up and hustled out of there. I didn't know it then, but I thought he must be a gangster or some big-time politician."

"Well, he never ran for office," Castor said. "Did she say anything about what the guys who raped her said to her while it was going on? I mean did they say anything at all to her, threaten her, her family?"

"Just that they'd kill her if she told anyone, like I just told you. That's all."

"Didn't mention the father's name, by any chance?"

"No, not that she told me."

"Thanks for the coffee," Morrison said. "Anything else at all you can think of that maybe we should know?"

"Not really."

"Well, if you do, I'd appreciate it if you gave me a call." He handed her a business card that she looked at and then smiled. "Sure, detective, anything to help keep our streets safe."

IN THE car, Morrison driving, Castor said, scratching his half-bald head, "You know, it's got to be one of two things, Joe, either a setup or, if not, just a couple of ding-dongs who wandered into the neighborhood. I mean no black guy around there would fuck with a white girl, not on Taylor Street."

The neighborhood Castor was talking about was unique, had been for years. An old-line Italian neighborhood that ran along Taylor Street and was filled with small restaurants, grocery stores, bakeries, cleaners, all with Italian names on their storefronts. It was like something out of another era, one before the big supermarkets and discount drugstores, an ethnic island that had turned out far more than its share of wiseguys. Surrounding the island, however, was a sea called the projects: ugly buildings, gang-infested, subsidized housing mostly for dirt-poor blacks. But the two factions coexisted, neither bothering the other, it was an unwritten and unspoken law, had been since the first tenant moved into the first project.

When he was much younger Castor had once asked the bartender at Gennaro's on Taylor Street if there wasn't a problem with all the blacks so close, and loved to tell the guy's response: "We got an understanding with them. They don't bother our women, our kids, or our cars, and we don't kill 'em."

"I think it just might be somebody with a vendetta for Tulips. Somebody brought these two guys in from Detroit or somewhere, just like a hit. Only they don't hit Facia himself, just hit him where it hurts the most and he's gotta live with the hurt forever. Everytime he looks at his little girl's face he'll see her being defiled by a couple of street animals."

"I thought you told me they never bother the women or kids. Kill each other, maybe, but the family's sacred."

"They never used to. But the young Turks, they're something else. They got their own rules these days."

Morrison shrugged. "I think it's more likely it was just a pair of assholes who didn't know where they were or who they were hurting."

"Could be. But I'd sure like to talk to the girl, see if they gave her any message. You know, like, 'Say hello to your dad for us.' Hell, we'll never get to talk to her now. The old man won't let her press charges, the lawyer'll keep her away from us. Unless we can come up with something to convince Tulips it'd be to his advantage for her to talk to us."

"Let me work on it," Morrison said. "So where to now?"

"The doctor, he lives out in Oak Park. His name's Naroum Punpatipal. You speak Hindu, Joe? Christ, where do all the American doctors go?"

"The language is Hindi, Norb. A Hindu is a person."

"How the fuck do you know all these things?"

"I work crossword puzzles."

"What's a four-letter word for snow? I'll tell you. S-h-i-t."

It was still coming down steadily, and Morrison was forced to guide the motor pool Plymouth through it at no more than fifteen miles an hour. "Why don't we hold off on Naroum the sawbones until the s-h-i-t stops?" Morrison said. "It'll take us at least an hour to get out there at this rate. Why don't we just go over to Taylor Street and see if we can dig up something? I used to have some people over there. Maybe they haven't killed each other off yet."

In his twelve years on the job Morrison had put together more of *his* people on the street than the rest of Area Six Homicide, Robbery, Burglary and Gang Crime combined. They had turned more than a few cases for him. They told him things, sometimes the truth, sometimes lies. He could usually tell the difference. After ten years in Homicide it wasn't all that difficult; you got to notice the bouncing Adam's apples, the restless eyes, the lips gone dry, things like that. Morrison's people—the finks, the favor-traders, the ass-protectors—there was a legion of them, and he had learned to orchestrate them like Toscanini, at least that was the way Tony Morano, the chief of detectives, once described Morrison's act.

"Why not. The Hindu can wait." Castor reached for the radio. "I'll call in and get someone to call him and tell him we can't make it. After Taylor Street, though, we should talk to that couple that took her to the hospital. They're a pair of yuppies, I'm told, live up in New Town in a loft. It's trendy these days to drive your BMW to Taylor Street for some pasta and white wine. 'Wasn't that the most boffo fettuccini you ever had, Muffy? Why, what do you make of that girl there stumbling around with the blood running down her legs? Perhaps we should help her.'" He shook his head. "Why the hell do I have a hard-on for everybody, Joe?"

"You've been on the force a long time."

6

THE FORD Maverick that Jo Kane's new friend was driving was badly rusted, silk-screened with a variety of scrapes and dents and needed a new muffler, but somehow it got them through the snowy, slippery streets. At Halsted and Belmont, she pointed to the only empty place on the curb, a bus stop, and told him to park there. "That's it," she said pointing across the street to Warner's Discount Drugs.

"Not that big a place," the man said.

"It don't have to be, Tommy. He don't need all that much room. He sells tons a medicine, drugs. I told you, my aunt says he's close to a goddamn millionaire. And he squirrels a lot of it away in his apartment. My aunt oughta know, she bedded him for a couple of years. He even took her to Florida once and they stayed in some real fancy hotel in Miami Beach right there on the ocean."

"Okay, okay, so let's go in and get a look at him."

"Not together, jeez." She shook her head. "You know, Tommy, if brains was lard you wouldn't have enough to grease your dick. *I* go in and *you* wait about a minute out here. I'll look around, maybe get a tube a toothpaste and when you come in I'll go back to where they got the prescription stuff. That's where Theo always is. You just gotta watch. The guy I give my aunt's note to is him. Get a good look at him so you'll recognize him later. Then after I leave buy yourself some toothpaste or something, and I'll see you back here."

Tommy, his pawlike hands still gripping the steering wheel even though the car was parked, watched her walk across the street through the snow. He waited a minute or so and then hauled himself out of the car. Tommy was about six-foot-four, weighed an easy 240 and below his broad shoulders had a paunch that was underwired by a wide cowboy belt. His hair was long and stringy and hung over the collar of the Eddie Bauer down jacket he had stolen a few weeks earlier. The sleeves were a little short but otherwise it fit fine and was warmer than he thought it would be when he first saw the man taking it off at the health club where he had been doing day labor moving equipment around. He didn't have to bother sneaking a peek at the combination, just waited until the guy loped off to the Nautilus room and then grabbed the lock and tore the entire handle off the locker.

Down in Georgia, there was a sheet on Thomas Alvin Bates that would take a speed reader about a day to digest, beginning with his first encounter with the law at twelve when he beat a school crossing guard with a softball bat in Valdosta, the town where he grew up or, as the sociologists would put it, metamorphosed from child to sociopath. The counts were all there: auto theft, breaking and entering, assault, battery, assault and battery, disorderly conduct—fourteen times on that one alone in Atlanta; most of them he got off of because witnesses were scarce or conveniently confused when it came time to testify against him. The biggest charge, though—manslaughter, for beating a steelworker to death in a fight outside a tavern in south Atlanta—got him six years at Reidsville and later an additional two for unruly conduct when he sent two prison guards to the hospital after they tried to break up a fight between Tommy and another inmate. When he got out two months earlier, he thought it was probably a good time to get out of Georgia. From what he'd heard, Chicago sounded like his kind of town.

He headed now across the street. Theo Warner's discount drugstore was actually misleading from the outside. It did not have a large frontage but the store stretched back a good sixty or seventy feet before it ended at the prescription counter. Jo was in one of the aisles, and when she saw Tommy come through the door, walked toward the back of the store. He followed her about halfway and stopped at a section of shelves with all kinds of shaving creams and after-shave lotions.

Jo spoke to a man behind the prescription counter who looked to be about sixty, which was about the age, Tommy remembered, she had told him that Theo was. The man was bald and wore reading glasses attached to a black cord that hung around his neck. Tommy noticed that he was doing most of the talking. Finally Jo nodded, turned and started back toward the door without having given the man the note. Tommy stopped at the counter at the front and asked the girl behind it for a pack of Marlboros and then he left too.

"He ain't there," she said as Tommy lowered himself into the car. "That's his brother, they both own the place. Theo won't be in till later, not till six. But he said he'd be in for sure because he's gotta pick up some stuff to take with him to Arizona. He's goin' out there tomorrow. He's gonna be gone a month, so we've blown it if we don't do it tonight."

"Why don't you just find out exactly where he lives and we go over there now and I'll just do it."

"I told you, Tommy, I don't *know* where he lives. Neither does my aunt. He moved about a year ago, which was about a year after he stopped fucking her. She knows it's a couple blocks from here, that's all. And he ain't listed in the telephone book. And I can't very well go in there and ask his brother where old Theo lives. That'd be just great. Then the next thing he finds out his brother's robbed there, for chrissake."

"So whaddya want to do?"

"Go back to the apartment. Then this afternoon we get Manford and come back here and wait for him. His brother said he's just gonna stop by, so we sit in the car and I point him out when he shows up and we follow him when he leaves and then you and Manford take care of it at the apartment and I wait in the car downstairs and then I drive us all home a helluva lot richer than we are right now."

Tommy shrugged and started the car's engine. "I still don't like the idea of the nigger bein' in on it."

"Fuck, Tommy, you need him more than I do. You only have to go down a flight of stairs now to get our stuff. Nigger or not, he takes care of you. Don't even have to go out on the street and buy it and find out you just made your buy from the Man. Plus I already talked about this with him before you ever came along. We were gonna do it together. He and Head and me. But I told him now it's just you and me and him. Christ, there's plenty there for all of us."

Tommy started the car's engine. "All right," he said, but he didn't sound like he meant it. Before pulling out into traffic, he looked over at her, his eyes tending to wall-eye as they always did when something was bothering him. "You sure you never got it on with that nigger?"

Jo turned and looked out the front window. "I told you before, I didn't. Just deal some drugs with him, just like you, for chrissake. And sometimes we went somewhere together, somewhere in the neighborhood to drink. That's all. But I don't do even that since you come along."

"I could be a real sonofabitch if I ever thought you nigger-fucked. That's one thing I could never abide in a woman."

"Don't worry yourself about it, Tommy . . ."

7

THE SNOW was down to a mild flurry by six o'clock and in spite of having stopped for several hours during the day it was still far ahead of the city's snow removal force; along Halsted Street, where the merchants had shoveled their walks, the embankment of snow was three feet high. Jo was at the wheel of the Maverick now parked directly across from Warner's Discount Drugs. Tommy was in the front seat next to her with Manford White in the back. They had been there about fifteen minutes when she saw the short man in the navy blue overcoat and black fur hat with ear flaps turn the corner at Belmont. She said quickly, "That's him, that's old Theo." Tommy strained to see him, White just stared indifferently from the backseat. "Now let's hope he don't stay in there too long."

"Fucking-A, he better not or we'll all be froze to death out here," Tommy said.

A half-hour later, however, Theo still had not re-emerged. Tommy was hugging himself. "Turn on the goddamn motor and see if we can get some heat, Jo. I ain't used to this kind of cold."

"Here, have some antifreeze," White said, passing a bottle swathed in a brown paper bag.

Tommy did not take it, just looked back over the seat

at White as if the man had just offered him a still-warm urine specimen. "I don't drink outa that bottle."

"Stay cold then." White took a drink from it, then held it out to Jo, who started to reach for it.

"She don't either."

"Since when?"

"Since now."

"You know, Tommy, I'm growin' to really dislike you," White said. "And I think you and me—"

"Knock it off, you guys," Jo said. "We come here for a job. So don't fuck it up before it gets started."

"I'll be right back," Tommy said, opening the car door and nodding toward the tavern a few doors up the street. "You want me to bring you somethin', Jo?"

"You can't do that, Tommy. What if he comes out? We gotta be ready to move."

Tommy was out of the car now, looking back in through the open door. "Won't matter. I'm just gettin' something to bring back out here, something that hasn't had somebody else's big lips all over it. Won't be more'n a minute. So you want anything or not, Jo?"

"Yeah, get me a half-pint of Comfort."

Tommy slammed the door and Jo watched him go into the tavern.

"Jokin, that man and I are not destined to cohabit on this planet," White said.

"Don't worry about Tommy, Manford. He'll be okay, just give him some time." She turned to look back at White. "In the meantime, gimme some of that stuff before he comes back out." He passed the bag up to her and she took a long swig. "What is it?"

"Beam."

"Not as good as Comfort." She took another drink and handed it back. "But it does warm you a bit."

BY THE time Theo Warner finally stepped out from his drugstore it was ten after eight and Tommy, Jo and Manford White were inside the tavern. They had gone in after Jo saw Theo's brother leave more than an hour earlier, Jo figuring Theo would now probably be the one to stay and lock up and if they weren't going to freeze to death they had better wait somewhere else than in the car. She decided she could keep watch through the window of the tavern, something that made Tommy happy.

As Theo walked to the corner and then headed east on Belmont, Tommy and White grabbed their coats and started out after him. Jo waited until they had turned the corner too and then walked out to the car.

The two stayed on the opposite side of the street from Theo and about thirty feet behind him. The snow and cold that they had been complaining about over the previous two hours had turned into their friend. Only two people passed them on the street, both with heads lowered. Theo walked east to Broadway and then headed south. When two blocks later he turned onto Barry Street, nearing home, they began to close on him.

AT THAT precise moment seven miles northwest, Joe Morrison was sitting by himself in the kitchen of his three-bedroom bungalow finishing a Stouffer's frozen meal, Chicken a l'Orange, which he didn't really like, and sipping a Miller Lite beer, which he did like. The girls were in the living room watching a rerun of "The Brady Bunch"; he thought maybe he could talk them into a game of Monopoly when he finished. Then another thought, the opportunity for something like that would not be around in another month, made him feel queasy. Joanne was in the bedroom, door closed, reading a Sidney Sheldon novel.

Four miles directly to the north, Norbert Castor was sitting in the living room of his one-bedroom apartment, the same one he had lived in for the past ten years since his wife divorced him, switching back and forth with his remote zapper between the Bulls-Lakers game and a middleweight fight on ESPN—Castor loved cable TV—and waiting for the nine o'clock movie on the golden-oldie channel. That night it was *Johnny Belinda*; he could hardly wait. Castor also loved old movies, the ones he never saw when he was a kid. The night before it was *The Third Man*. He had told Morrison the entire plot at lunch that day, much more about the sewers of Vienna than Morrison cared to know. He also told Morrison he thought Orson Welles was sinister enough to be a Chicago cop, but Joseph Cotten could never cut it.

JO KANE followed Tommy and Manford into Barry Street, driving cautiously down the narrow, snow-carpeted street, riding the brake to slow down when she felt she was getting too close to her accomplices, and worrying about skidding into one of the parked cars that were practically bumper to bumper on both sides of the narrow street. She saw Theo turn into the walkway of a six-flat, which she thought did not look all that fancy for a guy with the kind of money he had. Then she cursed because there was no place at all to park, a big Oldsmobile was even in the space opposite the fire hydrant, and at the street corner the cars edged over the crosswalk. Just across the street from Theo's apartment building was an alley, so she decided to pull into it and hope some squad car didn't come by with a couple of cops who might legitimately wonder what the hell she was doing sitting there in the cold. Actually it worked out pretty well. She could pull in just beyond the sidewalk and watch Theo's building on the other side of the street through the rearview mirror.

Theo, with some circulars in one hand that he had picked out of the basket beneath the mailboxes, was about to put his key in the inner hall door when he heard the noise behind him, the outer door opening. He turned to see who it was, a quizzical little smile on his face, but the expression changed instantly when he saw the two men wearing ski masks coming toward him.

He tried frantically to get the key in the door, but before he could manage it one of them had him by the arm and the other grabbed him by the back of his coat collar. He felt a gun barrel in his back just as he heard one of them say, "Not a sound, old man, or you're dead right here."

"What is this?" he somehow managed to say with surprising calm. "What's going on?" although he knew the answer.

"Just open the door," and he was shoved up against it and then pulled back. With his glasses slightly askew and his hand trembling he got the key in the door and they moved into the inner hallway. "What floor?" one of them said. Theo thought he sounded like a black man.

"The first."

There were doors to two different apartments on the first floor, and Theo hesitated between them. "Go ahead, old man, just open the fucking door." Theo, his keyring in hand, finally stepped toward one of the two doors, abandoning the thought of throwing himself screaming and pounding on the other, something he had considered for a moment but could not bring himself to do. When he got the door open they shoved him inside and closed the door behind them.

"Look, take anything you want," Theo said, trying to straighten his glasses and looking up at the two men, who appeared as giants to him, Theo being not even five-foot-six. "That's what you're here for, isn't it, to rob me?"

"You got the picture," the man he thought was black said. The man then tore Theo's topcoat open, wrenched it over his back and off. White reached inside Theo's suitcoat and pulled out a wallet. At the same time Tommy took the wallet from his back pocket, then said, "Shit, there ain't nothin' in here but credit cards, no money.'' Manford took three twenties and two tens from the other wallet.

''I don't carry any money in that wallet,'' Theo said to Tommy in a voice fragile and unsure. ''I've got a little more in the side pocket of my pants, just some . . .'' Tommy plunged his hand in and withdrew some folded bills, two fives and some ones.

Manford pushed him onto the sofa. ''Okay, now where's the money you keep around the house, old man.''

Theo suddenly thought of the gun that had been in his back and wondered why it was nowhere in sight. It did not really matter, he knew, he was in deep trouble with or without it. ''There isn't any money. I mean, maybe there's like fifty dollars in the desk over there. But that's all.''

''Bullshit, we know you stash cash here.''

''I don't keep money here. I don't know where you got that idea.''

''Where is it?''

''Not here. Look around if you don't believe me.''

Tommy grabbed him by the shirt and lifted him off the sofa. ''Where the fuck is it?'' and slammed Theo's back up against the wall.

''I'm telling you the truth.''

Tommy backhanded him across the face, leaving a dull sickening sound hanging in the air as the cartilage in Theo's nose collapsed. Theo screamed out more in shock at the blood rushing from his nose than from the pain. ''Shut the fuck up,'' Tommy said, and backhanded him again, this time the blow glancing off his cheek. Theo forced himself to be quiet, just groaned, and Tommy dropped him. On his hands and knees Theo dug a handkerchief from his pocket to try and staunch the flow of blood from his nose and crawled over to retrieve his glasses, which had sailed across the room when Tommy first hit him.

He had not gotten them on before Tommy had him on his feet again. His hand now clasped around Theo's throat,

"Get started tellin' where the money is or I'm gonna beat you to death right here."

"None" was all Theo could say.

"You're shittin' us," White said, kicking a little end-table out of the way as he approached Theo. "You gotta have money if you goin' away tomorrow. A man don't just up and go to Arizona with fifty fuckin' bucks in his pocket."

"That money I get tomorrow." Theo wondered suddenly how they knew he was going on vacation the next day. "In the morning, at the bank, I get traveler's checks. Please."

"I don't believe you, weasel shit," Tommy said, drawing his fist back.

"Don't hit me again—"

"Shut up, shut up, man," White said, afraid that someone in the next apartment would hear him, but Theo was already in a panic.

"Don't hit me. Somebody help me. Don't hit—" The punch from Tommy's fist to the side of Theo's face silenced him. Tommy let him fall in a heap on the floor. "Dumb fucker," he said.

"C'mon, Joe-ja, let's have a look around. If it's here I'll find it. I spent enough time in other people's houses before I became a respectable businessman that ain't nobody gonna hide a stash I can't find."

The two methodically and quietly tore apart the apartment. Then, almost through and in the back bedroom, Manford heard the noise, indistinct, meaningless to Tommy, but an alarm to White, who wheeled around and bolted through the door. When he got to the living room, Theo was at the front door but did not get it open before White knocked him back down.

Theo looked up at him, his eyes filled now with disappointment and dread, but said nothing.

"We're gonna have to do somethin' about you, old

man. You are not cooperating at all, not one little bit. Isn't that right, Joe-ja?'' to Tommy who was now in the living room as well. ''We are going to have to figure somethin' out here. This is just not goin' down as we expected, old man.''

JO WAS getting nervous, sitting there all this time. A few people had walked by, cars had passed, but at least no cops yet. There was bound to be a patrol car sooner or later, however, and that would be trouble. Tommy's car was such a wreck, they would check it just on general principles, she was sure.

''Chrissake, what's takin' them so long,'' she muttered out loud. They had been there for more than twenty minutes. It should have taken just five, not even that. Simple—take old Theo upstairs, grab the money, tie him to the sink or something and get the hell out of there. They had talked it over, for chrissake. Something had to be going wrong. Then she glanced into the rearview mirror as she had routinely for the past quarter-hour and suddenly her whole body tingled.

Moving toward her through the snow were Tommy and Manford, still ski-masked, each with a hand under the arm of Theo Warner, who was barely walking, looking like he was being dragged to the gallows by a pair of hooded executioners.

''B'Jesus,'' she said, and brought her hand to her forehead. When they got near, Jo slithered out of the car, trying to keep her face concealed behind her hand.

''Get him in the backseat,'' Manford said, ignoring Jo who was now standing beside the car glaring at them through her gloved hand. Tommy opened the door and they pushed Theo inside, Manford sliding in after him. ''Let's get outa here,'' he said, and pulled the car door shut.

Jo walked around the car to where Tommy was now standing, spotlighted under the streetlight with the snow gently falling on him. "What the fuck you two doin', Tommy? Jesus Christ and his mother, what's goin' *on*?"

"There ain't no money up there, Jo. Mebbe only a hundred bucks all told. We went through the whole goddamn place. Your aunt don't know shit, it turns out."

"So what the hell you doin' with him out here?"

"We're goin' back to his store and get what's there, that's what we're doin'. What you think, we're takin' him for a moonlight ride?"

"You dope, he's gonna know who the fuck I am."

"He ain't even gonna see you. I stepped on his glasses up there in the apartment." Tommy took a pair of shattered eyeglasses from his coat pocket, dangled them in front of Jo, then pitched them over the car into a snowbank down the alley.

"He could still know. He's not blind, you big dumb shit. He knows who the hell *I* am. Oh, Jesus."

"Shut up, Jo, get in the car and drive." He pulled her coat collar up and wrapped it around her face. "Just look straight ahead and keep your mouth shut and he won't know who the hell it is drivin'." He shoved her so hard she almost fell into the snow. "We'll take him in the store, you just stay in the car. Simple."

Jo got back in the Maverick and started the engine, put it in reverse and looked into the rearview mirror, where she saw Theo sitting next to Manford, his coat hanging open, the blood caked on his upper lip and chin and staining his shirt and tie, his eyes glazed, his hat tilted at a silly angle, one ear flap across his cheek. He was staring at her, she thought, and then she saw him bring the handkerchief back up to his face as the blood started to dribble out of his nose again.

8

THE SNOW had finally stopped somewhere around midnight and by Friday morning most of the expressways and major streets had been plowed. Morrison made it down to 11th and State by 8:30, thirty-five minutes, not bad. Norbert Castor was waiting for him. Morrison never asked what time Castor arrived, all he knew was that no matter how early he got there old Norb was already at his desk. "Wanna go across the street?" he asked before Morrison even got his coat off. "Grab a bite?"

Morrison shook his head. "I gotta start watching it. In a month I'm paying child support, rent, all the rest. I won't even be able to afford a friggin' cup of coffee, much less a breakfast."

"Sure you will, you'll adjust. Take it from someone who's been there."

"I don't know why it is but I keep saying *frig* these days. Do you think I'm getting so old I'm uncomfortable saying fuck?"

"Yeah, thirty-five's real old."

"Thirty-four." Morrison hung his coat on the hook behind the door.

"Tell me when you start forgetting your kids' names. Then I'll have some sympathy."

"You ever heard the story about when Tallulah Bankhead first met Norman Mailer?"

"What the hell does that have to do with anything, Joe?"

"It has to do with *frig*. She was supposed to have met him at a cocktail party back in the forties or fifties. Somebody introduced him as Norman Mailer who wrote the book *The Naked and the Dead*. She said, 'Oh, I read it. So you're the young man who can't spell *fuck*.' "

"I don't get it."

"In the book, Norb, all the G.I.s said *fug* or *fuggin'*. Back when that was written you couldn't use the word *fuck* in a book."

"Who gives a rat's ass? Get me a book on Florida. That's all I think about these days. I wonder if some old widow down there with maybe several hundred thou socked away is just waiting for the protection and companionship of a mature Chicago police officer to while away the winter of her life. Three years from now, Joe, when the old forms are processed and Norbert Castor, badge number five-four-six-eight-nine, is history, it's goodbye wiseguys. Kill each other off. I won't give a shit."

"Bull, Norb, you'll be bored out of your skull in a month."

"Not so, Joe." Castor looked at him with a certain intensity that was uncharacteristic. "It's what I been thinking about for ten years now. I been saving. I'm gonna get a place down there. I really am. And a boat."

Morrison poured himself a cup of coffee the color and consistency of ink. "This stuff is really swill."

"It's left over from the shift before. I thought we'd go to Dottie's so I didn't make any."

"Okay, get your galoshes. I'll probably go to pauper's prison next month, but what the hell."

Morrison had ham, eggs, toast, hashbrowns and a guilty conscience. They agreed to try and wrap up the street side of the Facia case, go visit Dr. Punpatipal, talk to the yuppie couple who they couldn't get hold of on Thursday, things like that.

After breakfast and a rather thorough rundown for Morrison on *Johnny Belinda,* Castor said he'd go back and make the phone calls if Morrison would pull a car out of the motor pool and meet him in front of headquarters.

MORRISON GOT the unmarked Plymouth and pulled up in front of the State Street entrance and watched the steady flow of lawyers, uniformed cops and others going in and out of the building. He could see them only from the chest up, looking out over the alpine ridge of snow that had been bulldozed onto the curb. He was thinking about the apartment up in Rogers Park he'd found, not far in fact from where Norbert lived. That was not the reason he chose the neighborhood, just a coincidence; in truth he had no plans whatsoever to hang around with his partner after work. They were very different people. But the place was perfect: furnished, one bedroom, a living room, big kitchen with an eating area and an extra room that somebody had fashioned into a kind of TV room. He had not yet signed a lease but knew he had better before the weekend or he was going to lose it and have to go through all the bullshit of looking for another. Signing on the dotted line seemed so final, though—he just had not been able to bring himself to do it.

Morrison's mind suddenly shifted into reverse. He saw the dog, the big Doberman that had been tethered in the backyard next door. He remembered his rage as his wife told him what happened that afternoon.

"Peggy just put her hand through the fence trying to pet him," his wife said. "That animal ought to be put away."

It had bit Peggy's hand and her mother had to take her to the emergency room and it took ten stitches to close the wound. Neal, the accountant who lived with the Doberman, apologized to Joanne for the incident. ''But you know what else he said to me, he said it was really her fault, she shouldn't have put her hand through the fence. Can you imagine that, a six-year-old, it's her fault?''

Neal stepped out on the back porch and was surprised to see Morrison glaring up at him. ''Hey, sorry about the little bite,'' he shouted over, the leashed dog straining, leaping frenetically at the sight of his owner, barking with deep-throated delight. ''Hope the little one's okay. Just tell her not to reach in there anymore.''

Morrison moved to the fence. ''Get rid of that goddamn dog.''

''Now wait a minute, Morrison. This was not the dog's fault. His territory was being invaded and he simply acted with natural instinct. There is a fence there, you know.''

''That animal bit my kid.''

''It didn't mean any harm.'' Neal shook his head at Morrison as if he were talking to a high school student.

''He bit a kid down the street two months ago. He's a goddamn menace to the neighborhood.''

''Don't worry about my dog. Go back to beating up prisoners or whatever you do,'' and he quickly vanished back inside his house.

Morrison walked back into the house, his wife a stride behind him. ''He's an idiot,'' she said.

''No shit,'' he muttered, ignoring her and going back to their bedroom. A moment later he was back out the door, scaling the three-foot fence with one hand for support and the move of an Olympic high jumper. In the other hand was his service revolver. Morrison approached the dog, which greeted him by struggling violently against its leash, its lips curled back and white slime gathering at the corners of its mouth, a low-throated, threatening growl coming out, until Morrison raised the gun and blew its head into a splatter of bone, blood and fur.

Which brought Neal rushing back out onto his porch, not in time, however, to watch Morrison unhook the chain that had tethered the dog and drop it on the grass. "My God, you shot my dog. You killed Shane."

"You bet your ass I did."

Neal was so flustered by the sight, the trauma of it, he could not say what he wanted to say, "I'll call the police," which did not make much sense because it was a policeman who had just destroyed his dog. Or "I'm gonna sue you." But Neal could not get it out, his suddenly shattered heart so overwhelming his mind at the sight of his dog lying there with only about a third of its head left.

"Too bad, Nealie, he was about to attack a kid who started to cut through your yard. I had to do it. You know," Morrison shrugged, "we're here to serve and protect, it's the job. You ought to have kept him on a leash he couldn't get out of."

"I'm going to get back at you for this," Neal said.

"Look on it this way, Nealie. Be positive. Your sacrifice will go down as a service to the neighborhood."

"You wait, Morrison. You just wait—"

"I just want to add one more thing, Nealie. If you get another animal like this one that so much as snarls at one of my kids, I'm not going to shoot it. I'm going to come over and shoot you."

Neal did not get another dog. Nor did Neal and his wife and the Morrisons get together for a lot of July Fourth cookouts or to exchange little Christmas goodies over the next few years. Neal finally moved away and, Morrison thought, probably got another vicious dog to terrorize some other neighbor.

Now Morrison was moving too, with the sudden hope it was not next door to someone who owned a Doberman or a Rottweiler or a pit bull.

He came back to the present with the sight of the hulk of Norbert Castor stalking out the front door of police headquarters, then stopping, trying to figure out how he was going to get over the four-foot snowbank that separated him from the car. Morrison pointed to the crosswalk down at Eleventh Street and Castor set off for it.

"The State's Attorney's office called, said Facia's lawyer told them the girl does not want to press charges. Surprise, surprise," Castor said after getting into the car. "Furthermore she is under medication and her doctor does not want her to talk to any cops. So the SA says to lay off, for now anyway."

"Little political pressure coming down, you think?"

"You bet. I was told Violent Crimes as of this morning has it as far on the backburner as you can get without being in the next apartment. And it's off the blotter. The press didn't get it, and they aren't going to if Facia's connections hang true, and as you can imagine they hang pretty high. The word coming down is no one, and I mean no one, leaks anything on this."

"You want to stow the car and go back upstairs?"

"No. Let's just lay off the kid, Joey. It's a felony, I told the SA, so of course we're gonna investigate it."

"It isn't a felony if she doesn't press charges and there aren't any witnesses around to testify that a crime was committed. I'd think that pretty well wraps it."

"I know. But I didn't tell him it was a fun felony. Not for the kid, I mean. I feel sorry for her. But it happened. And it's Rudy Facia, and because of that it's a fun felony. I mean investigating this shit is what makes the job worth coming to every day. I said, hey, we'll come up with witnesses. His attitude was, hey, don't waste the taxpayers' money, they're gonna take care of it themselves. They insist on it."

"Well, I wouldn't want to interfere with your fun felony," Morrison looked over at his partner, "but Norb, I get the feeling we got to go easy on this. We got to keep it *very* low key."

"I know, that's part of the fun." Morrison shifted into drive. "Wait a second," Castor said handing him a While You Were Out slip. "Here, you had a call. Terry Sawyer, from Six. You wanna give him a call before we go?"

Morrison looked at the note. "Yeah, I guess I ought to."

"Okay, leave the car in the alley. I'm gonna wait inside, shoot the shit with the boys in One, see if they had any good sex cases lately. This neighborhood gets some of the best. Last week they brought in some guy dressed like a broad who was walking around with a rubber dildo up his ass. What a guy, what a neighborhood."

MORRISON LIKED Terry Sawyer. He had been a good partner that last year in Homicide. Sawyer was only a year or two younger than Morrison, but he had spent a longer time in uniform and after trading it for plainclothes did not arrive in Homicide until after a four-year stint in Burglary. Morrison had been Terry's first partner and there was never a question of who was the senior and who was the junior of the partners that year.

Two things Morrison especially liked about Sawyer were that he always wanted to learn, was always picking Morrison's brain or anybody else's in Homicide who was handy, and he seemed to truly care about what he was doing. You had to care about the victim no matter who it was if you were going to be a good Homicide detective. Sawyer, he felt, had all the makings of a good one.

Morrison remembered that Sawyer was unhinged when he told him he had asked for and gotten a transfer out of Homicide; Sawyer even tried to talk him out of it, sounding like he was being abandoned. That had kind of touched Morrison.

THE TELEPHONE number was not Area Six Homicide, Morrison noted, and the voice that answered the telephone was not Sawyer's.

"Terry Sawyer there?" Morrison asked.

"Sure, just a sec."

"How you doin', Joe," Sawyer said when he got on the phone. "It's been a while."

"Yeah, can't complain, except the weather maybe, but what the hell, it's Chicago."

"You like OC?" Sawyer asked.

"It's a lot better than looking at a bunch of corpses. You still enjoying it over there?"

"Beats delivering pizzas for a living."

"I'm not so sure. So what's up? Where are you anyway?"

"At a drugstore over on Halsted. Warner's."

"Oh?" Morrison heard the touch of reticence in his own voice.

"You know, the one owned by the guy who was a friend of your dad's. We stopped in here a couple of times."

"Sure, Theo's place."

"Well, I got some bad news for you, Joe. Somebody did the little old guy in. His brother found the body when he opened up the place at seven this morning."

"Oh, Jesus."

" 'Fraid so. I thought you'd want to know."

"You gonna be there awhile? I'm coming over."

"I'll be here, fill you in when you get here. It's a nasty one, Joe, sorry to say."

"Yeah, see you in a bit, Terry." *They're all nasty,* Morrison thought as he headed downstairs.

CASTOR COULD tell something was the matter when Morrison walked up to him in the First District squad room.

"Hey, Norb. I gotta go up on Halsted Street. Somebody hit a friend of mine, mine and Dad's." Morrison shook his head, more in discomfort than mystification. "You don't have to go. I'll be back in an hour or two. I just want to see if there's anything I can do. I knew him since I was a little kid. He went to school with my old man."

"I'll go along."

Castor reached for the telephone. "Hang on, I'll call Punpatipal and tell him we're not coming this morning either." Castor ran his hand over the few hairs that lay crosswise on his balding head. "I told him we'd be there by ten."

"I bet he's beginning to think he's dealing with the Punjab secret police," Morrison said.

THERE WERE two squad cars, an Evidence Technician van and several unmarked cars outside Warner's Discount Drugs when Morrison and Castor pulled up. A small group were gathered outside sending vaporous tongues of breath at each other as they speculated about what must have happened inside.

Morrison found Bruce Warner sitting at a table by himself in the large room behind the prescription counter in the back of the store, staring at nothing in particular. The body was already gone, a fact that relieved Morrison immensely; and two crime lab technicians were dusting everything in sight for fingerprints. Several detectives were talking to each other, one of them eating a large-size Nestle's Crunch bar that he had appropriated from the candy rack up front.

"Oh God, Joe," Theo's brother said as Morrison approached him, "this is awful, somebody killed him . . ."

"I know, Bruce."

He nodded. "Your friend over there told me he was going to call you." He nodded toward Sawyer.

Morrison put his hand on the older man's shoulder, "I'm really sorry, you know how much I liked Theo."

"Why would somebody do something like this? Why would they have to kill him? Why couldn't they just take the money or whatever?"

"I don't know, but I'll tell you, Bruce, we'll do our damnedest to find out who did it and put him away forever."

Bruce Warner went back to staring off into his own special void again, and Morrison walked over to where his old partner was talking to one of the other detectives.

"This was a rotten one, Joe," Terry Sawyer said, pointing to a fifty-five-gallon drum in the back corner of the room. "That thing's half full of water. Somebody tied the little guy's hands behind his back with adhesive tape and dumped him head first into it. He couldn't get out, drowned. His brother came in and just saw the feet and legs sticking out. Real son of a bitch to do it that way."

Morrison grimaced at the thought of Theo gulping water instead of air and the panic he must have felt in those last awful moments.

"His nose was broken and he had some welts on his face like he was hit with a baseball bat." Sawyer shook his head. "The safe was open. His brother said there was probably three or four hundred dollars in it. And there's a lot of drugs missing. The pharmacist who works for them is taking inventory. Poor guy," Sawyer said, nodding toward Bruce Warner.

"They owned this store for about thirty years."

"A real shame. No sign of a scuffle, doesn't look like he tried to fight them off. Maybe he knew whoever it was. Or maybe he just thought they'd tie him up and leave."

"Nobody else in the store with him last night?" Morrison looked at his former partner, his eyes betraying a little disbelief.

"The last clerk to leave was a Miss Weisenhurst. She

said it was about eight and there was no one at all in the store, just the victim. He told her to get on home, he was going to close up early because of the storm. They ordinarily close at nine. Be careful because of the snow, he told her. How's that for reading it wrong?''

''She didn't see anybody outside when she left?''

''No. In the cold and snow all she was thinking about was getting home. We haven't got the whole thing down yet, but whoever it was ransacked his apartment too. No forced entry but everything turned inside out. I'd guess after they finished with him here they took his keys and went there to see what else they could grab. The old guy was supposed to take off today for some resort in Scottsdale, Arizona, a month in the sun. In fact he was getting out of the business altogether come June. Retiring—it was all set up, the way I hear it. That's part of the reason he was going to Arizona, to look for a place to live out there. The pharmacist''—Sawyer pointed to the young man in the white coat who was busy taking inventory—''was going to buy out his half of the store. Deal was already done.''

''I want in on this case, Terry.''

''Thought you never wanted to see Homicide again.''

''I didn't. But this is different. This is almost family. Theo helped all kinds of people, my old man especially. I want the bastard who put him away like this. I don't want the animal ever to see the street again.''

''Talk to Morano,'' Sawyer said. ''He's your buddy. If the chief of dicks can't do it, nobody can.''

''If I can't get on it officially, I want in on my own time.''

''I understand.'' Morrison turned and started to walk over to where Norbert Castor stood chatting with another detective. ''I got it,'' Sawyer said after him, ''tell your boss, Joe—word's out that Tony Spilotro had it done and it's OC has to get involved.''

Morrison looked back over his shoulder at him. "Spilotro's dead. Don't you read the papers anymore?"

"Oh, yeah, that's right. Well, dig up some live Mafia asshole then." Before Morrison turned again, Sawyer added, "Don't worry, Joe, I'll do anything I can to help. I know how you feel."

9

OUTSIDE MORRISON took a deep gulp of the cold air. He had started to get the stifling feeling in Warner's backroom, the awful angst that had plagued him so much in the last year of his career in Homicide. This time the cold perspiration had not come, nor the panic and tremulousness inside him, but it still felt good to be outside even if the wind-chill factor was fifteen below zero.

"Look, Joe, here's what I think we ought to do," Castor said, "it's almost eleven-thirty and I know this is bothering you. So what do you say we just take it easy a bit. Why don't we go over to the Ox and get a good meal. You always liked that place. They'll probably pop for a couple of drinks too. We can talk it over about how to get you on this thing officially. Okay?"

"Helluva idea, Norb."

The Golden Ox had sat on the corner of North Avenue and Halsted for as long as Morrison could remember. His father used to take him there when he was in high school, what seemed now ages ago, for the sausages, bratwurst, thüringer and knackwurst, usually on a Saturday around noon when it was not so crowded. His father always had the mushroom soup, he remembered, homemade, the best in Chicago, his father claimed, and only on Saturday. After he came on the force he found out that cops were always welcome there. The owner liked to have them around because the neighborhood was dangerous.

After lunch and a couple of steins of Dortmünder, Morrison felt a little better. From the Ox he had called his boss in OC, Lieutenant Roland, whom he got along with pretty well, told him the story, the situation, and asked for TDY on the Warner murder. The lieutenant said he would think about it, that he could not promise anything because it was a "precedent-setter" and he did not like anything that upset routine, "which inevitably serves no purpose other than to fuck up the functioning of the department." But he would mull it over and talk to Morrison at the end of the day. Morrison also put a call in for Tony Morano at Eleventh and State, in that big office on the fourth floor, but he was out.

"So let's go pay our visit to the yuppies," Castor said when they were back out on the street in front of the Ox.

Morrison looked at him, lost for the moment, far removed from Annette Facia and the crime committed against her, but it came back. "Oh, yeah."

"They're only about a mile from here."

"Hell, they're dinks, aren't they, double-income-no-kids? They won't be home on Friday afternoon."

"She will be. I talked to her on the phone earlier this morning. She always works at home on Friday, she told me. She's some kind of sales analyst or economist or some shit like that. They let her work at home on Fridays, on her own computer, she said. Shit, I wish Roland would let me work at home on Fridays. Anyway, she said she'd be there all day—slaving away at her console. I told her I didn't know what time we'd be by because at the time I thought we were going out to see Punpatipal first. What the hell, he'll keep."

HER NAME was Lynn Benson. She was about thirty, more than just attractive, and was wearing running shoes, designer sweatpants and a tanktop.

Morrison did a double-take after he stepped into the one vast room, perhaps eighty feet by forty feet, no partitions, just groupings of eclectic furniture set up as if they were in their own special rooms. The wall at the far end of the room was glass brick, which filtered light into the huge room in a strangely disorienting way, and itself seemed almost to glow. The other walls were raw brick. The whole effect gave Morrison the feeling he was standing in an enormous furniture showroom. The floor was polyurethaned oak checkered with scatter rugs and runners. The ceiling was high, maybe ten feet, and when anybody spoke the voice seemed to echo. The lighting was mostly track lighting hung in rows from all parts of the ceiling, giving Morrison the feeling that maybe now he was standing on the sound stage of a furniture showroom.

As both detectives looked around the room, a little overwhelmed, she noticed their reaction. "Never been in a loft before?"

Both shook their heads.

"It sure is, ah, open," Norbert said, and Morrison thought for sure he heard a resonant but diminishing "open . . . open . . . open . . ." flutter away toward the glass brick wall at the other end.

"It was a spring factory before. Springs for beds. But all the factories around here moved to the suburbs. Now it's all lofts."

"It's different," Castor said. "It'd be really great if you were . . . each . . . claustrophobic." He looked pleased with himself.

"Well, we've got some questions for you," Morrison said.

"Of course. Let's sit over there in the entertainment area," she said, pointing to a rather sprawling section of the room that had an L-shaped, white tufted Danish couch, some glass-topped tables and a variety of uncomfortable-looking chairs. "We have areas instead of rooms." She smiled. "That's what we call them, anyway."

As they walked toward the entertainment area she said to Morrison, "Actually maybe you'd be more comfortable in the den area. In fact that's where I left Bert's notes." She led them over to a far corner of the room, a section with a butcher block table serving as a desk, some teak bookshelves, an Eames chair and ottoman, a leather couch, a pair of endtables and a coffee table that seemed to be fashioned out of some kind of plastic; two frightening African masks hung on the wall.

"Bert your husband?"

"We live together." She paused, then added, "Not married."

"Modern times," Morrison said, and smiled at her.

"Bert made some notes about what happened. He and I went over it together so we wouldn't leave anything out. It was awful, the poor girl. We really would like to help if we can."

"Good." Morrison looked at the adjoining area set off by a row of two-drawer, multicolored file cabinets with expensive assortments of straw flowers and porcelain figurines gracing the top of them. "Quite a setup you've got there," he said, nodding toward what seemed to him to be at least five grand worth of computer equipment and another five in teak office furniture and bookshelves.

"We both use it as an office."

Morrison felt uneasy for a moment, thinking of the minicomputer he had wanted to buy for the girls, four hundred bucks, but Joanne had scotched the idea, telling him the kids could use the one at school and reminding him that they could not afford it now because in their about-to-change life they would need every penny they earned.

"I bring a lot of work home, so does Bert." She smiled

at him, kind of demure and sexy at the same time, and Morrison thought Bert, whoever he was, was probably one lucky guy coming home to that every night. "Does a detective bring work home with him?"

"No," Norbert said before Morrison could answer.

Morrison shook his head. "Some do. It's hard to forget the job."

"I guess I used to," Norbert added. "Before I got jaded. Isn't that what you told me I got, Joe . . . jaded?"

"I can't imagine how anyone in a job like yours could get jaded," Lynn said to Morrison. "I mean, there's a lot of danger, and I'm sure you're constantly encountering, well, a lot of ugliness and—what—vileness?"

"Yeah, we encounter a lot of ugliness, all right," Morrison said, thinking he sure wasn't at the moment. The vileness suddenly brought Sally Spermatozoa back to mind.

Castor lowered himself into the Eames chair, and Morrison sank into the soft leather couch. Lynn walked around the table-desk, sat in the chair behind it and picked up a manila folder to give to them. "Here's the notes."

Morrison took it and handed it to Norbert. "That's fine. We'll look them over." He gave her an appreciative smile. "Help make our job easier. But before we get into that maybe you could just tell us in your own words what you saw."

"We're big on firsthand impressions," Norbert added. "Let's get your ideas of what happened first."

"Sure."

"You were having dinner in that neighborhood, I understand," Norbert said.

"Right. We were going to go to Florence, a restaurant over there. Well, we couldn't get in there, I mean the wait was too long. So we decided to go up the street to Mategrano's instead."

"Where did you first see the girl?" Morrison asked.

"We were walking to Mategrano's, on the north side

of the street. It's a few blocks away from Florence and when we got up to the corner just before the restaurant, I heard this gasping sound from down that street and Bert and I turned and saw this girl standing in front of one of those public housing buildings, maybe twenty, thirty feet away. She said something to us but we couldn't make it out. Then she sort of stumbled and Bert said, 'I think maybe she's hurt.' He told me to stay there on the corner under the street light and he went over to her and then brought her back to where I was."

"Did you see anybody else around at all?"

"Well, there were some people on Taylor Street."

"White? Black?"

"I don't really remember. I think they were white. I think like there were a couple of couples, maybe."

"Did you see anyone at all on the street where the girl was?"

"No, there was no one there, except her, of course. I do remember that because I watched Bert the whole time and I didn't see anybody else there at all."

"Any car pulling away on that street that you noticed?"

"No, I'm afraid not."

"Did she tell you what happened?"

"She just said she'd been hurt—at first, anyway. And she did look like someone had hit her in the face, and she seemed, well, terrified. Bert said he'd better call the police and that maybe we all had better go into the restaurant and he would call them from there. But he didn't have to because just then a police car was coming down Taylor Street and Bert ran into the street and waved it down."

"She didn't tell you she'd been raped?"

"No. She really didn't say anything except just would we help her. I mean I think she was in shock. But when one of the policemen came over with Bert and asked what was wrong she said right out, 'I was raped' and then started to cry. The policeman took her over and put her in the backseat of his car. And then he asked us for our names and addresses and stuff. That was about it.''

Castor had been looking at the pages of Bert's notes while Morrison was keeping his own notes of what the girl was telling them. ''Can we take these with us?'' he asked.

''Oh, sure.''

''Also, do you have a phone I could use? Just a local call.''

''There's one over there on the desk next to my computer.''

Castor walked around the file cabinets to the phone.

Lynn got up and went around the table-desk and sat down at the other end of the couch from Morrison, crossing her arms as she nestled into the soft leather, which had the effect of uplifting her breasts, Morrison noted. ''I wish there was something else I saw that might help, but there wasn't. It was such a shock. I've never experienced anything like it before. Bert may remember something else.'' A little smile appeared at the side of her mouth. ''What about you? Have you been a detective long?''

''About twelve years.''

''Really? That long.''

''You make me sound ancient.''

''I didn't mean it that way. I guess I was thinking that's a long time to be in a job like that.''

Morrison looked at her and noticed she still had the traces of the smile. He was also having trouble keeping his eyes off her chest ever since he noticed the nipples standing out beneath her tank top. He liked her hair, too, reddish-brown, wavy, looking like it would be very soft to the touch. And the thought suddenly filled his mind that he would love to see her naked, sitting there like that at the end of the couch, arms folded, sort of cradling her breasts, legs outstretched and slightly apart. Maybe the bush was reddish-brown, too. ''It's not a bad job, you get used to it.''

"Has anybody ever shot at you?"

"No, not yet. But one of our own got it just the other day."

"Really? Shot?"

"Timmy Blake, a sergeant in Area Six. Been on the force over twenty years."

"Was he killed?"

"No, just got it in the foot—right through the foot, as a matter of fact. Poor guy'll probably walk with a limp for the rest of his life." Morrison noticed Norb was talking into the phone but looking over at him. "What do you do for a living, Ms. Benson?"

"Lynn, please. And I don't do anything exciting, I'm afraid. I'm a direct-mail marketing analyst. Who was it who shot your friend, I mean how did it happen?"

Morrison looked at her, shaking his head. "I'd rather not talk about it, if you don't mind. It's one of those things we on the force try not to dwell on, you know what I mean?"

She reached over and touched his hand. "I do, I can understand."

He thought of her naked again, patting him, her breasts swaying as she leaned over toward him—and then noticed Norbert hanging up the telephone, still watching him. "One more call, okay?" he shouted over. She shouted back "sure," which Morrison heard as "sure . . . sure . . . sure . . ."

"Well, back to business at hand," Morrison said.

"Are you married?" she asked, ignoring back-to-business.

"Sort of."

"Sort of?"

"I'm in the process of getting unmarried, divorced."

"I've heard that line before."

"Well, with me it's not a line. Next month it's all over."

"That's too bad. Or maybe it isn't . . ."

"It's got its good points and its bad ones. When will we get a chance to talk to Bert?"

"Not till Monday. He left on a mill trip this morning. He's in the paper business, taking some clients to see a paper mill in New Orleans. They go through the mill, then stay over the weekend and party. He comes back Monday morning. You'll probably get more out of him Tuesday, if I know those mill trips."

"How we doin'?" Norb asked as he rejoined the two.

"I guess we're pretty well done," Morrison said. "We'll have to wait till next week to talk to Bert. He's out of town. We'll take his notes along, though." Morrison stood up and drew a card from his inside coat pocket. "If anything else comes to mind, you can give me a call. Otherwise we'll call Bert on Monday."

"You know, if you want, I could go back over there with you, where it was that all this happened," she said directly to Morrison. "I don't know, maybe something might come back to me if I was there again."

"That's possible."

"I couldn't do it right now. I've got work to finish here, but I could tomorrow. It's Saturday, though. I don't know whether you detectives work on weekends?"

"Never," Castor answered.

"Not usually," Morrison said. "But, then again, when a case demands it, well, we do. Let me digest Bert's notes first and if I think it would help I'll give you a call tomorrow."

"Sure." She stood up and walked with them to the door.

IN THE car Morrison looked over at Castor. "Why've you got that big shit-eating grin on your face."

"You still got it, boy. That little boyish smile painted all over your face. I heard most of the bullshit. After twenty-some years on the job I developed that talent of listening in the telephone with one ear and to what the hell is going on around me with the other. Comes in handy sometimes. 'One of our own got it the other day.' Jesus."

"Well, I couldn't remember anyone else getting shot lately."

"Shit, if I wasn't along you'd probably be getting laid right now. Probably in the intercourse area. I think that was right next to the entertainment area, or maybe you'd get right down to business there in the den area."

"Norbert, you can be a very crass person."

10

VINNY GOT his first look at Jo's new friend when he walked into the Nashville Lounge on Friday night. The place was one of the less squalid saloons in Uptown where they cleaned the washrooms sometimes as often as once a week and even offered a little entertainment. Kenny and Karla sang country music on weekends. This being a weekend night the two portly entertainers in matching embroidered and bespangled cowboy shirts, Levis and fake snakeskin boots were on the little stage at the far end of the bar, their guitars sending out plaintive twangs as they sang about the grief a woman endures while rescuers dig for her man who is sealed in the local coal mine.

It was nearly midnight and the place was jammed, all the tables filled, the bar packed three deep and the entire place enveloped in a filmy gauze of cigarette smoke that hung in the air along with the odor of stale beer. Vinny studied the room but did not find a familiar face among the few that he could make out in the dark and the haze. He edged his way up to the bar and after a few minutes finally got a seven-and-seven. "You can make me another," he said as he put a ten down on the mottled bar, "this one took so long." The bartender gazed at him, his look for anyone he considered a wiseass, then at the bill on the bar and shrugged. A few minutes later he put another seven-and-seven in front of Vinny and five singles.

"When the hell you raise the prices?" Vinny asked.

"It's always two and a half a drink when we got entertainment."

"You call that entertainment," Vinny said. Kenny was now sitting in a straight-back chair on the stage smoking a cigarette and squeezing at a little cyst on the side of his neck while Karla sang a solo, "Too Close to Home," about a girl contemplating throwing herself into the Watahootchie River because she has just learned she is carrying a baby that was fathered by her brother.

"You don't like it, there's a hundred other saloons in the neighborhood."

"Maybe I'll get drunk enough to start likin' hillbilly music. Why the hell they dress like cowboys, they're from Arkansas, aren't they?"

"Maybe they think they're playin' Cowboys and Indians. In this neighborhood I could believe anything."

Vinny picked up four of the dollars and shoved the other back toward the bartender. It was when he turned back to the stage, where Kenny, who had exchanged places with Karla, was now singing a solo called "Thank God and Greyhound She's Gone," that he noticed the hulking figure at a table off to the side of the stage, just the enormous back with long hair worming its way in greasy strands over the collar of a flannel shirt.

When the big man got up to go to the washroom, Vinny saw Jo sitting at the same tiny table staring up at Kenny and Karla and blowing cigarette smoke in long spirals into the light on the stage. He watched her for a while and then moved down the bar closer to the stage until the hulk he took to be the new boyfriend who Manford White had told him about emerged from the john.

Vinny felt a kind of hollowness in his stomach, a sense of loss as he gazed at the table where the two sat, until he suddenly realized Jo was looking directly back at him. She had a dull sort of expression on her face, as if she were lost in some world of her own.

He looked away, embarrassed to be caught staring at her. When the song ended he was startled to hear his name called. He turned back to see Jo waving at him. "Hey, Vinny," she was yelling, now animated, almost bouncing in her seat. "Come on over." She got up with a little lurch, bumped into her own table and dragged an empty chair from the table behind her, saying, "You ain't using this, are you?" to the couple sitting there but not waiting for an answer. "Come on, come on, Vinny, you little sumbitch."

He knew she was drunk or stoned or both as he made his way toward her table, and he knew without a doubt he did not want to meet the animal sitting with her, but he was drawn to her anyway as irresistibly as sailors to the sirens. "How you doin', Jo," he said as he sat down.

"Just great, old pal. Just absolutely great. Fan-fucking-tastic, in fact."

"Quiet down," Tommy said.

Jo caught Karla glaring down at her from the stage and realized maybe she was shouting, although she had not been aware of it. She posed a pout, as if hurt by the reprimand, and looked even drunker to Vinny. "Vinny," she whispered, "this is Tommy, my good friend Tommy. Tommy, this is Vinny, friend of mine."

Tommy looked across the table at Vinny as if he were a bug splattered on his windshield.

"Yeah, glad to meet ya," Vinny said.

Tommy looked at Vinny's outstretched hand, then at his face. Finally he shook it and, turning to Jo as he did, said, "Who is this little shit anyway?"

Vinny tried to pull his hand back but it was clamped tight. "I'm a friend, okay? I live in the neighborhood. You mind if I get my hand back? I don't drink lefthanded too good."

"Funny little fella." Tommy had a kind of silly smile as he said it.

"Be nice, Tommy," Jo said, still whispering. "Vinny's okay. Might even be able to do you a favor some day."

"Doubt it," Tommy said, finally letting go his hand.

"Don't mind Tommy, he ain't into trustin' a lot of people."

Tommy had gone back to watching Kenny and Karla.

"We scored good, Vinny," Jo said, giving him a drunken wink. "Not as good as we thought we would, but still pretty good. Drugs. Pills. You should see the pills, Vinny. Ups and downs and all-arounds, for chrissake. Heavy stuff too. All kinds of shit. I might not come back to this world for a month, mebbe two."

"What the hell did you hit?"

She shook a finger at him. "Not to ask those questions. We just laid in a little supply for winter, okay?" She giggled. "I'm so high right now, I just love this whole shit. Tommy here, you Vinny, God, and Karla up there, I love her, too." Karla was now into her own scratchy-voiced version of "You Done Stomped on My Heart and Smashed That Sucker Flat." "But I was low before, real low. Goddamn, that's gone now. Tommy, get that cuntass waitress and let's have somethin' here. I'm empty, so is Vinny."

Tommy looked at both of them, at their empty glasses, then grabbed the waitress by the arm as she was passing with a tray of drinks. "Give 'em another. I don't know what the little shit's drinkin' but give him one."

"Thanks," Vinny said to Tommy after the waitress left. "I'll be even. Where you from anyway, Tommy?"

"What do you care?"

"For chrissake, Tommy, he's just tryin' to be friendly," Jo said. "I mean, get mellow. Have a good time like the rest of us." She reached under the table, her hand traveling up his thigh, a brief journey ending at Tommy's crotch.

"Come on, Tommy, be nice." Finding what she wanted there, Jo grabbed it, squeezing it, shifting him into neutral.

He looked over at Vinny. "The south. The land of cotton. Where niggers never used to cause any trouble and the jails were the assholes of the earth. Only half a that's true these days." Tommy gave Vinny that strange smile again.

Vinny wished he had gone in search of a little poker game or some craps instead of coming to the Nashville, never mind that Jo was being nicer to him than she had since that night of nights.

"By the way," Jo said to Tommy as she brought her hand back onto the table, "you give the piece back to Manford yet?"

"No. Maybe I'm not gonna."

"That's bullshit, Tommy. He loaned it to you. He helped us. Quit bein' so fuckin' nasty." She had her hand under the table again. "Just remember what we got now's gonna run out sooner or later. Be nice and just give it back, okay?"

"When I get around to it." He slunk back into his chair, enjoying what was going on under the table.

"But you will get around to it, right, Tommy?"

Vinny's street-sense told him to look as if Kenny and Karla had his full attention. They were now into a duet—"Thanks to the Cathouse, I'm in the Doghouse with You." He did not want Tommy to think he was hearing what they were talking about, and worse, he did not want to see what Jo was doing to Tommy under the table. Still, all he heard was the conversation between Jo and Tommy, and all he could think about was the groping and fondling that was turning Tommy on and not him. He also thought, as he looked at Tommy, that he was sitting with a creature that had crawled out of a swamp down South one dark night and somehow got on up to Chicago.

"Yeah, I suppose I will," Tommy said. "Sometime."

"Say, honey, I think yo' gettin' all worked up down

there.'' Tommy just grinned at her across the table. Vinny felt like throwing up.

The waitress brought the drinks, and suddenly Jo held up both her hands. ''Shush,'' she said, nodding toward Karla, who was now serious with the microphone, telling the uninterested audience that she was going to sing *the* song she had written herself. It was soon to be recorded, she said, something she had been telling audiences at the Nashville for the past two years.

''Tommy, this is the best song I ever heard,'' Jo said, her voice thickening. ''Ah cry every time Karla sings it. Listen up, both of you.''

Karla began strumming while Kenny sat down and lit a cigarette. And the words poured from her heart, her ballad about Jenny who had loved no one but Jimmy since their days at Pine Bluff High only to see him run off to Little Rock with the town tart. She sang of the lingering loss, the long days and longer nights, so lonely until Jimmy finally came back. Together again they made love as if time had stood still and her man had never gone away. But Jimmy was a rover and soon he was gone again, this time leaving her with another broken heart and a social disease.

When it was over, Jo's eyes were filled with tears and Kenny and Karla were leaving the stage for a break amid scattered applause.

''I'm gettin' real low again,'' Jo said. ''Let's get outa here.'' She looked at Vinny. ''Come on, you come along. We'll go back and do some drugs. We got pills galore, Vinny. We'll all feel great.''

Tommy reached over and put his huge hand on her arm. ''I think goin's a good idea. Doin' some drugs is a good idea. I think what else we are gonna do to feel good don't need no spectator. And I think we are gonna do lots of it.''

''Yeah, well, I couldn't make it anyway,'' Vinny said, getting up. ''Thanks for the drink, I'll catch up later.''

Jo was looking up at him, the tears still in her eyes.

"You come by tomorrow, Vinny. I'll give you some stuff you gonna love."

"Sure," Vinny said. "Nice meetin' you, Tommy. Maybe I'll see you sometime tomorrow." He walked down the long bar to the door that led back out into Uptown, feeling very sour in his stomach.

11

MORRISON FINALLY contacted Tony Morano late Friday after he and Castor had gotten back to 11th and State, reminding the chief of detectives that Morrison still held several chits for services past and would like to call one in. Morano, who played the game as well as anybody—something that had contributed more than a little to his successful ascent to the big office on the fourth floor at police headquarters—listened and then said okay, he'd talk to Lieutenant Roland about letting Morrison work the Theo Warner murder—part-time.

On Saturday morning Morrison went to Area Six Violent Crimes to look at the sheets on the Warner case. Not a lot yet. A lot of familiar faces came by, surprised to see him there sitting at a desk next to the rack of uncleared homicide cases. Morrison sensed he actually missed Area Six, not Homicide but the dicks who were on the street every day, who went out together afterwards, who inhabited one world, a part of their lives that outsiders rarely entered. It was much more somber on State Street, everybody more wrapped up in watching their own asses, except for Norbert Castor, maybe. Morrison had become pretty much a loner during the past year or two, he realized; it was not a good thought.

Timmy Blake was out of the hospital, Morrison learned,

doing fine or as fine as one could with a newly gouged hole through one's instep, but would probably be off the job for at least six weeks. Sally Spermatozoa had been advised to cool it around the district for a while, but word was that she had been sufficiently satisfied by the experience to last her until the whole thing blew over, which would probably be a week or two. Then he called Terry Sawyer at home. Sawyer was just on his way out to coach his kid's sixth-grade basketball team but agreed to meet Morrison around noon for a sandwich and a beer so they could talk about the case.

WARNER'S DISCOUNT Drugs was open for business when Morrison arrived at 10:30. Bruce Warner was not in, the only ones there were the young pharmacist and several clerks. Morrison talked with each, but none had anything of note to add. The funeral was set for Tuesday, he was told, with a visitation before it at the church, Wrigleyville Unitarian, a block from Wrigley Field. He had often gone to Cubs games there with his father, and once Theo Warner had gone with them, he suddenly remembered, back when he was in seventh or eighth grade. Funny how that game came back with such a special clarity. Maybe it was because it was so apparent that day that Theo Warner had little interest in baseball, unlike his father, and had just come along as a friend, not a fan. Morrison remembered that he spent half the game explaining what was going on to Theo, who tried hard to pretend interest. It was a game against the St. Louis Cardinals, the archrival Cardinals. The Cubs had a good team that year and he remembered thinking they might just go all the way, hell, they had Ron Santo and Billy Williams and Fergie Jenkins and Ernie Banks, but Ernie was pretty old then, shifted over to first base, in fact, so he wouldn't get into any real trouble in the field. And Leo the Lip, as everybody called Durocher in those days, was in the dugout ready to explode onto the field at any moment to shout down an umpire. But the Cardinals were better. Theo never could understand how Lou Brock was able to just race from first to second base when nobody hit the ball. Young Joe tried to explain stealing bases to Theo, but his spiel fell on unapprehending ears. Brock stole two bases for the Cardinals that day and Big Bob Gibson with that cannonball right arm of his beat the Cubs 4–2. Theo, however, went happily home, unmindful of the great catch Don Kessinger made of an Orlando Cepeda line drive that otherwise would have scored two more Cardinal runs or the home run Santo hit with one on in the sixth.

The memory still works pretty good, Morrison told himself—some things, anyway—then wrote down in his notebook the time of the visitation and the address of the church. Thank God it wouldn't be an open casket affair like all the Catholic wakes he'd been to over the years.

Morrison was surprised at how quickly the schema of homicide investigation came back—the dog-work first. Up and down the street, in the stores, the saloons; it was a start. He had about an hour before meeting Sawyer. But he got nothing. The only establishments within two blocks of Warner's that had been open the night of the murder were a couple of bars, an all-night convenience store, and a storefront restaurant specializing in Cajun cooking that had in fact closed down at 8:00 after the owner realized no one was going to venture out in the snowstorm in quest of blackened redfish or red-pepper rice. The bars had had a good trade that night, however, and Morrison left word with the bartenders that he would appreciate the favor—returnable, of course—if they would see if any of the regulars noticed anything out of the ordinary on the Thursday night of the murder. He would check back Monday, he told them.

VINNY HAD a terrible hangover that morning among other assorted pains. After leaving the Nashville he'd wandered over to J.J.'s, saw it was pretty full and went in, thinking he might find somebody to talk to and get his mind off Jo and the Neanderthal who had come into her life. He was throwing them down pretty good but he was in a funk and nobody seemed interested in talking to him. Clare, the waitress from the hashhouse, was there sitting at the other end of the bar with a hillbilly and his girlfriend, all three at this point just drinking and not talking to each other, lost in their own peculiar alcoholic reveries. In the back, two young but already wizened men who had probably caught on with Readyman that morning for a day's minimum-wage labor were playing pool under a cone of light that highlighted their leathery faces.

He tried to talk to the guy next to him, a wiry kid from Tennessee dressed in motorcycle boots, dirty Levis and a white T-shirt with a pack of cigarettes rolled into one sleeve like the boppers used to do in the fifties. On the front of the T-shirt was a message, the picture of two sizzling fried eggs captioned with: "These are my brains. Any questions?" Vinny should have picked up the message. The guy also had a tattoo of a dagger with a snake coiled around it on one arm and a bleeding heart with the words LOVE SUCKS under it on the other arm. He was with two other guys and seemed annoyed every time Vinny tried to join their conversation. The other two called the tattooed Tennesseean Winfred. Vinny didn't know whether it was his first name or last name, thought with the accent, though, that it was probably a first name. They named them funny down in the hills, Vinny had learned shortly after moving to Uptown. Sometimes it was a Bobby or a Billy, but just as often it was a Winfred or a Harlow or a Sanford.

He had gotten into it once with a Sanford, Sanford Stokes, a little guy with rotting teeth and reptile skin, Vinny remembered, but it was broken up before either could hurt the other. Sanford was now in Stateville doing one to three for making the mistake of trying to snatch the purse of an off-duty policewoman whose eye he blackened and nose he rearranged before she managed to get the snubnose .38 out of her pocket in the struggle, which ended it abruptly. Vinny thought Sanford must have gotten quite a reception when he arrived at the Town Hall stationhouse for booking with the bruised and bloody lady, the place she ordinarily spent eight hours a day or night working out of with her fellow officers.

Vinny was sipping on a straight shot of Seagram's Seven, which he chased with a glass of Old Style draft, while he was thinking about all this, and then got to staring at himself in the mirror behind the bar and trying to figure out why Jo didn't see the Tony Bennett in him and how instead went for a leadhead who looked like a slightly scaled-down version of the Incredible Hulk. He never did notice the man who sat down on the empty stool to his left. When the man ordered a bottle of Heineken, hardly a common order in J.J.'s where ninety percent of the customers didn't even know there was a country named Holland much less a beer that cost twice as much as Budweiser. Vinny looked over. The man was about fifty, dressed a lot better than the neighborhood warranted. One glance and Vinny pegged him.

"You with those guys?" the man asked, nodding toward the three sitting on Vinny's other side.

Vinny turned toward them and saw only the white T-shirted back of Winfred LOVE SUCKS, who was now talking in almost a whisper to his buddies, their heads all gathered together as if they were in a football huddle. "Yeah, but we're in the middle of a game," Vinny said. "I Got a Secret. It's my turn. I gotta guess what it is they're talking about." Winfred turned and glared at Vinny, who went back to staring into the mirror.

The man chuckled self-consciously. "You must be from around here." Vinny ignored him. "You like it, the neighborhood?" Vinny continued staring ahead. "Pretty tough turf." Coming from the man it sounded sappy.

"Look, if you're trying to pick somebody up, pal, you're in the wrong place," Vinny said. "Don't bother me, I got a lot on my mind."

"I don't mind paying for it."

Vinny looked him straight on. "Get the fuck away from me. Go down to Fagtown, Diversey and Broadway, you can find all the fruit you want there."

"I don't like that kind of stuff," the man said. "I like it rough." He looked at Vinny. "I'll do anything you want. You can do anything to me. I'll pay you well."

Vinny wheeled around on the bar stool and shouted, "I said get the fuck out of here, queerball."

Mason the bartender loomed in front of them, his face a map of fights past and with eyes as unflinching as a snake's. "What's the matter?"

"He's fruit," Vinny said.

The bartender looked at the man, sizing him, then jerked his thumb toward the door. "Get out." The man seemed about to say something back. "You hear me," the bartender added, his hand coming from under the bar and inching across it as if to grab the man. It was enough, the man got up and walked toward the door, never turning back.

The hillbillies had broken up their huddle to listen, and Winfred LOVE SUCKS said to Vinny, "Feudin' with your honey, huh," and laughed uproariously.

"Not funny, asshole," Vinny said, not even bothering to turn to look at him. The shot of Seagram's was halfway to Vinny's mouth when he was suddenly separated from it, the forearm adorned with the snake-encurled dagger smashing into him and knocking Vinny off the bar stool, the Seagram's splashing on his chest as he headed toward the floor, the shot glass bouncing along the bar. The hillbilly stood over Vinny and inquired, "What did you call me?"

Vinny stared up, unhurt and befuddled from all he had had to drink that night. "Nothing."

"The fuck you didn't."

As soon as he said it, Vinny knew he shouldn't have. But some deep primeval Italian instinct that he was helpless against took hold, and so he said it: "Fuck off." Then he followed it with a scream from the searing pain from LOVE SUCKS' motorcycle boot, which slammed into his side with the certified intention of restructuring Vinny's rib cage. Then Winfred was on top of him, fists flailing, a couple of them landing on the forehead, the cheek, the neck, the mouth, but somehow Vinny managed to scramble out from under and get to his feet, bleeding a little from the lower lip, the redness on his face rising before the swelling. But Winfred was between him and the door, and the other two guys were off their stools and behind him.

"Look, hey, take it easy," Vinny said as Winfred LOVE SUCKS took a step toward him. "I didn't mean nothin' by it. Just the booze talkin'." The guy had Vinny now, his hands with short staccato jabs pushing Vinny backward into the arms of the other two. Vinny did not know what to make of it when LOVE SUCKS suddenly dropped into a catcher's crouch before him. What is this fucker, some kind of kung fu nut, gonna jump up and kick me in the head? But as the guy sprang back up, Vinny saw that wasn't the case. He saw the knife that had come out of the top of the motorcycle boot, its steely gray blade long, double-edged, probably forged and honed to clean a deer in record time in somebody else's hand. LOVE SUCKS held it out in front of him; it looked like an extension of his arm, Vinny thought, like it was very much at home in the guy's hand, had been there before, lots of times.

"Howja like a taste of your ear. Howja like I just cut the thing off and stuff it in your mouth." The knife flashed in front of Vinny's face, a little Zorro action, but the blade didn't touch flesh. "With a fuckin' ear in your mouth mebbe you'd have trouble callin' other people names, huh?"

The noise startled everybody and the concussion rattled the bottles on the shelf behind the bar. Mason the bartender raised the sawed-off pool cue, two feet of lethal leaded stick no longer of any use in a game of eight-ball, and rapped the bar an ear-shattering rap to make his point. Fixing LOVE SUCKS with ice eyes, Mason flipped up the bar bridge and stepped around to the customer side. "Put the knife away. I don't want any of that shit in my place."

Winfred stared back, the coldness of confrontation holding him.

"I got no truck with you," the bartender said, opening it up for Winfred. "You put the knife away, you can sit back down and drink yourself crazy for all I care." He slapped the cue gently into an open palm. "But I ain't going to lose a license because you cut up somebody in my place. Sooner I'd send you to the hospital than let that happen."

Winfred looked at his knife, then at the bartender standing between him and the door. His scowl melted a little. "Awwright, we won't gut-up the asshole in your joint. We'll just take him on outside."

Mason shook his head. "You don't get it. You don't understand. You do something outside to him, it's like you do it in here. The cops come. They find out it started here. They got my ass and my license. Going outside ain't one of your choices. Your choices are you guys sit back down and Salerno here gets his ass out of here, or you guys leave and he sits back down. One or the other." Then the opening again. "Why don't you just fart the bug out of your ass and forget the kid's got a stupid mouth. You already let him know you don't like him. He'll know it when he looks in the mirror tomorrow too."

Winfred said, "Awwright," again. "Let him go," he said to his buddies. By the time LOVE SUCKS straightened up after sliding the knife back into his boot, Vinny had grabbed his coat and was gone, back out into the snow-covered street, relieved that both ears were still bookending his head.

IT WAS almost two in the afternoon when Vinny walked into the Tudor Arms. He hesitated before going upstairs, then rapped on the door to the janitor's apartment. The door opened about six inches and Head's massive rusty dome and sad-eyed face filled the open space.

"Your buddy around?" Vinny asked. "Manford?"

"He here." Head just stared out at him.

"Well, can I talk to him or do I have to make a fucking appointment?"

Head's dull stare turned to a dull smile and he shouted in the direction of the bedroom at the end of the hall. "Hey, Man, the little guy's here, the one with the connections. Wants to talk to you, Man. You wanna talk with him?"

Vinny could hear the footsteps on the bare floor, then saw Manford White's face replace Head's in the crack of the doorway.

"Well, sure, look who it is," White said. Opening the door all the way now, no shirt, only the gold chains around his neck.

In one hand Manford White was holding his cowboy boots, snake-skin with pointed silver-overlaid toes—killer boots, they were known in the trade—and a pair of orange socks in the other. "Come on in, Butter Cookie. We talk. You know I wouldn't want to get on the wrong side of the boys. So you is always welcome here. 'Specially if you want to do a little business." Head closed the door behind them.

"Maybe."

"Maybe you needin' something. You not lookin' too good," White said, his eyes on Vinny's face.

"I'm okay. Maybe I'd like a couple of packs of blow. If you got it, that is. And if the price is right."

White sat down on the ratty frayed sofa that had probably looked decent around the time of the Inchon landing and began putting on the orange socks. ''I got it. How many? Two? Three? Four?''

''Two.''

''That will require a C, Butter Cookie.''

''Forget it, I can get it for half that on the street.''

''Not the same stuff. This is pure as that heaven-sent snow outside, clean as the queen's pussy.''

''No,'' Vinny said, aware that his total net worth at that particular moment was the forty-two dollars he had in his pocket and the two twenties he had stashed back at his apartment. ''Maybe tomorrow. If I have a good night tonight.''

White shrugged. ''Well, the store be open then too.''

Vinny made no move for the door. Instead he screwed up his face a little and asked, ''You, ah, know that guy Jo's been hanging with. Is he living up there, too? With her?''

''Well, now, I think I'm gettin' the real message why you stopped by to see old Manford.'' White laughed. ''You know, Head, I don't think this young man wanted to make a little buy at all.'' Head nodded. ''Oh, hell, it don't matter. We friends, you, me, *the boys*. Would certainly wanna keep it that way.''

Vinny hated being put on and reached for the doorknob.

''Hate to break your heart but I'm afraid they are all comfy-cozy up in that little apartment. At least nightwise, anyway. He got something goin' in the daytimes, though. Gone most of the time. Boostin', probably.''

Vinny's interest perked. ''He up there now?''

''Don't think so. Thought I saw him hulk that big redneck out of here couple hours ago.''

''Thanks,'' Vinny said without meaning it and opened the door. ''Maybe I'll be by tomorrow.''

Vinny hoped White was right when he knocked on Jo's

door, and was ecstatic when he heard Jo say from behind it, "That you, Tommy?"

"No, it's me, Vinny."

"Damnation, what in hell happened to you?" Jo said when she opened the door and saw the bruise on his cheek, the knot on his forehead and the balloon lip. She grabbed him by the arm. "Come on in."

The room smelled of old cigarette smoke. Items of clothing, women's and men's, were strewn on the floor and over the few pieces of furniture in the small room. Glasses, a few dishes and an old pizza box with a few hunks of crust in it were on the sink in the little kitchenette at the corner of the room. The door to the bedroom was open, the bed unmade. It wouldn't be this way, Vinny thought, if she was living with me instead of the animal.

"You get rapped on the way home or what?"

Vinny waved it off. "It was nothin'. I just got into a thing with this asshole over at J.J.'s. Stopped there on the way home for a few more and a couple of games of pool."

"Sure looks like you got a lot more'n that."

"Guy sucker-punched me. Little asshole suckered me, then got a couple of shots in before I could get it together. Guy was with two other guys. Mason—you know him, the guy who owns the joint and could beat the shit out of the whole Marine Corps if he had to—held the other two off. The asshole isn't gonna sucker-punch anybody for a while. I did a number on his hands with a pool cue after it was over. I don't think he'll even see his knuckles for a couple of weeks. Got a couple of softballs stickin' off his wrists this morning."

"I shoulda brought you back here with me and Tommy. We had a good old time. Doin' a little this, a little that," she said, gesturing first as if she were smoking then popping something into her mouth then drinking. "Not much else. Tommy got in a poke, a two-minuter, but that was all after he found out my period started. Guess he don't like blood on his dick."

"Yeah, well, I just came by to see what was goin' on. Last night you said to stop by. Remember?"

"Lot I don't remember about last night. But I do remember you was with us listenin' to Karla."

"Yeah, you were tellin' me about all the stuff you got."

"Shouldn't have. That's what Tommy kept tellin' me. He weren't real happy about it, me telling you about it. But then he don't know you, Vinny." She motioned toward the bedroom. "Come on, Vinny, I'll show you."

Vinny followed her into the bedroom and watched while she pulled two boxes out of the closet. "Look at this," she said, taking a Zip-loc plastic bag from one box. "Snort. Christ be told, there it was, just waitin' to be scooped up."

"Where?"

Jo ignored the question, dropping the bag of cocaine back into the box and extracting a couple of plastic bottles of Demerol. "The real stuff. Couple of these little buggers and you could forget bein' gang-raped by a pack a German shepherds. Morphine too. And a shitload of uppers. And look at this," she said opening the other box. It was filled with four-ounce brown bottles. "G.I. Gin, that's what Tommy calls it. Says the old guy he celled with down in Georgia told him about it. Guy used to get it when he was in the army when he was sick or somethin'. It's cough medicine, but it's somethin' else."

Vinny picked up one of the bottles and looked at it. Printed on the label were the letters ETH & C, which stood for elixir terpin hydrate and codeine—forty-eight percent alcohol laced with four grams of codeine. Jo was not exaggerating its potency; Tylenol 3, prescription, had only a half-grain of codeine. And Tommy's old cellmate was correct too, it was why a lot of G.I.s in World War II and

Korea complained of wracking, chronic coughs bad enough to go on sick call as often as they could get away with it.

"Take it with you," Jo said. "Hell, we musta got thirty bottles of it. You'll love it. Goes great, better than vodka and Valium. It'll take you to faraway places, the only thing is you might not come back." She laughed. "But hell, everything you do in life's a chance, right, Vinny?"

He put the bottle in his pocket. "Yeah, I guess. A lot of chancy things, 'specially in this neighborhood."

When they heard the knock at the door Jo pushed the two boxes back into the closet. "Probably Tommy," she said. Several organs inside Vinny's body cringed.

12

TERRY SAWYER was already sitting at a table in the Candlelight Lounge, a pizza-and-sandwich place on the far north side, sipping a bottle of Coors Light when Morrison walked in. Sawyer lived on the far north side, in west Rogers Park, a nice section of the city with more homes and bungalows than apartment buildings, about as close to the suburbs as one could get without actually being in them, which were off-limits as far as living went for a Chicago cop because police policy mandated all Chicago policemen had to live within the city limits. Being Catholic, however, Sawyer would never say he lived in west Rogers Park. If asked, he would say he lived in St. Margaret Mary's parish. Catholics in Chicago saw the city geographically only in parishes. Where did you grow up? Not the north side or the south side. Not Lincoln Park or Woodlawn or Beverly or some other nominated neighborhood as the city was legitimately divided. In Chicago a Catholic grew up in St. Ignatius parish or St. Sabina's or Queen of All Saints. Non-Catholics, as the Catholics referred collectively to all other Chicagoans, recognized neighborhoods and aldermanic wards as the places they were born, raised, or currently lived in. Morrison, a lapsed Catholic, when asked, grew up in St. Tim's parish, also known as St. Timothy's, but was now looking for an apartment in Rogers Park.

"You bring home a winner this morning?" Morrison asked as he sat down.

"Don't ask."

"It matters not whether you win or lose, it's how you play the game. Grantland Rice, I think it was, said that."

"Bullshit."

"That's what Mike Ditka said."

"Forty-two to sixteen. How the hell can they play four quarters of basketball and score only sixteen points?"

"How'd your kid do?"

"He scored four points. Two lay-ups." Sawyer gave a half-hearted shrug. "No Michael Jordan yet."

Sawyer, a sports nut, coached kids' basketball in the winter, the neighborhood Little League team in the summer. When he and Morrison were partners they had gone to a couple of Cubs games together, and Morrison had come up with a pair of tickets for a Bears game one freezing December Sunday, endearing himself forever to Sawyer, who took his kid. Morrison had not the least inclination to bundle up and sit in great discomfort in the fierce cold of Soldier Field when he could watch it at home on television.

Sawyer was also a physical-fitness nut, Morrison remembered. Worked with weights, jogged, drank only a few beers now and then. It was how he expunged the job from himself after work, pump the weights in his basement or take on the Nautilus over at the YMCA until all the day's anxieties and horrors and frustrations were purged out through his pores and then toweled away along with the perspiration. Probably a lot healthier than drowning it out in some cop bar, Morrison had conceded but never considered emulating. Still, in a way, Morrison had envied his junior partner, how he could routinely dispatch the job when the shift was over and arrive so fresh for the next one. He had wondered how long it could last.

Taking him in from across the table now—lithe, energetic, involved, still anticipating the challenges—the formula was still working, Morrison thought.

"Let's eat," Morrison said, waving at a waitress. Both ordered the All-American lunch—cheeseburgers, fries and beer. "I made a quick run through the neighborhood this morning. Nothing. Just the stores and saloons. Monday Castor and I'll hit the apartments there, above the stores, and then his neighbors over where he lived."

"We already talked to his neighbors. Nobody saw or heard anything. The old couple who lives right next door weren't even home. They'd been at their daughter's house during the day and she insisted they stay overnight so as not to have to drive back to the city in the snowstorm."

"Fingerprints?"

"A lot of his. In the apartment, anyway. But nothing else. Whoever turned the place upside down wore gloves. All kinds at the store, like you'd figure. They're being sorted out."

"You think this was a professional?" Morrison asked.

"No. No. It's got all the make of a drughead, but not a dumb one. He knew what he wanted in the line of prescription medicines. We got the inventory of what was missing late yesterday. Which brings me to another point."

Morrison took out his schoolboy notebook and a ballpoint. "Go ahead."

"They grabbed the usual crap—Valium, codeine, stuff like that, you know, Percodan, Demerol, Dilaudid, some of that codeine-laced cough syrup. I didn't even know they dispensed that anymore. Jesus, it makes Wild Turkey seem like three-point-two beer. That was about it, according to the pharmacist and the brother, Bruce. But they got pretty good amounts of it. The Warner boys had a pretty good-size business over the counter, it seems."

"They did all right, I think."

"But wait, here's the hitch. You know the back room,

where they made up the prescriptions behind the racks, where the body was?''

''Yeah.''

''Well, the back wall had shelving, floor to ceiling, you know the kind, steel shelves you can adjust, make 'em a foot apart or eighteen inches or whatever, about three-feet wide. There were three of them. The one on the far right, I noticed, was a little taller than the other two, about an inch or so. The reason being it was on casters. Inquisitive minds like mine and those that read the *Enquirer* prompted me to roll it out to see what was behind it. There was a door. No knob. Just a keyhole. So I asked Bruce about it and he told me it was just a storeroom where they kept stuff they didn't want laying around. He said whoever ripped them off didn't find it because nothing was missing from it.''

''What'd they keep in it?''

''That's it. He seemed like he'd prefer I just drop the subject. Nice about it, but something didn't seem quite kosher. So I asked him to open it up, and he did. It was like a linen closet, about three feet deep and it had some shelves at the back. That's where they kept the good stuff—pharmaceutical cocaine, morphine, some pretty heavy stuff. And a helluva lot of it to have on hand, I thought.''

''Anything contraband?'' Morrison said uneasily.

''No, everything was legit for a pharmacy. He said they supplied a number of clinics and nursing homes in the neighborhood on a regular basis. The coke they mix up with some other stuff for certain medicines. I got the names, and they checked out with the lab as legit. Ophthalmologists use the stuff too, Bruce told me, and that checked out with the boys in the lab.''

''But something's still bothering you?''

''Yeah. I can see the stuff hidden. That doesn't bother me. It's how *much* of it they had. I took a count and it seemed high. The boys downtown thought it was too.''

Sawyer took out of his back pocket some folded and stapled sheets of paper. "Here's the inventory. Take a look for yourself."

Morrison looked at the quantities and descriptions. "Does seem a little much."

"I got to wondering if maybe they didn't have a little something going on the side. From what I'm told you can make a form of speedball from morphine and pharmaceutical cocaine, fancy stuff, cleaner and much better, safer than you'd find on the street. Maybe they were dealing a little and one of their customers got dissatisfied or maybe just knew the stuff was there and when he couldn't find it and Theo wouldn't tell him where it was he showed him just how displeased he was. It's a theory, anyway."

"I don't see Theo or his brother dealing. They're not the type," Morrison said.

"Well, I'm not saying they are. It could be a possibility, to my way of thinking, that's all. I hope I'm wrong. Hell, I've been wrong enough times before. You were the one who never seemed to be wrong, as I remember. Why don't you do the city a favor and transfer back?"

Morrison smiled. "No thanks."

After lunch Morrison walked over to the pay phone in the Candlelight, looked in his notebook and dialed a number. When he heard the hello at the other end he asked, "Lynn Benson?" although he recognized the soft voice immediately. "This is Detective Joe Morrison."

"Oh, sure."

"I decided to work today, a murder case, but thought I might put some time in on the Facia rape. You still think something might come back if we went over to Taylor Street?"

"Could be. Can't promise, but maybe. Can you give me about an hour?"

"Pick you up about two."

TOMMY GAVE Vinny a look as if the little guy had just pissed on Tommy's foot, which was in fact wet from the snow he had been trudging through. "What's he doin' here?" Tommy asked Jo.

"Just dropped by. Member, I told him to last night."

"Don't remember. Somebody gave you a little face job, huh?" he said to Vinny.

"I came out of it okay, better'n he did."

Tommy grinned. "I know, on the way home you just threw open your coat and showed some girlie that little pecker of yours and she took one look and then whaled the shit out of you."

"Hang on, Vinny," Jo said suddenly and then disappeared into the bedroom. Vinny fantasized Tommy lying there on the floor of the apartment, clutching his stomach, the blood oozing through his fingers from the holes left by a couple of hollow-nosed .45s, a pitiful pleading death moan rolling over his lips and pervading the room but falling on uninterested ears. Reaching out now with a bloodied hand, trembling for a last touch of something human but grasping only air. Then the convulsions. Then—

But Jo was back, a handful of capsules in each hand. "Here's somethin' to make your day, wild and wicked or soft and sleepy. Your choice." She handed them to him and smiled. "Now you behave yourself. Fightin's for guys like Tommy. He'd as soon fight as fuck."

Tommy grinned in agreement.

"But you, Vinny, you should be usin' your brain instead."

As Vinny walked out into the sunless afternoon, the pills in one pocket, the G.I. Gin in another, the now dirtied snow everywhere adding to the grayness of his mood, he thought: just one big score, something special, a brain-play—he had the brain, she'd said it herself—then he'd be back. He'd show Jo the money, the roll as big as a baseball, and no ones fattening it up. And that just to carry. Come on, let's get out of here, he'd say. To L.A. No, to Vegas. Hell, wherever Sinatra was playing or Bennett or Deano. That's where they'd go. Just the two of them.

13

NORBERT CASTOR was in an especially ebullient mood Monday morning, telling Morrison about the double-feature he'd watched over the weekend—*The Razor's Edge* and *Forever Amber*—as they drove to the neighborhood of Warner's Discount Drugs. Morrison nodded from time to time but was thinking more about one of the last homicide cases he had worked on, one, he felt, that stretched any definition of irony. He was thinking about it because he had read in the *Tribune* that morning the Grateful Dead were coming back to town in the spring for a concert out at Poplar Creek west of the city and all the Deadheads, as their followers liked to be called, would be streaming in to camp out, snarl traffic, aggravate the local police and annoy the otherwise laid-back suburbanites of that area.

The Deadheads who followed the GD around the country to their concerts were holdovers from the 1960s—Woodstock revisited, long-haired, marijuana-smoking, free-loving dropouts who wore tie-dyed shirts, Levis and Jesus sandals if they wore any shoes at all. The cops did not like arresting them because they all had dirty feet.

A year and a half before they had enraged the city's White Sox fans because they literally tore up Comiskey Park, where the Pale Hose, as Chicagoans liked to call the ballclub, played baseball when the Grateful Dead were not performing in their stadium; desecrated it by turning the infield into something that looked like an Arizona landscape, arroyos and all, tearing clumps of grass out of the outfield, relieving themselves in various ways in the grandstands instead of the washrooms and leaving an assortment of litter that would gag a garbageman with twenty-five years on the job. The Sox, who had played out of town that Friday, had to have the games scheduled for the following Monday afternoon and Tuesday night postponed because it took that long to clean the mess up and get the field in shape.

Six of the Deadheads, however, made the mistake of wandering into Bridgeport, a neighborhood not far from the ballpark, the day after the concert. Bridgeport, a strongly segregated bastion of Irish and Italians, was home to a lot of politicians—the late legendary mayor of Chicago, Richard J. Daley, had lived there all his life—and an assortment of working-class families. It was a place where most looked upon hippies or anybody resembling them with the same degree of compassion as Heinrich Himmler had shown for the Jews. When the Deadheads tried to buy some hot dogs at a local stand, they got into a little fracas with some of the local youths, leaving five of the Deadheads beaten up, three of them badly enough to merit a visit to the local hospital's emergency room.

The sixth, faster than the other five, had outrun the others only to be run over by a car in an alley about three blocks away. Since it was broad daylight and the alley was a wide one with nothing to obstruct a motorist's view, and since the youth driving the car was a friend of the other youths who'd beaten up the other Deadheads, the newspapers implied it might not have been an accident. As a matter of fact they implied it so strongly that the case was turned over to Violent Crimes and Morrison and his partner got it because the Deadhead died a few hours after the accident from extensive brain injuries. But there were no witnesses and so the young driver, who happened to be the son of a bigwig with Streets and Sanitation, was charged only with reckless driving and failure to yield the right of way to a pedestrian. It was the Grateful Dead fan, Morrison mused, who proved to be the ultimate Deadhead.

"I don't think you're giving me your undivided attention, Joe."

"Sure I am, you especially loved *Forever Amber*."

"I didn't say I loved *Forever Amber*. I said I loved *The Razor's Edge*. I loved Linda Darnell in *Forever Amber*, though. Jesus, she's got a body. You know where she died?"

"I didn't even know she was dead."

"She died out in Glenview," Norbert said referring to the suburb just to the northwest of Chicago. "In a fire. Can you imagine that, Linda Darnell, dying out there? You know, you'd think you'd hear she died in, what is it, Cedars of Lebanon Hospital or some other place out there in Beverly Hills, not Glenview."

"The world is filled with small ironies," Morrison said, thinking again of the Deadhead of whose corpse he had made the acquaintance in the not too distant past.

"You know the other thing about *Forever Amber*, it came out when I was a little kid, maybe twelve or thirteen. It got a lot of publicity because it was Adults Only, and it got a B-rating by the Legion of Decency. The only thing worse was a C, for Condemned. Did they have that when you were a kid, the Legion of Decency, I mean?"

"Nope."

"Jeez, it was something. The nuns talked about it all the time. You went to see a C-movie and it was a mortal sin, anybody, adults or anybody. An eternity in hell, they used to tell us. A fucking eternity of the worst pain and suffering you could imagine. And how long was an eternity? Sister Donna Marie always gave us the story. If a bird over in Africa took just one grain of sand from the Sahara Desert every ten years and dropped it in the ocean, she'd say, by the time the bird finally emptied the desert and dropped the last grain of sand, it wouldn't even be one second in eternity. Shit, *The Outlaw*, which I saw about a month ago on TV, was C. The worst pain imaginable you could suffer for longer than it took that fucking bird to clean out the desert just for looking at Jane Russell's cleavage. I think that comes under 'cruel and unusual,' don't you, Joe?''

''A little harsh.''

''It was tough growing up Catholic in those days. Speaking of cleavage, though, did you by any chance take the little lady of the loft back to the scene of the crime Saturday?''

Morrison looked over at Norbert, then back out the window, not saying anything.

''I knew you did. You sly dog, you.''

''You don't know anything.'' But Morrison was smiling.

''So what happened?''

''Nothing. She looked around Taylor Street but she didn't come up with anything new.''

''No, I mean what happened with her. Give me all the dirty details. I know you got in her pants.''

''Even if I did, Norbert, it is not gentlemanly to kiss and tell. You know that.''

''Fuck, you may dress like a dandy but you are not no gentleman. You are a cop.'' Norbert waited but got no response. ''So was she a good lay?''

''They're a different breed these days. It sure wasn't like that when I was in my twenties. Talk about taking the ball in your own hands.''

''Balls, in this case.''

''My favorite philosopher and theologian, Warren Beatty, said it and I used to believe it. How did it go? Men use marriage for sex, and women use sex for marriage. That sure as hell isn't the way it is anymore.'' Morrison shook his head. ''I was just along for the ride. I sure didn't do any of the driving. I mean, I take her back to that arena she lives in, she says come on up, gets a bottle of chardonnay out of the refrigerator, hands me a glass of it, bumps hers against mine, kisses me, and then says right out, 'Would you like me to suck it?' Just like that.''

Castor looked dreamily off into the distance. ''I gotta quit hanging around cop bars and get out in the real world. The only piece of ass I had in the last year was Darlene, you know, in uniform now, used to be undercover. She works out of the first district, they tried to use her as a decoy in the Loop for a while but she was so ugly not even the subway freaks would try to cop a feel. Jesus, I must have been drunk that night. But don't let me interrupt, go on.''

''I mean one kiss, one sip of wine, and she's unbuttoning *my* shirt, *my* pants, and at the same time telling me every detail of how Bert introduced her to oral sex. And how she and Bert have an agreement, an arrangement, about sex.''

''Darlene said she'd have to have a lobotomy before she'd let somebody stick his thing in her mouth.''

''It wasn't all you'd think it was.''

''Why not?'' Norbert asked.

''First of all, she's big on moaning and talking about what the hell's going on. 'Put it in. Oh, do it, do it. Faster. Ah, ooh.' All that. And in that place, it echoed. It was like somebody was giving a play-by-play from the ceiling. It was distracting to say the least. I finally said why don't you put on some music. So she put on a Bruce Springsteen CD in this zillion-dollar setup they've got. Loud. Loud as hell. Then it was like doing it in the middle of a rock concert at Chicago Stadium.''

THEY PARKED in front of Warner's drugstore but did not go in, instead hit the street. It was on the seventh call that they got lucky. A little elderly lady answered the door. Her apartment was above a video rental store almost directly across the street from Warner's. She was perhaps sixty-five with hair the color of chablis, the ends of it in curlers. She wore a flowered housecoat over a patterned dress, giving a whole new dimension to the concept of clash, knee-high stockings and sensible shoes. She seemed delighted to have visitors. Morrison noted the framed photograph of a man in his early fifties in a bus driver's uniform on an endtable. There were plastic flowers in little vases on either side of it. Morrison took him to be the lady's late husband.

"Are you aware that a major crime took place across the street last Thursday night?" Morrison began.

"Certainly am," she said. In spite of her rather frail appearance she had a strong, whiskey-throated voice. "Poor Mr. Warner. Killed in his own store. I knew him. I go there all the time for my needs."

"Did you see anyone go into or come out of the store that night, say, sometime after eight o'clock?"

"No, but I do know they closed up early. They always stay open to nine, but I looked out at eight-thirty and the sign was off and it was dark in the store. I just figured they closed up early because of the snow."

"Had you been in the store that day?"

"No."

"You didn't hear or see anything out of the ordinary that night, anything that might be a little suspicious?"

"Well, uh, no, not really. As I said, I just saw they closed early."

Morrison had picked up the hesitation. "Are you sure? It's very important. This was an ugly murder of a very nice man."

"Oh, I know he was nice. As I told you, I went in there

often and he always said 'And how are you today, Mrs. Otis?' Very friendly."

"Well, if there was anything at all that you noticed out of the ordinary that night it would be helpful if you told us. No matter how small. It might give us a lead, it might be something we could hook to other information and help us." Morrison looked at her, the soft approach.

"Well, there was . . ." Then she shook her head. "No, I guess not, that was nothing."

"Mrs. Otis, I think maybe you did see something. Are you afraid to tell us?"

"No, no, it's just, well, I . . ."

"It is important, Mrs. Otis," Morrison said. "Even if it doesn't seem important to you it may be to us—"

"Mrs. Otis," Castor interrupted, "if we think you might have some information that would be pertinent to this investigation and that you are concealing it, we will have to take you over to Area Six headquarters for official questioning."

"Well, I did notice something, but it was much earlier." She paused.

Morrison picked up the trace of fear in her voice. "Go ahead," he said.

"It was just after six o'clock. I was coming back from getting some milk and a few other things at the little convenience store in the next block. You know the one, it's called Quickee Shop?"

"We know it."

"Well, I wasn't going to go out because it was cold and the snow was coming down real hard but then I thought I'd better in case the snow kept up and maybe nothing would be open the next day. You know we've had those big snowstorms here before and everything's closed." Morrison nodded. Castor did, too, suddenly thinking of Florida and sitting at one of those outdoor bars on the beach with the thatched roofs drinking a piña colada.

"When I was coming back, there was this car parked right in front of the door downstairs—illegally, I might add. Because of the streetlight I could see in it. There were three people just sitting there, kind of hunched up. Cold, for sure. Well, I recognized the girl in the front seat, the driver's seat. I've seen her before. And the man in the backseat, I'd seen him with her before. He was colored. That's why I remember them, seeing them together, thinking what a shame. She was not a bad looker and he was, well, a flashy colored."

"Who was the third person? Sitting where?"

"It was another man, in the front seat. He was white, but that's all I noticed. I didn't pay any attention to him. It was the colored fellow. He was drinking, too, out of a brown paper bag. They all do that, you know."

"Where had you seen them before?"

"Why, in Warner's."

Morrison looked at Castor then back to the lady. "When?"

"Oh, a couple of times. Not recently, but a month or so ago, maybe. Two or three times I saw them before that. I just thought it was awful. More than just friends, I'd say."

"Can you describe the car?" Castor asked.

"It was old, didn't look in very good condition."

"The make?"

"Oh, I wouldn't know."

"Color?"

"I'm sorry, I just didn't pay any attention to it. I think it was a light color maybe, but I really don't remember."

"Do you know how long they were there?" Morrison asked.

"Oh, yes. It was a while anyway. But they weren't in the car all that time."

"Where were they?"

"In the tavern, the one two doors down. Frankie's Place."

"How do you know that?"

"Well, after I came upstairs and had supper I went down for a little nightcap. I do that most nights, but usually later, after the good television shows are over. I just have one whiskey and ginger ale. It helps me sleep. Sometimes I have two . . . but not that often. That night, though, I decided to go right after supper, about seven o'clock. And they were in there, the colored and the girl and the other one, sitting over by the window. Well, I noticed them but paid them no attention and went to the bar and had my drink. When I left about a half hour later they were still there. That's all I know. And I just know they're not the right kind of people, especially for this neighborhood." She looked at Morrison. "Do you think they might have had something to do with it, you know, the killing?"

"Don't know," Morrison said, "but it's a lead we didn't have before."

"Oh, and I do know when they left." Morrison had been about to ask but she preempted him. "Actually I don't know exactly when, but I know they were gone by eight-thirty because I looked out my window then. I know it was eight-thirty because it was right after "The Newhart Show." It's my favorite show, and when it was over I went to the window to see how the snow was doing. That's when I noticed the drugstore was closed up. I also looked down and their car was gone."

"LUNCHTIME," NORBERT said when they were back on the street.

"Christ, it's only eleven-fifteen."

"Where I'm taking you will take a while to get to."

"What do you mean, taking me?"

"Remember, Joe, we're on this thing part-time. We got another case we're supposed to be investigating. Remember the one you were so interested in you devoted a major,

major part of your day off, Saturday, to, um, interviewing a key witness?''

''What does that have to do with lunch?''

''I think we should go out to Allegorio's. It's a den of bent-noses. Plus Facia eats there himself almost every day, he and his cronies. In fact he owns a piece of the place. Maybe we can have a word or two with him.''

''Okay. But first we talk to the saloon-keeper while we're here.'' Norbert shrugged. ''The food any good at this place?'' Morrison asked as they started down Halsted Street to Frankie's Place.

''The food's great—expensive, but first class. It's only the clientele that's rotten.'' Norbert clapped a hand on Morrison's shoulder. ''And don't expect any discount out there unless you're on the take from the Outfit and I don't know about it.''

When they walked into Allegorio's the maître d' recognized Castor immediately. ''Well, to what do we owe this honor, the visit of an esteemed police officer?''

''We're in the mood for dago food, Salvatore,'' Norbert said.

''Well, you couldn't have come to a better place.'' He picked up a pair of menus. ''Smoking or non-smoking?''

''Wherever the most bent-noses are. I like watching them whisper to each other.''

Salvatore led them through the bar and Castor noticed the corner banquette, the one Rudy Facia usually occupied, was empty. In the main dining room Salvatore put the menus down at a tiny table at the far end of the room but only Morrison was with him. Norbert had stopped at a table where four men sat around a bottle of Orvieto Classico. They tried to ignore him but couldn't when Castor said, ''Hey, if it isn't Tony Baloney.'' One of them looked up and forced a smile. ''How's the chop-shop business these days?''

''I'm in the used car business, Castor. You know that.

You wanna buy a beater? That why you came all the way out here? I got a good one, one-owner, driven by an old schoolteacher who used it just to drive to and from the classroom. Make you a helluva deal, you bein' a man of the law and all, makin' the streets safe for all of us."

"Can't afford it. But I'm sure it's a beauty. Probably a Cadillac with a Lincoln Continental engine, Chrysler transmission, Oldsmobile drive train, Mercury carburetor . . ."

"Funny man. I thought all cops lost their sense of humor after bein' on the job a couple of years."

Castor looked over at one of the others, who was staring into his linguine Romano. "And you, Francis, when did you get out? Last I heard you were residing in the penitentiary."

Francis's expression was sullen, looking up at Castor. "Two months I been out."

"How was it in Stateville? The gangbangers leave you alone?"

"I was in Sandstone."

"Sandstone. Oh, the country club. I forgot it was a federal rap. How the hell you swing Sandstone? Thought that was just for politicians, judges, guys fixing the stock market."

"I was convicted of a white-collar crime."

"Since when is running a gambling operation a white-collar crime?"

"Can't you see, I'm white collar," Francis said pointing to the collar of his white-on-white shirt, which was two buttons open to reveal a mat of curly black hair and a gold chain. "It's class, white-collar class. Custom Shop, a hundred twenty-five bucks, I got a closet full of 'em." He pulled the sleeve of his sportcoat up to show the monogram FJN on the cuff. "If you don't get the monogram you can get the shirt for maybe fifteen bucks less, just in case you wanted to know."

Castor smiled at Francis, who continued to stare sullenly up at him. "I don't give a shit about your wardrobe. But maybe you can tell me the spread on the Bulls game tonight. They're playing the Knicks at home."

"I wouldn't have any idea. I'm not in that business anymore. Learned my lesson. White-collar crime does not pay."

"Oh, and what business are you in now, Francis?"

"The dry-cleaning business."

Castor laughed. "That's wonderful, a perfect place to launder money. You guys think of everything." He got no response. Turning back to Tony, "You not going to introduce me to your other two friends? That's not polite."

Tony nodded to one of them. "Joey Scalise, meet Officer Norb Castor, who has a desk job downtown and is very nosy for a cop." Then nodding to the other, "Bruno Benedetti, Officer Castor."

"Well, it's a pleasure meeting you." And then to Tony, "And, of course, chatting with you. But I better go join my partner, he's dying for some greaseball cuisine. Anything you want to recommend?"

"How about cyanide Vesuvio," Tony said.

"WHO WERE those guys?" Morrison asked when Castor sat down at their table.

"Tony Baloney I call him, the guy with the white sportcoat and black shirt. I call him that because he's so full of shit. I think the only time he ever told the truth in his life was when his girlfriend asked him if he wanted to fuck. His real name's Tony Santori. The other guy's Francis Nicoletti, the one with the curly hair. I call him Francis of Assisi because he only associates with animals. He just got out of the joint, got pinched for running the gambling operation in Jefferson Park. I think he got two years, served maybe eight months. The other two I never seen before, didn't recognize the names. Probably from out of town. Let's eat."

CASTOR, SATIATED after a platter of spaghetti and Italian sausage, four pieces of garlic bread and a scoop of spumoni, grabbed the check when the waitress brought it. "I got a deal for you today, Joe. You leave the tip and I take care of this. It was my idea. Leave her three bucks; she wasn't worth more than ten percent."

On the way out Norbert and Morrison stopped by the table of the four he had talked to before. "I just want you guys to meet my partner, Joe Morrison. Used to be a great homicide cop. Probably even investigated some of the homicides you guys pulled off."

"You oughta come out here more often, Norb," Tony Baloney said. "We don't get many comedians at lunch."

"Well, I just thought it would be nice for you guys to be on a first-name basis now that he's working Organized Crime."

Tony threw his arms up in the air, a big smile on his face. "Organized Crime? Organized crime, *what* is that?"

"Try your corporate affiliation," Norbert said.

"Come on. I never heard a nothin' called organized crime. You pullin' my leg, Norb. You ever heard of anything like that, Frankie?" Francis just shook his head, sullen as ever. "Wait, maybe I did hear that once," Tony went on. "Yeah. It was back in the days of Hoover. Old J. Edgar said somethin' about it. I think he made it up to justify all the money they were payin' all those agents of his."

"See you around, Tony," Castor said as they started to walk away. "And by the way, you're as full of shit as ever."

"Likewise, I'm sure," Tony said, still smiling.

When they passed into the bar, Norbert nodded toward a short squat man built like a high school fullback gone to pot and standing at the bar talking to two other men. "That's Facia," Norbert pointed out. The man had a mop of black hair sprayed into place and wore a green blazer and cream-colored slacks, a couple of gold chains exposed by the unbuttoned silk sportshirt. The other two hardly looked like they made their living on LaSalle Street.

"Let's go say hello," Norbert suggested.

Rudy Facia looked distinctly annoyed when the two approached him, but he introduced Castor to the other two anyway and Norbert introduced Joe Morrison.

"You here on some kind of business?" Facia asked.

"Not really," Castor said.

"Then if you don't mind, we're in the middle of something important."

"I can imagine."

Facia turned back to the other two, expecting Castor and Morrison to leave. But Norbert said, "Well, there is one piece of business. We'd like to talk to you about what happened to your daughter the other night down near Taylor Street. We're sorry about it, but we—"

Facia turned quickly back, his eyes ablaze. "Nothing happened to my daughter, nothing that would concern you. There was no crime, no charges. I don't want to talk about it to you or anybody else. You want to talk, talk to my lawyer, Tom Dungen, One-two-oh South LaSalle Street." Facia suddenly snatched the lunch check from Norbert's hand and gave it to the bartender. "Comp these guys," he said. "Now if you don't mind . . ."

Norbert reached across the bar and grabbed the check back. "Mr. Facia, I must tell you that this is perhaps the only restaurant in Cook County where I would never eat on the cuff." Then to Morrison, "C'mon, Joe, let's get out of here. I can only stay in the gutter so long."

"He's not a really friendly guy," Morrison said when they were out on the street.

"He's scum. They're all scum. Rich scum, but scum. And I'm stupid."

"What do you mean?"

"I shoulda let him pay for the goddamn meal."

AT SIX headquarters, Terry Sawyer was in the squad room two-finger-typing a report when Morrison and Castor walked in. "Got something," Morrison said, sitting himself on the desk next to Sawyer.

When he finished telling Sawyer Mrs. Otis's story, Morrison added, "I have a hunch those people weren't on the street to admire the beauty of fresh-fallen snow."

Sawyer shrugged. "They were in the saloon, I thought."

"I know. But they were sitting at the window, which gives a perfect view of Warner's drugstore. We stopped in the joint after talking to her. The bartender was the same one who worked last Thursday. He vaguely remembered the three. Said they came in, took a couple of stools from the bar and sat by the window. He didn't pay much attention to them because the place started to fill up and he was busy. But he said when they first came in he wondered maybe if she wasn't a hooker and the shine her pimp maybe. They were there for at least an hour, he said, but he didn't know what time they left. It was a pretty busy night, a lot of antifreeze going down the old tubes."

"Well, it's worth following up. I got one for you now, Joe."

Norbert brought Morrison and himself Styrofoam cups of coffee.

"That Weisenhurst dame who works at Warner's, the last one to leave that night, she called in because she said she remembered something over the weekend and thought she should report it. She said one of the last people in the store was a guy who comes in regularly, maybe once a week, to get prescriptions. He was there not too long before Theo told her to pack it in for the night, in the back with Theo, and when she thought about it she didn't remember seeing him leave. That she thought was strange because she was up front at the cash register near the door."

"Does she have a name on him?"

"No, but we do. From the prescription log. The last entry was for a guy named Dennis Courtland. He had a standing prescription for Valium, picked up thirty of the little suckers. We got his address from the doctor who issued the prescription. It seems they're friends, neighbors anyway. Now get this, they both live in the Carlyle, you know, that very fancy, very expensive joint on Michigan Avenue kitty-corner from the Drake Hotel."

"I know it," Morrison said, immediately wondering why someone would regularly travel about four miles to have a prescription filled when there was a drugstore in the hotel just across the street.

"He came all the way over there in a snowstorm that night. He's gotta be a little potty upstairs from the tablets to do that, right? Or maybe he had another reason?"

"A guy living in the Carlyle does not seem like your ordinary drug thief. He could buy the damn drugstore if he wanted. On the other hand, maybe there was something else and he took the other stuff to make it look like a druggie robbery."

"I'll go see him tomorrow," Sawyer said, looking at his watch. "It's after five already."

"Give me his number. I'll give him a call. Maybe I can go over there now. Hell, I don't have anything else to do."

Sawyer shook his head knowingly. "The divorce still going through, huh?"

"You bet. In fact, we might be neighbors. I gotta look at an apartment up in your neighborhood."

Sawyer handed him the sheet of paper with Dennis Courtland's address and telephone number. "Why don't you check out if they've got any empty space in the Carlyle? You'd fit right in, you dapper devil, you."

14

AS EVENING began to settle on Uptown, Manford White was in the vestibule of the Tudor Arms on his way out when he saw Tommy's car pull up in front. He decided to wait.

"You been rather elusive lately, Joe-ja," he said when Tommy walked in.

Tommy just looked at him, his expression of indifference changing to annoyance. "What business is it of yours?"

"Well, it's not that I'm missing your company, you bein' such a fuckin' pleasure to have around, but there is the little matter that you've got something of mine which I want back, like a three-fifty-seven Mag."

"You'll get it."

"When?"

"When I want to give it back."

"That's not good enough, Joe-ja. Why don't we just go upstairs together and you give it back to me and everything'll be fine?"

"It ain't upstairs."

"Where the hell is it then?"

"I got it stashed."

"Well, how 'bout unstashin' it?"

"What's the rush? You plannin' on shootin' somebody tonight?" Tommy grinned, pleased with his humor.

"Tomorrow," White said, pointing a finger at Tommy. "I am not shittin' you. I want it tomorrow." Tommy didn't say anything. "You understand." Tommy still didn't say anything, just turned toward the stairway. "Don't let little Jokin distract you so much you forget, now. She is one helluva lay."

Tommy turned back to look at White, about to say something but before he could White said, "She still run around the apartment just in those little panties? That was a sight. Nothin' on but them little panties, pink ones I liked the best."

Tommy's eyes wall-eyed, the thought registering that Jo did spend much of her time upstairs walking around in nothing but panties. "What are you, a fuckin' peeping Tom?"

"Come on, man. I know Jokin for a long time. We been buddies. Real buddies."

"Bullshit." Tommy took a step closer to White.

"Bullshit yourself, Joe-ja. She ever tell ya why she got them little ladybugs tattooed on her thigh?" Tommy didn't say anything, overwhelmed for the moment with the thought of the three ladybugs in black and orange on Jo's inner thigh. "Some guy she shacked with got her to do it. A real, and I mean real, drughead. Used PCP most of the time and when he was really blown he used to see ladybugs all over, the walls, ceiling, floor. Liked 'em, I guess. So he got Jokin to get some tattooed near her bush so he could look at 'em when he was havin' lunch, so to speak. I thought they were kinda cute."

Tommy lunged but White slipped out of the way, a matador move. "You don't want to do somethin' stupid, Joe-ja." But he did. Tommy swung but White got his head out of the way and Tommy's punch caved in one of the old mailboxes on the wall. White, forced back against the marble wall, got a knee into Tommy's groin but it wasn't quite on target. It was enough, however, to enable him to slip out from being pinned against the wall.

Tommy came on swinging. White dodged, ducked and fended off the punches with his arms, intent on finding the opening that would let him take the big man down. Then Manford White made a mistake, something he ordinarily never did in a street fight; he misjudged how fast Tommy was. Just as he was about to lash out with a kick to the shin, the easiest target, a White tactic that would stall Tommy just long enough to get the kick to the balls that would indeed change the course of the fight, Tommy had him. White was stunned with the quickness of Tommy's move and struggled furiously to get out of his grasp. The two lurched into the outer door, which never closed all the way, slamming it open, and they tumbled down the two front steps onto the snowy sidewalk, legs and arms flailing.

White managed to extricate himself and bounced to his feet, ready now, dancing, his shoulders loose, fists clenched but down, daring, Sugar Ray Robinson, Sugar Ray Leonard, cocky. He had been here before and he always walked away leaving somebody bleeding and hurting. "You started somethin', Joe-ja, you are going to regret," he taunted as he jabbed with a left that caught Tommy on the forehead, danced away, then came back, another left, this one landing on the side of Tommy's neck, and a right that seemed to land almost simultaneously it was so quick that it glanced off Tommy's head. "And when I'm done, Joe-ja," he said a little breathlessly, the vapor in the cold coming from his mouth in spurts, "maybe I'll go up and give Jokin one for you because you won't be able to." A kick caught Tommy in the knee but didn't faze him. The follow-up, aimed for the groin, never got more than a half-foot off the ground. Tommy, with a move that surprised White with its speed, lunged forward and sent a right smashing into White's chest, a shot that sent White careening into the snow drift four feet behind him. White felt the pain in his chest as he scrambled to get back up because Tommy was coming down on him, eyes afire and so wall-eyed they looked like they might burst.

There were people now, standing around. They just materialized suddenly as they always did when a fight broke out in Uptown. Usually it was outside some bar or in the alley next to one, but when it started they came to watch, silently, restlessly. They appeared, growing in numbers in spite of the cold and the Chicago wind. They sensed this was a fight beyond the normal. This was one where somebody was going to get hurt very bad, maybe so bad it wouldn't even matter except maybe to the next-of-kin if either had one who would admit to the relationship.

Tommy got one of his huge hands on White's throat, but only for a second. White whipped a right to Tommy's face that split a lip, then scrambled away. Tommy rolled with it but White was on his feet first and got another kick in, this one catching Tommy in the ribs as he was halfway to his feet with enough force to send Tommy back into the snow.

White moved in now, fast, one more shot and the man was his, he thought, and the man was going to suffer, the big redneck was going to feel pain like he never did before—

Tommy erupted from the snow and smashed a fist into White's pelvis. An inch lower and Manford White would have sounded like Roberta Flack for the rest of his life.

The crowd, grown to maybe eighteen or twenty now, didn't seem to respond to what was going on. Witnessing one of the most savage fights ever in the streets of Uptown, they just stared, no gasps, no heys, no my Gods. They winced now and then, that was all. Then suddenly through the muted crowd two police emerged, one male, one female, the flashing blue light from their squad car behind the crowd giving the scene a kind of Hollywood opening-night flavor.

The male cop was shouting, "All right, that's it. Break it up." He had his nightstick out. Tommy turned his attention from Manford White, who was getting to his feet a little unsteadily, to the police officer and grabbed the nightstick, wrenched it from his hand and threw it back in the direction of the flashing blue light of the squad car. The female cop had the good sense to follow the nightstick and leap into the car and call in a 10–1, policeman in trouble—which one was as Tommy leveled him with one punch after pitching the nightstick out into the street.

Which gave a somewhat stunned but still deadly dangerous Manford White the moment he needed to get it back together. He swung, the punch coming, it seemed, from a block away and smashing into the side of Tommy's face. It would have ended just about any other fight, but it only knocked Tommy back two steps and caused him to sway a little from side to side before he reacted, charging with fists swinging and a guttural sound coming from deep in his throat. White did manage a solid kick to the knee and landed a few punches himself before they clinched and grappled to the ground.

White realized it was bad trouble being on the ground, his speed and deftness now useless. He understood just how bad it was when Tommy raked at his face, trying to tear at his eyeballs. White managed to stop that by biting Tommy on the thumb. Tommy was on top now and threw a wild left that glanced off the side of White's head. As he wriggled to free himself from under Tommy, White felt a brick in the snow gouging him in the side, managed to get hold of it and swung it, hitting Tommy on the side of the face and opening a gash on his cheek. He still had the brick in his hand, but Tommy had his arm pinned to the ground . . . it took the hands of four newly arrived policemen grabbing at Tommy to pull him off.

The street was now a parking lot of police cars, their occupants trying to keep Tommy and Manford White apart. Eventually it took six of them to do it, two on White and four trying to subdue Tommy. The policewoman was tending to her partner, who was sitting on a snowbank now but thought that he was somewhere in Minnesota ice fishing. The four wrestling with Tommy could not keep his arms behind him long enough to get the cuffs on so they settled for cuffing them in front, to which Tommy responded with one sudden thrust that actually managed to snap the steel chain. Which was when the two plainclothes cops used the saps on him and were finally able to get his arms behind his back and cuff him again.

The sergeant from Town Hall district was talking to Manford White. The two knew each other, the sergeant having been the recipient of a little bag money from Manford on a somewhat regular basis over the past few years. White told him the fight had been over a girl. "But you better keep that animal off the street for a while," White told the sergeant. "As you can gather, he didn't especially cotton to the idea that his little white girl liked some black dick once in a while, which he just found out, which is why we were having our little scuffle." White nodded toward Tommy, who, still dazed, was leaning up against a squad car surrounded by policemen who still had their saps and nightsticks out. "Keep him locked up, at least until he cools down. A nice cell with extra-thick bars and maybe give him a double dose of animal tranquilizers." The sergeant seemed to be mulling over the request. "C'mon, you owe me a couple," White said in almost a whisper.

The sergeant looked at White, then over at Tommy. "Okay," he said to one of the officers standing behind him. "Take the cuffs off this one," nodding toward Manford White. He walked over to the police standing around Tommy. "Take this one in and book him for battery and resisting arrest." He walked back to White. "We probably won't hold him for more than twenty-four hours.'' He jabbed his finger into White's chest. ''You find the girlie and tell her what went down. I don't want her surprised when the ape over there gets out.''

''I surely will, sergeant, I surely will.''

''Okay, get the hell out of here.''

White walked over to Head, who had been a spectator but had not taken off like most of the others when the squadron of cops came. ''That is one mean dude,'' White said. ''One mean, strong, nasty dude.'' And in a whisper, ''C'mon, Head. We got to go get me another gun. Right after I talk to Jokin. We got to talk to Jokin. Believe me, Head, we do.''

15

IT WAS just past six o'clock when Morrison pulled his own beater into the driveway of the Carlyle, the uniformed doorman looking rather disdainfully at it. Norbert Castor was on his way home, not wanting to miss *Angels with Dirty Faces*, which was scheduled to air at seven on the Turner Movie Channel. Morrison got out of the car and flashed his identification. "To see Mr. Dennis Courtland. He's expecting me."

"I'll have your car put in the garage," the doorman said as he signaled to a young man in the lobby who was also uniformed. As the youngster hustled outside, Morrison thought if the kid had a pillbox hat he could pass for the old Call-for-Philip-Morris boy.

"That's okay. Just leave it here. I won't be long."

The doorman looked over at the car. "I would prefer it in our garage."

"Have it your way." Morrison shrugged and handed the keys to the young car hiker. "Try not to nick it up."

Dennis Courtland's apartment was on the twenty-fourth floor with a sweeping view of Lake Michigan from four of its eight sprawling rooms, Persian rugs scattered about the floor, oil paintings on the walls, statues on pedestals, Chinese vases, all the accoutrements that would catch the eye and approval of a Robin Leach. Courtland himself looked like he could afford it, dressed in a navy blue cashmere blazer with a colorful foulard in the breast pocket, a Ralph Lauren sportshirt, oxford gray slacks and Bally loafers with little tassels, and with crisp salt-and-pepper hair styled and molded with hair spray. Morrison wondered for a moment what it would be like to be able to afford to buy any clothes you just saw and liked and never have to worry about what they cost.

"I can't tell you how shocked I was when you told me about Theo Warner on the telephone," Courtland said as soon as Morrison was in the apartment. "I'd read or heard nothing about it."

"It wasn't front-page news, just another murder. We get seven, eight hundred of them in a good year, or bad year, should I say." Morrison turned when he heard the high heels on the parquet floor to take in an exceptionally attractive blond-haired young woman.

"Linda, this is Mr. Morrison, the man who called about the murder. Linda Tate," he said to Morrison.

Morrison took all of her in. She had a beautiful mouth, he noticed, thin slashed at the sides, reminding him of Jamie Lee Curtis.

"You're a detective?" she asked.

"Shows, huh?"

She smiled. "Not really. But who else would want to come over and talk about a murder?"

He smiled back. "Did you know Theo Warner?"

"No, never met him. I just heard Dennis speak of him once or twice." Morrison could see anger in her eyes when she looked at Dennis Courtland. "So there is nothing I can help you with. And as it is, I was just leaving—"

"Linda, please wait," Courtland said. Then to Morrison: "I said on the phone this wouldn't be a bad time to talk, but as it turns out it is."

"It's not a bad time," Linda Tate said. "There's nothing more we have to talk about." She looked at Morrison.

"If you'll excuse me." She forced a polite smile and after Morrison nodded she turned and walked swiftly across the room and down a hall and turned into one of the other rooms.

Courtland sighed. "A little domestic dispute with my friend. Do you think we could have this chat maybe some other time?"

"I just have a few questions. It won't take long."

She came out of the room, a Louis Vuitton suitcase in one hand and a full-length raccoon coat draped over the other arm. She dropped the coat on a chair next to Courtland. "You can keep this. The jewelry is on the dresser." She walked to the closet, took out a cloth coat and put it on. "Nice meeting you, officer."

"Linda, please," Courtland said, exasperation in his voice. But she was out the door.

"Goddamn women," Courtland said. "Well, let's sit down, but as I told you on the phone I really know nothing about it."

"You were in the store that night, last Thursday?"

"I was in there one night last week, Wednesday or Thursday, I can't really remember."

"The woman at the counter said she saw you come in Thursday night, the night it snowed so much."

"Is she sure it was Thursday? A lot of people come in and out of that drugstore."

"She was sure. The pharmacy log also listed that you picked up some Valium Thursday night."

"Then it must have been Thursday."

"What time was it?"

"Must have been about seven or seven-thirty."

"Who was in the store?"

"Well, let's see. There were hardly any customers. It was a real bad night, now that I think of it. The woman you mentioned, she was there, and, of course, Theo. He got me my prescription. I have a standing prescription for Valium."

Morrison nodded. "You take it all the time?"

"No." Courtland seemed slightly embarrassed. He smiled. "You think I'm a drug addict maybe? Well, I hate to disillusion you. I take the Valium when I need it, that's all. I'm in a very stress-filled business, the commodities market. There's tremendous pressure, we deal in some very large figures. So I need to wind down. I don't drink anything but wine, so my doctor prescribed Valium. It helps."

"At about what time did you leave the store."

"I was there about ten minutes, I guess."

"Nobody else in the back? Bruce? The other pharmacist?"

"No, they'd gone home early, because of the snow, I suppose." Courtland shook his head. "I'm trying to think if there was anyone I saw in there. I wish I could but I can't."

"Did Theo seem at all nervous, on edge or anything?"

"No, just his normal self. We chatted for a few minutes, I wrote him a check and left. That was it."

"Did you know Theo well?"

"Rather well, yes."

"And his brother, Bruce?"

"Yes, as a matter of fact I know Bruce better, longer."

"How long have you been patronizing the Warners' store?"

"Four or five years now, I'd think."

"What puzzles me a little is why you'd go all the way over there on a fairly regular basis. It's hardly around the corner from here."

"I'm a loyal customer." Courtland seemed amused by his answer. "You see, when I first moved to Chicago I lived in that area. That was maybe five years ago when I first got started in commodity trading. I didn't have much then. I used to go in there all the time. Then when I started to make it in trading, and as you can see I made it fairly well, I moved. But I kept going back to Warner's. I liked Bruce, he was always interested in what I did. He was always looking for investments to make some quick money. Theo was the conservative of the two. Anyway, I liked both of them, even made a few dollars for Bruce on a couple of occasions. So I kept going back. That's just the way I am."

"You must have needed your Valium pretty bad to go all that way that night. It was almost a blizzard."

Courtland looked at Morrison with a little condescension, not liking the tone of the question. "It was a bad day in more ways than one. Especially bad. I lost eighty-five, eighty-six thousand dollars, all on pork-belly futures. I needed to calm down. I'm not normally a loser." To emphasize his point Courtland looked around the room at the expensive furniture and the bay window that offered such a beautiful lake view. He smiled conspiratorially at Morrison. "But don't worry, I've already made it back and then some."

"I'm not worried. I'm just trying to find out who killed Theo Warner."

"I'm sorry. I wish I could help."

"Have you always been in the commodities business, Mr. Courtland?"

"No, just the last five years or so."

"What did you do before that?"

"The brokerage business. I was with Merrill, Lynch down in Florida."

"Nice down there," Morrison said. "What prompted you to give up the sun for the snow? Usually it's the other way around."

"The commodities market." Courtland seemed pleased with himself. "I saw the opportunity, the potential of the market here, and I grabbed it. That's what life is all about, officer."

"Where was that in Florida?"

"Tampa–St. Pete. Actually my office was over in Clearwater, near the beach."

"Must have been a big change for you."

"It was. Change and challenge."

"I'd imagine," Morrison said, nodding. "I won't take up any more of your time." Morrison handed him his card and gave Courtland the same kind of conspiratorial smile Courtland had given him a moment ago. "I know it's valuable. If you can think of anything that might help in the investigation, I'd appreciate it if you'd give me a call."

"Be glad to."

IN THE lobby, the girl was standing there next to her suitcase, the doorman outside whistling for a cab. Morrison walked up behind her. "Kind of tough to get a cab in this weather."

She turned. "You aren't kidding."

"You know Dennis Courtland pretty well, I take it."

"Too well. Maybe you ought to put it I *knew* Dennis pretty well."

"I picked that up," Morrison said glancing down at the suitcase."

"Was he of any help? In your investigation, I mean."

"In a way, yes. You know, after talking to him, I thought as I was coming down on the elevator that I might like to ask you a few questions."

"As I told you upstairs, I didn't even know the man who was killed. I was never even in his store."

"My questions aren't about him. They're about Mr. Courtland."

"Well, I'll be happy to oblige." She looked at him like she meant it, which made her look even more attractive, her hazel eyes captivating. "But I've really got so much on my mind right now. This has not been a good day."

"I gathered that, too."

"And if he ever gets me a cab, I just want to get out of here."

"Where are you headed?"

"To my sister's, up in Evanston. Stay with her for a while."

"Nice suburb, Evanston." Morrison suddenly added, "Say, how about if I give you a ride up there? Got to go sort of that way anyway and maybe we could just talk on the way."

But as he said it, a cab pulled into the driveway and the doorman waved to her and then came back to open the door.

"That's kind of you, but he's got one for me now. And as I said I really don't want to talk about Dennis right now."

"Sure." Morrison took out his little notebook. "Where can I reach you?" She gave him her sister's telephone number. "Tomorrow be okay to call?"

"How about Wednesday? Not too early, though."

He watched her walk out to the cab, his eyes traveling from her blond hair curled over the collar of her coat down the back to the sculpted calves sheathed in sheer, slightly glistening nylon all the way to the delicate three-inch heeled pumps. She got in, then surprised Morrison by waving back at him through the window. He thought that was a nice gesture.

As he waited for his car, his thoughts went back to the now mistressless Dennis Courtland. His chief thought—he did not believe him.

IN THE morning Morrison told Norbert just that. Told Terry Sawyer the same thing on the telephone. Sawyer said he would run a check on Dennis Courtland, see if there was anything about him they should know, anything in his past.

When Morrison hung up after talking to Sawyer, Norbert said, "We work OC today, okay?" Morrison just looked at him, his mind elsewhere. "Or at least I do. The murder's part-time, remember." Still no response from Morrison, whose mind was in Homicide, not Organized Crime, at the moment. "For chrissake, Joe, am I talkin' to the wall?"

"Sorry. What'd you say?"

"I said we work OC, or I work OC anyway. Roland sees how little time we're putting in on what we're paid to do, we're gonna end up on midnights in Woodlawn watchin' them bring in gangbangers, drugheads, AIDS-ridden prostitutes and other assorted community leaders." Castor looked at a taciturn Morrison. "Remember, we were going to talk to Bert today, Bert of the loft, the loft of the lady, the oohs, ahs and echoes."

"How could I forget, Norbert?"

"So do we do it, or do I do it alone?"

"We do it. Just let me make one telephone call first."

"Awright, I'll go pull a car. Pick you up in front."

Morrison dialed, got the drugstore and asked for Bruce.

"Joseph, you caught me on the fly," Bruce said. "I just came in to open the store and get things going. We're closing at two today, you know. The services are at three. Will you be there?"

"Of course, Bruce."

"That's good. You know how much Theo thought of you and your dad, God rest his soul too."

"I do. Bruce, can I ask you a couple of questions now or is this really a bad time for you?"

"No, go ahead, Joseph."

"How late did you stay at the store that night, Thursday?"

"I think it was around six-thirty. Why?"

"Were you out front or in the back?"

"Well, actually I was working the counter. Theo was in the back that night."

"Did you by any chance see a white girl, mid-twenties,

with a black guy and another guy, white, in the store that night?''

''No. Not that I remember. There were so few people in there because of the snowstorm.''

''No mixed couples?''

''No, I'm sure.''

''Okay. By the way, I talked with Dennis Courtland last night. Were you still there when he came by that night?''

''No. I was gone by then. I saw from the log that he was in, though.''

''You've known him pretty long.''

''Yes, a number of years.''

''What do you know about him?''

''A fine man, always comes back to us for his prescriptions and buys a lot of other things too. He's very successful, you know. Made millions, I've heard, on the market. Commodities.''

''How did he get along with Theo?''

''Well, just fine. Why?''

''He was, at least to our knowledge, the last person in the store that night. Would there be any reason to suspect him in this?''

''Dennis? Oh, no. He's a gentleman first-class. Why would he rob us? He's got more money than all of us put together. No, he's not the kind to hurt anybody.''

''Do you think there's any chance he might have had a drug problem?'' Morrison noted the pause.

''Well, he took Valium regularly. But other than that . . . I certainly don't know. He's a good man, Joseph. He really is.''

''I'm just trying to check out every angle, Bruce. Look, I won't keep you any longer. I know this is a tough day for you.''

''The toughest. I'll see you at the chapel, Joseph. Oh, and afterwards, we're having a little get-together back at my place, some food, some drink, just for the good friends. I hope you'll come."

"I'll stop by."

NORBERT HAD driven up onto the snowdrift at the curb in front of 11th and State, the lopsided car looking as if it might roll over if a gust of wind whistled in off the lake. He did it so Morrison could clamber in instead of having to walk down to the corner. He'd be in deep trouble if somebody like a deputy superintendent came in or out of the building and saw it hunkered that way. Coincidentally, he was reading a story in the *Sun-Times* about a judge in California who had found a beach bum not guilty of rape because the girl he had penetrated had been dressed skimpily—"provocatively," was the way he put it—and therefore had in fact enticed the man. In order to remove the judge from his seat on the bench NOW was preparing an all-out frontal assault so devastating that it would have made Genghis Khan weep with pleasure.

Morrison had to climb the snowbank, open the door and then kind of hurtle himself into the front seat because of the car's angle. "You know, I really should do all the driving, Norbert."

"Hey, fine with me. I hate to drive. You wanna switch?"

"Yeah, but pull off the glacier first."

THEY MET with Bert in his office, a new all-glass edifice that was overshadowed by the world's tallest building, the Sears Tower across the street. Trendy neighborhood, Castor observed. He remembered the area just west of the Loop as derelict heaven when he was growing up. You would go over here to look at the bums lying on the sidewalk, or standing in line in front of the Madison Street Mission in hopes of a free meal, or gathered in little groups next to the liquor store/bar that offered shots for a half-buck, beers for a quarter and a carry-out bottle of muscatel for less than a dollar, paper bag included. Now the drunks and the bag ladies were gone from there, relocated to other areas of the city to accommodate the downtown expansion—replaced with men of purpose and ambition in Mark Shale suits with racquetball equipment compartmentalized in their leather duffel bags, and women on the move who came to work wearing running shoes and bobby sox over their nylons and carrying briefcases instead of grease-stained shopping bags. The saloons and flophouses and pawnshops had given way to glass-walled office buildings, high-rise motor hotels, little restaurants that featured pasta primavera for lunch and a wine list that replaced muscatel and Thunderbird with soave and sauvignon blanc. As they pulled up in front of the building that housed Bert's office, Castor reflected, "This neighborhood sure has lost its character."

Bert was tall, slender, indeed had a duffel bag and racquet in the corner of his office, several modern-art posters on one wall and framed certificates from things like the Printing Industry of America and the American Paper Institute on another wall, like a doctor might display his degrees and associations. It was not an imposing office by any means, and Bert seemed a little unsettled by it. He greeted Morrison and Castor. "This is just my nest in the forest. I spend very little time here but I have to have an address." He smiled broadly at two unresponsive faces. "I added some things to the notes Lynn gave you. We talked it over last night and so I just jotted them down." He took a manila envelope from a gunmetal-gray file tray that also sported a label, THANKS FOR NOT SMOKING, and handed it to Castor, who was closest to him. Norbert took the pages out of it, sat down and began to read.

"Understand you and Lynn returned to the scene of the crime Saturday," Bert said to Morrison.

"It didn't help any, as I'm sure she told you."

"It helped Lynn."

"Pardon?"

"It helped her," Bert said, a decibel or two above a whisper. "She said it was a great day." Morrison looked at him. "Said you two had a great time." Bert's eyebrows arched. "It's all right," he said. "I understand. You see, Lynn and I like to see each other happy. It's a sad world in too many ways and we don't want to be part of that aspect of it."

"That's nice," Morrison said. "About the rape of—"

"Life is short," Bert interrupted. "Youth is even shorter. So we enjoy it. She said you were very good." Norbert looked up from Bert's notes. "Both times, both ways."

"Look, we need to talk about Miss Facia, the young lady you met after she had been raped," Morrison said. Norbert went back to reading the notes.

WHEN THEY were outside, Castor, breaking into a broad grin, said, "You seemed a little unnerved up there. Not like you, old boy."

"Can you believe that guy?"

"Sure. You told me they got an arrangement."

"Life is short, youth shorter. So you just go out and screw around and then come home and talk about it. Jesus." Morrison shook his head, then looked over at Castor. "Modern times."

"Well, I'm glad to hear you're good, *both* times, *both* ways. May I ask what the second way was? You told me what the first one was."

Morrison ignored him. "Incidentally, I think I've got a way we can get Facia to talk to us. I don't know how much we'll get, but I think I can arrange the talk."

16

THEY RELEASED Tommy at 6:45, twenty-three hours and fifty-five minutes after they had booked him for battery. Actually they could have kept him for seventy-two hours, but that was a lot more paperwork, plus they did not want him, even behind a set of bars. He collected his personals—a weathered wallet, $142.28 in cash, two sets of keys, a belt, the rawhide laces from his workboots, and the Eddie Bauer down jacket he had stolen from the health club. He got the items from the sergeant in a cubicle just off the main holding area of the Town Hall station. Tommy, more sullen than usual, appeared about to say something and the sergeant knew it was not going to be "thanks for the hospitality." So he pointed a finger at Tommy and said, "You say one fucking word that I don't like and you're right back in there," pointing now across the room to the door that led to the detention cells. Tommy glared, but did not say a word, just turned and walked out. He had things to do that night.

After several stops, Tommy reached the Tudor Arms just in time for the ten o'clock news, but he was about as interested in that as he was in soliciting contributions for Mothers Against Drunk Drivers.

It was dark in Jo's apartment when he let himself in, the only light coming from the cold blue winter moon that filtered in through the bare window on the wall opposite the door. He flicked on the light. Everything was in its natural state of disorder. The ratty furniture was there. Grimy glasses on the table. Unwashed dishes in the sink. Overflowing ashtrays. His clothes were strewn about the room. Jo's weren't. They were gone, like she was. So was the money she kept in the bottom drawer of the chest in the bedroom, so were all the drugs they had relieved Warner's Discount Drugs of. The only thing that remained were four empty bottles of G.I. Gin with the telltale labels still on them. "Dumb ass," he muttered to himself, and put them into a brown paper bag he found on the kitchen floor.

Outside, Tommy walked back to the alley, dropped the bag and then stomped the contents into ground glass and left it there with the other garbage that littered the snow. He went back into the building and rapped on the door to Manford White's apartment, standing away from the peephole that had been drilled into it. But there was no response after several tries and so he went downstairs.

There was light coming from under the door to the janitor's apartment on the ground floor. Open for business, Tommy thought. He walked over to the door; it, too, had a pinhole drilled through the wood at eye-level. He paused there, thinking.

Only one of the two lightbulbs in the hall was working. Tommy went over and stood under it. He couldn't reach it so he went to the little utility closet down the hall to see if there was something to stand on, which there was not. He took the mop that was there, the one Head was supposed to use but never did, walked back to the light and swatted it. There was a hissing sound and the tinkle of the shards of fragile glass as they fell to the marble floor, and now there was almost total darkness in the hall.

Tommy went back to Head's apartment, knocked three times, counted to three, one more knock, counted to three, two more knocks—the code—and waited. Nothing. Did it again, harder this time, and heard someone come up to the door. He could feel the eye at the pinhole, but he was not in front of it.

"What you want?" he heard from inside, Head's voice.

"Jo Kane wants to buy something," Tommy said in the most unsouthern accent he could muster. "Sent me for it. And she sent a package for Manford White. He ain't upstairs. She said if he wasn't around I should see you."

"What this Jo Kane want?"

"Dick Tracy"—that week's codeword for cocaine. "Two dime bags."

The door opened three inches, the heavy chains at shoulder and knee level drawn taut. Head's face was there peering out into the darkness. Tommy took in Head standing in front of the crack, from the top of his Afro to his bare feet, saw he had nothing on but a pair of white jockey shorts.

"Who you?"

"The guy she's stayin' with for a while. C'mon, I can't stand here all night."

"Gimme the bread and the package and I'll see what I can dig up for this Jo Kane."

"The package ain't gonna fit through here."

"Then just the bread and leave the package out there."

"You don't know what's in it. If you did you'd know I ain't leavin' it outside *anywhere*. I either give it to Manford White or you or it goes back with me. And White is gonna be one pissed person if I have to do that."

Head was not overbright. The door closed and Tommy smiled as he heard the chains slide out of their runners. The door opened again and Tommy pushed in, closed it behind him. The look on Head's face was one of consternation, trying to figure out what was happening. It was slow going under the basketball.

"Get you out of bed?" Tommy asked, looking up and down the nearly hairless, wiry brown body. "Least you got your shorts on." Tommy sniffed the air, it was the unmistakable odor of marijuana. "Been smokin' a little, too?"

Head was still trying to figure things out. "Where's the package?"

"There ain't no package, dimwit. Just want to find out a few things, like where Jo went. You know where?"

"No. Didn't even see her go. Man told me she just left last night in a big hurry. Wouldn't be back, leastways for a while."

"Where is Man? He ain't upstairs."

"Don't know. Must be out somewheres."

From the back came a fuzzy voice. "What's goin' on out there Head?"

Tommy's eyes wall-eyed at Head, then he shoved him out of the way and half-ran down the hall to the bedroom in the back where Head often stashed drugs for Manford White.

He saw Manford White, naked, just getting to a sitting position on the edge of the bed. The smell of marijuana was even stronger in the bedroom. "Holy shit," White said when he saw who was in the doorway. White's eyes, dull before, lost their haze.

"Jesus in Georgia, you're *queer*," Tommy said, then laughed. "A couple of nigger queers." Tommy whirled around suddenly and grabbed Head, who had followed him down the hall, clutched him by the back of the neck and shoved him into the bedroom. "Lover boys. And I thought you had something goin' with Jo. Where is she, faggot?"

"Don't know, asshole," White said, on his feet now, but aware of his vulnerability, barefoot, naked. Even it up, he thought as he snatched a four-inch switchblade that was on the table next to the bed, snapped it open. "And if I did know, you'd be the last to get the word, my man."

Tommy looked at the knife. "You *are* gonna tell me where she is. That blade ain't gonna help you." White was edging toward the door to the closet, which was slightly ajar, about three feet away.

Tommy took a step toward him.

"You want your innards all over Head's floor, Joe-ja, you take one more step," White said. He had his left arm up, chest-high, elbow crooked at a ninety-degree angle. Beneath it he moved the knife slowly side to side, a practiced motion; he had been here before.

"Where is she?"

"She's gone, man. Maybe went south for the winter, like the birdies do. Suggest you do the same thing." He took another step toward the closet.

"I'm askin' you only one more time, faggot. Where is she?"

"First of all, Joe-ja, I already answered that. Second of all, I don't like that name. You just don't understand. You probably a little retarded, bein' from Joe-ja. Some of us like it both ways. Variety, spice of life. Jo didn't mind. She know I do her sometimes, sometimes I do Head." He took another half-step toward the closet. "Fact, once I did Head, then went upstairs and did Jo. Didn't even stop to wash it first."

White saw it, knew in that split-second the knife was inconsequential now. About to make a leap for the closet door, he never had a chance. The bullet from the .357 drilled into his chest, past the rib cage, through the heart, hit bone, then ricocheted downward, lodging in White's mass of lower intestines. The impact sent Manford White into the closet door, bouncing off as if it, as if he were made of rubber. He was dead when he met the floor.

Tommy turned to Head, whose eyes now resembled two silver dollars with a little black dot centered in each. He grabbed Head by the Afro and dragged him over to the bed and forced him to sit on the edge. Before Head could mouth a plea Tommy let go of his hair and grabbed him by the neck, heard a gurgled, garbled noise that sounded like "no, no," jammed the barrel of the gun into Head's mouth and pulled the trigger, the wall behind the bed suddenly becoming a Jackson Pollock in red, yellow and white with an embellishment of curly rust-colored strands plastered against it.

Tommy moved quickly. He pulled a pair of wool gloves from a pocket of the parka and put them on, then carefully wiped down the gun. Head lay across the bed now, his basketball forever deflated. Tommy placed the gun in Head's right hand, which he wrapped carefully around it, index finger across the trigger, the safety on, then pressed the hand firmly to absorb Head's fingerprints; satisfied, he flipped the safety off and dropped the gun on the bed next to Head. "When you fag lovers spat, you spat," he said softly. Then looking over at Manford White crumpled on the floor, he added, "Told you I'd give you your gun back."

He picked up the knife, closed it and put it in his pocket, then went over to the closet, opened the door, saw the other gun on the top shelf and realized now why White was trying to make it over there. He stuck the gun in his pocket, went back to the living room, latched both chains on the door from the inside, went over to the window, opened it, then the storm window, and climbed out into the alley. No one out there in the darkness and the cold, no noises even. He shut the windows tightly and loped off down the alley.

17

MORRISON WAS late getting to 11th and State Wednesday morning, greeted by "Where the hell you been?" from Norbert Castor.

"Stopped by Six to talk with Sawyer. I thought you were my partner, not my mother."

"Part-time, Joe. Remember, part-time."

"I also have a terrible hangover so don't give me any crap."

"Where were you?"

"I went to Theo Warner's funeral, then back to his brother's where I drank just enough scotch to make me think it was a good idea to stop by Flannery's"—a cop bar near Area Six headquarters—"for a nightcap where I managed to kill at least several thousand more brain cells. Schnapps with beer chasers. I should have my head examined."

"You got a couple of messages there." Morrison picked up the two While You Were Out slips. "So what you got going with the ward committeeman DiFranzo?"

"You *are* my mother. Screen my messages. What time's curfew tonight?"

"Just asking. He's connected, you know."

"I know. You think I'm going to get a talk with Facia going through the Red Cross?"

Castor understood now.

The other note was from Bruce Warner, bereaved yesterday afternoon, somewhat drunk by evening's approach, as Morrison remembered.

"I'm going over to see the good Dr. Punpatipal today. If you want to join me, you're welcome. You do remember we sometimes work Organized Crime."

Morrison gave him a patronizing smile, then picked up the telephone and began dialing.

First-ward committeeman Anthony DiFranzo, when reminded he owed Morrison a major favor—a major-major favor—said he would see what he could do to set up a meet with Rudy Facia.

Bruce Warner did not sound any better than Morrison felt. "I called you, Joseph, because I remembered something this morning. Yesterday morning you called and asked me if I saw a black and white couple in the store the night Theo was murdered. Well, I didn't. But this girl came in that day and asked for Theo, wanted to give him a letter or something. He wasn't here at the time so she left. And I remembered this morning she used to come in here with a black man, he was her boyfriend, I think. Don't know whether that means anything or not but I thought you should know."

"Could be something. Do you know her name?"

"I think her first name was Joan or maybe Jo. Never did know her last name."

"Where's she from?"

"Uptown area, I believe."

"That's a lovely part of town. How did she know Theo?"

"Oh, her mother or her aunt had a thing going with Theo a few years back. You know how Theo was with the ladies? Well, the woman got arthritis real bad a while back and Theo would give her the medicine free. He was like that, you know. And the girl would sometimes come in to pick it up.''

''Do you know the woman's name?''

''No. I never got involved in any of Theo's personal life. I'd seen her a few times but never was introduced. Theo kept his women pretty much to himself.''

''So you don't know where she lives?''

''No, sorry.''

''Did the girl leave the letter?''

''No. Said she had to give it to him personally.''

''She was alone?''

''All by herself.''

''What time was it that she came in?''

''In the morning, about eleven maybe.''

''Did she come back later? See Theo?''

''I don't think so. At least I didn't see her. But then I left earlier than Theo.''

''What does she look like?''

''Not bad. Nice figure, brown hair, shoulder-length, about five foot six. Doesn't dress very well.''

''What about the black boyfriend?''

''I don't really know that he was her boyfriend, just assumed it. But he was a flashy dresser, cocksure of himself.''

''What did he look like?''

''You know, black curly hair, big eyes, big lips. In his thirties. He was good sized, over six feet, well-built, like an athlete. They hadn't been in together in the last month or so, though.''

''Thanks, Bruce. I'll follow up on it. You just might have something here.''

''Well, I hope it helps. Keep me informed about the case, will you, Joseph? I sure would like to see you catch the person who did this to Theo.''

''We would too. I'll let you know if we come up with anything.''

Morrison told Castor, then called Terry Sawyer over at Six.

"I think I'll go snoop around Uptown a little today," he said to Sawyer, "see if I can find out anything about a salt-and-pepper couple that might just be drug-rich lately. Norbert's working OC today."

"Why don't you swing by here and pick me up? My partner's off today. I'll go over there with you."

IN UPTOWN Morrison and Sawyer hit several bars on Broadway, a pawnshop and a liquor store on Lawrence Avenue but came up with nothing. As they turned onto Sheridan Road from Lawrence, Morrison suddenly shouted, "Over there," pointing at a slender man hunched over walking into the wind.

He threw a U-turn that left Sawyer's stomach on Lawrence Avenue and pulled up, double-parking just in back of the man, and was on the street almost before the car stopped. Sawyer was out the other door almost as quickly, automatically following but still a bit bewildered. Morrison grabbed the man, pushed him up against a parked car. "Hands on the car, Vinny," he said. "Lean, you know the routine." Vinny spread-eagled, holding himself in a push-up position off the car. He did know the routine. Sawyer stood back, surveying, right hand inside his coat now unsnapping the holster hasp on his left hip.

"What's this?" Vinny said, looking back over his shoulder and suddenly recognizing the man. "Morrison, for chrissake, what's going on? I ain't seen you in a year, year and a half."

"Shut up, Vinny," Morrison said as he ran his hands around Vinny's torso, then up and down each leg. "I want to talk to you. You prefer I just walk up, throw my arm around you and personally escort you into the squad car? Let all your friends on the street know we're real good pals, huh." Vinny sighed. "Just look pained, like I'm a real pig of a cop harassing you." Morrison turned him around, stood him up, unzipped the jacket, took it off, threw it on the hood of the car, pushed up Vinny's sleeves to look at the inside of his arms. "Well, at least you're not mainlining yet." Morrison handed him back the jacket and said quietly, "Now, where do we meet, like old times?"

Vinny did give him a pained look now. "Come on, Morrison, I got enough troubles on the street."

"I'm not fucking around, Vinny. I want to talk to you. You want to go to the car now, broad daylight, sit in the back?"

Vinny thought for a moment. "The alley, just west of Clarendon, between Windsor and Sunnyside. Halfway down it. Just drive in, I'll come out. Gimme fifteen minutes."

"You got a deal, pal."

"You remember where Clarendon is, Morrison?" Vinny said, kind of brushing himself off, trying to regain his street dignity. "You ain't been around here in a long time."

"Same old Vinny, kid with the smart mouth. Be there. Or I'll come find you and drive you around the neighborhood like you were the grand marshall of the Columbus Day parade."

BACK IN the car, Morrison explained to Sawyer that Vinny was a snitch who worked both sides. Vinny had been one of Morrison's "people," one, like a lot of the others, who he kept solely to himself. Morrison had availed himself of Vinny's services more than a few times when he was working Homicide out of Six. He'd got some things from him, two of them were good enough to close out a pair of bad cases. On the other side of the flip sheet he once got Vinny off a substance-abuse charge, possession with the intent to sell—that's the way it looked, twelve double-dime bags of freebase on him, you don't carry twelve on your person on the street unless you are going to sell them. He talked to the judge, explained the situation, asked to keep Vinny on the street as a pal and got Vinny probation instead of a year at Stateville, where he would have had one bodily orifice restructured to resemble the Rapid Transit subway tunnel. Vinny owed him a lot for that one.

As Morrison edged the car down the alley he saw Vinny's head peer out from between two garages. He stopped there and Vinny, crouching, made his way to the car like an infantryman advancing on the enemy. He climbed in the back and curled up on the floor as Morrison hit the gas pedal and sped out of the alley.

"We'll take a little spin up to Rogers Park. You know Detective Sawyer here?"

"No."

"So how you been, Vinny? Still living on the fringe?" Morrison asked.

From the back floor came, "I ain't won the lottery, if that's what you mean."

"The big score still out there, waiting for you, right?"

"It's there, one of these days. And then I'm out of here. So what's the big deal you want?"

"A little information if you've got it. If you don't, maybe a little snooping around for me."

"Am I ever gonna be even with you?"

"Probably not. I'm looking for a salt-and-pepper, black guy, white broad, supposedly living here in Uptown."

"Yeah, probably about five hundred I could give to you. Discrimination we don't have in this neighborhood. Hatred maybe, but no discrimination."

"The black guy is in his early thirties, built like an athlete, six-one, two hundred pounds, maybe, flashy. The girl's in her twenties, not bad-looking, brown hair. Might be a hooker."

"That narrows it to about four hundred."

"They're probably into drugs."

"That brings it back up to five hundred."

"Come on, Vinny, cut the cute talk."

"What can I tell you. There's loads of salt-and-pepper shakers in Uptown, a lot of whores, and a helluva lot of 'em into drugs. You been gone a while, Morrison, this place ain't turned into a suburb, you know."

"Vinny, I'm beginning to get a little pissed."

"You got anything more? I mean, maybe there are a hundred fits the description. Five hundred was an exaggeration, but still . . ."

"Any one of them come to mind that might have gotten a little windfall of drugs lately?"

"All the salt and peppers around here are into drugs one way or another, but I haven't heard of anything special."

"We think the girl's name might be Joan or Jo or something like that. Ring any bells?"

A carillon. But Vinny didn't say anything.

"You still back there, Vinny?"

"Yeah, I'm thinking. Don't think I know anybody by that name that hangs with a pepper. What's this all about, anyway?"

"A murder."

"Here? The one in Uptown last night?"

Sawyer said to Morrison, "He's talking about two blacks who went down last night. One shot the other, then shot himself. Seems they were sexually related, at least that's the way it appears according to the Medical Examiner's report—finding fecal matter on the dick of the guy who was shot and semen in the asshole of the guy who did the shooting. And chemically speaking, they were a perfect match."

"Some romances just don't work out," Morrison said. Then to Vinny, "That's not the one I'm talking about. One I want went down at Belmont and Halsted. A drugstore robbery, somebody killed the druggist there last Thursday night. You heard anything about it?''

''Not a thing. That's out of my territory.''

''You can still hear things.''

''I can, but I didn't. You think this salt and pepper did it?''

''We don't know. Just want to talk to them. You think you can nose around a little, see if there is any word about the robbery down there, any salt-and-pepper couple that might fit what I told you?''

''Sure, but if I haven't heard anything about it by this time chances are there isn't any word going around. I'll keep it in mind, Morrison.''

''That would be nice, Vinny.'' Morrison reached back over the front seat. In his hand was a card and a twenty-dollar bill. He dropped both of them to Vinny on the floor. ''I've got a new number, Vinny. I want to hear from you in the next two, three days. Sooner if you've got something.''

Vinny looked at the card. ''You downtown now, Morrison. State Street. Got yourself a big promotion or something?''

''A lateral move, Vinny. Don't forget, I want to hear from you. Where do you want out?''

''Where are we? It's tough to tell from down here.''

''Just coming to the intersection of Wilson and Broadway, the heart of beautiful Uptown.''

''Any alley.''

VINNY MADE his way from the alley back to the street, looked in the window on the door of J.J.'s, saw no known Tennesseans with tattoos on their arms, then went inside.

''A shot of VO,'' he said to Mason. ''Splurge today, tomorrow we may all be dead.''

Mason put the shot glass in front of Vinny, filled exactly to the white line. ''You're gonna be dead, you don't control that mouth of yours. The other night that hillbilly was all set to gut and hang you up like a side of beef."

"What an asshole." Vinny looked down at the glass in front of him. "Thanks, Mason."

"Just think before you open your mouth, kid. You'll live a lot longer." Mason drew a draft beer from the tap. "Here's a wash," he said, and walked down to the other end of the bar.

Vinny sat there looking at the glass, then looking at himself in the mirror behind the bar. Jo had a lot of drugs, got them somewhere. But kill a guy for them? No, Jo wouldn't do that. Plus she was with a white guy these days. No way Tommy could be mistaken for a black—a gorilla maybe, one of those midbrain wrestlers on televison maybe, but not an African/American. But, Jesus, he thought, if the thing had gone down and the animal killed somebody and she was there, she would go away for a long time for just being with the asshole. Vinny downed the shot of VO, sipped slowly on the beer. No, this just doesn't go down right. Jo is too street-smart to get into something like this. Plus, she's not a killer, she's a lover. What a lover. The memory brought about as much pain as the Tennessean had dealt him in the same place a few nights earlier.

18

BACK AT Eleventh and State, Castor told Morrison the only things Dr. Punpatipal could contribute were that the Facia girl had indeed had sexual intercourse just prior to being brought to the hospital, seminal fluid was found in her vagina, that she was a newly deflowered virgin and appeared to have sustained no real injuries except for a few contusions. Castor brought up the possibility of genetic fingerprinting, something he had read about recently in the *Daily Bulletin,* but Punpatipal, whose command of the English language was minimal, could not really understand him, especially when he got into polysyllabic words like genetic and fingerprinting. Castor had tried to explain the little he knew about it but got nowhere, leaving Punpatipal finally and ultimately confused, trying to figure out why the police would want to dip somebody's fingers into his own semen. That issue totally unresolved, Castor went on to find out that the girl had not talked to the doctor about being raped. Punpatipal was about to question her about it, he said, but did not have time in the emergency room before her father arrived and took the girl out of there. That was it. Dr. Punpatipal also informed Castor that he was a certified graduate of the University of Peshawar in Pakistan, and proudly displayed the certificate attesting to that fact. He was happy to be working now as a fully accredited intern in the United States and was hoping to set up practice here and buy a house in Lake Forest.

Morrison listened and agreed with Castor that they were not getting very far in the Facia fiasco, as he now called it. He went over and sat in a barrel-back chair at the Formica desk that was his when he chose to use it and looked through his messages. He saw that Alderman DiFranzo had called.

When he got on the line DiFranzo said, "Morrison, this was not a popular favor. Rudy is wacko about this."

"Understandable."

"He's got a bad temper. Anyway, I explained to him the situation, and told him maybe it might even be in *his* interest to talk to you. Who knows, right? We all need favors now and then, right? But I talked. For you."

"So."

"So it's set up. Friday afternoon, four o'clock at his lawyer's office. That's Thomas Dungen, One twenty South LaSalle, Suite Sixteen hundred."

"You aldermen do get things done."

"Oh, and he said don't bring the fat cop with you—Castor, I think Rudy said his name was."

"He's my partner."

"No matter. Rudy agreed to just you coming. He was adamant on that."

"My partner's not going to like it. Neither do I."

"That's the way it falls sometimes. You alone, or nothing."

MORRISON GAVE Norbert the bad news.

"The greaseball knows I live to put him in the penitentiary, that's why he's doing it," Norbert said. "He knows I know he's scum. He knows I die to be there for the talk, so he stiffs me. What a son of a bitch."

"Nothing I can do about it, I'm afraid."

"I know." Castor shook his head in disgust. "You

know, he was a helluva leg-breaker in his early days. And I'd say he was in on at least seven, eight hits in his heyday. He came up working for that maniac, that certified psychopath, Sam Agronso. Even the wiseguys would have trouble with some of the stuff Agronso could come up with. They whacked Agronso because he was so out of control he scared *them.* Remember, about twenty years ago he left the Turf Club out in Cicero one night and wasn't seen again until his body parts bobbed up in a couple of plastic bags in the Sanitary Canal a couple weeks later." Morrison didn't remember. "Agronso was some kind of guy," Norbert continued. "Once he was ticked off at his wife, so he picked up two winos from North Clark Street and brought them home with him. Tore off her clothes, threw her on the floor and made them urinate on her while he watched, then sent the guys on their way. One of the guys beefed because he thought they might get hit on sexual assault or something. They were scared to death she'd beef to us. I got the job, investigated it, but there was nothing to do. She wasn't about to press any charges. She understood the lunatic who gave her the rent money every month. She was a beauty, too. And that's who Facia was apprenticed to. Anyway, I'll do up a dossier on Facia so you can go over it before your meet."

Morrison, looking at his little notepad, dialed another number, got Linda Tate, who was just leaving to go downtown to do a little shopping before meeting her sister for dinner, she said. But she agreed to meet Morrison, suggested the lobby of the Westin Hotel on Michigan Avenue.

MORRISON WAS standing in the lobby near the main entrance to the Westin when Linda Tate walked in at 5:15.

"Sorry I'm late, but it was next to impossible getting a cab from the train station."

"That's okay. I'm just glad you could make it. We got enough time until you meet your sister?"

"How long are we talking about?"

Morrison took her in from pointed patent-leather shoes to soft, furled hair. Four, five years if everything works out, he thought.

"I'm meeting her at seven over in Water Tower Place."

"Why don't we go sit down over there," Morrison said, pointing to the cluster of tables and chairs in the main part of the lobby, most of which were already occupied.

They found a small table with two chairs. "You can get a drink or coffee or anything you want," Morrison said. "What do you think?" he added when the waiter approached.

"I don't know. Are you going to have something?"

"Sure. A Jack Daniels on the rocks with a splash of water," he said to the waiter.

"I'll just have a glass of white wine." After the waiter left she said, "So how can I help you?"

"Well, I'd like to know a little more about your friend."

"Former friend."

"Right. I don't want to get too personal, but . . ."

"I lived with him for about a year, if that's what you're asking."

"That's what I was asking. My interest in Mr. Courtland has to do with a homicide case, as you know."

She nodded. "I know, the drugstore owner."

"That's right. You see, Mr. Courtland was, we think, the last customer in the store that night, that's why I wanted to question him about anything he might have seen."

"Well, all I can tell you is he seemed flabbergasted when you told him on the phone."

"Did you know before that he regularly went to Warner's?"

"I knew he got some prescription drugs there. I don't know how regularly he went."

The waiter brought the drinks. "First one today," Morrison said as he lifted the glass of Jack Daniels. She lifted her glass too. "Same," giving him a little smile. He noticed she had a little molelike birthmark on her cheek.

"Your friend—former friend, I mean—he had a standing prescription for Valium over there. Did you know that?"

"I knew he took it a lot. I guess I didn't pay much attention to where he got it."

"Did he take any other drugs?"

She paused, took a sip of the wine, then looked a little uneasily at Morrison. "He drank a lot. That's all."

"What do you mean by a lot?"

"Just that, a lot. Before dinner, during dinner, half the time after dinner. I don't think he drank during the day, though."

"What sort of things did he drink?"

"This is beginning to sound like an AA interview."

"It might have a bearing. We've been known to grasp at straws, as they say. Catch enough of them and maybe you can weave something out of them. That's the theory, anyway."

"Well, let's see, maybe a couple of martinis before dinner or sometimes scotch manhattans—what do they call them, Rob Roys? Wine with dinner—he has very good wines, expensive. Scotch after dinner, sometimes cognac."

"AA aside, what you told me is in fact helpful."

"How's that?"

"I don't really want to go into it just now. I want to catch a couple more straws first." Morrison cocked his head to the side and gave her a slightly mystified look. "You know what I'm curious about? Why Mr. Courtland went all the way over to Belmont and Halsted to get his Valium all the time. That's maybe four miles from the Carlyle. There's a drugstore in the Drake across the street, another one on Rush Street two blocks away, no doubt one near the Commodities Exchange."

"I really don't know why. I know he did know the people there. I think he used to live in that neighborhood."

"Yes, he told me that. Another thing that puzzles me is why he went over there *that* night, Thursday. If you remember, it was a near blizzard."

"Lord knows why Dennis does what he does."

"What do you mean?"

"Dennis does a lot of things that defy explanation." She looked at Morrison. "You don't think Dennis had anything to do with this, do you?"

"I have to look at it from every angle, and there are a lot of angles. Dennis is just one of them because he was one of the last people in the store. That's all."

"Well, Dennis can do a lot of strange things, a lot of things that might drive someone crazy, but I can't see him killing somebody."

"You're probably right. And I do want to make it clear that at this point he's not considered a suspect in the case. It's just that certain things don't exactly add up and I'm trying to get answers so they will. You can understand that, I'm sure." Morrison took the last sip of his drink. "Plus I enjoy talking to beautiful women." She started to say something but he hurried on, "Especially those who are pleasant and have a good sense of humor."

"Are we getting away from police business?"

"See, that's what I mean, pleasant, good sense of humor." It was the hazel eyes, radiant, distracting. "Getting away from it, you sure are right, maybe you should be the detective. Sorry."

"You don't need to be sorry." A smile.

"Another question. Do you remember what time your former friend got home that night?"

"About ten-thirty."

"You have any idea where he was, say, between eight and ten-thirty?"

"No."

"You saw him when he came home."

"Unfortunately."

"Was there something wrong?"

"He was stoned."

19

MORRISON CALLED Sawyer first thing Thursday morning to tell him about his conversation with Linda Tate. He did not know why Courtland lied to him about drinking; why Courtland said he only touched wine, but it was significant that he had lied. Both agreed they would like to know his whereabouts from eight to ten-thirty the night of the murder and where he got whatever it was he got stoned on. Morrison said he would get hold of Courtland and try to set up a meet after the Commodities Exchange closed that day and suggested it might be a good idea if both of them went. Sawyer agreed.

He walked over to Castor's desk. "Got a deal for you, Norb."

Norbert looked up from the *Cable Channel Guide* he was reading. "Any time I hear something like that I know it's gonna cost me."

"What say we work the street today?"

"What say we don't. Somebody's got to work OC. No disrespect meant, but the mob has not shut down operations in memoriam to your father's friend. The lieutenant's gonna have a shit-fit when he sees how little time we put in this week on OC cases."

"Wait a minute, Norb. I'm talking OC, at least half the day. I think we should work Taylor Street in the morning, all morning. We've got almost nothing except a vague secondhand description of the two guys who raped Facia's kid. Right?''

Norbert nodded. ''We been there once. Your people, let me say, were less than helpful, as I recall.''

''I don't mean we should work my connections on Taylor. I thought we might have had a chance the day after, before the whole story covered the street. Now I agree, if the Italians have anything at all that might help, it's already gone Fed Ex to Facia. My idea is let's work the darker side of the street. I used to have a good one in the Abla Homes there, the project, a gangbanger, doper, his street name was Ballbat, his weapon of choice. He wasn't all that into our national pastime. His real name was Lemuel, Lemuel Davis, but he knew a helluva lot about what was happening on the street. I turned him myself about two years ago. There's also some colored bars off Taylor we could look into. If somebody there has got something, they sure as hell aren't going to give it to the Italians. That's the code of Taylor Street. That's how they coexist. They each pretend the other doesn't exist. Maybe we'll get lucky.''

''Joe, you old Homicide dicks like to go door to door more than the Jehovah's Witnesses. At least you go to more interesting places. So, okay. You wanna stop at Dottie's for a little something first? I always work better on a full stomach.''

Morrison was already putting on his coat. ''Then we work Uptown this afternoon for Theo Warner.''

''I figured as much.''

''Just till maybe four or four-thirty. Go on over to Dottie's, I'll meet you there. I got one phone call to make and then I'll get us signed out for a car so we can leave just as soon as you've stuffed your face.''

VINNY GOT up a little after one in the afternoon. He had worked Wednesday night after seeing an obituary earlier that week in the *Tribune*. Vinny religiously read the death notices, not because he cared who died but for leads. He knew it was a lost cause these days to try to hit a decently fashionable place during a wake or funeral because the richies had learned. You leave somebody house-sitting, the undertakers told them that, the pricks. But the not-so-rich, they weren't always that smart, or didn't pay attention. This one, however, was a natural. Long obit about one Murray Sanderson, eighty-one years old, founder of Sanderson Assemblies, which employed more than two hundred people. He had died in Sarasota, Florida, had moved there after retiring ten years earlier. Funeral services were set for Thursday morning in Florida with interment following at the St. George Cemetery in Sarasota. He was survived by his wife, Estelle, and a son, Stanley Sanderson of Winnetka.

Sure enough, in the white pages of the north suburban telephone directory, there he was: Stanley Sanderson, 684 Yellowstone Drive, 256–4817. Stanley had no doubt gone down to his old man's funeral, Vinny figured, taking the family with him, boarding the golden retriever or Irish setter or whatever fancy breed they had in Winnetka. Gone down to be sure to console the old lady so when she dropped there was no problem with the will and all that shit—and Vinny would bet, if he had it, a four-figure note that Stanley did not understand there were people like him out there.

He took the train up to Winnetka late in the afternoon, walked off it, like all the other commuters, found the house, red brick Georgian, eight, nine rooms—worth maybe half a million in today's market—cased it from the front and the back. Great, there was an alley behind it, a church parking lot about two blocks away, an easy entry looking at the back porch with the slanted roof that led to a second-floor bedroom. Vinny could climb. They all made it difficult on the first floor, security systems sometimes, but the second floor, they didn't understand, they thought only Superman could get in up there, the assholes.

He went back to Uptown, made the obligatory telehone calls to the Sanderson residence, got the answering machine: "Sorry, we're not in at the moment but if you'll leave your name and number after the beep we'll be happy to return your call." After four of those between six and ten o'clock he felt secure enough to call Hertz to rent a car for the trip up to Winnetka, then got on the el to O'Hare, where he would pick it up dressed right—suit, tie, briefcase, a tired airline traveler just arriving on a late-nighter from Los Angeles. Vinny liked that thought—maybe he was in town to do a deal for Vic Damone at the Chicago Theater, maybe something for Sinatra's kid, Frankie Junior, a favor.

That's what he was thinking about as he stood at the Hertz counter trying to look weary as he filled out the forms. He gave the girl a fake driver's license and a fake American Express card—he knew they wouldn't run it through until he returned the car and then he would take it off the card and pay cash. He got the car. Full-size. A Chevrolet Lumina. He had never heard of it but it seemed nice and it had great trunk space.

Just outside Winnetka he stopped at a gas station that had an outdoor pay phone and called the Sandersons once more, same recording. At a little after three in the morning he parked in the church parking lot, up close to the side entrance. You can't park on the street in Winnetka at night, Vinny knew—a car parked on one would draw more than a few suspicions from a cruising cop and they did cruise up there, burglary being their biggest worry next to kid's beer parties, Vinny thought. As he walked down the dark street carrying his briefcase, which contained a flashlight, a couple of plastic garbage bags and some tools for jimmying a window, anxious to get to the alley, he wondered how a Winnetka cop would make out working a day in Uptown.

There was no one on the street, no cars, everything was dark, even the moon was blocked by clouds. It was an easy climb, no problem with the storm window, and the inside window was not even locked. He was out of the cold less than two minutes from the time he started to climb. In the house he found $646 in cash—$400 in a bedroom, the rest downstairs; a Rolex wristwatch; some nice jewelry but not as much as he had hoped to find—the broad must have kept the really good stuff in a safe deposit box, Vinny figured. There was a camcorder, CD player, VCR and a helluva nice set of silver among other fencable items. It did not take long to fill the trash bags. Then he just walked out the back door, the trash bags over his shoulders, and deposited them like any good citizen next to the garbage cans at the alley, went to get his car and, of course, drove back to pick up the trash. He was in Uptown by 4:30; since the bars were all closed, he went home. It had been a very good night.

MORRISON AND Castor's trip to Taylor Street got off on the wrong foot. They could not find Ballbat. And when they asked around—he was wanted for questioning, they told those they asked so as to keep Ballbat clean, or dirty, however you looked at it—they found out that they would not ever be finding Ballbat. Ballbat had taken several shots in the chest on the street six months earlier, delivered by a Latin Disciple in a ceremonial act of gang revenge; Lemuel Ballbat Davis was DOA at Cook County Hospital on a warm, early August night just when a lot of other Chicagoans were packing up the old station wagons to go to Wisconsin or Michigan for vacation.

But it got better, much better. As they were pulling up to Nat's Place, a hangout for the lower life of the Abla Homes project, Morrison saw the transaction going on before they saw him. "Let's grab 'em" he said to Castor, and was out of the car so quick—in hand the five-battery flashlight foot-and-a-half long, big rounded head, the basher—that the two startled young kids did not have a chance to bolt. Castor was out right after him, only a little slower.

One of the two kids threw something that landed about ten feet down the alley by a telephone pole before Morrison had both of them spread-eagled against the alley wall of Nat's Place. "Over there by the telephone pole," Morrison said to Norbert, who went over and retrieved a small aluminum foil packet that contained a different variety of snow than that on which it landed. He showed it to Morrison, then stood to the other side of the two young men, who now appeared to be holding up the alley wall to Nat's Place, so neither one could break and take off down the alley.

Morrison patted down the thrower. Nothing. "What's your name?" he asked.

"Kenneth, Kenneth Waters. Say, what is this anyway."

"Shut up, Kenneth. How old are you?"

"Sixteen."

"How long you been using the stuff?"

"Say, I don't do that shit."

"Kenneth, you just tossed a pack of cocaine down the alley."

"Yeah, but I didn't know what was in it. We just found it here in the alley and Larue here picked it up and was showin' me."

"Sure, and Detective Castor here is Santa Claus and I'm his elf."

"No, that's the God's truth. You see, you know, I don't got nothin' on me. I just tossed it cause I thought it might be somethin' bad and I didn't want to get stuck with it, you all jumpin' on us like that."

Morrison ignored him and began patting down the other

kid, the one who seemed edgier. "And what's your last name, Larue?"

"Washington."

"How old are you?"

"Seventeen."

"Ah, the teenage years, puppy love and proms, sodas at the fountain." When he reached the calf, Morrison felt the bulge and pulled up Larue Washington's pants leg. Inside the sock were six more aluminum foil packets. "Well, look at this, Norb. Would you believe it, this boy found a packet of coke in the alley and six of its friends just started crawling up his leg to be with their buddy . . . Larue, you are in big trouble."

Larue did not say anything. Morrison turned to Kenneth. "I think, Kenneth, you were making a buy from this dealer here."

"No, sir, as God is my witness, I thought Larue found the stuff. He just showin' it to me, like I told you."

"Kenneth, you're full of shit. But I don't see we have a case with you, so get the hell out of here." Kenneth pushed himself away from the wall and started to back out toward the sidewalk. "Thank you," he said. "Thank you much."

"And Kenneth, remember," Morrison added, "just say no to drugs."

"Say what?"

"Get the fuck out of here." Kenneth took off running.

Morrison got the handcuffs from his belt and cuffed Larue's hands behind him, took him by the arm, led him to the car and pushed him in the backseat. He and Norbert got in the front.

"Larue, you know what possession with the intent to sell gets you these days?"

"No."

"You're seventeen. Know what that means? They try

you as an adult at seventeen for a felony, which is what you just committed.''

''I weren't goin' to sell it.''

''You *were* selling it, Larue. We saw you. We saw you take that twenty-dollar bill, put it in your jacket pocket there and hand Kenneth a packet that just happened to have cocaine in it. That's the way it's going down, Larue.''

Larue was silent, but Morrison could see fear in his eyes and that's what he wanted to see.

''Now, Larue, we want to talk with you before we take your ass in and send it off to Stateville for, what shall we say, reconditioning.'' He got no response. ''Larue, you understand what I'm saying?''

''I do.''

''I do! Well, I guess we're married.''

''How much time I gotta do for this?'' Larue was accepting the reality of his situation.

''More than you want. Could be a couple of years, depending on the judge and his affection for Nancy Reagan.'' Morrison had his arm draped over the front seat, looking back at Larue. ''Now, Larue, maybe we can work something out—something that will save your asshole from getting much, much bigger.''

''Yeah.''

Morrison put the car in gear and pulled away. ''We're on our way to the Monroe Street stationhouse where you're going down. But if you can answer a few things for us on the way . . . it might turn the whole thing around for you. Know what I mean?''

''Yeah.''

''You hear anything in the neighborhood about a rape last week? Two guys involved. Nice little white girl, got it from two animals. In the basement of a building over on Ada just off Taylor.''

''No.''

''Larue, let me make myself perfectly clear. Monroe

Street is a way station to Stateville, where people serve some bad, bad time. We are offering you maybe an alternative. You think you can understand that, Larue?'' Morrison pulled the car over to the curb. They were about four blocks from the lockup at Monroe and Racine. He looked back again at Larue in the backseat. ''Last chance.''

''You mean I give you somethin' on that, you let me walk?''

''If it's worthwhile, yes. If it's bullshit, no.''

''There was talk.''

''So give it to me.''

''How I know you let me walk?''

Morrison held up the key to the handcuffs. ''You got to learn to trust the police, Larue. You give us good information, I unlock those things and you can hitchhike back to the project, free as a bird. You don't give us anything we can use, I start up the car and deposit you at Monroe Street and Norb here and I then sit down and do all the goddamn paperwork and hand it over to the State's Attorney and you, Larue, go to that wonderful school in Joliet, Buggery State.''

''There was two guys talkin' it up. Said they got some nice white chick real good. Even had her wallet, said it had two Cs in it along with some other cash. Thought it was real funny, gettin' paid for it. Gettin' money from the girl, know what I mean? More than a hundred each. That's what I heard.''

''Where'd you hear this?''

''Just on the street. Some were talkin' about it. Say they heard 'em braggin', that's all.''

''You didn't hear it from them, then.''

''I didn't even know 'em. Never even saw 'em myself.''

''Who were they?''

''Don't know. Just heard what I heard.''

''Come on, Larue.''

"That's all, man. That's all I know."

"That's not enough to walk, Larue. Sorry." Morrison started the engine up, shifted into drive.

"Awright," Larue said. "They weren't from here. Just passing through, way I heard it. Nobody around here goin' to do what they did to who they did it to. They didn't know, that's what I heard. When talk came 'bout who she was, everything shut down. Nobody talked to nobody. And they gone, took off quick."

Morrison shifted back to park. "Larue, you are getting close to walking out of here. But you're still a stride or two away."

"They just drifted in, and they gone now. I told you."

"So who were they?"

Larue fidgeted in his seat. "Don't know their names." He looked at Morrison and Castor; both staring back at him. "Honest to Jesus, I don't know who they was. All I know is they was stupid studs. Everybody said that."

"Come on, give us the whole thing, Larue," Morrison said, again dangling the key to the handcuffs.

"I'm walkin', right?"

"You're getting close."

"Well, what I heard, they was roommates together in Pontiac, got out around the same time, hooked up and ended up here. Decided to have a little fun. Didn't know what shit they was gettin' into. That's all I know."

"That's not all you know, Larue. Why were they here? What's their connection? They didn't just come up here for the scenery."

Larue's fidgeting turned to squirming, but he knew he had to finish it. "You gotta promise me this goes nowhere. What I tell you could end me up worse than Stateville anybody ever finds out."

"Nobody will ever know, Larue. I guarantee we'll protect your vulnerable ass."

"From what I heard, the black brother was Rose Shaman's cousin. You know who she is?"

Morrison did not. "Should I?"

"No, guess not."

I should, Morrison thought. "Where do we find her?"

"She lives across from Union Park. They came up to see her, get something going, some cash flowin', and then they went and did that thing. Well, they got the word they better get the fuck out of the neighborhood, the city, pretty quick, and they did. That's all I got, honest to God."

"You invoke God a lot, Larue."

"My father was a preacher."

"Where exactly is Rose Shaman's place?"

"On Laflin just north of Lake. A two-story she works out of—I mean, lives on the second floor."

"Address?"

"Don't know. But it's the second house from Lake, west side of the street."

Morrison got out of the car. "Get out, Larue." He unlocked the handcuffs.

"I don't get the stuff back?"

"Jesus, Larue, you're out of here. You think I'm going to give you your dime bags back? Are you nuts?"

"Just asked." Larue started running down the street, a beautiful gait, smooth, effortless; Morrison watched him go and wondered how good an athlete he might have been had he stayed in school, worked at it. No one would ever know, Morrison thought.

"Let's go visit Rose Shaman," Morrison said as he got back into the car.

WHEN THEY pulled up in front of the old graystone two-flat where Rose Shaman lived, two bleary-eyed men in their early twenties were just coming out and stepped aside looking nervously at the two detectives, then started to walk quickly down the sidewalk.

Morrison yelled to them, "Hold it."

They knew it was the Man. They stopped, turned around slowly, looking disconsolate.

Morrison did not bother to identify himself, he knew it wasn't necessary. "You live there?" he asked, referring to the building they had just come out of.

"No, sir," one of them said.

"What were you doing in there?"

"Just visitin' a friend."

"Miss Shaman?"

"Yes, sir," the spokesman said warily.

"Have a nice visit?"

"Yes, sir."

"She was home?"

"Yes, sir."

"Be careful," Morrison said as he and Castor turned toward the apartment building, "this isn't the safest of neighborhoods."

The two-flat had probably been an elegant apartment building sixty years earlier when it was built, when the neighborhood just west of downtown was a nice place to live. Now the vestibule smelled of urine, the walls were cracked and filthy, the stairs uncarpeted, unswept, rotting, there was dried vomit on two of them. Upstairs, when they saw the door, both Morrison and Castor shook their heads. It was made of reinforced steel.

"Well, now we know how our little friend Larue knows this Miss Shaman," Norbert said quietly.

Morrison nodded, then rapped on the door with his basher, making a clanging sound. No answer. The second time he pounded, somebody could hear it a block away. "This is the police," he shouted. "We want to talk with Rose Shaman." No answer.

"She may think we're a couple of stick-up guys," Norbert said. "They're more worried about them than they are about us." They heard the toilet flush inside. "I guess she thinks it's us.'' They heard it flush again. ''Busy place, that bathroom.''

Morrison pounded again. The toilet flushed again. Morrison shouted, ''We do not have a search warrant. We do not want to come inside. We just want to talk to Rose Shaman or whoever is in there. We'll do it in the hall out here.'' Still no response.

''Wonder how much dope just entered our sewer system,'' Castor said.

Morrison was getting irritated, ''If you don't come to the door in ten seconds I'm going downstairs and radio over to Monroe Street and get a patrol car to come over here and sit out in front until I can go downtown and get a search warrant and come back and break down the goddamn door.''

They heard a sound behind the door, then a woman's voice. ''I want to see some identification.'' The door opened as far as the chains would let it. There was no one there. ''Show it to me,'' she said, still behind the door. Morrison pulled the wallet from his back pocket, opened it to show the badge and the ID card and stuck his arm through the partially opened door. ''Okay,'' he heard, then withdrew his arm. The door closed, then reopened, this time without the chains. A black woman in her thirties, attractive, wearing jeans and a Harvard sweatshirt, stepped out into the hall. ''So what do you want.''

''You Rose Shaman?''

She stared idly back at him, finally said, ''Yep.''

''You have a cousin who was recently released from the penitentiary down in Pontiac.''

''I have a lot of cousins.''

''I'm talking about this one in particular.''

''I didn't know any of my cousins was in Pontiac.''

''The one who was up here last week to see you.''

She shook her head. ''Weren't any relatives up to see me. Don't know where you got your information.''

"In Pontiac, couple of their buddies said your cousin and his cellmate were going up to Chicago to see Miss Rose Shaman. Maybe get a job working for you."

"Well, they didn't show up. What you want with my cousin, anyway?"

"We want to talk to him."

"Sorry, I can't help you."

"All right, Miss Shaman, you seem like an intelligent woman, so let's cut the bullshit," Morrison said. "We've got an undercover agent working this neighborhood. She heard on the street that this pair might have had something to do with a rape that took place over near Taylor Street. She heard that one of the pair was your cousin."

"Well, whether she got it right or wrong, I don't know. If it was a cousin of mine I don't know which one 'cause none of them have been by here lately."

She was quite used to bullshitting the cops, Morrison thought, did a good job of it, too. But she was thinking, Morrison could tell—thoughts maybe turning to worry behind those rich brown eyes that now were not quite as stone-cold as they had been a few moments ago.

"Did you hear anything about a rape over on Taylor Street?" Castor asked, but before she could answer and knowing what the answer would be, he added, "Oh, never mind, let me tell you about it. It was a young Italian girl, happened to be the daughter of Rudy Facia. Ever hear of him?"

"No."

"Well, he's a big man in the Outfit, you know, that group they sometimes refer to as the Mafia. A captain. Used to be a real hellraiser, an enforcer, a lot of his contemporaries walk with noticeable limps the result of dealing with him, some don't walk at all, don't even breathe. Now he's big time. Others do those kinds of things for him. And he is really not happy about what happened to his daughter."

Rose Shaman looked from Castor to Morrison, who

added, "You could say it is perhaps his main mission in life right now to find out who did this."

There was worry in her eyes now.

Morrison continued, "Now, our undercover heard about your cousin talking about it and she heard on the street that shortly thereafter your cousin and his buddy were gone as soon as word came around just who the rapee was."

"I told you, I don't know."

"Well, how would you like to tell *them* that, too? You know, it would only take one telephone call and I'm sure Rudy Facia or his representatives would arrange an interview with you regarding your family tree. You know, find out for sure if you really didn't know your cousin was walking around the neighborhood, find out just who that cousin might be."

"You wouldn't do that."

"I wouldn't bet on it." Morrison pointed his finger at her. "Look, you give your cousin to us, we talk to him. Maybe he didn't have anything to do with it. If that's the case he walks away. If he did, and you know this as well as I do, he's in a lot better shape with us than he would be with *them*. And look at it this way, if our undercover picked up something relating it to you, how long you think it will be before *they* pick something up? Think of that."

"Okay, I'll give you what I got but it's not all that much. My cousin was up here with this guy named Harper, don't even know his first name."

"This Harper, was he black?"

"No, white. You had it, he was with my cousin in Pontiac."

"What's your cousin's name?"

"Johnny Jonnell."

"Spell it." She did. "Where are they now?"

"I don't know. And I don't know whether he had anything to do with that rape. I do know he was talking it but I don't know whether he did it."

"He left town the day after it, right?"

"He and Harper just disappeared."

"And you don't know where they went?"

"I never talked to him after the word went out who it was got raped. He wasn't staying here. I heard they just went. I don't think anybody knows where."

"You got maybe a little suspicion in the back of your mind where he might have gone?"

"Not Johnny. That boy could turn up anywhere, and when he does there's always some kind of trouble." She paused, caught Morrison's eyes, passing a streetwise look. "He lived in East St. Louis before he went to Pontiac, that's all," another pause, "he's got family in East St. Lou, though."

"That's it?" Morrison said.

"That's all of it." Morrison could tell, nodded. She said, "You know, if the others come around, I tell them just what I told you because that's all I got to tell. I want to preserve *my* ass. I'm gonna tell them I told you the same thing . . . hope you'll stand up to it. I know what they can do, I just don't want them doing it to me."

"We'll help you—in this. Any visitors, let me know." Morrison handed her his card.

ON THE way downstairs Castor said, "You want me to call Narcotics or you want to do it?"

"You do it, Norb. But I'll bet my ass she's out of here by tomorrow . . . after this. And that fucking armored-tank door will be gone with her. Moving day coming up. New apartment, same door . . . new toilet, too."

20

VINNY WAS walking down Wilson Avenue just after three o'clock Thursday afternoon, on his way to the Chevy Lumina he had parked on a side street east of Broadway some ten hours earlier. He had two fences to meet, one for the jewelry and silver, the other for electronics; specialization had even snaked its way down into his world.

It was there on Wilson Avenue that Vinny ran into the one person he least wanted to encounter in the whole world. He tried to avert his eyes. No luck. Tommy, standing in front of the door to the Backstage Lounge, yelled at him, and Vinny, still with a swagger, reluctantly walked over to him.

"How goes it, Tommy," he said, trying to appear he was happy about the chance meeting while, at the same time, noticing Tommy's face was kind of a mess, big scab on the side of it, a couple of nasty bruises. Vinny hated to think what the other guy must look like.

"It goes shitty."

"Who'd you duke it out with?" Vinny thought it was a friendly thing to say.

"Why the hell would you want to know?"

"Just thought it was anybody I know, I might want to go to the funeral." Vinny thought it was funny.

Tommy ignored it. "You know where Jo is?"

"Jo? I thought you were livin' with her."

"I was but she's gone. I want to find her."

"Jeez, I didn't know she went anywhere. She's gone?"

"That's what I said, you don't hear good?"

"Why'd she go?"

"Because I think she thinks I might break her fucking neck if I get my hands on her." Tommy grabbed Vinny by the shoulder of his coat, pulling him closer. "You sure you don't know where she is?"

"Honest to God, Tommy. I haven't seen her since the day I was over there and you guys gave me that stuff."

"If I find out you're lying to me, you little dago, your face gonna become a pizza."

"Take it easy, Tommy, if I knew I'd tell you," Vinny lied. "Like I said, I didn't even know she left." Vinny desperately wanted to change the topic of conversation, so when Tommy let go of his shoulder he said, "Whatcha think of White and his buddy? Word I heard, they were queer."

Tommy nodded. "Couple of freaks, deserved each other, deserved what they got, too."

"Say that Head blew White away, then blew his own brains out." Vinny shook his head. "Never thought Head woulda had the balls to do that."

Tommy grinned. "When you're in love strange things sometimes happen, dick gets in the way of your brain."

"Yeah, ain't that the truth. Well, I gotta get goin', Tommy, got some business to attend to."

Tommy, grin gone, grabbed Vinny by the shoulder again, this time lifting him to his tiptoes. "I'm stayin' in Jo's apartment. You get any word where she might be, you better hot-ass it over and let me know. You come lookin' for me till you find me. You don't and I hear about it, I come lookin' for you. You understand."

"Sure. I hear anything, I'll let you know."

Tommy let him go, then stalked into the Backstage.

Vinny turned toward the street and saw the car double-parked about three cars down, saw Morrison at the wheel, somebody sitting next to him he didn't know, and said to himself, Oh, Jesus, what a day.

Morrison signaled with his finger for Vinny to come over. Vinny walked out into the street to the driver's side of the car, looked around nervously.

"Anybody asks, you tell them I just wanted to know who it was you were talking to. You got anything for me? If you do we'll pick you up the same place as yesterday, take another little drive."

"Not a thing." He held his hands up, palms facing the lead-gray sky in melodramatic submission. "Absolutely nothing."

"Keep your little eyes and ears open, Vinny." Morrison started the car's engine. "And remember, I want to hear from you in the next couple days. *Capisce*?"

Castor leaned over toward the driver's window to look out at Vinny. "You heard anything on the street about Rudy Facia's daughter getting raped?"

"Anything, jeez, that word's all over the city. They want those guys bad. But I ain't heard anything. Wish I did, a man could do himself a lot of good pickin' up some word on that deal."

"Who was that guy, anyway?" Morrison asked. "Looked like he might not like you a real lot."

"He doesn't like anybody. He's a fucking street ape, up here from Georgia, name's Tommy Bates. Been here a month or two. Look, I ever get anything on him I can give you, you got it gratis. He should be livin' over in Lincoln Park Zoo instead of Uptown."

"You better get goin', Vinny, and don't forget me."

"You got it, Morrison."

MORRISON LOOKED at his watch. "It's three-thirty, you might as well go back to State Street, Norb. I got a meet set with Courtland at five at his apartment. Sawyer's going with me. I figured you wouldn't want to at that hour."

"You got that right. I'm eight to five. Say, did I tell you about *Angels with Dirty Faces* I saw the other night. Jimmy Cagney, Pat O'Brien. Cagney's goin' to the chair. Puts on a show, screamin', chickenshit, but it's all an act . . ."

"Twice, Norb. How about dropping me at Six?"

SAWYER WAS on the street when Morrison walked into Violent Crimes in Six, so he just made himself at home. Been gone only a little over a year now and half the detectives in the squad room he had never seen before, but the in-house uniform hadn't changed—white shirt open at the neck, the tie hanging down in two strands or, at best, tied and lowered to sternum level. He bullshitted with them for a while in the squad room until Sawyer and his partner returned.

Sawyer seemed surprised to see him.

"I was in the neighborhood," Morrison said. "Norbie dropped me off. Thought we could go in one car from here."

Sawyer introduced Morrison to his partner, another new face, then said, "I got something for us on this Courtland guy" as they both walked into the Homicide office. "Don't know if it means anything," he said when they sat down at one of the empty desks, "but I checked him out pretty good. Nothing wrong up here. One moving violation, speeding, two years ago, that's all, not even an outstanding parking violation. Credit's Triple-A-One. His business is rock-solid. Owns that condo in the Carlyle outright, has another place on Amelia Island in Florida and some real estate holdings in Colorado. No problems with the feds. Not a big socialite but he has a lot of charitable interests—

a giver, I'm told. Pillar of the community, as they say, and a rich one."

"So why does he tell lies?"

"Maybe because he wasn't always a pillar. I talked with the guy who's the head of the Merrill, Lynch office down in Tampa. He wasn't when Courtland was there, but he knew of him and said he couldn't give me any information about him. Anything about Courtland I'd have to get from the security section at their headquarters in New York. I got through to the head of security. He's the only one, it turns out, who's authorized to give out any information about Courtland.

"It seems Courtland left the company in the wake of a little scandal. He and his wife fell off a boat down there and she drowned. They were on this yacht, a forty-six-footer, he told me, with four other couples, partying. About midnight some of them were out on the deck in the back and Courtland and his wife were dancing around together out there and the next thing the others heard was a big splash and the Courtlands were gone. They went to the back of the boat, couldn't see anything in the dark but heard Courtland yelling.

"Somebody went inside and told the captain and he circled around. They spotted Courtland and threw him a life preserver and dragged him in. But they couldn't find the wife. In the meantime the captain radioed the Coast Guard and they showed up. In all the excitement the others didn't think to clean up their little mess and the Guard found some cocaine and some very high quality hash on a counter in the ship's galley. The Guard later testified that most on the boat were sailing in more ways than one. At any rate the wife's body washed up on the beach on Longboat Key the next morning. The autopsy showed she'd been drunk, a one-point-eight alcohol-blood reading, and they found cocaine in her system. At the inquest some of the people on the boat testified that Courtland's wife was flying high but that Courtland seemed to be in control, although he had been seen snorting some of the stuff earlier.

"It made all the papers. Some of the people on the boat were pretty prominent down there. You know the headlines: DRUG PARTY ENDS IN DEATH ON HIGH SEAS; SOCIALITES, DRUGS AND DEATH; that kind of thing. It was ruled an accident after the inquest, and the drug thing was just kind of washed aside.

"According to the guy I talked to, Merrill, Lynch suggested Courtland might be happier in another line of work and so he took what they called early retirement. Off the record, the guy told me there was an investigation about foul play because it was a known fact down there that Courtland and his wife weren't the happiest of couples. But they were never able to come up with anything.

"He got two hundred thousand dollars from her life insurance and moved to Chicago."

Morrison looked at his watch, got up. "Let's go talk to him."

DENNIS COURTLAND seemed a little dazed when he let Morrison and Sawyer into his apartment, about fifteen milligrams of Valium worth, Morrison figured. Must have been a tough day in the pork-belly market.

"Can I interest you gentlemen in a drink?" Courtland asked. They declined. "It's after five, work day's over."

"Not ours, but thanks anyway," Morrison said.

"Well, I'm not quite so disciplined." Courtland walked over to the wet bar and took a bottle of Puligny-Montrachet from the refrigerator there and poured himself a large glass. "Nothing beats a good wine." His voice had a sing-song tone to it, different than the other evening.

"Yes, you told me that," Morrison said. "That's all you drink, you said."

Courtland looked at him somewhat absently. "Yes, that's right, hardly a vice, a little wine." He smiled. "Now what else can I do for you? I told you everything I know the other night.''

''Think back to the night you were in Warner's,'' Morrison said. ''You said you didn't see anybody else in the store.''

''I didn't say there *wasn't* anybody in the store. I just said I didn't notice anyone else.''

''I understand. You would have noticed a salt-and-pepper couple—black man, white girl—if you saw them, wouldn't you?''

''I would, I guess.''

''But you didn't see such a couple?''

''No.''

''How did you get to Warner's that night?''

''I drove.''

''Bad night for driving. I guess I'm having trouble understanding why you would drive all the way over there in a snowstorm like that.''

Courtland gave him that look of condescension. ''A little snow doesn't stop me if there's something I want. When I want something I get it.''

''Well, there was more than a little snow. Did you go over there from here or come out from downtown?''

''Here.''

''How long did it take?''

''Only about fifteen or twenty minutes. There wasn't much traffic and Lake Shore Drive was pretty well plowed. Why?''

Morrison ignored the question. ''And you said you left the store about seven-thirty or eight, correct?''

''About then. I don't remember exactly.''

''And you went home then?''

''That's right.'' Courtland looked from Morrison to Sawyer, then back to Morrison. ''I don't see what this has to do with your case.''

''How long did it take you to get home?''

"About the same time, fifteen, twenty minutes."

"So you got home about eight-thirty?"

"I'd say that, yes. What does this have to do—"

"You're sure of that, eight-thirty?"

Courtland's condescension turned to anger. "I'm sure of that. Otherwise I wouldn't have said it. I don't like the way this conversation is going. It's almost accusatory."

"Well, Mr. Courtland, some of the things you've told us don't exactly add up."

"Like what?"

"We have reliable information that you did not arrive back here until at least ten-thirty that night."

Courtland went over and took the bottle of Puligny-Montrachet from the silver ice bucket and poured himself another glass. "Well, quite frankly I don't really remember what time I got home that night. I may have stopped off. I have a lot of friends, a lot of acquaintances, a lot of places I drop in to. I may have stopped off at the Coq d'Or Bar over in the Drake and had a glass or two of wine or maybe a cup of coffee. Come to think of it, I did stop by there one night last week. I think it was Thursday, the snowy night . . ."

"It was Thursday night, then?"

"Look, I have a lot on my mind every day, detective, that's why I do as well as I do. I don't spend a lot of time thinking about where I've been on a particular night some time ago. I think of buying and selling commodities and futures, I think about investments." He gave Morrison a look of incredulity. "Are you in some way trying to implicate *me* in this case of yours?"

"We think you may have lied to us on a couple of matters."

"Lied. You mean because I said I got home at eight-thirty, that's a lie? That's ludicrous."

"You said it."

"I also said I may have stopped off across the street at

the Coq d'Or. I do it several times a week. Who told you I didn't get back here until ten-thirty anyway? Linda?''

''No,'' Morrison lied. ''You mean the woman I met here the other evening?''

''Linda Tate, yes.''

''I haven't talked to her. Should I?''

''No, I just thought maybe she said something. She gets confused. Drinks a little too much sometimes.''

''It was another source, and, as I said earlier, a reliable one.''

''Look, I'll give it some thought, see if I can remember if I went some place after, if that'll make you happy.'' Courtland's attitude had turned from angry to nervous.

''That would be good. We just want to establish your whereabouts. We have to, you were one of the last persons seen with the deceased.'' Morrison had changed tactics as Courtland had shifted gear. ''It's our job. You can understand that, I hope.''

Courtland appeared to relax a little. ''I understand. Are you sure I couldn't offer you a drink of something?''

''Positive,'' Morrison said, reaching into his inner coat pocket and coming out with the weathered notebook. ''I just want a couple more things for our records and then we'll get out of your hair.'' He tried to make it sound like a friendship was budding between them. ''Your company's full name and address?'' Courtland gave it to him and Morrison scribbled in his notebook. ''This is your principal residence?'' Courtland nodded, but also told him about Amelia Island and a condominium in Vail he was thinking of picking up. ''And you're not married?''

''No.''

''Any family in Chicago?''

''No. I have a sister in California—Long Beach.''

''Were you ever married?''

Courtland looked at him. ''Once.''

''Divorced?''

"No, my wife died."

"Sorry to hear that. Recently?"

Courtland shook his head. "Before I moved to Chicago."

"Illnesses can be devastating, not just for those suffering them."

"Yes, they can, they certainly can."

"I hope it wasn't a long one. Those are the worst."

"Mercifully, it wasn't."

Morrison closed his notebook and stood up. "Thanks for your time, Mr. Courtland."

Courtland walked with them to the door. "Good luck in your investigation," he said as he held the door open for them.

DOWNSTAIRS MORRISON said, "You got time for one at the Coq d'Or?"

"Sure, if you're buying."

WHEN THEY walked into the Drake Hotel Morrison nodded at the pay phone just off the entrance. "Go on down there, I need to make a call. You know where it is?"

"The Drake is not my usual hangout."

"Just follow the hall. It's on this level at the other side of the building. Make friends with the bartender. I'll be there in a few minutes."

Morrison dialed, got an unrecognizable voice at the other end. "Can I speak with Linda Tate, please?"

"She isn't available, can I take a message?"

"Tell her Joe Morrison called. You her sister?"

A kind of cold "Yes."

"Well, I'm a detective, she knows who I am. Just tell her not to talk to Dennis Courtland until I've had a chance to talk to her first, would you please?" There was a pause at the other end. Finally Morrison said, "Are you still there?"

"Yes, yes, I'm sorry. It's just that he just called, looking for—" She sounded suddenly like she just realized she had given away a major military secret.

"Did Linda talk to him?"

"No. She doesn't want to talk to him."

"Good. When do you expect her back?" Another pause. "Look, this is important. As I said, Linda knows who I am. Will you please get the word to her."

"Hang on just a minute." It was about ten seconds. "She said she could call you in about fifteen minutes if you leave a number."

"Tell her I'm downtown, at the Drake. I'll call her back in fifteen, twenty minutes, okay?"

"I'll tell her."

"Thanks."

Sawyer was at the bar, only one other person at it, a few tables filled, but otherwise a very quiet night in the Coq d'Or. "As long as you're buying I'm having Jack Daniels," Morrison said as he sat down.

"What do you mean, *me*? It was your idea we come here. Otherwise I sure wouldn't have ordered Johnnie Walker Black."

"Jesus, all *right*, I'll have the same," Morrison said to the bartender. "Just a splash of water in mine and a twist."

"He works here Monday through Thursday, nights," Sawyer said after the bartender went off to get the scotch. "And Sunday, days." Sawyer then added with a smile, "And he did work last Thursday night, four to midnight. The rest I leave to you, Joe."

The bartender slid the drink in front of Morrison, a glass of water with it.

"Always this quiet?" Morrison asked him.

"No, this isn't usual at all."

"How about last Thursday night, the night of the big snowfall?"

"Oh, God, that night. It was crowded, jammed. Closed

up at midnight, got out of here about quarter to one, didn't get home until two. You guys cops or something?"

"You are an observant fellow, Chuck," Morrison said, looking at the brass nameplate on his lapel. "Do you know a man by the name of Dennis Courtland, lives across the street in the Carlyle?"

"Oh, sure. Nice man. Stops in fairly often."

"Remember last Thursday night, crowded as it was, did you notice if he was here?"

"No, he wasn't."

"You're sure."

"Positive. I tried to get here early, taking into account the snow and all. I was here about three-thirty and at that time it wasn't crowded. I know he wasn't here, it didn't start to fill up until around six or so."

"But later do you think he might have been here, say, between eight-thirty and ten-thirty?"

"No, he never comes here in the evening. The only time Mr. Courtland comes in is in the afternoon, three, four o'clock at the latest. Never stays more than an hour. Has a few pops and leaves."

"Pops being?"

"Usually Absolut on the rocks, twist, and a Perrier chaser."

Morrison looked over at Sawyer. "Chateau Absolut, a great white wine, from the vineyards of Sweden." Then back to the bartender, "And you're sure he didn't come back that night in particular?"

"Positive." The bartender looked from Morrison to Sawyer. "What's this all about, anyway?"

"Just a little investigation we got going." Morrison finished the last of the drink in one gulp.

"Well, Mr. Courtland's a good man . . . very good tipper too. Say, you two want another?" Morrison looked at Sawyer, who gave him a pained smile and said, "Yeah, one more, put it on a separate check."

"No, no," the bartender said. "Who you are, these are on the house. Don't flash it around, though, okay?"

"I got to call Courtland's old girlfriend again," Morrison said to Sawyer, "be back in a few minutes. Don't touch my drink."

LINDA TATE was there when Morrison called, this time from the pay phone just outside the lobby entrance to the Coq d'Or.

"What's this all about?" she asked, an edginess in her voice.

"I just wanted to let you know that your former friend has not told us the truth about several things we asked him. I told him I thought he might be lying to us. He may suspect you told us some things."

"Like what?"

"The time he got home that night. He told us eight-thirty. Well, that didn't jibe, and I told him so."

"So he thinks I told you that?"

"I told him I haven't talked to you, that I got it from another source, but he might suspect it. He called you earlier, just after I left. My guess it's either to talk you into coming back to the commodities bin on Lake Shore Drive or to find out if you did talk to me. My bet is the latter. I just wanted to tell you before you talked to him that I didn't compromise you."

"Well, I don't have any plans to talk to him about *anything* anyway."

"Just wanted you to know. If he gets to you, tell him I haven't talked to you. Save yourself the hassle."

"I appreciate that."

"On the other hand, I do want to talk with you again. After our little session with Courtland, there are more and more things here that I feel I need to pin down. You available tomorrow by any chance?"

"You can't do it over the phone?"

"Look, I'm at a pay phone in the lobby of the Drake, my partner's inside at the bar waiting for me. Plus it just works better face to face. I promise not to be trouble."

"Okay."

"Where will you be tomorrow? I can come up to Evanston, or if you're going to be down in the city . . ."

"I'm coming downtown. I've got an appointment at ten o'clock."

"Looking for a job?"

"You detectives can be so insightful."

"Yeah, it's the job. Didn't mean to pry."

"That's okay, Detective Morrison."

"Can the detective stuff, okay?" There was a pause. "So where are you going to be downtown?"

"On Michigan Avenue, Ohio Street."

"Not a lot of employment agencies there."

"I'm not going to an employment agency, Morrison, I'm going back to a modeling agency where I worked two years ago. They want to see if I still have what I once had. Translation—they want to see if my legs and boobs are still firm. That enough?"

"Plenty. What time do you get through the physical?"

"Probably about eleven-thirty."

"How about I buy you lunch afterwards? We could talk then."

There was the pause, calculating, ascertaining, as Morrison might say. Finally, "Sure, why not."

"Good, where do I pick you up?"

"Six twenty North Michigan, just north of Ohio."

"I'll be out in front. In a Plymouth, Chevy, or Ford that will look exactly like a police car but without the blue-and-white veneer and strobes on top. Should I wear a carnation or something so you'll recognize me?"

"I'll recognize you."

"That's the nicest thing I heard all day. See you tomorrow."

21

THE DOSSIER on Rudy Facia was on Morrison's desk when he arrived at 11th and State Friday morning. ''Good reading, if you like horror stories,'' Castor said. Morrison opened the folder and took out the ten typewritten pages, four arrest reports, mug shots of Facia when he was a young hoodlum, mug shots when he was an older made man in the Outfit, a newspaper photo of Facia leaving the federal court building with his attorney.

''You been workin', Norb.''

''A labor of love. Just wish I could be doing the same thing for the warden at Leavenworth so as to prepare him for welcoming a new guest.''

Morrison looked at the four arrest reports. ''Only one conviction.''

''Yeah, hijacking, grabbed a truckload of liquor with Tony Tortorelli when he was twenty-five or so. Tortorelli drove it under a viaduct on North Avenue. Only trouble was, once you got past the incline of the street the viaduct was a few inches shorter than the semi. Good old Tony just drove right under and wedged it in there like a cork in a bottle. Couldn't go forward or backward. Not only was Tony a lousy truck driver, his timing wasn't so good either. Just as he scrunched it in, a squad car was going by the other way, which stopped, and the rest is history. They each got six years and went to the federal pen at Terre Haute. Facia served two years, Tony stayed for four because he got caught with some dope somebody smuggled in to him.''

Morrison read the bio Norbert had typed for him. He remembered the story of the tulips. There was also a story that a young, twenty-two-year-old Rudy Facia was reputed to be one of the good fellas that ambushed Roger Touhy in front of his sister's house on the far west side back in 1959, another that he had been one of the hitmen who whacked Manny Skar in an alley behind his swank apartment building on Lake Shore Drive in 1965. Big-time mob hits, Morrison thought. Smooth ones, too, so smooth the cops or the G never had anything but rumors from a couple of snitches on the street. No wonder he rose so high in the ranks. There was another that he was a member of the party that impaled a 260–pound juice loan shark on meathooks in the back of a meat-packing plant on Fulton Street, where the guy hung for two days while the boys took turns torturing him. They'd work on him for a while, then go play cards, then come back and put out a couple of cigarettes on him, run various instruments into his various bodily orifices, smack him a few times with a baseball bat, give him a couple of shots with a blow torch, then go out and get a bite to eat, come back, play a little more gin or pinochle, revisit their meat-hooked guest, having a good time all the while. After he finally passed away they left his burned, bruised, bloody body in the backseat of his car in a supermarket parking lot on the near north side so that it could be found—a serious message to others about what could happen if you cheated the Outfit.

''What a warm soul, this Facia,'' Morrison said when he was finished reading.

''Yeah, Tulips was a real sweetheart.''

''I'll give him your warmest regards.''

''Do that. Tell him I had something better to do. Tell him I opted to go over and inspect the toilet bowls in the

Greyhound Bus Terminal. Incidentally, I got the East St. Louis cops looking around for Johnny Jonnell. They had a stack of sheets on him."

"Good. On another issue—"

"Let me guess. It wouldn't have anything to do with a homicide, would it."

"Norbert."

"Let me have a T. Yes, there's one T. Let me buy an E. Yes, there's two Es. I think I'd like to solve the puzzle—Theo Warner. Ah, the lights flash, the music plays. I should definitely be on 'Wheel of Fortune.' "

"Are you finished trying to piss me off?"

"Come on, I'm just kidding around. Don't be so serious."

Morrison said, "Okay."

"That Vanna White is something though, you gotta admit."

"I don't watch the show."

"You ought to, for her if for nothing else. I beat the asshole contestants most of the time, and I don't have to clap my hands or jump up and down and act like a nut. Then again I don't win any money or trips to the Bahamas either."

"Norb, are you going to listen to me or not?"

"Sure, Joe, shoot."

"You know Sawyer and I went over to see Courtland, the commodities guy, the last guy in Warner's the night of the murder. Well, he lied to us about not drinking anything but wine. Now why would he do that? Maybe because he doesn't want us to think he's a first-class substance abuser, and that maybe he was getting something else under the counter from the Warners besides Valium." Morrison leaned back in his chair, propped his feet on the desk. "Then he told us he got home at eight-thirty. His girlfriend said he got in at about ten-thirty and was stoned. Now we know she doesn't like him anymore, but I doubt she dislikes him enough to lie to make him a murder suspect. When we told him we had a reliable source that said he didn't get back to the Carlyle till ten-thirty, he said he probably stopped at this bar across the street in the Drake. Only the bartender at the Drake was sure he was *not* in there that night."

"Sounds like Dennis Courtland is trying to hide something," Castor said.

A uniformed cop came into the room with a manila folder in his hand. "Here's the evidence technician's report you asked for," he said, handing the folder to Morrison.

Morrison opened it, began to read again. When he finished he said to Castor, "You know, there are no fingerprints in the apartment except Warner's and some they could tell belonged to a woman as yet unidentified, but hers weren't on anything that was thrown around so she obviously wasn't the one ransacking the place. Probably one of Theo's girlfriends."

"A ransacker who wears gloves, professional," Norbert said.

"In the drugstore, according to this, there were a number of elimination prints—Theo's, Bruce's, that pharmacist's, but no others. So much for that." Morrison got up and walked over and sat on the edge of Castor's desk. "Now let me tell you about Courtland and his former wife."

"You thinking it might be this Courtland guy?" Castor said when Morrison finished his tale of doping and boating in the Gulf of Mexico.

"Anybody who lies to me I've got to think is a suspect. Anybody whose wife departs like she did, who knows what he's capable of?"

"He'd have to be after drugs. Sure as hell wouldn't have been money."

"Could be. But on the other hand, Theo wouldn't have kept drugs at home. Or would he?"

"I wouldn't think so. But then I thought Rock Hudson and Doris Day were made for each other."

Morrison went back to his desk, picked up the phone and dialed the interoffice number of the Bureau of Identification. "This is Joe Morrison up in OC. Run a complete check on Dennis Courtland." He pulled out his notebook, riffled through it. "Current address, The Carlyle, Ten forty North Lake Shore Drive. He's a commodities broker over at the Board of Trade. And fingerprints—maybe security over there at the board requires them. If you don't come up with any, feed it into the G's computer. See if they've got a set on him. Thanks."

Then to Castor, "Worth a shot, see if they can find something Terry missed." He picked up the phone again and got Terry Sawyer. "Where they keeping Warner's clothes?"

"I'll have to check. Why?"

"I'd like the lab to go over them. I'm into some longshots."

"I'll call you back."

Five minutes later he did. "They're over at your place. Crime lab's already got them. Don't know if they did anything with them, though."

"I'll go up and see. I want to look at them myself anyway."

The technician in the crime lab brought the clothes in two boxes and put them on a stainless steel table for Morrison to look at. "What have you done with these so far?" Morrison asked.

"Just a cursory exam. We didn't get a request for anything in particular. We looked them over, didn't find anything that seemed out of the ordinary."

"Well, you've got a request now. I'll send the form up later this morning. I want you to go over these fiber by fiber, see what you come up with; I'm especially looking for traces of drugs. Check the shoes, belt, the leather flaps on the hat, the buttons on the coat for fingerprints. I want this thorough as you can get, okay?''

The technician shrugged, ''You got it. Just get me the form.''

''By the way, where are his glasses? Theo always wore them.''

''There weren't any with his personal effects.''

Morrison made a note to ask Sawyer about that.

MORRISON WAS parked at the curb when Linda Tate walked out of the 620 North Michigan Avenue building at 11:30. He reached across the front seat and opened the door for her. ''You get the job?'' he asked as she settled into the seat.

''It wasn't a job interview. I wanted to see if the agency would represent me again, get me some modeling jobs.''

''That's right, you told me that. So did it go okay?''

''They told me they'd be in touch. I think that's like get lost.''

''Maybe not. So where would you like to have lunch?''

''Anywhere's fine with me.''

''How about the Golden Ox over on North Avenue? Ever been there?''

''No.''

''My old man used to take me there as a kid.'' Morrison turned on the ignition and moved the car out into traffic.

The police radio band was on, the calls coming over in their staticky codes.

''I've never been in a police car before.''

Morrison reached down and turned the radio off. ''That's what you get for living a good clean life.''

''Maybe I just never got caught, Morrison.''

Morrison looked over. ''You can call me Joe,'' at the same time thinking if that modeling agency didn't take her back it had to be run by the Hadley School for the Blind. ''What kind of modeling did you do, anyway?''

"Catalogs. You know, Sears, Spiegel, those kind and some of the specialized ones they send out before Christmas like Marshall Field's."

"What did you model?"

"A little of everything. Dresses, sweaters, lingerie."

"You mean you posed for those bra and panty things, garter belts?"

"Sometimes. You spend a lot of your time going through catalogs looking at women in their underwear?"

"Not anymore. When I was a kid I liked it better than the comics."

In the restaurant they sat at a corner table under the head of an antlered elk; the surroundings—dark oak beams, Dürerlike paintings, beer steins, cuckoo clocks—prompted her to say, "Reminds you of Munich."

"Never been there. Only been out of the country once and that was to go down and pick up a little Mexican who'd decided to swim back across the Rio Grande after killing an old man and his wife in their bakery over on Cermak Road that the kid was trying to rob. We heard he went back to Mexico City, the cops down there found him for us—more than a surprise, a miracle, knowing them—and we got him extradited and my partner and I had the honor of flying down to escort the little slimebag back."

"You lead quite a life."

"Well, it's not your mainstream accountant job. Our ledgers are more interesting." He waved at a waitress. "Speaking of jobs, a part of mine is I get to talk to wealthy commodity traders—and beautiful women." The waitress loomed above them and asked if they wanted something to drink—a Perrier for her, a beer for Morrison. It wasn't all business and no play, he said. When the waitress left, he picked up where he left off. "As I said on the telephone, I need to ask you some more questions about your former friend."

"You said he lied to you."

"He did. And I don't know why."

"I don't know why he would either. What did he lie about?"

"First he told me he didn't drink anything except a little wine. You told me different. So did a bartender in the Drake where he was known to stop off."

"Well, if he told you he didn't drink, that's a real whopper."

"But why would he lie about that?"

"I don't know. Maybe he's self-conscious about it, feels guilty about it." She shrugged. "Maybe he figures you'll think less of him. That's one thing about Dennis, he's a peacock and wants everybody to think of him as something special. He has an ego, believe me."

"But, you see, *he* offered the lie. I never even asked him whether he drank. I couldn't have given a crap whether he drank or what he drank. He told me without my asking. Then you told me the opposite. The lie sends off a siren with me. So then I get to thinking maybe this gentleman has a substance-abuse problem, one that might in some way connect with Warner's drugstore."

She looked at Morrison. "Well, I told you he drank a lot, a lot more than the average drinker and he takes Valium regularly. I don't know whether that qualifies him as an abuser."

"Did he use any other drugs? Snort a little coke now and then, anything like that?"

She did not answer right away, stared into her Perrier, then looked up. "Do I have to answer that?" Before Morrison said yes, she added, "I'm through with Dennis for good. In fact I flat-out dislike him, but I don't want to get him into trouble."

"You won't get him in trouble by answering that question. I'm not looking to bust him for using narcotics. I'm investigating a murder."

"Did you ask him?"

"No."

"Well, maybe you should."

"I probably will. But I also asked you. And I would like an answer."

She sighed. "He'd take a line or two from time to time, at parties. Some of the parties we went to everybody did."

"Did he ever use it at home?"

"Occasionally." Linda Tate seemed to be getting a little nervous.

"Where did he get the stuff?"

"They don't just trade wheat and corn down at the Board of Trade."

"How often, at home?"

"Like I said, occasionally." She now looked like she was getting annoyed.

"You said he was stoned that night. Stoned on what? Do you know?"

"No. He was a case, though. Logy one minute, hyper the next, and abusive."

"Physically?"

"No. He never did anything like hit me, if that's what you mean. If he had I'd have been out of there in a second. That wasn't his way. But he could be verbally abusive, you know, rant and rave, try to make you feel like an asshole. That's one of the reasons I finally left him for good."

"What were the others?"

"That's a little personal, don't you think?" She took a sip of the Perrier. "Oh, hell, Morrison, I guess it doesn't really matter. I just got tired of his ego trips, his ups and downs and believe me, he had them—his ups and downs are a lot higher and a lot lower than yours or mine or most everybody, for that matter. I don't know, maybe he's a manic-depressive or something, or maybe it's all the booze and Valium together." She looked at Morrison as if for some kind of response, but he was just listening. She suddenly seemed a little self-conscious. "And I just got fed up with myself, living like that."

"Living like what?"

"You know what I'm talking about. I was just his mistress. And I finally realized I'd degraded myself. I did it because I was dazzled at first. The trips to Europe, St. Thomas, Cancun, Las Vegas, the fur coats, jewelry." She shook her head. "I grew up in a two-bedroom apartment in a blue-collar neighborhood in Cleveland, then made a decent living in Chicago modeling but living not much more than paycheck to paycheck. Suddenly I'm flying first class, calling room service for anything I want, eating lobster, drinking Dom Perignon, shopping like there's no tomorrow, and all I had to do was be there, be pleasant in public, on-call in private and when the call came be good in bed. Before all that I always had good thoughts about myself. I thought *I* was something special. It took me a year to find out I'd lost the self-respect I'd had before I took up with him. So I left. Now I'm trying to get it back." She looked like she was on the edge of tears.

"You already have. By leaving."

"Well, I don't think that's quite true. But thanks, anyway." She was back in control of herself now. "You're a pretty good detective, getting things out of people . . ."

"Sometimes. Sometimes, Linda, people just want to get it out of themselves . . . has nothing to do with me."

"So what else did he lie about?"

"He said he got home about eight-thirty, I've already told you about that."

She nodded, giving Morrison a little smile. "Well, that's another." She brushed her hair back with a smooth sweep of the hand. "We had reservations for dinner at Spiaggio, across the street, for eight-thirty with another couple, friend of his from the Exchange, Tom Downing and his wife. They called at nine, wondering where the hell we were. I told them I didn't know where *he* was. Tom said something about it must have something to do with the weather, probably got held up in traffic. I said, sure, that's probably it.''

''This Tom Downing . . .''

''I know, you want his telephone number. You can check with him, you'll find out *I'm* telling you the truth.'' Morrison felt bad, but reminded himself it was part of the job. ''But I don't know his number or where he lives. You can find it easy enough though, he's a big deal on the Board of Trade, just check there.''

''Okay. And after that?''

''They called back about nine-thirty. I said he still wasn't home. Tom said they were just going to go on and eat. I said fine, I thought they should do that. At ten I gave up, put on a nightgown to watch the ten o'clock news.''

''And he came home, what, ten-thirty?''

''It was just after the news, ten-thirty, quarter of eleven.''

''Did he even know what time it was?''

''If he didn't when he walked in he did after I told him about Tom calling twice from the restaurant. I went out to the living room and listened to him babble on for a while, then he sort of fell asleep in a chair. I went back to bed. He came in a little later, flying high, talking about going down to the Caribbean to get out of the snow and cold, maybe take the Downings along to make up for that night. He was as excited as a little kid who'd just found out he was going to Disneyland. Then he turned around and went back into the living room. In the morning I found him curled up asleep on one of the couches there.''

The waitress reappeared. ''Give us a minute to look at the menu,'' Morrison said. ''But you can bring me another beer. You want another one of those?'' he asked Linda Tate. She didn't.

Looking at the menu, she said, ''Oh this will help me

get back into modeling: knackwurst, bratwurst, pork shanks, potato pancakes, strudel."

"They have fish. On the other side of the menu."

"I think I'll just have a salad, in case by some slim chance they call me to come down and put on a bikini for the summer special mailer for Spiegel's." Morrison ordered the thüringer with sauerkraut.

Throughout the lunch they talked about a variety of things other than Dennis Courtland. Morrison found out she had gotten married in Cleveland when she was twenty-one to a guy who had been the quarterback of the Case Western Reserve football team. After he graduated he went through five different jobs in two years, plus several girlfriends before she divorced him and moved to Chicago. She had been here five years now and really liked the city. She told him a little more about her present disillusionment. Morrison said not to feel alone, then told her about his upcoming divorce, explained that police had among the highest rates of divorce, alcoholism and suicide, said he definitely qualified for the first, was worried about the second, but thought the third was a little bit of overreaction. She agreed. He told her about his two kids. She told him she had had a miscarriage while still married to the quarterback. He told her how his mother died when he was fifteen, his father ten years later. She told him she had a younger brother who had gotten a few bit parts on television out in Hollywood and was getting by as a waiter at a small restaurant in Beverly Hills.

After lunch Morrison got back to business. "Do you think there's a possibility that if Dennis Courtland was on one of his upper-downer swings he could commit a violent crime? I mean, you've seen him under the influence. Do you think he could lose control?"

She paused before answering and avoided Morrison's eyes for just a moment, then said, "No, I really don't."

She looked him down now. ''You mean like kill that man in the drugstore?''

''That's what I mean.''

''It would come as a major shock if I found out he did. I lived with him for a year. He's capable of a lot of upsetting things, but murder—I can't imagine it. Sorry, but I really can't.''

''Did you know he'd been married?''

''Yes, that was a while ago.''

''Do you know what happened to her?''

Linda seemed uncomfortable with where the conversation had wandered. ''I don't know what this has to do with what we're talking about.'' She dabbed at the corner of her mouth with the napkin, returned it to her lap. The silence hung there for a moment, Morrison waiting. Finally she said, ''She died. He didn't like talking about it.''

''Did he tell you how she died?''

''Yes. Cancer. It was a long drawn-out affair, seven or eight years ago.''

Morrison pushed the empty plate in front of him off to the side and sat back. ''Okay, no more Courtland questions.''

''Good.''

He leaned forward, his elbows on the table, chin resting on his clenched fists, ''Did anyone ever tell you you have beautiful eyes?''

''No, but my dentist said I had the healthiest gums he'd ever seen.'' Her eyes trailed from Morrison to the empty plate and then back to him again. ''So how was the thüringer and kraut?''

''Great, except for the after-effects?''

She looked at him. ''After-effects?''

''Yeah, every time I come here and eat a meal like this, afterwards I get this overpowering urge to invade Poland.''

He asked the waitress for a check. "You'll have to excuse me for a second. I better call in and see if I've got any messages."

There was one, call Terry Sawyer over at Area Six—important.

22

MORRISON DROPPED Linda Tate off at the Northwestern train station and then went back to Eleventh and State to call Sawyer.

"I've had a busy morning," Sawyer said when Morrison got through to him at Area Six Homicide. "Been over in Uptown. Remember the murder-suicide there last Tuesday that your snitch mentioned . . . couple of black queers?"

"Vaguely."

"Well, it seems the guy who got whacked by his lover was a dope dealer. He was in his lover's apartment when the thing went down. The shooter was the janitor of this tenement over on Sunnyside, the Tudor Arms, lived on the ground floor. The dope dealer lived in an apartment one story above. Seems he dealt out of the janitor's apartment too. Anyway, the dicks on this one found a good stash of shit upstairs in the dealer's apartment—the usual double-dime bags of coke, PCP, freebase, Ludes. But there was some other stuff, too.

"Now get this, the other stuff was drugs from a drugstore: morphine, pharmaceutical coke, Valium, codeine, stuff like that. And there were about a dozen bottles of G.I. Gin—labels had the the name Warner's Discount Drugs on them." Morrison was feeling better by the minute. "And this is just the beginning. The dealer was a good-sized guy, flashy as a pimp, judging from the wardrobe in his closet—he was naked, by the way, when they found him, which was not so flashy—and he fit the description we got on the pepper the old lady saw with the salt across the street from Warner's.''

Morrison was making notes on a yellow legal pad as Sawyer told the story.

''Now, the autopsy report on Manford White—he's the dealer who got shot—showed various contusions, like he'd recently been in one helluva fight, the coroner thought. But not with the guy who blew him away. There was nothing to link that asshole with it. In fact his hands were were so smooth and soft he could have done a Revlon commercial if they put a little high-gloss ruby red on the nails. But Joe, it linked with a fight that half of Town Hall responded to . . . the night before.''

''Half the district turns out for a street fight?'' Morrison sounded dismayed.

''It was more than that, Joe. This was a real one. The guy the dealer was fighting was one major street animal. He was a redneck with a ream of sheets on him down in Georgia. They ended up booking him over at Town Hall on battery and resisting arrest, held him twenty-four hours, then let him out on an I-bond. He tried to break the RO's jaw, didn't succeed but sure as hell rearranged some brain cells with one punch.''

''So what does the fight have to do with what we're talking about?''

''Everything, Joe. They were fighting over a girl, a *white* girl, the sergeant at Town Hall told me. The redneck was living with the girl I found out, but she used to hang around with the dealer. I guess he went both ways. They all lived in the same apartment building. I went over there. She and the redneck lived together on the third floor. The apartment is in her name. And now get this, her name is

Jo, Jo Kane, like in the Jo or Joan who was in the drugstore looking for Theo Warner the day of the murder, like the Jo who in the past had frequented Warner's with a flashy black.''

''You grab either one of them?''

''Nobody home. But I got a warrant, was just waiting because I thought you'd like to come along.''

Morrison looked at his watch. It was two o'clock. ''I'll leave right now. Meet you over there. I've got to be back downtown by five. What's the address?'' Sawyer gave it to him. ''Should be there in about twenty minutes.'' Morrison grabbed his coat and headed for the police parking lot next door.

SAWYER WAS sitting in an unmarked police car in front of the Tudor Arms when Morrison pulled up. ''The young lady has a record,'' he said as they started for the building. ''I ordered up the sheet and her mug shot, should have it later this afternoon back at Six. Nothing big, pinched for prostitution once but it didn't stick. Another, petty theft, got her probation. The dealer did time down in Pontiac, three years for armed robbery, another year for burglary at Stateville. The gun his lover used to blow him away, incidentally, was traced to that burglary. It had never been found, until the other night, of course.'' Inside, Sawyer pointed out the janitor's apartment. ''This is where Romeo and Juliet met their maker,'' he said. ''They got a new one living in there already, some guy from Nigeria,'' Sawyer said. ''I talked to him earlier this morning. He doesn't know anything, just started on the job yesterday.''

Sawyer rapped on the door. The Nigerian answered it. Sawyer showed the man the warrant and told him he wanted the man to come along and let them in with a passkey in case no one was in the apartment upstairs.

But someone was. Tommy opened the door, standing there barefoot wearing just a pair of tan washpants and an undershirt. "What the fuck you all want?" he said with his natural sincerity.

Morrison recognized him immediately as the man who had been talking to Vinny on Wilson Avenue the day before. The little son of a bitch, he thought, figuring he now had his Saturday suddenly planned tracking the little snitch down.

The two detectives showed Tommy their identification. Sawyer turned to the janitor and told him he could go now.

"You must be Thomas Alvin Bates, formerly of the state penitentiary at Reidsville, Georgia," Sawyer said by way of introduction.

Tommy gave him an ugly look. "So what?"

"We want to talk to you and your girlfriend," Morrison said.

"And we want to have a look around," Sawyer said, holding up the search warrant.

Morrison put his fingers on Tommy's chest and pushed him backward a step so they could get into the apartment.

"Keep your fuckin' hands off me," Tommy said, glaring at Morrison, who stared back at him.

"Shut up, asshole," Morrison said.

Inside the apartment now, Morrison asked, "Where's your girlfriend?" Tommy did not answer, just continued to stare down Morrison. "You got a little hearing problem?" Still nothing. "I asked you where your girlfriend was. Jo Kane."

No answer. Sawyer said, "Answer the man. Or would you rather we haul your ass over to the station and persuade you to talk to us there?"

Tommy broke into a huge grin. "He told me to shut up. So that's what I'm doin'."

"Oh, you're a riot," Morrison said. "I bet you had them rolling all over the catwalks in the penitentiary." Morrison held him with his eyes. "So where is she?"

Tommy's grin faded. "Don't know."

"When's she coming back?"

"Don't know that either."

"You really want to go to the station, don't you," Morrison said.

"I'm telling you what I know. I don't know where she is. She moved out. I ain't seen her all week. Look around, you don't believe me. You won't find anything of hers."

"We'll look, don't worry."

"So what's all this shit about, anyway?"

"You had a little fight the other night with a gentleman who lives, or should I say lived, downstairs."

"The faggot, yeah."

"What was it over?"

Tommy grinned again. "We didn't like each other."

"We hear it was over a girl, your girlfriend, who also was the former girlfriend of the gentleman you were fighting with."

"What the fuck does it matter to you what we were fightin' over?"

"He's dead now."

"So what? His little honey shot him."

"Did Miss Kane want to take up with him again? He did go both ways, we understand. Is that what the fight was about?"

Tommy's eyes dilated, then wall-eyed. Both detectives could sense the sudden rage. "She'd never take up with that nigger fag. She was mine. Fight had nothin' to do with her. Do I gotta write it out for you, asshole?"

"I'd be amazed if you were capable of that," Morrison said. "Why did she move out?"

"Don't know."

"Bullshit."

"We had a little argument, that's all."

Sawyer suddenly asked, "You ever been in a drugstore over on Belmont and Halsted, Warner's Discount Drugs?"

Tommy looked at him, did not answer right away. "Where's that, Belmont and what?"

"Halsted. About two miles south of here."

"Never heard of the place." Tommy looked from Sawyer to Morrison and back to Sawyer. "What's so special about it?"

"There was a robbery there, week ago last night," Morrison answered for Sawyer. "And the owner was murdered."

"Murdered?" Tommy hesitated, then said, "Too bad. Nasty city. I guess I don't know just what the fuck this has to do with me." There was more caution than anger in Tommy's voice now.

"Well, that's what we're trying to find out."

Tommy shook his head. "Don't know nothin' about it, don't even know where the place is. What makes you think I might know something about it?"

Sawyer spoke up: "The guy you got in the fight with, Manford White, dope dealer downstairs, some of the drugs taken in the robbery were found in his apartment."

Tommy shrugged. "Maybe he and his honey did it when they weren't suckin' each other off."

Morrison pointed to a ratty armchair in the corner of the room that had a tear in the cushion where some yellowish stuffing was poking out. "Sit down over there and keep your mouth shut," he said. "We're going to look around for a while." Tommy didn't move, just stared at Morrison with a mix of hatred and fury in his eyes. Tommy had this thing about authority. "You hear me, get your ass over there," Morrison shouted. Tommy finally started to move toward it, his eyes never leaving Morrison, then sank down in the chair, knowing he had no other choice unless he wanted to go back to Town Hall where the cops the other night had given him more than a little pay-back for cold-cocking one of their brethren. He remembered it as he sat there seething, remembered standing there in the interrogation room, one hand cuffed to the railing along the wall, the cops coming in, taking their shots, one after the other, mentioning their buddy's name as they did it. Nothing he could do, except maybe hate. He focused it now on Morrison, the man who pushed him, the man who told him what to do, the man who did not seem to be afraid of him. Maybe he could change all that, Tommy thought—the right time, the right place, later. It was the only comforting thought he could hold on to at the moment.

Morrison and Sawyer scoured the apartment. Tommy was right, there was nothing that belonged to a woman there. And there was nothing contraband—no drugs, weapons, nothing.

Tommy sat through it all, his surly expression never changing. When they finished and came back into the room where he was sitting, he said, "You done?"

"We're done," Sawyer said.

"Good, then how 'bout gettin' the fuck out of here so I can finish my nap."

"Finish your *nap*?" Morrison said. "Holy Christ, I can't believe this guy."

"There's nothin' in this place. You looked around. So get the fuck out."

"Get up," Morrison said.

Tommy looked at him like he was crazy. "I'm comfortable where I am. Just close the door on your way out."

"Get the fuck up, asshole," Morrison said. "You're going with us back to Six. Couple of people I want to look at you." Then to Sawyer, "You want to read him his rights?"

Tommy did get up, looming over both of them, glowering down at Morrison especially, Morrison thinking, My God, I sure would not want to go one-on-one with this cretin. Sawyer already had his .357 out, with regulation .38 caliber bullets in it—couldn't use the higher caliber ones, only the bad guys could do that, departmental orders—

aimed directly at Tommy's knee. "You want to drag your leg around like it was a log for the rest of your life?" Tommy looked at the gun and understood his options. Sawyer read him his rights.

"Get yourself dressed," Morrison said. "It's a little nippy out there."

Tommy went over to the couch where his boots, socks and shirt were in a heap on the floor. He put them on, then the Eddie Bauer down jacket, after which Morrison stepped around behind him. The nozzle of Sawyer's gun had never wavered from Tommy, and he was staring at it now as Morrison put the cuffs on him. Tommy turned his head, looking over his shoulder, and said in almost a whisper, "This is gonna be evened up." Morrison ignored him.

"I'll follow you back to Six," Morrison said to Sawyer, "but then I've got to get downtown. I've got a meet with Rudy Facia at five."

"The mob Rudy Facia?"

"None other."

"You are not keeping especially good company these days."

"I know, comes with the territory. You can get the little old lady to come over and see if she recognizes this ape. And the bartender from that saloon across from Warner's. The lady can look at the mug shots of the salt and pepper, too, if they've gotten there. Keep Mr. Congeniality overnight at Six, I'll bring Bruce Warner by in the morning to take a look at him." Then to Tommy: "You'll like it there, a clean, dimly lit cell. Maybe you can continue your nap."

"I don't forget," Tommy said.

23

MORRISON TOOK the elevator to the sixteenth floor, stepped out of it and could not miss the office he was looking for; dead ahead was a pair of paneled mahogany doors, next to which was a brass-framed plaque, the shiny brass letters against a black marble background announcing:

1600
Kendall, Roth & Dungen
Attorneys at Law

He was ten minutes early but opened the door and went in anyway. It was a handsome reception area, richly furnished, everything in expensive wood and leather—two huge black tufted couches, one on each side of the reception room. Embracing each were French armchairs with rounded backs, seats and little armrests in burgundy-red leather perfectly positioned at each end of cherrywood coffee tables. On the two coffee tables at each side of the room magazines were neatly fanned out, and there were endtables with ornate brass lamps, a lot of fresh flowers in Chinese vases, oversized ashtrays without a trace of ash in them. In one corner, Morrison noticed, a four-foot porcelain vase with Chinese art all over it was sitting on one of those black ebony tables that had the same moldings as the facades of buildings in Chinatown. It reminded Morrison of one he had seen once in the Asian collection of the Art Institute, when he used to go there, take the girls; he had not done that in a long time . . . Many, many bucks, Morrison thought, as he took it in. In the middle of it all sat an attractive woman, maybe forty-five, maybe fifty, neatly coiffed black-and-gray hair, a creamy silk blouse and pearls draped around her neck, looking at him over a pair of reading glasses from behind an enormous cherrywood desk. She had some papers in a neat pile in front of her, a multi-buttoned telephone to her left, a typewriter-stand extension of the desk to her right supporting a massive IBM Selectric. A large seascape oil painting in an elaborate frame hung on the wall behind her. "Can I help you?" she asked pleasantly.

"I've got an appointment to see Mr. Dungen and his client. Joe Morrison's the name."

"And your company?"

"The Chicago Police Department."

She picked up the telephone and relayed the message, then said, "Mr. Dungen's secretary will be with you in a minute."

Morrison walked over and sat in one of the burgundy leather chairs next to the magazines—*Forbes, Business-Week, U.S. News and World Report, Fortune, Chicago Law Review;* no *People,* no *Readers Digest,* no *Sports Illustrated.* Morrison thought it would be fun someday to slip a copy of *Hustler* in there between *Fortune* and the *Chicago Law Review.*

After ten minutes went by the secretary emerged from a door just behind and to the side of the receptionist, who now had her purse on the desk and was getting ready to leave for the day. The secretary spoke in a nasal monotone. "I'm sorry, Mr. Dungen's been tied up with some important business. He said he was sorry, it would be another ten minutes. Could I get you some coffee, a soft drink?'' Morrison suddenly saw Lily Tomlin, sitting at the switchboard on ''Laugh-In.''

''No thanks.''

She disappeared back behind the door. Morrison hated waiting. Lawyers always made you wait. Unless they wanted something from *you*. He started thinking of the lawyer jokes that were always floating around 11th and State. The one he liked best: How can you tell the difference between a dead snake and a dead lawyer in the road? The skidmarks in front of the snake.

It was more like twenty minutes before the secretary reappeared to tell Morrison in that Lily Tomlin tone he could now follow her down the corridor.

Tom Dungen's office was enormous and somber. Walls paneled in burled walnut, English hunting prints on one wall, a pair of eighteenth-century portraits on the wall behind the desk, the other wall a built-in bookcase filled with law books. A large Persian rug was on the floor. Besides the stately mahogany desk, there was a sitting area, leather chairs and a couch surrounding a square glass-topped coffee table with a Steuben glass figurine in the center of it.

Dungen, a good-looking man with prematurely gray hair and wearing a navy blue suit with a blue tie with tiny white polka dots and a matching foulard fountaining out of his breast pocket, was standing next to the desk when the secretary led Morrison in. He put down what he was reading and stuck out his hand in Morrison's direction. ''Detective Morrison,'' he said. ''Sergeant, isn't it?''

Morrison shook the outstretched hand. ''That's right.'' He took the room in, there was something missing. No Rudy Facia.

''Sorry you had to wait but I was in the middle of something that just couldn't be interrupted. I hope you can understand.''

''Where's Facia?''

"He's still in the conference room." Dungen pushed a button on the desk console. "Denise, would you tell Rudy that Sergeant Morrison is in my office. And that will be all for today."

A minute later Rudy Facia walked into the office, dressed as expensively as his attorney but from a different league, one as far from the Ivy as Chicago was from the Vatican: light gray silk suit that sort of shimmered in the light, matching gray shoes, gray silk socks, a white-on-white shirt with a white tie that appeared only as an outline against the shirt, all in contrast to his black hair and bushy black eyebrows. He did not extend a hand, just looked at Morrison, then went over and sat in a corner of the couch. Morrison and the attorney joined him around the coffee table.

"So Tony DiFranzo owed you one," Facia said to Morrison when they sat down.

"More than one."

"That's good, I like that. Tony's a good man."

"I didn't come here and wait a half hour to talk about Tony."

"So what is it you do want to talk about?"

"You don't know?"

"I think I know. And if it's what I think, it's something I don't want to talk about." Facia looked over at Tom Dungen, nodded, then back to Morrison.

"Look, your daughter was sexually assaulted. You know it. We know it. So let's quit the bullshit."

Facia's eyes came alive, like someone threw a switch and the kliegs burst into light. "My daughter was not assaulted." He turned to Dungen. "Tom, you see any charges go down on something like that?"

Dungen looked over at Morrison, "Sergeant, no charges have been filed. Nor is there any reason for any to be filed. The girl, according to her father, took a tumble down some stairs, banged herself up, then hallucinated. That's all.

When she got over the shock of it she realized she had been hallucinating and admitted it to her father. No crime was committed against her."

"I understand, and Al Capone was just a good beer salesman."

"You heard the man, no crime was committed," Facia said.

"As you can understand, my client, Mr. Facia, for the sake of his daughter would not want *anything* made public that would falsely lead people to believe that his daughter in any way had been violated."

"Here's what I understand," Morrison said. "Word is all over the street your client, Mr. Facia, wants the two guys who did it more than the Israelis wanted Adolf Eichmann. Word has also filtered down that we should back-burner this, and that no word of it should leak to the press under pain of spending the rest of one's law enforcement career cleaning up the dog shit in the Canine Patrol kennels." Turning to Facia, "All this I can understand. I've got two daughters myself. The guys probably deserve to be caught by you and your buddies. But you've also got to understand where we're coming from. We want them off the street before they do something like that to somebody else. We are not going to sit around and wait to see if the Outfit finds them." He stopped for just a second, shook his head. "If you do, you do. We're saved a lot of paperwork and the taxpayers won't have to foot the bill for their room and board for, say, ten, fifteen years. But we're not going to stop looking for them."

The kliegs in Facia's eyes had faded. "My lawyer has explained my position—"

"My client agreed to this meeting," Dungen interrupted, "with the hope of clearing the air on this matter, of bringing you and your partner to the understanding that there is no need for the police to investigate this alleged assault. After all, you and your partner are the only two actively investigating it. You are aware of that, aren't you?"

"Area Four Violent Crimes is also investigating it."

"I said *actively* investigating it."

Morrison nodded his head in understanding.

"I checked you out with some friends of mine," Facia said to Morrison. "Heard you were street-wise. Good Homicide dick."

"*Was* Homicide. As you know, I now work Organized Crime."

Facia gave him a look of distaste at the words. "With that lardass you were with the other day, Castor? I've always hated that asshole."

"The feeling's mutual, I assure you."

Caring less, Facia continued, "What I guess I don't understand is why, whatever this thing is with my daughter, you two would be involved in the investigation in the first place."

"Because it was *your* daughter. And you are reputed to be a ranking official in that organization known as Organized Crime."

"There has never been evidence of any sort to link my client to Organized Crime," Dungen said with a straight face.

"Get off it, Dungen, we've got a file this thick on Rudy Facia," Morrison said, holding his thumb and index finger about two inches apart. "And the reason we got the case along with Violent Crimes is that there just might be some link involving Organized Crime. Maybe somebody in the organization wants to send Mr. Facia a message. Or maybe get even. Either a possibility, Mr. Facia?"

Facia looked at Tom Dungen. Dungen said, "You're making an assumption with no valid basis, sergeant."

"That's right," Facia put in, then sat back. "But let me put something to you, Morrison. Suppose, just suppose, that you and tubass find something that would lead us to discover that my daughter's hallucination was not, say, a hallucination. Know what I mean?''

''Do I look stupid to you?''

''No, I'm just bringing up a suppose. You know in this world all kind of strange things happen.'' He gave Morrison a look as if he had just imparted some new deep philosophical truth. ''Tony DiFranzo owed you a couple, you probably owe somebody else a couple. I figure you know the game.'' He paused, waiting for something from Morrison but just got a stare. ''So say my daughter did get roughed up a little, and you got word of who the guys were . . .'' He let it trail off, left it to hang in Morrison's mind. Tom Dungen appeared edgy but did not say anything.

''Is it possible we've quit playing games?'' Morrison said, looking from Facia to Dungen.

''My client is talking about a supposition,'' Dungen said. ''Nothing more.'' Then speaking directly to Facia, ''Which I don't think is really going anywhere, Rudy.''

Facia ignored him. ''I make you to be about mid-, late thirties, Morrison. Am I right?''

''Mid-.''

''You said you got a couple a kids, so they must be still kinda young, got college ahead of them and all. You know how expensive college is these days?''

''Very. I also know they won't ever go to college on money I get from you for tipping you off about who assaulted your daughter.''

''I'm sure that is not what Rudy had in mind,'' Dungen said.

Both Facia and Morrison ignored him this time. ''So maybe you don't like money, to each his own,'' Facia said. ''You are in the favor business, I know, call 'em in from time to time. And favors come in all sizes, small to extra-extra large . . .'' Again he let it trail off, waiting for a response, and again did not get one unless you counted Tom

Dungen's visible discomfort. "So let me give you a small one. Back to my suppose. Suppose two dumb fucks did bother her. It wasn't no message, no vendetta. I can tell you that."

Morrison nodded.

"Now I could owe you an extra-large one," Facia said.

"You could, but you won't. We find the two guys, we grab 'em and they go through the system. They end up in Stateville or Pontiac."

"You think they'd be safe there?"

Morrison paused. "Probably not."

Facia got up, indicating the meeting was about to be over. "Do me a small favor, think about my suppose."

Morrison got up too. "I already did. And I already forgot about it." Morrison took a step toward the door, which Tom Dungen was opening for him, then turned back to Facia. "I haven't got any sympathy for those guys. I can guess what will happen to them if you find them before we do, and I don't really give a shit, but if any innocent person gets hurt in this, my partner and I are coming after you. *Capisce?*"

"Sure, sure," Facia said.

"I'll show you to the elevator," Dungen said as Morrison walked toward the door.

"Don't bother."

Facia stepped into the doorway, looking at the back of Morrison in the outer office on his way out, "You got any leads so far, sarge?"

Morrison, the trace of a smile on his face, turned back to Facia. "A couple."

"You do?"

"We do."

"You close?"

"I'd say so, pretty damn close, as a matter of fact."

Morrison felt good riding down in the elevator, even if he had lied a little.

ON HIS way home Morrison stopped at Flannery's for a drink and called Norbert Castor as he had promised he would. Norbert was watching *Brute Force* when the phone rang, enraptured with Burt Lancaster moving with that trapeze-artist grace and pent-up violence as he walked across a prison yard, just released from solitary confinement, thinking now of nothing but prison break. Lancaster *was Brute Force*, Norbert thought, his eyes still to the screen as he edged across the room to pick up the ringing telephone. He would not have answered it except he knew it had to be Morrison.

"He does not like you, Norb," Morrison said.

"I do not like him either."

"I told him that."

"You call just to tell me my social relations aren't all that strong?"

"The only thing he gave me was, it was not family."

"Well, that stiffs one theory."

"Needless to say, he wants us to give him the dirty duo. I told him we wouldn't. I also told him we were going down to the wire with this one. But Norbert, we have to do this with velvet gloves. He already has seen to it that Violent Crimes redirect their attentions to crimes elsewhere. We are probably going to get some shit on this the next day or two."

"So what else?"

"Nothing. He doesn't seem to have a tit to touch. He's groping. We just have to Harpo Marx this."

"Understood. That's it?"

"That's it, partner."

"Okay, I gotta get back to my movie. Helluva show, *Brute Force*, right now they're shooting blowtorches at some guy's face in the prison workshop. Those guys in prison have all the fun. Lancaster's something else in this one."

"Before you go back, I'm going over to Uptown tomorrow, which I know is our day off. I want to run down Vinny the snitch. I could use a little help. I think we could write it off, overtime or time off."

There was silence at the other end, then acquiescence. "You gonna get the car?"

"I'll get the car. Pick you up at your house, say eight-thirty?"

"Jesus, Joe, eight-thirty?"

"It won't hurt you, pal."

"I gotta go, Joe. Flashback, Lancaster's with Ann Blyth. She's in a wheelchair. Being a nice guy. What's he doing in prison anyway?"

AFTER HE hung up Morrison slipped another quarter into the pay phone and dialed Terry Sawyer's home number. Found out there was good news and bad news.

Sawyer told him that the little lady, Mrs. Otis, looked at the mugs and said definitely that Jo Kane was the girl she had seen in the drugstore with a colored man before and was the girl in the car across the street the night of the murder. And Manford White was indeed the man she had seen Jo Kane with in the drugstore on several occasions, and he was the man in the backseat of the car that night. The bad news: she could not pick Tommy out of the lineup.

Sawyer told him he had an APB out on Jo Kane and her picture would be on the front page of the *Daily Bulletin* in every district stationhouse in the city the next morning.

The bartender had not been able to recognize either Jo Kane or Manford White from their mug shots, reminding Sawyer that it had been a busy night. He was not sure but he thought he recognized one of the men in the lineup, was not positive, he cautioned, but thought that the third man from the left might have been in his place that night. The third man from the left was Detective Joe Patkowski from Area Six Burglary.

Morrison went back to the bar, got another Old Style Light, then called Bruce Warner, who said he would be most happy to go over to Area Six in the morning with Morrison and look at pictures and live street animals.

24

VINNY WAS on the street early Saturday morning—nine o'clock was early for him, unless, of course, he was just getting home, which was not uncommon. He was looking for someone who might know where Jo was, knowing now he had to get to her before Tommy did, had to warn her about the cops nosing around Uptown, too, about a drugstore burglary and murder. Vinny saw it as his chance. He could help her with the two thousand dollars he got fencing all the trinkets good old Stanley Sanderson had bestowed on his wife and the fancy silver and all the other stuff. Maybe it was just what he needed to get them out of Uptown for good, together.

Vinny had spent most of Friday afternoon and some of the evening bar-hopping through Uptown looking for someone who might have any idea where she had gone. Nobody did.

He learned two things, though. Jo had an aunt she saw pretty regularly, but no one knew where the aunt lived. And he heard that Tommy and Manford White had been in one helluva fight over her the night before White took a .357 round in the chest. Given Tommy's nature, Vinny wondered now whether White and Head really had a quarrel with such fatal consequences. Thought of Tommy after he heard about the brawl and was truly scared for Jo, maybe for himself too.

Vinny had gone home early Friday night, early being about one in the morning for him. More often than not Jo was a morning drinker, hit the bars around nine, nine-thirty and had a few with the janitors and day laborers who did not get hired on for the day and other assorted lowballs. Maybe one of them knew where she went. They were a separate crowd in Uptown, but a lot of them knew Jo. Helped her occasionally to pick up a little bread of her own from the janitors who made pretty good money and were sometimes horny in the morning—right there in the can, couple of minutes, take the twenty bucks, go back to the bar and gargle a vodka and soda for mouthwash—but Vinny did not like thinking about that.

MORRISON AND Castor picked up Bruce Warner at his drugstore about the same time Vinny walked into Carmen's and ordered a shot of VO with a Bud chaser, VO because he had a bunch of fresh dollars this morning; go for the best, he said to himself, what the hell. Breakfast of champions, he called it.

Morrison explained to Bruce, sitting in the backseat of the unmarked police car, just where they were at. "We found some of the drugs from your store in the apartment of a black man in Uptown. We can place him and a girl named Jo Kane in a bar across the street from you on the night of the murder. There was another man, too, a white man we believe to be one Thomas Alvin Bates."

Bruce was excited at the news. "Have you arrested them?"

Morrison looked into the rearview mirror, saw the anticipation on Bruce's face. "The black man's dead, got himself shot the other night. The girl's disappeared. Bates is over at Area Six, where we're going now. You can take a look at him in a lineup, see if he might have been in your store that day or any time before that. And I want you to look at some mugs, see if you can find the girl who was in there looking for Theo earlier that day. I've got more than a hunch that it was Jo Kane.''

They took Bruce upstairs at Area Six, through the sprawling squad room that served the entire Violent Crimes division with its islands of desks, each with its own manual portable typewriter for all the two-finger typists in the department. Homicide was a smaller room just off it at the far end. In the room there were four desks, one of which was occupied by the shift sergeant, Andy Hardy, whose real name was Tom, but he had been known as Andy from almost the first day he moved to Area Six eight years earlier, because he had a round boyish face that he probably did not have to shave more than a couple of times a week and he looked a lot like Mickey Rooney.

''Detective Morrison, what a pleasure,'' Hardy said, looking up from a case sheet as Morrison and Castor walked in with Bruce behind them. There was another detective in the room whom Morrison did not recognize. ''It's been what—more than a year?''

''Just about.'' They shook hands.

''Heard you couldn't stay away from Homicide. Sawyer tells me you come back to it like flies to you know what.''

''Personal. That's the only reason.''

''I heard that, too. Welcome back anyway.''

''You know Norb Castor, OC, State Street?''

''We met a couple times,'' Hardy said.

''Not in a long time,'' Norbert said. ''Used to see you in the Pineyard,'' which was a cop bar just down Clark Street from the Rogers Park stationhouse.

''They used to see me in a lot of those joints.''

''Not anymore?'' Castor asked.

''Not since I saw the light.'' He introduced Morrison and Castor to the other detective.

''This is Bruce Warner, Theo Warner's brother.'' Bruce

turned from the bulletin board with its composite sketches and fact sheets of those souls the police wanted badly, the list of currently popular smash-and-grab intersections, announcements of retirement parties, new regulations, stuff like that. Bruce nodded to the sergeant. "Want him to look at some mugs. Sawyer said he left them with the Warner file."

"Yeah, he left it out for you," Hardy said, pointing to a wire basket with two fat manila folders in it on one of the empty desks.

"I'd like him to look at a lineup with Bates in it too, Thomas Alvin Bates. You arrange one on such short notice?"

"Hey, Joe, for you, anything. After all, you're an esteemed alumni."

"Alumnus."

"Whatever." Hardy sat back down behind his desk. "By the way, we can't keep that asshole too much longer. We got nothin'."

"Not yet."

Hardy lifted the telephone to request a lineup. They would do it downstairs.

"Why don't you sit down over there," Morrison said to Bruce, indicating the desk with the wire basket, then walked over to Hardy's desk, picked up a copy of the *Daily Bulletin* and saw Jo Kane staring back at him, and in profile staring at herself in the picture next to it. He thought she was typical of the breed, a hardness, a bitterness in the face that always seemed to come out in mug shots, but then it came as no surprise considering the kind of boyfriends she chose and the neighborhood she inhabited. Above the photos:

Wanted for Questioning, Homicide
Warrant on File

He read the description beneath the frontal and side portraits of Ms. Jo Kane:

Female, Caucasian
Complexion: Light
Age: 23
Height: 5 feet 5 inches
Weight: Approximately 130 pounds
Hair: Brown
Eyes: Brown
No visible scars, birthmarks or tattoos
Former charges: Prostitution, Petty theft,
    Possession of a controlled substance (marijuana).
Known to frequent taverns and other establishments in the
    Uptown area
Last known address: 908 West Sunnyside

There was also a description of the crime in which she was wanted for questioning. Morrison did not bother to read that. He put the *Daily Bulletin* back, grabbed a folding chair, unfolded it and sat at the side of the desk next to Bruce Warner. He took the files from the wire basket, opened the one with the mug shots containing twelve of "Caucasian females," twelve of "Negroid males."

He handed the stack of females to Bruce Warner. "Take a look at these. See if you can find the girl in the store that day."

Andy Hardy was explaining to Castor the merits of Alcoholics Anonymous, pointing out that certain of the AA meetings were as loaded with cops as the old change-of-shift parties. Norbert listened, nodded occasionally—as unreformed as he was, he did not much like reformed drinkers.

Bruce Warner was taking his time, studying each. At the seventh one he looked over at Morrison, "This is *her*."

There was no doubt in his voice. "The same one who used to come in with the colored fellow."

"You're sure?"

"Absolutely, Joseph."

"Sergeant," Morrison said to Hardy, handing him a form sheet, "you want to verify for me that witness Bruce Warner identified this woman—four-five-eight-seven-nine (the number at the bottom of the photo)—as being in his drugstore the day of the murder of Theo Warner, having asked for Theo Warner specifically, and having been in there on various occasions preceding it. Number four-five-eight-seven-nine being one Jo Kane, sheet on record, and warrant out for her questioning in regard to the burglary of Warner's Discount Drugs and the murder of Theo Warner."

The telephone rang and Hardy picked it up, then looked over at Morrison. "They say they can come up with four, the lineup." He looked at Morrison skeptically. "That enough, you think?"

"Hell, no. You mean in all of Area Six headquarters you can only scare up three guys besides Bates to stand?"

"Easy, Joe," Hardy said, his hand cupped over the mouthpiece of the telephone. "It's Saturday morning, quiet time around here, and last night I hear was a quiet time in the zoo out there, all the animals behaving themselves, so we're a little short in the cages this morning."

Castor said, "Let me go down there, see what I can do. I'm not doing anything up here."

Hardy nodded, said into the telephone, "Detective Castor from Eleventh and State's coming down there, wants to see if he can help. Four's not enough, this is a homicide, you know. Give Detective Castor all the cooperation you can." He paused, then added, "Before he goes back down to Eleventh and State."

"I bet we'll come up with a couple more," Hardy said to Morrison. "Maybe a whole chorus line."

Morrison turned back to Bruce Warner. "Let's see if you can make it two in a row. The black man who accompanied Ms. Jo Kane to your store on previous occasions, tell me if he is one of these," and handed the other stack of mug shots to Bruce.

It appeared this time that Bruce Warner was struggling. He went through all twelve photos, looked over at Morrison. "Coloreds are harder to recognize, Joseph," he said.

"He's not in there?"

"I didn't say that." Bruce brought his hand up to his cheek. "I'm just not as sure as I was with the girl. A lot of these look not too much different from each other. You know what I mean, Joseph?"

"Maybe you should look through them again."

"There is one. One I would pick." He brought his hand back from his cheek to the pile of photos. "But let me look again." He went through them as slowly as the first time. When he finished he let out a sigh, looked at Morrison and said without conviction, "I think it's this last one," and handed the photograph to Morrison.

Morrison looked at it, then checked the key sheet just to be sure: 86213, Manford White. "Bingo," he said, both to Bruce and Andy Hardy. "Strike two. One more and we're out of this inning."

The phone rang again. Hardy grabbed it, listened, then said to Morrison, "It's your buddy Castor. How's eight?"

"Perfect." He motioned to Bruce Warner. "Come on, Bruce, you got a strike-out going. Let's see if we can get it."

Morrison handed the mug shot and the key sheet to Hardy.

"Who does all your paperwork downtown?" Hardy asked.

"I have a secretary, looks exactly like Raquel Welch but younger, nicer tits, too." Then, over his shoulder as he was ushering Bruce Warner out of Homicide, "Good seeing you again Andy. Drop by you ever get downtown, third floor. Just look for the beautiful secretary. Of course she's no Judy Garland, Andy, but you might like her anyway.'' And they were gone.

''I DREDGED up the last two from Narcotics, just going off-duty,'' Norbert said to Morrison. ''You can tell which, they're the two seediest-looking.''

The eight men entered the room in single file and ambled along a pale green wall, squinting under the brightness of the floodlights, and turned when a voice from the darkness said, ''All right, face out this way and don't move around.''

''Just like on television,'' Bruce said to Morrison.

''Sure, where did you think they got their material? Now, Bruce, I want you to look at these men carefully and see if you recognize any of them as having been in your store.''

Bruce, standing in the darkness between Morrison and Castor, slowly ran his eyes up and down the line of men, all of whom looked either bored or put upon. Finally he looked to Morrison, ''One of them you think was with the two who murdered Theo?''

''We don't know whether any of them committed the robbery and murder,'' Morrison said. ''They're just a lead at this point. Any of them look familiar?''

Bruce went back to scrutinizing the eight men. ''I can't be sure, but maybe that one in the middle.'' He pointed at a scraggly, unshaven man wearing a grimy flannel shirt and jeans.

''The one fourth from the right, that the one?''

''That's the one, but I'm not positive, Joseph. Just seems I've seen him before.'' Bruce was looking up at Morrison with an expression like he was waiting to see if he had won the lottery.

''Anybody else?''

"No."

"Okay," Morrison said to the uniformed cop who had brought the men out. "That's all." The cop led the men in the lineup back out of the room and, when they were all out, flicked a switch at the door that turned the regular lights on, then another that doused the floods.

Norbert took Morrison by the arm and led him out of earshot of Bruce Warner. "Undercover Narcotics, name's Filchock, first name's Dan, I think. I told you they were the seediest-looking."

Morrison shook his head. "Goddamn Bates is going to be out of here before you and me."

Norbert held his hands palms up. "Win some, lose some." He clapped Morrison on the back. "We get the girl we got a good chance of gettin' him. If they did it, that is."

"If we get the girl," Morrison repeated.

Bruce Warner came over to them. "Well, was he the one, Joseph?"

"No strike-out today, Bruce. But you did good, two strikes, we're still ahead of the batter."

Bruce Warner, confusion now in his eyes, was about to say something when Morrison's beeper went off.

"Hang on, Bruce. We'll take you back to your store in a minute. I have to call downtown first."

"SOME BROAD called," said Detective Faverly at OC when Morrison phoned in. "Said she wanted to talk to you, asked for your home phone. Told her we don't give those out. Asked if I'd call you. Did. Your wife said she didn't know where the hell you were. So I thought you might be working, dedicated public servant I know you to be, and gave you a beep."

"I take it the lady left a name and number and you being an astute detective and all wrote it down."

"You betcha. Even printed it, seeing as how I have

trouble reading my own handwriting . . . in the morning anyway. It's Linda Tate.'' He gave Morrison the telephone number. ''Said if you couldn't call before eleven to try after two, she was going out.''

Morrison looked at his watch, 11:15. ''Thanks,'' he said. ''Anything else?''

''Not a thing.''

''Anything for Castor? He's with me.''

''Nope.'' There was a pause. ''My God, how'd you get him out on a Saturday?''

''Good influence. Rubs off.''

''LET'S HEAD over to Uptown, Norb. See if we can find that little snitch. I think he knows more than he's telling me.''

''What about lunch? You got me on overtime. Am I supposed to fast too?''

''I'll buy you a Whopper. There's a Burger King on the way with a drive-thru.''

''You always go fancy on the weekends, huh?''

In the car driving to Uptown Morrison said, ''You're right about finding the girl. If this merry trio did in fact do in Theo, she's our only hope. See if we can turn her. She left the animal for some reason. Maybe she's afraid of him. Maybe she hates his guts now. Get the State's Attorney to offer her a deal if she gives us Bates.''

''On the other hand,'' Castor said, ''maybe they didn't do it. Maybe they were just in the neighborhood, had a drink with the black guy, went on their way and he did it alone. Or maybe he bought or stole the stuff he had in his apartment from the person who did it. We don't really have a whole helluva lot.''

''That's true. But it's our best lead so far.''

''What about the Courtland character? I thought you were interested in him.''

"I still am. He's covering up something, I just don't know what."

"But Joe, would you make this megabucks commodities guy to be someone who'd crack around a little old druggist, tie him up and dump him into a barrel of water to drown?"

"Would you make John Wayne Gacy in his clown costume to be a serial killer? There are a lot of maybes, I admit."

"You got an address on the snitch we're going to see?"

"Last known is on Broadway, Forty-six-forty-three, that's between Lawrence and Wilson. I ran a check on him after Sawyer and I drove him around the other day just in case he doesn't call like I told him to do. But who knows if he still lives there? He did when they dragged him in for boosting nine months ago. But those guys don't stay in the same place too long—you know, moving target's tougher to hit. But we can start there. Doesn't have a telephone. Had one but it was disconnected about a year ago. Didn't pay his bill. If he isn't there we're just going to have to look around, maybe ask around, tell whoever we're from Burglary. It wouldn't surprise the misfits over there to think a couple of Burglary cops were looking for Vinny Salerno."

They passed the Burger King on Ashland Avenue. "Aren't you forgetting something?" Castor asked.

"Oh, yeah, food."

"We just passed it."

Morrison slowed down and cut a sharp U-turn, causing a CTA bus to pitch its twenty or so passengers just short of whiplash as the driver slammed on his brakes to avoid broadsiding Morrison's car. "I'm a man of my word, Norb."

They lucked out after lunch, finding that Vinny not only still lived at the address but had just gotten home.

"Jesus, Morrison, don't you ever take any time off?"

Vinny said as he opened the door a slice. "I don't see you in maybe two years and all of a sudden we're going steady."

"I'm not in the mood for any smart-mouth crap. We want to talk to you."

"So talk."

"How about inside."

"You got a warrant?"

"Vinny, you want I should grab you by that scuzzy shirt, pull you out of there, drag you down the stairs and drive you over to Area Six?"

"C'mon, Morrison, I'm just kidding." He opened the door wider. "Your buddy can come in too. We'll have a party."

The two detectives stepped inside, looked around.

One room, a kitchenette with just a half-stove, refrigerator, sink and three small cabinets, and the world's smallest bathroom, Morrison judged, taking it in because the door to it was wide open. In the one room there was an opened sofa-bed with a crumpled army blanket on it in the corner, an old stuffed chair on the other side of the room that the Salvation Army would not bother to take, a card table and two folding chairs. On the housing spectrum, Morrison thought, Vinny Salerno was at the exact opposite end from Dennis Courtland. On the card table was about a quarter of a greasy hamburger, the waxed paper wrapping underneath it saturated—it was what was known around the city as a slider, one of those so lubricated with fat it could just slide down your throat—and some fries with grease that had already congealed sitting next to the balled-up brown paper bag in which Vinny had toted the meal home from the diner over on Wilson. There was also a can of Old Milwaukee on the table.

"Nice place you got here, Vinny," Morrison said.

"Yeah, well, if I knew you were coming I'd a spiffed it up some. I was just getting ready to take a nap."

Morrison looked at Norbert. "Jesus, everybody in this neighborhood takes afternoon naps." Castor gazed back, his look one of uncomprehension. Morrison explained, "Sawyer and I disturbed another nap over in this neighborhood yesterday. Tommy Bates is a napper, too."

"You guys want a beer?"

"This isn't what you would call a social visit," Morrison said.

"Sure," Norbert said.

"Why not?" Morrison said. "We're not here to bust you, although I'm sure we could probably find cause on fifty or so counts if we had to."

"Me?" Vinny said. "One of our town's upstanding citizens whose taxes pay your salary? You got to be kidding." He got two more Old Milwaukees from the refrigerator.

"Vinny, that guy you were talking to Thursday, the guy hassling you a little on the street—" Morrison started after he popped the beer can open.

"Yeah, Tommy. I can't say we're big buddies. He ain't big buddies with anybody, and I mean anybody."

"I can understand why." Morrison sat down on one of the folding chairs. "Especially with a black man named Manford White, who he got in a fight with the night before this Manford White got himself shot by his boyfriend."

"Yeah, I heard about the fight. Supposed to have been some battle."

"You know this Manford White, too?"

"Knew him. Never liked him either."

"You know he dealt dope?"

Vinny looked at Morrison. "Heard something about it."

"I'm sure. What exactly did you know about him?"

"Like I said, I heard he was into dealing. Tough guy. I didn't know he went both ways until after he got blown off." Vinny smiled at Morrison. "A little double-meaning there. Pretty good, huh?"

Morrison crossed his legs, leaned back in the chair. Castor was leaning against the wall, enjoying the tingle of the Old Milwaukee as it sprinkled down onto the two Whoppers digesting in his stomach. "Vinny," Morrison said, "you know this Tommy Bates . . . you know this Manford White. Right?" Vinny nodded slowly, waiting. "Then you probably know their girlfriend, name of Jo Kane."

Vinny summoned a look of innocent ignorance. *Fake*, Morrison picked up immediately, and knew now just where he was going before Vinny said, "Uh-uh. Girlfriend?"

"That's who the fight was over. That's who was living with this Bates creature. The girl used to pal around with White before that, been a denizen around here for some time." Morrison watched him closely. "Vinny, I don't think you've been honest with me since we started talking a couple of days back. And I don't like that. I don't know why, but I'm beginning to put bits and pieces together."

"What do you mean? I didn't give you any bullshit. I didn't give you *anything*, in fact."

Morrison sat upright, leaning across the table now. "We talk now, straight, okay, or you are going to get yourself into a big mess of trouble. The girl."

Vinny hesitated. "Yeah, I know her. But she ain't around here anymore. Just disappeared about a week ago." Vinny was clearly nervous now.

"How come, Vinny, when I asked you the other day if you knew a salt and pepper, white girl named Jo or Joan, you said you didn't?"

"Didn't come to mind, salt and pepper. That was a while back when they were together." Vinny felt some inner panic like he sometimes did coming down from a real high.

"Not convincing. You trying to protect her for some reason?"

"Hey, no. What would I do that for?" Vinny took a

gulp of his beer, then looked back at Morrison. "What're you interested in her for anyway?"

"We have reason to believe the three of them might be involved in a robbery and murder."

"That drugstore thing?" he asked, at the same time thinking, Holy Christ, what has Jo gotten herself into with those two? If she was with them when they did the druggist, she would do some very hard time in the joint for ladies down in Dixon. God, he had to find her. "I can't see her being messed up in something like that. That Tommy, sure as hell could. White maybe. But not Jo Kane." Nervous pause. "You pull Tommy in yet?"

"We talked to him."

"You still got him?"

"Why do you care?"

Vinny shrugged. "Nothin', the street's a little cleaner, safer, that ape's off it. That's all."

"Back to his girlfriend," Morrison said. "You have any idea where she might be now?"

"No. Why would I? I just saw her around the neighborhood now and then." Vinny's mind was whirling. They were probably looking for her all over the city. They'd probably find her. Tommy'd find her. Jeez, poor Jo.

"If I find out you're lying to me about this, Vinny, you could go down along with them, witholding information. We're talking a homicide here. And I'd see to it you went . . . personally."

Vinny looked over at Castor, then back to Morrison, holding him with his eyes. "I'm telling you guys, *I* don't know where she is." Vinny took another swallow of his beer, draining it. His helter-skelter thoughts suddenly focused. Looking down at the empty beer can on the table, he said, "I did hear a rumor. Now I got nothing but rumor on this, which is why I say *I* don't *know* where she is, but I heard she might have been done. Her boyfriend, that guy Tommy. Pissed because she was through with him, thought she was gonna take back up with White. Word floating around he killed her and tossed her body in a dumpster in the alley behind those stores on Wilson Avenue.''

''When?''

''I don't know, sometime after the fight. I just heard about it yesterday. Hell, I didn't even hear about the fight till yesterday.''

''Why didn't you call me, Vinny?''

''Morrison, I said it's just a rumor and I didn't put it with what you were looking for. I didn't see no connection. I hear a lot of things on the street.''

''Keep listening, Vinny.''

OUTSIDE, MORRISON said to Norbert, ''Let's get some help from Town Hall and go through the dumpsters in the alleys on both sides of Wilson Avenue.''

''Hey, what a way to spend my day off.''

25

After dropping Castor off at his apartment in Rogers Park, Morrison stopped in a drugstore to call Linda Tate. It was nearly four o'clock.

"Sorry to have bothered you at home," she said.

"I'm not at home. In a drugstore. We worked today."

"Well, Morrison, I just wanted to thank you for the lunch yesterday, and for your ear. I felt a lot better getting it all out of my system."

"Say, Tate, you've got a pretty good ear yourself. Maybe you should consider becoming a detective instead of letting every farmer in Iowa see you in your underwear."

"There you go again, that fixation. And what's with this Tate? Nobody's ever called me by my last name, not since junior high, anyway."

"You call me Morrison, I call you Tate. On the other issue, blame it on the job, reading all those sex crime reports. Maybe it'd be better you didn't become a detective."

"There was another reason I called, too. I talked to Dennis last night. He wanted to know if I was the one telling you things about him."

"I thought he might call."

"Well, he did. I made the mistake of answering the telephone."

"Did you tell him what I told you to tell him if he called?"

"I told him I hadn't talked to you."

"That's good. He say anything else I should know about?"

"We talked a long time, or maybe I listened a long time. There were a couple of things."

"Say, are you doing anything right now? I mean in the next fifteen, twenty minutes?"

"No, why?"

"I'm up on the far northside, probably not more than ten minutes from you. How about if I came by and we talked a little? It's always better, remember, face to face."

She paused a moment. "If you want, sure, come on by." She did not sound displeased. "You know how to get here?"

Morrison had his spiral notebook out, the telephone cupped against his shoulder, paging through it, stopped, and said, "I've got the address, see you in a bit."

VINNY DECIDED to forego the nap, too much running around in his mind, too much frustration, too much figuring what if anything he could do. He had had the last can of Old Milwaukee just after Morrison and Castor left, ate what remained of the now-cold hamburger and picked at the fries. Now he sat there on the couch pondering his ever-growing dilemma.

Planting the thing about Jo maybe being dead was a stroke, just pulling it out of his mind like that, thinking on his feet, laying it on them. Vinny congratulated himself on that one. Get the dumb cops looking for a corpse instead of a real live girl. Maybe they would even haul Tommy in for questioning, keep him a while, get him off the streets in case Jo did decide to suddenly show up in Uptown.

The troublesome thought, however, was if Jo had gone along with them on that screwball robbery that had a murder hanging over it, she'd be the only one who could give the cops Tommy, White being dead. God, if Jo didn't have a big enough problem with Tommy before, how about now, when the animal knows they're closing on him and her. He decided he would be better off getting out, looking around, asking around, doing something.

THE APARTMENT was only about six blocks into Evanston, just west of Sheridan Road, maybe a two-block walk to the Lake Michigan beach. A grand old building, three-story, six apartments. *B. Tate* was on the second floor, according to the mailbox in the lobby. Morrison rang the bell. Over the squawk-box he heard a female voice ask who was there. "Joe Morrison." The voice said she would buzz him in. A grating ear-shattering noise came from the door to the hall and he hurried over to open it before the screech stopped.

Upstairs, at the open door, he said to her, "You sound like Louis Armstrong on that thing."

Stepping back to let him in, she said, "Must have the reverse effect coming up, you sounded like Pee Wee Herman." She took his coat and hung it in the hall closet, then walked into the living room.

It was a large apartment, tastefully furnished, the kind they used to call a railroad apartment: a large living room with a bay up front—the engine—a long corridor with bedrooms and bathrooms off it, emptying into the dining room, then the kitchen and finally the back porch—the caboose. The living room was especially large, with a wet bar built into one corner, which saved you the trek all the way down the hall to get an ice cube. Easy eight hundred a month rent, Morrison figured. There were enough potted and hanging plants to qualify it as a Park District conservatory.

"You always work on Saturdays?" she asked.

Morrison remembered hearing something to that effect a week earlier and in his mind he suddenly heard Bruce Springsteen and the echoes and the talk, then thought of

Bert . . . Modern Bert. "Just lately. Had a great time. Spent most of the afternoon rummaging through garbage cans down in Uptown."

"That doesn't sound very appealing." She sat down in the corner of a long L-shaped couch. She was wearing a paisley nylon blouse with a large bow, tan slacks and black flats, one of which she dangled from her toes after crossing her leg. Morrison sat kitty-corner from her.

"Actually they were mostly dumpsters."

"What were you looking for?" She cringed a little. "I think maybe I'll be sorry I asked that."

"A body."

"That's kind of what I figured. Whose?"

"A girl, one we want for questioning. We got a tip she might have gotten whacked herself and dumped down there."

"Did you find her?"

"Nope. It's in the hands of the garbage cops now."

"The garbage cops?"

Morrison nodded. "Yeah. See, they could've picked up the garbage between the time the body was dumped and today. So we find out where they take the garbage from that particular area, which garbage dump, and a couple of cops go out and dig through it. It's one of the lesser joys of police work. Usually goes to the newer guys on the job. Sometimes takes 'em a couple of days to get the smell out of their uniforms."

"By way of changing the subject, would you like a drink or anything?"

"I would."

She got up and headed toward the wet bar. "What would you like?"

"What've you got?"

"Come on over and see for yourself."

Underneath the bar there was a wide assortment. He put the bottle of Jack Daniels on the bar. "Just a glass and some ice cubes. I'm easy,'' then he moved around to the other side of the bar and half-sat on one of the stools. She handed him an ice-filled glass, then poured about two ounces of Sambuca in a snifter and dropped an ice cube in it for herself.

He took a sip. ''Sure beats dumpster-diving.'' They walked back to the couch. ''Where's your sister?''

''Up in Door County, cross-country skiing.''

''Sounds healthy.''

''Sounds cold to me.''

''So what about Dennis Courtland?''

''Well, to begin with he was upset. He sounded funny, jittery. I think he believed me when I told him I hadn't talked to you. He said that you probably would try to talk to me now, the way things were going. As I said, he sounded on edge.''

''Did he ask you to alibi for him?''

''No. He just kind of meandered around about who might have told you he didn't get home until late, if I didn't. I told him it could have been the doorman or the car-hiker or even a neighbor. That seemed to satisfy him. But you would think he would have thought of that himself. He's not himself, I tell you.''

''Why do you think he's upset?''

''Well, for one thing, he *is* worried about what you think. He went on about how these detectives made it clear they didn't believe him, maybe even suspected him of having something to do with the crime. He said that was ridiculous. But he said, 'I was the last person in the store, maybe the last to see the man alive.' ''

''How did he know he was *the* last person in the store?''

''He said this Warner said he was closing up as soon as he left.''

''Did you ask Courtland where he was between that time and ten-thirty?''

"No, I don't really care."

"Anything else he said?"

"He asked me what I was going to tell you if you did come talk to me."

"What did you tell him?"

"The truth, I told him. Whatever you asked me, I'd tell you the truth, that's all."

"What did he say to that?"

"Oh, then he got real nice, giving me a little bull, but he said at the end—emphatically—that he had nothing to do with the murder. Then he started to go on about it all being like a bad dream, being in the wrong place at the wrong time, being suspected of something he had nothing to do with, being persecuted, I think, is the way he put it. Then he started talking about us getting back together, a little more bull, then about how you all were mistreating him, rambling on like that. I finally said I had to go. He said he'd call again and I said I wished he wouldn't. That was it."

"You think he was on something when he called?"

Linda hesitated, met Morrison's eyes. "I think he probably was."

"Any idea what?"

"No."

"Well, if he calls again just tell him we haven't contacted you. There's no need for you to get involved."

"I am involved, though, aren't I? I mean, you have talked to me and I've told you things that don't quite jibe with what Dennis has told you."

"He doesn't have to know it—not now, anyway."

"He won't bother me."

"You never know. You said he was acting funny. We know he's on some stuff—Valium, booze, who knows what else. They get on enough of it or on it too steady or maybe mix up the wrong things, they can do some weird things. Believe me, I've seen it happen too many times. Unfortunately it's the results of it I usually get to see."

"You're starting to make me worry."

"Maybe you should." Morrison took a healthy belt of the Jack Daniels. "He lied to you, too."

"Lied to me about what?"

"His wife. She didn't die of cancer."

Now there was more than puzzlement on her face, like she was about to hear something she did not want to hear. "She didn't?"

"No, she drowned. She and Courtland fell off a yacht down there after blitzing themselves with coke and booze and who knows what else. There was an investigation." He told her the whole story.

When he finished, she sat there, stunned. Finally she just shook her head. "My God," was all she could say. She reached over to the coffee table and picked up the snifter of Sambuca, finished the few drops that were left in it. "I thought I felt bad before. Now I find out I was even more stupid than I thought."

"Let's change the subject," Morrison said. "What's the B for in *B. Tate* downstairs?"

"Brenda, my sister."

"What's she do? Whatever it is, she must do it well, judging from this," he said, waving a hand in a circle indicating the apartment.

"She works for an advertising agency down in the city, a big one. I don't know exactly what she does but she makes good money. The condo here came after her divorce a couple of years ago. No kids. No-fault divorce. They just split everything down the middle, sold their house out in Deerfield and she bought this with her share."

"You're pretty close with your sister, I gather."

"We get along fine. She's two years older. I introduced her to the guy she married when she came over from Cleveland to visit me one time. She's forgiven me for that. Actually, he's not a bad guy. They just didn't get along after a while.'' She looked at his empty glass. ''You want another?''

Morrison hesitated, looked at his watch. It was a quarter after five.

''Got to get home, huh?''

''No.'' He shook his head, bringing things together. ''The kids have already eaten. They eat at five. And Joanne, well, we only talk about two things these days, the kids and divorce details. Tomorrow's my day with the kids. Maybe I'll take them to a museum or something.''

''Divorce is not one of life's little pleasures.''

''Sometimes it's better.''

''At least you get out with your self-respect.''

''I was looking at my watch because I was thinking of stopping to grab a little Italian on the way home, a place over on Touhy called Positano, near California, not too far from here. You ever been there?''

''Never heard of it.''

''It's small, has great pasta. It's also cheap and always crowded. You get there early, though, before six, you've got no problem. Later you could wait an hour, hour and a half.'' Morrison gave her a friendly grin, the detective now buried somewhere deep inside. ''If you've got nothing better to do, why don't you join me?''

She caught the change of tone in his voice—not as honed; fishing, not searching. ''I think I'd better not.''

''Your sister coming back?''

''No, she's up there for the week. Some resort.''

Morrison took her in, thought he would take one more shot, and said, ''You going out somewhere then?''

''Well, not really.''

''You going to eat by yourself?''

''That was the plan.''

''You like to eat alone? I hate it.''

''It's been so long since I have. Life with Dennis was

like writing the Restaurant Guide in *Chicago* magazine. And with Dennis calling last night and what you just told me . . ."

"Well, that's maybe why you should get out. This place is good. Neither of us would have to sit alone and brood." He paused. "No strings." Morrison looked at his watch again. "What do you say? I can get you back by seven-thirty or eight if we leave now."

She stood up, one easy fluid movement, and hovered there in front of him. He stared up at her, waiting for an answer.

"Maybe you should have been a salesman instead of a detective."

"So you'll go?"

"I don't think I like to eat alone either. Give me a few minutes to change into something else."

"This is not a fancy place. You're fine just as you are."

"You have a coat and tie on."

"Have to. Departmental regulations, detectives on duty must wear a coat and tie. Makes it a lot easier for the bad guys to pick us out when we work places like Uptown."

She smiled again. "Well, let me put a skirt on anyway. Ten minutes, okay?"

"Sure." He stood up, picked up the glass. "Maybe I'll take you up on that other drink now."

"Help yourself," and she disappeared down the railroad-car corridor.

I should work Saturdays more often, Morrison thought as he poured several ounces of Jack Daniels into his glass.

26

VINNY, DECIDING there was at least one thing he could do, put on his coat and went out, heading south on Broadway. It was dark now, the vapor streetlights emitting their goldish glare illuminated the dull gray, dirt-streaked snow that rose in banks on either side of the sidewalk and the street, giving it a kind of bronzed look. The streets had all been plowed now and most of the sidewalks were shoveled, but none of the rest of the snow that covered the flotsam and jetsam of Uptown had melted. Instead it had taken on a crisp, icy coating.

It was still too early, 6:30, for the night people of Uptown to be out making their way to the dingy haunts on Lawrence and Wilson and Broadway. He turned on Wilson and headed east. The street was especially quiet in the bitter cold—an occasional car, a lone pedestrian here and there, not like a dark summer Saturday night when the streets teemed with the victims and the predators, the dopers and the dealers, the drinkers and the drunks. Cars with suburban stickers would be cruising, the drivers in their murky quest to buy some sex from girls or guys. The side streets and the alleyways in the shadows of walls spray-painted with gang symbols would be alive with clusters of the young, huddling, whispering, planning something.

He looked in the window of the sandwich shop where

he had gotten his hamburger and fries earlier. The place was nearly empty, two men several stools apart sat hunched over the counter and only a couple of tables were occupied. The lone waitress was talking to the cook by the grill where the burgers and the bacon and eggs and hashbrowns and assorted other diner delicacies were greased, splatterings of which were vividly painted all over the cook's apron.

He walked past J.J.'s without bothering to look in the window. He knew Mason was there behind the bar, Mason who proved to be a friend the other night. Vinny liked Mason, one of the few people he really watched his tongue with because he knew Mason did not like it. Mason was kind of like a father-figure to Vinny, whose real father he vaguely remembered before the man went off to Menard for armed robbery when Vinny was six, the three-to-five sentence turning into a death penalty when he ended up on the wrong end of a shank in the prison yard. At Sheridan Road he walked south to Sunnyside, then east to the Tudor Arms. Vinny rapped on the door to the janitor's apartment.

A moment later the door opened, the chain on, and the Nigerian peered out. Behind him Vinny could see a two-year-old boy not quite as dark as the Nigerian sitting on the floor looking about the room.

"You the new janitor, right?" Vinny asked. The Nigerian just nodded, looking at Vinny suspiciously. "The girl who lives on the third floor, apartment Three-F, she hasn't been around, right?"

The Nigerian shook his head. "No girl livin' in Three-F."

"Not now, I know. But it's her apartment. She's the one who rents it."

"Man lives there. Big one. No girl."

"I know. I know. Jeez."

"That's the apartment the police come to."

"They did? When?"

"Yesterday. They have paper says they can search the apartment."

"They searched it?"

"Big man was there. They go in. I go back downstairs. They take the man with them when they go."

Vinny thought of the drugs that were in there before, stashed in the closet. "They take anything from the apartment besides the moron?" The Nigerian just looked at him. "They take a box or a bag of something, anything like that?"

"Don't know. Just saw the man in handcuffs."

"He still gone?"

"No, he come back this afternoon."

Vinny thought he better get his business done and get the hell out of there. "Look, this girl, she might come back. If she does I want you to give her this," pushing an envelope through the opening of the door. The Nigerian took it, looked at where Vinny had written *Jo Kane.*

"How do I know her?"

"That's her name on the envelope. You see a nice-lookin' girl heading upstairs, early twenties, about this tall"—Vinny held his hand up in a salute at eyebrow level—"brown hair, great body"—Vinny drew an hourglass with his hands—"that you can understand, I bet. Sometimes wears a fake fur jacket." When she's working, Vinny was about to say but didn't. "Other times she wears a long coat, kind of grayish. You see her, you ask if she's Jo Kane. You tell her you got a very important message for her and you hand her this envelope."

The Nigerian stared at the envelope. "Okay," he finally said.

"The one thing you *don't* do is show this to the big guy up in Three-F now. Absolutely not. You do and you're gonna look like a melted Hershey bar when he's through with you."

"Melted Hershey bar?"

"Never mind. Just don't let him know about the envelope or he'll get real mad. Understand?" The Nigerian nodded. "Only give it to the girl if she shows up, nobody else." Vinny turned and walked back out through the lobby into the street.

Nothing more he could do, he thought. Just hope Jo doesn't come back before Tommy leaves . . . and that might be pretty soon, the cops hassling him like they were. If Tommy had a brain bigger than a walnut he'd already be headed somewhere far from Uptown, far from Chicago, Vinny thought, before they got something hot and heavy to tie him to that drugstore deal. Christ, he had a car, a jalopy, sure, but it could get him out of town, or he could just leave it here and take a bus to Detroit or Newark. He'd fit in great, definitely Tommy's kind of towns.

Vinny turned south on Sheridan Road. At Montrose he went into the Tip Top Tap. The bar was about half full. Nobody turned as Vinny walked down it to where Warren, the night bartender, stood, arms crossed on his stomach, eyes on the television above, which was tuned to a rerun of "Bonanza." Warren, big in a sloppy fat sort of way, was in his early thirties but could easily pass for fifty, his face already into meltdown. He was from Pigeon Forge, Tennessee, in the shadow of the Great Smoky Mountains south of Knoxville. He was one of the friendlier bartenders in Uptown, but was downright nasty when he was on the other side of the bar partaking instead of dispensing. Warren had worked the Tip Top Tap for about two years and lived in a small apartment above it that he occasionally let Leroy Tolliver use for his poker games—for a fee, of course. Tolliver took a half-dollar out of each pot for Warren, but Vinny did not think he gave all of it to Warren.

"Jo Kane been in lately?" Vinny asked.

Warren moved his gaze from the television set to Vinny, his eyes brightening. "Well, say, you been scarce around here lately,'' he said. ''Where you been sippin' the suds, Vin? Some fancy place downtown?''

''Been busy, Warren. Got a few deals goin'.'' Vinny waited for a moment, then said, ''You forgot something, Warren?''

''Forget something?''

''Like the question I asked. Jo Kane, you know, like in the girl that brings all the drool to your mouth whenever she comes in, she been around at all?''

''No, ain't seen tit or ass a her in some time.'' He pointed to the bottles on the counter behind the bar. ''That old Southern Comfort bottle ain't gone down an inch in weeks.''

''How about Tolliver, he been in today?''

''Oh, yeah. Earlier. He's comin' back. Game tonight.'' He raised his eyes toward the ceiling. ''Upstairs.''

''You know if he's got an opening?''

''That I do not know. But he said he'd be back around seven, nearly that now.''

''Okay, I'll stick around for a while.'' Vinny took off his coat and hung it on a rack on the back wall, then sat at the bar in front of Warren, whose attention had reverted to ''Bonanza.'' ''Let me have a beer. Whatever you got on draft.'' As Warren went down the bar to draw the beer Vinny headed into the men's room, a slotlike cell that was only five feet wide and consisted of a sink, urinal and stall in tandem. He saw a boot under the partition to the stall when he stepped in and was immediately overwhelmed with a ferociously fetid odor. Standing at the urinal, he tried not to breathe.

His beer was sitting on the bar when he finally escaped the john, and Vinny drained half the glass, hoping to cleanse his nasal passages.

When Warren came back to the other end of the bar to reattach himself to ''Bonanza,'' Vinny crooked a thumb toward the door to the men's room. "Whoever's on the crapper in there, Warren, has died."

"Oh, hell, that's just Tommy. He takes a mean dump."

With the name, Vinny felt a sudden flutter in his chest that had not even begun to subside when he heard the door to the men's room behind him slam open. He turned at the noise, only to see Thomas Alvin Bates surveying the bar, his Eddie Bauer down jacket slung over his shoulder, then feeling the flutter gain in velocity as their eyes met. Tommy walked over to him.

"Hey, Tommy," Warren said, "old Vin here hardly got his pecker back in his pants he tried to get outa there so quick. Musta been all that chili we put away last night." Warren gave a high-pitched laugh that made his jowls move up and down.

Tommy burst into a grin, then looked at Vinny. "What'd you expect, lilacs?" which sent Warren into another spasm of laughter. "Warren, when you stop yelpin', gimme a double Early Times with some ice," Tommy said.

Vinny was trying to force a smile, join in the merriment. He managed a chuckle. "Lilacs, that's a good one." He watched as Tommy pulled a roll of bills the size of Vinny's fist out of the side pocket of his Levis and peeled off a five-dollar bill and put it on the bar. Where the hell does he get all the money, Vinny wondered, thinking there had to be at least five hundred dollars there, maybe more.

Tommy clamped a hand on Vinny's shoulder, turning him sideways on the bar stool. "You hear anything on Jo Kane?"

"Not a thing, Tommy. Been keepin' my ears open, though."

"Your mouth too, so I heard. You been askin' all around about her, what I heard."

"Yeah." Vinny was scrambling now. "Doing it for you. You know, you told me you wanted to find her. Doing it for her, too, warn her the cops've been around lookin' for her. You heard that?''

''I heard that.'' He dug his fingers into Vinny's shoulder and Vinny almost came off the bar stool.

''Hey, easy, Tommy,'' he said wincing, ''that hurts.''

''The first thing you do, you hear where she is, you come to me. You don't go tellin' her nothin' about the cops. I want to see her before them, you understand that?'' Tommy's hand tightened again. This time Vinny did lose his balance and came off the stool, his shoulder angled downward under the pressure from Tommy's hand.

''Sure, sure. You get the word first.''

''Hey, don't be pickin' on the little guy, Tommy,'' Warren said. ''Vin's a regular 'round these parts.''

Tommy let him go. He put his jacket on the stool next to Vinny, sat on it and grabbed up his drink. He turned, facing Vinny. ''The cops talk to you?''

''No, Tommy. When I asked around the neighborhood about her a couple of guys said the Man was looking for her, too, that's all.''

''Say what for?''

''Something about the drugstore stick-up. That's all I know. Maybe they think she knows something about it.'' As soon as he said it he wished he hadn't.

Tommy nodded, showing Vinny he had already thought along those lines. ''Maybe she does,'' and he gave Vinny one of his patented unnerving grins.

Vinny definitely wanted away from the subject but said anyway, ''Heard they were hassling you a little the other day, too.''

''Who'd you hear that from?''

Vinny was sure as hell not going to tell him the coppers he talked to nor the rookie janitor over at the Tudor who had the note he had written to Jo telling her that Tommy would probably kill her if he got his hands on her and that the cops were looking all over the city for her in regard to a robbery and murder and that maybe he could help her if she would just let him. ''Just somebody over at J.J.'s, said they saw a couple of them taking you out of the Tudor. Said it probably had something to do about that fight with White.'' Vinny looked at him, working up an expression as if to ask for confirmation, which he did not get, just Tommy's empty eyes staring back at him, the grin coming back slowly. This guy is a certified lunatic, Vinny said to himself as he grappled for a way to get himself out of the Tip Top.

Looking beyond Tommy toward the front door at the other end, Vinny saw Leroy Tolliver come in with two other black men. They stopped at the curve of the bar up front. Warren went to tend to their needs and Vinny saw him say something to Tolliver and gesture toward his end of the bar. Tolliver came down.

''Warren says you might be interested in a little gaming tonight,'' he said to Vinny.

''Might be, you got an opening?''

''Got five put together so far. Leaves two.''

Tommy looked at Tolliver, his eyes traveling from the face down the fur-collared leather jacket to the tapered gold slacks that cuffed tightly at the ankle to the pointed-toe, black patent-leather boots, then retracing the path. When his eyes concluded their journey at Tolliver's face again, Tommy's expression resembled that of a road-kill collector his first morning on the job.

''Straight poker?'' Vinny asked.

''Straight, my man. Five-card, stud or draw; seven stud; Chicago stud; that's it.'' Chicago stud was seven-card stud with the winnings split between best hand and high spade in the hole. ''No hoke, no joke. Last card, pot limit. Half-buck to Warren from each pot.''

''Sounds like my kind of game,'' Vinny said. ''Check me in. What time?''

''Should kick in about ten.''

Vinny suddenly noticed Tommy staring at Tolliver and felt he should do something. "By the way, you know Tommy Bates," he said to Tolliver. Tolliver shook his head. Vinny turned to Tommy. "This here's Leroy Tolliver, Tommy. Gets some good card games going around the neighborhood."

"I bet," Tommy said, taking in the man, then turned back to the bar and his Early Times.

"Tommy's a man of few words," Vinny said, then, catching the bulge-eyed glare from Tommy, added, "but one helluva lot of action if need be."

Tommy finished his drink and picked up the two dollars' change that Warren had left on the bar, wrapping them around the wad of bills he took from his pocket, which did not go unnoticed by Leroy Tolliver.

"How about you?" Tolliver said to Tommy. "You like a little gaming? We got one opening left."

Tommy said, "With you?" in a tone that sounded like Tolliver had just asked him to go skinny-dipping in a pit of sewage. Tommy shook his head in disbelief, got up, put on his coat and motioned for Warren to come down the bar. When Warren got there he said, "Be back about two, like we talked about."

Warren burst into a big smile. "You got it, Tommy." He looked up and down the bar. "Whyn't you make 'er about one. I think I might close this sucker up early, business bein' what it is lately."

Vinny thought, my God, he does have a buddy.

"One's okay," Tommy said. "But I don't wanna be sittin' around here for an hour waitin' for you. We got things to do." He looked over at Vinny, gave him that death grin again. "Places to go."

Tommy was standing now. He was a good four inches taller than Leroy Tolliver. Looked down at him. "I don't do *nothin'* with niggers." He turned to Vinny. "And you remember, little shit, you hear *anything* about Jo, you get hold of me first.'' Vinny did not say anything and the silence hung there. ''You understand, that girl is mine.'' Vinny nodded. ''I get her first. Jo is *mine.*'' He reached into the side pocket of his Eddie Bauer jacket, his hand emerging with a gun, looked to Vinny like an automatic, the kind that could make jelly of your innards on impact even if you were wearing one of those bullet-proof vests and blow most of your insides out your backside if you weren't. ''And if I ever find out you knew somethin' about Jo's whereabouts and you didn't tell old Tommy,'' he said pointing the gun at Vinny's crotch, ''I'm gonna blow that little pecker Warren told me about right off you.'' Pointing the gun lower now, ''Then I'm goin' to use your kneecaps for target practice. But that shouldn't bother you, little shit''—Tommy was grinning again—'' 'cause you won't need those legs to get you to the whorehouse 'cause you won't have the apparatus to do anything there anyway.'' Tommy laughed at his own humor. Nobody else did.

Warren, who had sensed something, hustled down to that end of the bar and said almost in a whisper, ''Criminy, Tommy, put that thing away. You want us all to go to the jailhouse?''

Tommy put the gun back in his pocket, then put his hand on Vinny's shoulder, the grin still lingering on his face. ''Just wanted to get across a message to the little guy here.'' He started for the door, turned. ''See you about one, Warren.''

''Lookin' forward to it,'' Warren said. Looking at Vinny and Leroy Tolliver, ''Don't take Tommy too badly. He comes on a little strong sometimes, but he's good people.''

When Warren moved back up the bar Leroy Tolliver shook his head. ''Who the mother was that guy?''

''One you don't want playing in your card games,'' Vinny said.

"That Jo he's lookin' for," Tolliver said, "that Jo Kane, the one you been talkin' about all the time?"

"That's the one, Leroy."

"What's he want with her?"

"I think he wants to kill her."

Tolliver raised his eyebrows at that. "Explains why," he said, nodding now in understanding. "Why's he want to do that?"

"A long story. Something to do about her takin' up with a man of your color. That man is now dead."

"He do it?" the eyebrows rising again.

"Don't know. I said it's a long story. The cops think the guy's boyfriend did it—he went AC-DC. The other guy did it, then did himself, that's what they think. I'm not so sure." Vinny eyed Tolliver. "What'd you mean when you said 'Explains why'?"

Tolliver looked back at Vinny. "You don't know where she is?"

"Hell, no, Leroy. I spent the last couple days trying to track her down, warn her."

"You got a mind to tell him where she is if you find her?"

"Jeez, Leroy, that's the last thing I'd do in this world. I want to *help* her."

Tolliver sat down at the stool that Tommy had vacated. "Would it surprise you," he said, "I tell you *I* know where she is."

Vinny could feel his heart beating. "Where?" was all he could say.

"She's workin', Vinny. That's the word I heard."

"Where, Leroy?"

"Wait a minute, my man. Let me explain." Tolliver patted Vinny on the thigh. "You gotta calm yourself down. Understand the sit-u-a-tion." Tolliver removed his hand from Vinny's thigh and shook a finger at him. "I got word from two of my ladies about her. They're unhappy. She just showed up last week and, well, she's takin' away some of their business. They don't take to that. You can understand. So they let me know, bein' their representative and all."

"You talked to her?" Vinny asked, not calmed at all.

"Was goin' to last night, but the little girl was nowhere to be found. I was out there late and neither of my ladies had seen her. Surprising, 'cause Friday night's a good business night out there."

"Out where?"

"Mannheim Road. Out 'round Stone Park, Melrose Park. She's workin' independent, they tell me. One night she was in the Black Beaver Lounge where my Lola Lust"—Tolliver smiled at Vinny—"working name, pretty good one, if I do say so. The Beaver's what Lola calls home these days. Another night your Jo was in the Club Havana, Tonya told me. But Friday she not around anywhere. I wanted to talk to her about the sit-u-a-tion."

Vinny was not thinking about the sit-u-a-tion. He was trying to figure out how he was going to get all the way out to Mannheim Road without a car. Probably have to go out to O'Hare again and rent one, but that meant taking the subway downtown, then switching to the Kennedy el to go all the way out to the airport.

"Cancel me out of the card game, Leroy. I'm goin' out there, see if I can find her." Vinny put a dollar bill on the bar for Warren and got up. "What's your other girl's name, besides Lola Lust, the one at the Havana?" he asked as he climbed off the bar stool.

"Tonya, Tonya Turner. But it won't do you no good talkin' to them."

"Why not?"

" 'Cause they won't tell you nothin', they not knowin' you. Not unless I tell 'em it's okay."

"How about you tellin' them that then. Call 'em, tell

'em I'm coming around in maybe an hour and a half, two hours."

Tolliver shook his head. "Can't call. They still wouldn't talk to you, my callin'. Hell, you could be sittin' next to me holdin' a gun to my head. These ladies know the action, they don't trust nobody 'cept, of course, their representative."

Vinny sighed. "How much it cost me for you to drive out there and introduce me to your whores?"

Tolliver looked at his watch, a little after 7:30. "I gotta be here at ten," he said, shaking his head. "Money to be made, my man."

"I'm not askin' you to go out there on a double-date. All I want is you to tell 'em it's okay to talk to me. Then you can turn around and race your old pimpmobile back here. You be back by nine-thirty. So whaddya say, Leroy? How much?"

"Gasoline's mighty expensive these days."

"C'mon." Vinny dug into his pocket, pulled out a clip of bills. "How about fifty?"

Tolliver looked at him, then at the bills. "You double that, a C-note and you got yourself a chauffeur."

"A hundred. Since when did you add robbery to your sheet?"

"Otherwise it's not worth my while." Tolliver shrugged.

Vinny took the clip off the bills and put five twenties on the bar in front of Tolliver. "Okay, bandito, we're out of here."

THE WAY Morrison remembered the evening as he sat in front of his television drinking a glass of schnapps and watching the ten o'clock news was this. The food at Positano was good. She had pasta primavera, he had linguine with white clam sauce, they split a bottle of Pinot Grigio recommended by the waiter although Morrison drank most of it. They did not talk about Dennis Courtland or Theo

Warner. They did talk about some of life's disillusionments, they also talked about some pleasant things. He did not, maybe could not, hide the fact he was attracted to her. She seemed to enjoy the attention, at least she did not appear to object to it. He walked out of Positano with a Visa card receipt for $42.80.

In the car on the way back to her sister's apartment he told her he would like to see her again, on a nonprofessional basis. She said she thought she would like that. He parked in the No Parking space directly in front of the apartment entrance and mentioned it was still pretty early, Saturday night, America's date night. She did not invite him in but she made no move to get out of the car. He kissed her. She accepted it, became part of it, moved against him, her hand going up to the back of his neck, her mouth opening, together now in rhythmic motion. The taste of her lipstick, the scent of jasmine coming from her. He could feel her breasts pressing against him because her coat was open. When they kissed again, he put his hand on her breast. It was firm and the nylon of her blouse felt soft, sensual, rubbing against the nylon of her bra. He could feel the hard nipple pressing out against both. When she drew away slowly, she told him she felt like she was back in high school sitting in a car, making out. They kissed again, tongues exploring. Then she told him.

"I haven't really been candid with you, Joe, about Dennis Courtland," was the way she put it. She sat with her back against the car door now so she could face him. The sexual feelings dissolved as the detective in him came back. "Maybe *honest* is a better word than *candid*." There was a plaintiveness about her now, he noticed, like she was dredging up some buried sorrow.

"In what way?"

"I don't know why I didn't tell you this before. In the beginning I guess I was just trying to protect Dennis—he had meant something to me, for a while anyway—and I knew it was something you probably did not want to hear, after your telling me about your feelings about the man in the drugstore.'' She looked at him, as if asking for forgiveness.

''Go ahead.''

''Dennis wasn't just getting Valium over there. He got cocaine, too. Actually it was some kind of speedball, that's what he called it, cocaine mixed with something else.''

Morrison nodded. ''Heroin or morphine. If he got it there it was morphine.'' Morrison felt empty inside thinking about it.

''He paid a lot for it, he told me that, but it was worth it because it was pure and he didn't have to take the chance buying it on the street where he didn't know what he was getting. Which he never did, by the way. And he didn't want to buy it regularly over at the Board of Trade—his reputation, you know.'' She let out a deep breath. ''He wanted me to try it. That's probably what he was on that night. I've seen him before when he mixed a speedball with alcohol. It was like that, up and down, really disoriented, hyper then dozy then hyper again until he'd finally just pass out.''

''How often did he use the junk?''

''On the weekends, almost every one.'' She reached over and put her hand on Morrison's arm, which was resting on the back of the front seat. ''Are you upset with me not telling you?''

''I wish you had before. But I'm glad you finally did.''

Morrison saw in his mind little Theo Warner in the back of his pharmacy sitting at the aluminum table there with his Bunsen burner and test tube and paten concocting some gourmet speedballs so Dennis Courtland could fry his brain. He wondered how many clients like Courtland Theo had. ''You mentioned he tried to get you to do a speedball. You ever do one?''

She shook her head. ''Never.'' She could not tell

whether he believed her or not, the way he was just kind of staring at her. ''Well, I've got to got now, Joe. Thanks for the evening,'' she said. ''It was a nice restaurant. And it was nice being back in high school, even if it was for only a couple of minutes.'' She leaned over and brushed a kiss across his lips, then opened the car door, wondering as she said goodbye if she ever would see him again . . . nonprofessionally.

Morrison watched her clutching the unbuttoned coat to her chest, her heels clattering as she walked swiftly up the sidewalk, his eyes on those perfect legs. He waited until she let herself into the apartment building, then drove home, a lot on his mind.

27

VINNY KNEW he liked the Black Beaver Lounge the moment he walked in the door. Never been there before, but he had been to others like it. It was the kind of place he sometimes day-dreamed of running: an office in the back, big desk, big couch with fold-out bed, he personally picking the personnel. He knew it was Outfit-owned or at least they had a major piece of it, all the strip joints and rendezvous clubs along this stretch of Mannheim Road had their ties.

The monster at the door had nodded to Leroy Tolliver when they walked in, and Leroy, a ten palmed, shook hands with him, said, "How goes it, Rocco?" It reminded Vinny of the old neighborhood and how most of the guys named Rocco down around Grand Avenue, and there were more than a few, never saw their thirtieth birthday. Roccos seemed to screw up for some reason. Not the Tonys or Sammys or Brunos. Roccos, they always seemed to end up underneath an asphalt driveway or in a car trunk or swimming with the carp in one of the branches of the Chicago River.

Inside it was big and dark. A bar stretched all the way down to the left of the enormous room. There, over the bar, sure enough, standing on a little platform was a three-foot stuffed beaver with its flat, ping-pong paddle tail propped up and sporting a coat of fur that had long ago lost its luster. Tables and chairs formed a broad U around the spotlighted stage against the opposite wall, where a girl with huge breasts and pasties with dangling tassles shook them to the tune of "Are You Lonesome Tonight," from which the Elvis Presley estate was surely not getting any royalty.

The place was doing a good business, Vinny noticed, thinking at the same time the world was not lacking for suckers. All these guys come in, pay fifty bucks for a bottle of rotgut champagne or ten bucks for a watered-down whiskey so they can watch some naked broad fake orgasm up there under the lights or have some other broad sit next to them, stroke their thigh, pucker up her lips, talk dirty and if they were really on a roll go into the backroom where there were some booths (a box of Kleenex on each table) so they could get jacked off for forty, fifty bucks, or *really really* on a roll, leave the place with one of the hostesses, as they liked to be called, for one of the mattress motels along the strip and drop maybe another hundred and fifty for ten, fifteen minutes of entertainment.

Lola, an attractive black girl with dreadlocks who could not have been more than twenty, was lounging on a bar stool, her back to the bar, between two Oriental men who were talking animatedly with her. When she saw Leroy Tolliver, she waved. The two Orientals turned, big smiles on their faces, heads bobbing. Tolliver gestured for her to come over.

"I don't want to lose those, Leee-roy," she said as she sidled up next to Tolliver. "We're talking *some* dollars here." She nodded back toward them. "They both in love with me. One of them said his name is something like Kum Quat. Ain't that a vegetable or something?" She flashed a big smile at both Tolliver and Vinny. "He said he got the runs for me. I told him it was the hots, at least I hope that's what he meant. You wanna meet them, Leee-roy?"

"No. This is Vinny. He's lookin' for that Jo Kane. She been around?"

"Nope. Haven't seen her since the other night. We don't need no more girls round here. We the ones get hurt. Management don't give no shit, long as she scores. Hell, between their cut, your cut, I'd be better off walking Lake Street or Madison, even in this weather."

"You have any idea where I could find her?" Vinny asked.

"Nope."

"No idea where she's staying?"

"I do know she took a trick or two to the Star Dust."

"Where's that?" Vinny asked Tolliver.

" 'Bout a block and a half south of here."

"You see her," Vinny said to Lola Lust, "you tell her to call Vinny, Vinny Salerno. I'll get her outa here for you. Okay?" He did not wait for an answer. He pulled a piece of paper from his pocket and a ballpoint, wrote down a number. "Tell her to call J.J.'s, leave a message with Mason where I can call her or meet her. Tell her it's very, very important."

She looked at him, then at Tolliver, who nodded, saying softly, "Do it."

"I gotta get back to my friends," she said, taking the slip of paper and sticking it in the cleavage of her strapless black leather dress that measured about two feet top to bottom and covered her from just above the nipples to about two inches below the *labia majora*. Then, looking at Tolliver, "We may gross three, four hundred here tonight on these babies alone," she said, gesturing toward the two Orientals. "Already had two bottles of the sparkly. Talkin' a double-header. Unless they get kinky and decide they want some white trash instead." She gave a little hip-wiggle and walked back to her newfound friends at the bar.

Tonya Turner was not of much more help, but she too took the telephone number of J.J.'s. She suggested, however, that Jo might be working the ordinary taverns instead of the clubs. There were five or six along the strip, working-class hangouts. She said Jo told her she needed money bad, needed it to get out altogether. Things were bad. Tell me, Vinny said to himself.

Vinny tried to talk Tolliver into staying there on Mannheim with him so he could check the taverns out, but Tolliver would not. So Vinny trekked the strip alone in the awful cold for the next two hours, hit every saloon along it but there was no Jo Kane in any of them. The bartender in a little tavern next to the Star Dust Motel, however, figured he knew who Vinny was talking about and said a girl who fit the description had been in there a few times earlier in the week but he hadn't seen her in the last couple of days.

The desk clerk at the Star Dust, a frail little old man with Coke-bottle-bottom glasses and a pencil mustache and who sounded like he was in the last round of a battle with emphysema knew nothing about her, or so he claimed. Vinny just stared at the man, his eyes telling the man he did not believe him. The man raised his hands in front of him, palms turned upward, telling Vinny that's the way it was, sorry. A ten Vinny put in one of the palms got verification between coughing spells that a young lady who could have been Jo Kane had been a guest in the motel several times early in the week. A ten in the other palm got Vinny the information that she had never stayed overnight there and in fact had not visited the establishment since Wednesday night.

Looking at the little sign standing on the desk,

Adult Movies
Available
in All Rooms

and the one tacked on the wall behind the wheezer,

Ask About Our Special 4–Hour Rates

VINNY THOUGHT they ought to rename the Star Dust something like Herpes Heaven.

Vinny considered taking a room there, hang around just in case Jo did turn up, but decided that it would probably be a waste of time and money. The overwhelming aroma of roach-kill spray helped contribute to his decision.

About midnight Vinny gave up, took a bus down Mannheim Road to the el station at O'Hare, then the Kennedy el downtown and finally the Howard Street el back to Uptown. It was one-thirty in the morning when he got off the train at Wilson Avenue. He went home worrying that maybe the cops had already found her, thought maybe he would call Morrison later in the morning to see if he could wangle a line on her out of him. Then another thought crept into Vinny's mind, a horrifying one. Maybe Tommy found out where she'd gone, came out and found her. Maybe he was just playing dumb to throw everybody off the track, asking around as if he hadn't found her. Maybe the thing Vinny had made up and dropped on the police wasn't a lie after all. He took that thought to bed with him.

CASTOR TALKED Morrison into going over to Dottie's for breakfast on Monday morning so as to work out a plausible story to lay on Lieutenant Roland when he ruptured over how little time they were spending on Organized Crime cases—*his* department, *their* department—Castor said, trying to imitate Roland's raspy voice. Norbert guessed they had until maybe ten that morning before the eruption.

Morrison listened, diddling around with his fork in the scrambled eggs, wishing in a way he had not ordered the sausage but looking at the links with a certain savory passion. But the rote Organized Crime cases in his wire-wicket basket across the street were far from his mind. Norbert could sense that.

"Well, the Courtland character's a druggie," Norbert said, understanding where his partner's mind was at. He wiped some pancake syrup from his chin with a paper napkin. "And little old Theo was his supplier. Guess you can't trust anybody these days."

" 'Fraid so."

"You think his brother was in on it?"

"Don't know. Linda didn't know who he dealt with over there. All *I* know is Theo was the only one there when he went to get the stuff that night. Bruce and the other pharmacist were long gone home. The clerk was the only one in the store, and according to her, Theo was going to close up as soon as she left." Morrison threw his hands up in the air. "Off the top of my head, I'd say Bruce probably knows. But then sometimes you got a little scam going you just keep it to yourself, don't tell your wife, your mother, your brother."

"How you gonna approach Courtland?"

"Don't know yet. I don't want to jeopardize Linda Tate in case lurking behind that cool snob-rich exterior is a druggie capable of murdering for the stuff. But I want to talk to him today."

"Hey, that's it. Whyn't we tell Roland we think this Courtland guy's laundering Outfit money through soybeans and winter wheat and we being good OC dicks are checking out every angle. It's just a wild coincidence that he figures into a little unrelated homicide at the same time."

"Norbie, finish your pancakes and let's go back across the street. It's nine o'clock."

Detective Joe Faverly was the only person in OC when Morrison and Castor walked in. "Anybody looking for us," Norbert asked him, "like maybe the lieutenant down the hall?"

"Haven't seen him. I heard he's in a meeting up in the

deputy superintendent's office. I hear some indictments are coming down from the grand jury today. You had a call, though, Joe, some guy but he wouldn't leave his name. Same guy as called yesterday morning, sounded the same anyway. Said he'll try again later."

Morrison went over to his desk, sat down and plucked the two messages impaled on his spindle and dropped them on the faded blotter that place-matted the desk. Norbert grabbed his mug, which carried the imprint I ♡ PEORIA on one side and on the other AND ELECTRIC SHOCK THERAPY, and walked out into the squad room to fill it with some oily-black liquid that masqueraded as coffee.

"By the way," Faverly said to Morrison, "the Loo did send somebody over for your file on that Facia kid's rape. Guy said the Loo wanted everything you had so far on it. I gave him the case file. That's all there is, right?"

"Right." Castor appeared in the doorway. "You hear that," Morrison said to him, "Roland pulled our Facia fiasco file."

Castor hit himself on the forehead with the heel of his empty hand, some coffee sloshing out of the mug in the other as he did.

"I told you he's gonna be all over our ass for spending so much time on your homicide." He walked to his desk, muttering, "And here all I wanted was to spend my few remaining years in this asylum free from stress, free from aggravation. Not out in a car cruising some Puerto Rican neighborhood at four in the morning looking for some gangbanger dope dealer who can only say 'My name is Hay-zoos. Do I do somethin' wrong, Mister Officer?' The only—*only*—words I wanted to hear from Roland was maybe some kind ones at my retirement party."

"Why do you think he wanted the file, Norb?"

Norbert took a sip of the coffee. "I don't think for its literary value." He shook his head. "Who knows? Maybe he wants to see if we've done anything at all on it." He arched his eyebrows at Morrison. ''On the other hand, maybe we ruffled some feathers, as they say.''

Morrison thought of the meeting with Facia and his attorney, decided he'd have to run it back through his mind and see if he'd missed something. ''Well, we'll find out, won't we?''

''I wager we will.''

Morrison pushed the two messages aside and from one of the desk drawers pulled a folder labeled *Theo Warner*, more than an inch thick now. Inside were Xeroxes of the original report, which was over at Area Six Violent Crimes. He leafed through it until he came to the paper-clipped set of pages devoted to Dennis Courtland. The top page was an information form, the vitals concerning the person interrogated. He found what he was looking for and then picked up the telephone and dialed the number of Courtland & Associates at the Board of Trade.

The woman who answered said that Mr. Courtland was not in the office. When Morrison asked when he was expected, there was a pause and then the woman told him not that day. When he inquired where he might reach Mr. Courtland the woman said she could not—meaning *would* not—tell Morrison where and suggested that perhaps he might wish to talk to one of Mr. Courtland's associates.

''How about his closest associate?'' Morrison said.

''Just a moment.'' A click, then some elevator music, a velvety orchestral arrangement of ''You Are My Lucky Star,'' and then a rather sharp voice came on the line saying *Benderman-* or *Banterman-Can-I-help-you*, the words coming so fast they seemed strung together as if they were one long one.

Can't waste a second when the trading pits are open, Morrison thought. ''You can if you can tell me where I might reach Dennis Courtland.''

''He's not here today. Can I help?''

The voice, in spite of its hurriedness, its impatience,

sounded quite young. ''I already told you how you could help.'' Police unanimously are a little short-wired when talking with abrupt twenty-eight-year-olds making maybe a hundred thousand a year more than they are. ''Is Mr. Courtland at home?''

''No.'' A silence that predisposed irritation at both ends hung over the wire. ''Can I ask who this is?''

''Sure, Sergeant Joe Morrison, Chicago Police Department.''

There was a pause. ''Hang on,'' then some muffled words at the other end as Benderman or Banterman, his hand clamped over the mouthpiece, began talking to someone else in the office of Courtland & Associates. When the hand came away from the telephone the presumably close associate said, ''All we know here is Mr. Courtland's not going to be in today. You want to leave a message, I'll see he gets it when he does come in.''

''No one there knows where the boss is or when he is going to be back?'' Morrison asked, accenting his disbelief.

''No, sorry.''

The guy was a lousy liar, Morrison thought. Good that he chose a career in commodity trading instead of law or tax accounting. ''Look, I can't believe that no one over there knows where to reach your Mr. Courtland. And it's important we talk with him—today.''

The voice that came back was both wary and pretending irritation. ''In the first place, even if I had it I can't give out information like that over the telephone. I don't even know whether you really are a police officer.''

''Fine, tell you what you do. You hang up the telephone and look up the general number for Chicago police headquarters, Eleven thirty-one South State Street. Then you pick the phone up again, dial that number, and ask for Sergeant Joe Morrison, Organized Crime Division.'' He articulated the last three words, let them sink in, then said, ''And if I don't hear from you in the next five minutes my partner and I will come over there and personally ask each and every person in your office if they know where Mr. Courtland is. And if they don't, we'll toddle on down to the trading floor, identify ourselves and ask around there. And maybe there's a chance some of your bigger clients might know where we can reach Mr. Courtland."

There was no immediate response, but finally a "I'll be back to you."

"Five minutes," Morrison said, and hung up.

Four minutes later the telephone in OC rang. Norbert picked it up. "It's for you, Joe, a Hurley Whiteside from Courtland and Associates." Hurley? Norbert muttered to himself, shaking his head.

"I'm calling at the behest of Fred Banterman," Hurley said. Hurley's voice was as haughty as Banterman's was sharp. "I'm a limited partner with Dennis, second in line, you might say."

Might I? Morrison thought.

"You wish to reach Mr. Courtland, I understand."

"Not wish, Mr. Whiteside, we intend to. I thought I made that pretty clear to your Mr. Banterman."

"Indeed."

Morrison listened, making notes on a yellow legal pad as he did. When he finally hung up, Morrison stood and walked over to Castor, who was reading the transcript of a wiretap on the office telephone of Aldo Patrick, *né* Patrici, alleged to be the Outfit's Chicago liaison to Las Vegas. "This guy Patrick's gotta be real horny," he said as Morrison approached. "All he talks to are broads. He's got one stashed in an apartment over in Sandburg Village, and when he isn't talking to her he's setting something up with some other babe to meet her at the Ritz Carlton or he's on the line to Vegas—he's got a couple of bimbos out there."

"Well, Norbie," Morrison said, "we found a legitimate approach to our friend Dennis the druggie. He's in the detox unit out at Lutheran General. Checked himself in Saturday morning. You up to a trip out to Des Plaines?''

As he said it, a uniformed cop came in. ''Glad I caught you guys,'' he said. ''Lieutenant Roland wants you two in his office at ten-thirty, sharp. He'll be through his meeting upstairs by then, he said.''

Morrison and Castor looked at each other. ''Well, I was a half-hour off,'' Norbert said. ''That's not too bad.''

LIEUTENANT ROLAND'S meeting did not end until a little after eleven. Morrison kept himself busy in the meantime, but not on Organized Crime cases. He went back over the Theo Warner file page by page; he wanted to review it in light of the confusing issues that were now emerging. Courtland was an insipid character. But was he capable of killing a little old man? Had he killed his wife? If he had he sure as hell was capable of killing Theo Warner. The Uptown three, now two. Where the hell was the girl? He admitted to himself that they had not yet turned that corner, the one in any investigation like this where you suddenly realized you could head straight down the street and you were home.

Morrison thought back on the other years when he did this kind of thing every day. So many homicides were so easy. In the family. In a brawl. The other gang. The mob hit. The last was never easy, though. Impossible, in fact. They had never solved a single one of them. Maybe *solved* was not the right word. Maybe it was better said they had never seen anyone convicted for one.

Rudy Facia came to mind. The non-rape rape. The one that Facia did not want settled in a courtroom.

28

IN THE washroom over at the Medill city garbage dump at Clybourn and Fullerton the young uniformed cop was retching at the toilet bowl. He had gotten rid of everything in his stomach out on the dump site when they opened the garbage bag. Now, after bringing it inside and watching his partner put the contents on an empty table, he was, it seemed, trying to rid himself of the inner lining of his stomach. Meanwhile his partner was out in the main office on the telephone trying to reach Joe Morrison. Next to him, on a table lying on the dark green plastic garbage bag were a pair of human legs chopped off just below the hips.

Faverly stuck his head into Lieutenant Roland's office, where Morrison and Castor were still waiting for the lieutenant's meeting upstairs to end. "Joe, the garbage cop's on the phone, says he's got something for you."

Morrison walked back with Faverly to their OC cubicle. The garbage cop told him they had found two adult female legs that were now yellowish-brown and as stiff as baseball bats.

"You're sure they're female?"

"Looks that way," the cop said, "them being shaved and the toenails painted red."

"Nothing else, just legs?"

"There was a pair of high heels in the bag, too. Otherwise that's it. We dug all around there but couldn't find anything else. There's gotta be a body and a head somewheres but we sure as hell couldn't find it."

"Any idea how long they've been there?"

"According to the dumpmaster—can you believe it, that's what the guy calls himself, dumpmaster—anyway, he says judging from where we dug 'em up they probably been there two or three days. The dumpmaster's got some of his guys going through the crap again to see if they can find anything else but I doubt it, I think we covered it all, at least all the stuff that hasn't been ground up yet."

"Okay, pack them up and take them over to the ME's office. I want a full pathology report. They should be able to determine age and height from the bone structure."

"Gotcha. The report goes directly to you downtown, sergeant, right?"

"Right."

Morrison called Area Six and asked for a couple of beat patrols to nose around the alleys and under the back porches near Wilson Avenue and to look into the sewers for a female torso or head or arms or all of the above that might be wrapped in a plastic bag or bags.

He remembered, for the moment, back in the days when he was first on the force, the same kind of detail sent out by the Homicide dicks, himself in a well-pressed uniform then, grunging through the putrescence of other people, opening the garbage can, finding a human head staring back at him, the neck just shivers of skin loosely surrounding the severed white spinal cord, blood all over the garbage beneath . . . and nothing else. In those early days on the force that awful confrontation of life and death augmented, certified, his desire to become a Homicide investigator, he recalled. Later, with an even stronger impetus, it ushered him out of the unit.

Morrison was in the process of explaining to Castor

about the legs with their painted toenails when Lieutenant Roland hustled into his office and interrupted with, "How you boys doin'?" Roland sat down behind his desk and let out a tired breath. "Busy, busy," he said. "Couple of bag men going down today." He rapped his fist on the desk in a gesture of triumph. "And a couple of dippers in the Tax Appeals Board office, two lawyers, all the result of our own Anthony Alderino," nodding to Castor, "with whom you are acquainted, I believe."

"Mad Anthony," Castor said.

"Mad Anthony is now in the Witness Protection Program. And more to come, much more. The first grand jury indictments are coming down right now over in the Federal Building. Watch the six o'clock news. You'll get the whole story." Lieutenant Roland opened the top drawer to his desk and took out a file. "Won't keep you long, boys." Morrison looked at his watch and saw that they had already been in the lieutenant's office forty-five minutes waiting for him. "This little deal here with the Facia girl."

"The rape of the Facia girl," Castor corrected.

Roland looked at him, annoyed. "I don't recall seeing any charges of a felonious sexual assault having been filed in regard to this," he said, tapping the file with his finger.

"Whether or not there were, there was still a rape. Just because Rudy Facia doesn't want it known around town—"

"Look, Norbert," Roland said, his threshold of patience never being very high, "I don't have the time or the inclination to quibble here. And I'm not saying there wasn't a sex offense committed against the girl." He looked from Castor to Morrison and back to Castor again. "I've read everything that's in here. It doesn't seem you've gotten anywhere so far." His tone had turned mellow now. "Is this all there is?"

"That's it," Castor said.

"You're sure? There mightn't be anything that's floating around . . . not logged yet in here?"

Castor shook his head. "What makes you think that?"

"Nothing. It's just that I heard through the grapevine that you had made some strides here, had a lead or two, but I didn't see anything in the file here that might corroborate that."

Morrison and Castor looked warily at each other. Morrison spoke up. "We don't have anything that you could call a lead yet. I spoke with Facia and his lawyer, as I gather you know if you read that." Morrison pointed at the file. "I wrote it up. All I got was they don't think it has anything to do with the Outfit, no vendettas or anything. It seems it was just a couple of transients who hit on the girl and then moved on. What else can I tell you?"

"You can tell me if you *do* get anything. This is a touchy issue. There are some people over in the Hall who do not want this to become public. Favors being pulled in. Can you two understand that?" Roland did not expect an answer. "I want this file kept in the office here with me. You got anything to add to it, you come in here and add it. I want to know everything you get as soon as you get it. And I don't want either one of you talking about this thing to anyone else, in or out of the department. Do we understand each other?"

"We sure do, lieutenant," Castor said.

"Keep in touch," Roland said.

ON THEIR way back to OC Norbert said to Morrison, "Not a word, can you believe that, not a word on the fact we've spent about fifteen minutes in the last week on OC and about sixty hours on your homicide."

"Will you quit referring to it as my homicide." Then, shaking his head, "You know what that was all about, don't you?"

"I think I do. I hate to think I do."

"I take it you didn't write up anything on Johnny Jonnell."

"Wrong. The sheets I wrote up on him and Rose Shaman and my contact with the *po*-leece down in East St. Louis are right here," he said, pointing at his inside coat pocket. "You don't spend all these years down here on State Street and come away thinking you can trust anybody."

"Norbie, you are a cop's cop."

"Thank you. So now where do you think he got the inkling we got a lead, you and me being the only ones that know about Johnny?"

"Let me put it this way. The only time I even remotely implied to anyone that we had a lead was in Facia's lawyer's office, when I was leaving. I should have kept my mouth shut. But it was just too good not to lay it on the creep. Couldn't resist." Morrison threw his arm around Castor's enormous shoulder. "Tells you something, doesn't it?"

"Yeah," Norbert said. "Small world, isn't it?"

THE DOCTOR out at Lutheran General was not immediately responsive to Morrison's request that they talk with Dennis Courtland. She explained that no one, not even family members, were allowed to visit with the patient during the first week, the most crucial period of the detoxification process, she said. But after Morrison explained that it was a homicide they were investigating and that they had just received some information pertaining to it that they very much needed to discuss with Mr. Courtland, she reluctantly agreed, with the stipulations that she be present when they saw him and that she would have the right to end the interview if she thought it was "in any way adversely affecting my patient." Morrison agreed. How many times had he done this before. By the time she decided her patient was being adversely affected, Morrison figured he would have gotten what he came for. "He is under some sedation,'' she added as they walked to the elevator, ''but should be fairly lucid.''

Courtland was in a private room in a wing on the third floor that was set off from the rest of the hospital by a pair of swinging doors, one of which bore a large sign that said No Admittance, Authorized Personnel Only. Inside the doors a young man in a grayish blue lab coat sat at a desk, monitoring, Morrison gathered, anyone who came in and keeping anyone from leaving who shouldn't be leaving.

Morrison and Castor were more surprised when they saw Courtland than he was at seeing them when they followed the doctor into his room. ''These two men are from the Chicago Police Department, Dennis,'' she said. ''They want to have a few words with you.''

Courtland nodded, recognizing Morrison. He was sitting in a chair by the window, which looked out on a shopping center across the street. The bed was made, the room rather sterile with its institutional light green walls. There was a large pastoral print framed on one wall and an embroidered scroll in script on another that read One Day at a Time. Courtland had on a plaid bathrobe and yellow silk pajamas. It was his face that momentarily startled Morrison and Castor. His right eye was a nasty black and purple, swollen almost shut, just a slot left to look out from. A large bandage covered the other side of his head, including the ear. He appeared especially pale and there was a noticeable tremor in his hands.

''Now if you find this interview getting to a point that is upsetting to you, just let me know and we'll end it,'' the doctor told him.

''I can't offer you a seat,'' Courtland said. ''We're only allotted one chair.''

''That's fine,'' Morrison said. ''We'll stand. What happened to you?''

''A little unpleasantness Friday night. As you can see, I didn't win.'' Courtland forced a little smile and as he did he turned in his chair and suddenly winced. He pointed at his chest. "Couple of cracked ribs to boot."

"Mugged?" Morrison asked.

"I guess you could call it that."

"Where?"

"Just off Division Street, west of Wells—Franklin, I think the street was."

"What were you doing in that neighborhood at night?" Actually Morrison had a pretty good idea already, aware of the kind of neighborhood it was, only a few short blocks from the gang-held, dope-ridden Cabrini-Green housing project, one of the most violent in the city.

Courtland sighed. "It's all part of the story. I intended to call you, clear the air of all this. But I thought I'd wait until I was in a little better shape. How did you find out I was here?"

"Your office. Hurley . . ."

"Ah, yes, Whiteside. I phoned him at home yesterday to tell him I wouldn't be in the office for the next six weeks or so and that he would be unable to reach me at all this week. The rules." He nodded toward the doctor, who was now sitting on the edge of the bed. "Hurley and I are good friends as well as business associates. He knew I overindulged in various things. I told him where I was and asked him to make something up for the rest of the office, our clients, anyone else. I'm surprised he told you."

"It was either that or everyone in your office and on the trading floor knowing you were avoiding a couple of detectives who were investigating a homicide."

"Well, you're here, so I might as well get on with it." Courtland raised a shaky hand to make a point. "Let me preface it. When we last talked, you implied—in fact said—you did not believe I was being totally forthright with you. Well, you were right, I wasn't. But only on two points."

"Only two?"

Courtland ignored the question, seemed removed for the moment, adrift in his own thoughts. Finally he said, "Let me tell you the whole story." He cleared his throat. "As is apparent, I have a substance-abuse problem. When you asked me certain questions I did try to mislead you. All of us who have the problem try to do that. Denial." He looked over at the doctor. "Isn't that right, Dr. Spanner?" She nodded in agreement. "I wouldn't admit it to myself, so how could I admit it to a stranger? So I tried to lead you to believe I was a moderate drinker and just a sometime Valium user. That was, of course, untrue."

Courtland seemed frail all of a sudden, the trembling in his hands more accentuated.

"What were you using?"

"Alcohol and Valium regularly. Cocaine on occasion. That's about it. But to an extent that I was addicted." He seemed to have difficulty saying the last part.

"That's why you went to Warner's in the snowstorm?"

"Yes, the need often overwhelms common sense. I needed my Valium and that's where the prescription was held, so I went there and got it."

"What else did you get there?" Morrison asked, a sharpness now in his voice.

"What do you mean?" Courtland tried to look bewildered.

"Look, Mr. Courtland, I'm going to level with you," Morrison said. "We have good reason to believe you were getting other drugs from Warner's, without a prescription and on a regular basis. In other words, that Warner's was a source of supply for you."

"Now where did you hear something like that?"

"We'll reveal our source at the proper time. Do you understand the implications of this?" Courtland looked at him nervously but did not answer. "You want to explain it to him, Norb?"

Castor took Courtland in. "You're fast becoming a

solid suspect in the murder of one Theo Warner, Mr. Courtland. Dealing drugs with the man illegally. The last person to see him alive. Arriving home stoned several hours, several unaccountable hours after the murder took place.'' Courtland seemed stunned, just staring back at the large detective as though trying through the sedation to understand what he was hearing. And when it did seem to come together in his mind he clearly appeared nervous, even frightened. ''I think I had better read you your rights, Mr. Courtland,'' Castor added. ''You have the right to remain silent—''

''Now wait a minute,'' Dr. Spanner interrupted, rising from the bed and stepping over beside Dennis Courtland. ''This is really more than I expected. It's out of line at this time and under the circumstances. You are upsetting my patient. You told me this was going to be an interview, not a third-degree.''

Morrison looked at her, saying to himself, You worry too much about your malpractice insurance premiums.

Courtland waved her off, looking at Castor and finally Morrison. His voice was weaker than before. ''I've got to clear this up . . . totally.'' He shook his head. ''You're correct that I have been getting something other than Valium from Warner's. For the last four or five years, in fact. But I want to say here and now I had nothing whatsoever to do with what happened to Theo Warner. He was in fine health when I left the store, looking forward, he told me, to his trip to Arizona the next day.''

''So what was it you got there besides Valium?'' Morrison asked.

''A mixture of morphine and cocaine. On the street they call it a speedball. Addictive, as I can attest to. But not something you need every day, if you have other things at hand to keep you numbed, that is.'' He had the look on his face as if he had just betrayed his best friend. Like he was digging into himself and finding it was painful.

"And that's what you really went over there for that night?"

"Well, actually, I went for both, the speedball and the Valium."

"And Theo Warner provided you with both that night?"

"No, no, Theo didn't have any made up. The Valium was easy but the other wasn't. Needless to say, you don't make up a batch of speedballs and leave them sitting around with another pharmacist back there and clerks coming in and out."

"Theo then made some up for you?"

"Theo never made them. I don't know if he even knew how. He never liked the idea, it was Bruce I normally dealt with. In fact, Theo even got into some big arguments with his brother from time to time over it. But Theo went along with it, I paid them handsomely, a lot more than one would normally pay for such. It was worth it to me, the safety, the convenience. Theo just tried to ignore the whole business. I think it was part of the reason he was planning to retire early."

"So you left without the speedballs?"

"Not exactly. I got Theo to call his brother at home just in case he had made them up and maybe had them with him or maybe had them hidden in the store. Well, he hadn't. Theo said I'd just have to come back in the morning, Bruce would be opening up the store. I got on the phone and, well, you know, the need I mentioned, I pleaded with Bruce to make me some. I offered him twice what I normally paid, said I'd give him a thousand dollars. That's two hundred fifty dollars a speedball! Well, he said okay, but he had this neighbor couple over and it would take him a little bit to get rid of them. But then he'd brew up the four for me. I said I'd come over. He lives down the street on Belmont next to the Belmont Hotel. He said no, that I should go over to the hotel and he'd meet me in the bar there whenever he finished. He warned me it might be an hour or so. I said I didn't care, I was just so relieved, and so I went over there and waited."

"Why is it the clerk up front at the cash register didn't see you leave?" Morrison asked.

"I went out the door in the back. The door back there opens into the alley. I often used that door when I came or left, being part of the family, so to speak." Courtland, now looking directly at Morrison, said, with emphasis, "And, please believe me, Theo Warner was alive and well when I left."

"What time did Bruce bring you the stuff?"

"That became my problem." He shivered even though the room was warm. "I took a Valium while I was in the store, then had several vodkas at the bar at the Belmont. Bruce didn't get there until about a quarter of ten. I had had perhaps five drinks by then and another Valium. When he finally got there I went into the john, into a stall, and shot up a speedball. I had all the paraphernalia with me. This is rather humiliating. But I had my needle and spoon and pack of matches. Whap, did it. Then I had one quick drink with Bruce back at the bar and drove home. How I made it, I'll never know. The speedball kicked in, mixed with the other stuff—I don't know. Things exploded. The only thing I remember is almost driving through the plate glass into the lobby of the Carlyle. I swerved in the driveway and rode up onto the sidewalk." He paused. "The doorman tell you that? I scared the hell out of him even though he was inside the building."

Morrison said, "The doorman told us he didn't even see you come in that night."

"I'll have to remember that next Christmas."

The doctor asked, "Are you getting tired? Would you like to continue this later?"

Courtland, very pale, said, "No, let me just finish up."

Morrison, who had been writing everything down in his pocket notebook, said, "That's a good idea. Get it all out."

"I wouldn't have wanted anything to happen to him." His voice now had a crack in it. "Theo was a nice gentleman, so is Bruce. I was the one who brought them into this." He seemed to lose it for the moment. Morrison and Castor waited. Then he reared up, coughed, settled back and said, "I wouldn't do anything to hurt them. I *needed* them. Do you understand that? *Needed* them." There was an uncomfortable silence. Then Courtland continued, his voice wavering. "I called Bruce after I heard about his brother. Told him how sorry I was. Then Bruce told me that the deal was off for the time being, no more speedballs. The police were in and out of the place. Everybody was eyeing everybody around the store since the murder, everybody nervous."

"So you went to the street?" Morrison asked.

Courtland looked like he might cry as he nodded his head. "I called Bruce again on Friday afternoon. Begged him. It was degrading. But he refused. He said maybe later after whoever did it was caught and the thing had blown over. But not now. So that night I went over to Wells and Division, just south of Old Town. You know where that is. I'd heard they dealt stuff right on the street around there, out of cars. I'd never done something like that before, didn't really know what I was doing. But I was desperate. I figured I could just look around, ask somebody. I stood there on the corner. It was freezing. Then I walked up and down Wells and on Division, back and forth. Finally these two black kids appeared from out of nowhere and asked me what I was looking for. This was right on the corner there. I told them and they said they could get me some freebase or some dime bags of coke. They said there was a drug house a couple blocks west of there where they could buy some. They'd do it if I gave them fifty dollars apiece above the cost of the stuff. I wasn't dumb enough to give them the money but I *was* dumb enough to go with them.'' Courtland tried to choke back a sob.

''Take your time,'' Morrison said.

''I went with them up to Franklin and they said the house was a block north. We got about half a block and suddenly they were hitting me, beating me. They took all the money I had, maybe a thousand dollars, and my watch, a Baume and Mercier. And after getting all that they started kicking me in the stomach, the legs, the ribs, while I was lying there next to the gutter. And then they ran off. I can't tell you the horror of it, the degradation I felt. It was so silent and dark there, that's what I remember after they left, lying there by myself on the sidewalk in this wretched neighborhood, any semblance of dignity destroyed. All I could hear was my own breathing and my groveling in the snow trying to get up. I managed to get back to my car and drive home.''

Courtland was crying now.

Dr. Spanner said, ''This *is* enough.''

But Courtland stumbled on. ''I got home, left the car on the street so I didn't have to go past the doorman, got the elevator at the lower level. I went upstairs and proceeded to drink myself to sleep. In the morning I got up and knew I was in trouble.'' He pointed again at the ribs. ''The pain was terrible. I looked at myself in the mirror and wanted to throw up. And so what did I do? I started drinking again until I *did* throw up. That's when I called my neighbor, a doctor, Donald Thorsen, an internist, got his wife and she knew immediately something was wrong. She got hold of him at his office and he came over and they brought me out here in an ambulance. It's all so mortifying . . .''

Morrison nodded to Courtland. ''That's it,'' he said and turned, and Castor and the doctor followed him out of the room.

Morrison looked at the doctor, some sympathy in his eyes. "Really bottomed-out," he said.

"That's the way we ordinarily get them," she said.

Norbert looked at both of them. "Better living through chemistry."

The doctor looked back at him. "You police have a peculiar sense of humor."

"NORBERT," MORRISON said as they were leaving the hospital, "I think your humor was wasted on the doctor."

"Who cares?" He was putting on his heavy leather jacket. "Let's get out of here . . . You think they never laugh, the doctors, make jokes about what they see every day like we do? They're human, aren't they? Aren't we all?"

Morrison didn't answer.

29

"YOU BELIEVE him?" Castor asked when they were in the car headed back to 11th and State.

"I've gotten to a point, Norb, where besides you I don't think I believe anybody anymore." The snow was melting, the temperature having reached into the forties that afternoon and still hovering there. The grimy snow was now turning into even grimier slush on the streets and sidewalks, reflecting wetly in its own murky way in front of the beams of the car's headlamps in the dim, late winter afternoon. Morrison was driving, passing cars by swerving into the left-turn lane and then jutting back in or roaring out into the oncoming traffic lane when there was a maneuverable space; Castor thought he would feel more comfortable if Morrison just threw the flasher on up top the car and kicked in the siren. At least let them know out there who they were dealing with.

"You know, Joe, I watched *Patton* the other night. And I swear you were one of the guys driving a tank up there, hell-bent on saving Bastogne. How 'bout giving my little ticker a break—11th and State is not under siege."

Morrison eased back into the flow of traffic. "I got to admit he sounded pretty straight up," he said. "I didn't pick up any signs of lying. But you make a big mistake if you start believing drugheads or anybody for that matter who has major reasons to lie to protect his ass.''

''You going to talk to Bruce about it?''

''Not yet. But later, I guess, I've got to.''

BACK IN Organized Crime, Morrison looked at the two messages on his desk, untouched since the morning. There was nothing new on his spindle. One of them was from the crime lab upstairs. He called and the evidence technician there told him they would have the results of all the tests he wanted typed and ready for him by noon the next day.

The other message was from Bruce Warner at the drugstore, and Morrison dialed the number.

''Just wanted to know how you were doing on the case, Joseph. Anything more on that girl and her boyfriend, the black?'' Bruce asked.

''We're still looking for her, Bruce.'' Morrison's mind wandered momentarily. After their talk with Dennis Courtland and the sudden vision of Thomas Alvin Bates that loomed in his mind, he realized he had to find the girl—alive. Then he thought of the legs with the painted toenails over at the Medill city garbage dump. ''We've got a countywide APB out on her. The sheriff down in her hometown, Mound City, he's keeping a running check to see if she shows up there. That's about all we can do for the moment.''

''Well, I just wish there was something I could do.''

Morrison saw Bruce Warner in his mind's eye mixing up speedballs under a lonely pyramid of light, hunched over a table all by himself in the night, dumping each into a plastic packet, pristine-pure, bowing slightly to Dennis Courtland as he handed them over, pocketing the thousand dollars, probably ten crisp hundred dollar bills, serial numbers in sequence, straight from Courtland's ample checking account downtown. Then he saw Bruce, sorrowful and defeated, sitting in the back room of his drugstore the morning of the murder, lost to all the police hubbub going on around him.

"You know, Bruce, I went through Theo's apartment the other day, looking through his papers, checkbooks, things like that, even went down to the Lake Shore National Bank where he had a safe deposit box. I was trying to find a name for the girl's aunt, thought Theo might have had something, some correspondence, a check written to her, but I came up empty. Is there any other place I might find something on her, anybody else who might know who she was? Did they ever go out with anybody else?"

"Well, not that I can think of offhand. Theo was always pretty much a loner with his girls. But let me think on it and if I come up with anything I'll sure let you know."

"Fine, Bruce. If we can locate the aunt we got a shot at finding the girl."

VINNY WAS talking to the Nigerian in the hall, learning that the note remained undelivered because the girl known as Jo Kane had not shown, when Tommy came lumbering down the steps, his cowboy boots clacking on the uncarpeted steps. Vinny groaned silently.

"You got something for me," Tommy said, "that why you over here?"

"I go," the Nigerian said, his eyes betraying the fact that he did not want to be around Tommy any more than Vinny did. He swiftly disappeared back into his apartment. They could hear the deadbolt turn, the chain screeching into its slot.

"Sorry, Tommy. Not a word to be heard."

"So what're you doin' over here?"

Looking for Jo, Vinny said to himself, so I can tell her the brain-dead ape from Georgia is still around and the cops are still looking for her, what do you think, you moron. "Aw, I just wanted to check with the spook there," nodding toward the Nigerian's apartment, "see what they get for rent over here these days. I think I gotta get out of my place the end of the month. You're still livin' up there?''

''Sometimes. Sometimes I shack up other places, things turn out right, you know what I mean.'' Tommy licked his lips.

''I'd be a little careful, I were you,'' Vinny said. ''The cops are really hot on that drugstore hit. They're all over askin' about Jo, askin' about you, too.''

''They got nothin'. Tried to have somebody ID me. Couldn't, so they got shit. And White's not talkin'.'' Tommy grinned. ''And Jo, she ain't goin' to do no talkin' either.''

''Oh, hey, Tommy, she wouldn't talk to cops. Believe me.''

''She wouldn't take up with niggers either, huh?''

''That's different. I mean that was the past. She got over all of that. She wouldn't do anything against you.''

''You keep in mind what I told you.'' Tommy patted the side pocket of his Eddie Bauer down jacket. ''You remember, over in the Tip Top.''

''I do, I sure do.''

Tommy turned and walked out.

Vinny headed straight for the pay telephone in the Wilson Avenue el station.

IT WAS shortly after five-thirty when Morrison picked up the telephone in OC.

''You're a hard person to get hold of, Morrison.''

He recognized Vinny's voice. ''You the mysterious caller the last two mornings, Vinny?''

''You got it.''

''So what's up?''

''I been hearin' some things, and I got a goodie for you.''

''Can you give it to me over the phone?'' Norbert was putting on his coat and Morrison gestured for him to wait.

Vinny looked around at the rush-hour jam of people hurrying in and out of the el station. "Sure. Maybe you'll take care of me later."

"Maybe."

"Actually what I'm givin' you is a freebie. Remember, I told you I ever got something on the street animal I'd give it to you gratis. But first let me tell you what I been hearin'. I heard it was Tommy and Manford White, you know, the spook who got himself killed, that did the drugstore job. Did it for the drugs. Don't know which of them iced the old man, but if I were a betting man I'd put my stash on Tommy. That girl, the one you're lookin' for, I heard she didn't have nothin' to do with it."

"That girl, Vinny, we place with the two of them across the street from the drugstore the night of the murder."

"Well, I'm just tellin' you what I heard. Maybe she found out what they were up to and left 'em. I don't know." Vinny could see it: the first, the very *first* words he would say to Jo when he found her would be "Give 'em Tommy." *Tommy* and *White* did it—*alone*, he'd tell her. You knew about it, Jo, and ran away 'cause you were scared of them. You weren't there. Don't worry about Tommy. They'll put him so deep in the pen he won't get out till he's eighty.

That is, if he found her alive.

"Vinny, you got something going with this girl?"

"Me? You kiddin'? What'd give you an idea like that?"

"I keep getting these little protective signals, and the only ass I ever saw you protect before was your own."

"You never did read me right, Morrison."

"I know, you're a closet philanthropist and it's been lost on me the past couple of years."

"A what?"

"Never mind, Vinny. You want to get on with it?"

Vinny did, wondering why Morrison was throwing

these two-dollar-bill words at him; not knowing what they meant, he didn't like that. "Anyway, like I told you, I also heard she might be like totally departed." Vinny then said warily, "I gather you don't got anything on that yet."

"Maybe we do, don't know for sure yet."

The alarms went off inside Vinny's head. "You do?"

Morrison ignored the question but noted the sudden rise in Vinny's voice. "Who'd you hear all this stuff from, Vinny?"

"Just street talk, Morrison. Pieced it together for you."

"That all of it?"

"No, Morrison. Now I'm gonna give you the freebie. You want this guy, Tommy Bates, right?"

"We do."

"Well, you got him. He's walkin' around with a piece on him, carries it in the side pocket of this parka-coat he wears."

"How do you know that?"

"He flashed it around in a saloon I was in the other night. Had it with him no more'n ten, fifteen minutes ago, too."

"How do you know that?"

"I just talked to him, jeez. It was fallin' out of his pocket. Believe me, he's carrying."

"You know what kind it is?"

"Looked like maybe a forty-five. You know, I don't know a lot about guns, not being a violent person . . . but it looked like an automatic, close as I could see."

"He still staying in the girl's apartment over on Sunnyside?"

"That's where I saw him, in the lobby, on his way out."

"What were you doing over there?"

"Jeez, everybody asks me that question. Can't a guy go apartment-hunting without havin' to answer to everybody and their brother about it?" Vinny was thinking would people ask Tony Bennett what he was doing in Tahoe if he just happened to tell them he was there? Hell, no.

"Okay, Vinnie, I owe you one."

"I already got it marked down and underlined."

"By the way, Vinny, this Jo Kane, who you seem to know pretty well, you know if she paints her toenails?"

Vinny thought for a moment, then said, "Yeah, I think she did. Why you ask a question like that?"

"I got a foot fetish."

"HOW ABOUT working a little overtime with me tonight?" Morrison said to Castor after he put the phone back in its cradle. "Our friend Tommy Bates is walking around the streets with a gun in his pocket."

"Oh, great."

"You don't have to, Norbie."

"I know I don't *have* to." He sank back into his chair, coat on, muffler hanging out the front, put his feet on the desk. "I'm just a dedicated public servant who would not let his partner wander around in the snow by himself."

Morrison called Area Six looking for Terry Sawyer, only to be informed that he had already checked out for the day. He told the detective in Violent Crimes that he wanted the search warrant Sawyer had ordered for the apartment in the Tudor Arms on Sunnyside a few days back, which had to be with the original file on the Theo Warner uncleared homicide case. He explained they were going after a prime suspect in the case who they now believed was carrying a concealed weapon—Morrison always hated putting it like that, nobody since the old west carried an *un*concealed weapon, but it was part of the jargon, part of the procedure. He said he would also like a pair of backup cops from either Homicide or the tactical unit, whoever was available.

IN THE squad room at Area Six Morrison, the search warrant now snug up against the spiral notebook in his inside coat pocket, explained to Castor and the two tactical-unit detectives how he would like to handle it. "I want to take it *on him*. I want him on the street with it." He looked at the two tac officers. "This guy's a real wild man. And he feels about cops the way you'd feel about genital warts."

"He served time down in Georgia for beating some guy to death in a fight," Castor added, wanting to be more than just an onlooker to the two tac detectives. "We don't know if he's used the gun to kill anybody yet, but we figure he's not carrying it for show."

Morrison said, "There's also a possibility if we ever find the carcass that goes with the two legs the garbagemen picked up in the vicinity of Uptown the other day we might find a bullet or two from that gun in it." He could see the tac detectives didn't follow him. "We heard from a snitch that this Tommy Bates may have whacked his former girlfriend who may have been involved with him in the drugstore homicide over on Belmont and Halsted about ten days ago."

"He's a real charmer. Wait'll you meet him," Norbert said.

THEY DROVE to the Tudor Arms in two cars, parked across the street, and all four went into the lobby. Morrison rapped on the janitor's door.

"Who there?"

"Police. Open the door."

The Nigerian did, the chain still on. Morrison showed him his badge and the door closed and then opened without the chain. Probably the only thing that frightened the Nigerian more than Tommy Bates was the sight of the four plainclothes detectives facing him.

"The big guy on the third floor," Morrison said,

"Tommy Bates. in Three-F, you know who I'm talking about?"

The Nigerian nodded.

"Is he up there now?"

"Don't know." The Nigerian looked from one detective to the other, his eyes asking something like when were they going to start beating him with clubs. "Look like he goin' out about a hour ago. Had a coat on. Don't know if he come back since."

"Your telephone over there," Morrison pointed to it, sitting on a small table across the room. "I need to use it."

The Nigerian stepped aside and Morrison went over to it. He noticed the woman standing at the entrance to the hall, light-skinned black, dreamy, cautious eyes fixed on him, the two-year-old next to her, one hand clutching her dress, the other with the thumb stuck in his mouth. There was an odor of food cooking, some kind of vegetables boiling that Morrison could not identify. He looked in his notebook for the telephone number he had jotted down the other day when they searched Jo Kane's apartment. He let it ring ten times. No answer.

"Don't go anywhere," he said to the Nigerian back at the doorway. "We might need you to let us in up there."

Out in the hall Morrison said to one of the tac officers, "You stay here, watch the front." Then to the other he pointed down the corridor. "There's stairs and a back entrance down there at the end just around the corner, kind of an enclosed back porch, you take that, it's the only other way out. We'll go up and see if anybody's in there who isn't answering the phone. If he's there I'll give him some bullshit: we're just checking, heard the girl was back in the neighborhood, give him that to suck on. Then we'll come back down here and stake out until he hits the street and take him outside. If he's not up there, maybe a couple of us can wander the neighborhood and the others can wait here for him."

Upstairs Morrison and Castor walked down the dimly lit hall to apartment 3-F. Morrison pointed to the light coming out from under the door. "Could be somebody's home or else it's Motel Six leaving the light on for you." His voice carried an echo in the empty, bare-floored hall. Morrison rapped loudly on the door to 3-F with his fist. They heard nothing inside. They waited, then he knocked again. This time Morrison thought he may have heard something. Norbert said he thought he did too, but wasn't sure it came from inside the apartment.

Morrison hammered harder this time. "This is the police," he shouted at the door. "If someone is inside, open the door." Nothing. "One more time," Morrison said to Castor. Pounding, "This is the police." Still nothing. He tried the knob but the door was locked.

"I'll go down and get the janitor," Morrison said. "I think maybe we should have a look around inside," and headed back down the hall to the stairwell.

Norbert waited. Then he heard it. The wailing scrape of wood on wood from inside the apartment, the unmistakable sound of an old window being opened. His heart jumped as he fumbled to get the .38 Smith&Wesson from his hip holster, a gun he had not drawn in the line of duty for more than ten years. With his other hand he hammered at the door. "Police, open the goddamn door." He heard the sound of the window being forced open again. "Open or I'll kick the goddamn thing in." Nothing. Gun out now and held in front of him with both hands, he raised his foot, aimed the size 12 triple E at a point just to the left of the doorknob.

Downstairs Morrison, search warrant in hand, was just about to rap on the janitor's door when he heard the muffled sounds of gunfire as they rolled through the corridors and down the stairs of the Tudor Arms, a fusillade of five or six shots fired rapidly, and then silence except for the noise of the tac detective throwing open the lobby door and running inside.

Both went for the stairs, pulling out their own guns as they ran. The other tac detective heard the shots, too, and held his ground at the back entrance, kneeling now behind a metal garbage can just inside the door to the alley, gun drawn, eyes on the stairs.

At the third floor hallway they stopped; Morrison in front peered down it, seeing only a silhouetted hulk slumped in front of the door to 3-F. He took off toward it, the tac detective held back, covering him. Morrison skidded to a stop on his knees in front of Norbert Castor, whose glazy eyes made contact. ''Oh, Jesus,'' Morrison said, then looked from Castor, whose hands were clutching his lower abdomen, to the still-shut door with the oblique line of holes and the splinterings around them that walked about a twenty-five-degree grade across the door. Morrison slid him away from the door as gently as he could.

''Heard somebody, thought they were going out the window,'' Castor said, his voice weak, strained.

''Take it easy, buddy.'' Morrison was tearing open Castor's coat. He could see the bleeding down where Castor had been clutching himself. The tac detective was now standing above both of them, his radio out, shouting into it: Ten-one, ten-one, police officer shot. Sunnyside Avenue, Uptown. He was stymied for the moment. Morrison, rolling his scarf into a ball, looked up. ''Nine-oh-eight Sunnyside, third floor,'' he said, then went back to Castor. ''Can you press this down, hold it there,'' he said as he pushed the rolled-up scarf onto Castor's bleeding abdomen. Castor nodded, clamping it down. ''Everything's numb down there, Joe.''

''Paramedics'll be here any second, Norb. Hang in there and keep that thing held tight.'' Morrison was on his feet now, standing to the side of the door. He motioned the tac detective to the other side. ''Cover,'' is all he said and then shot the lock off. When he knocked the door open it snapped off the bottom hinge and dangled listlessly. They were greeted by a waft of frigid air blowing in from the open window directly across the room.

The tac detective moved to the side of the bedroom door, then went into a crouch. Morrison went to the window. It was only a short jump to the roof of the four-flat next door. In the moonlight that glimmered on the slush-paved roof Morrison could see the track churned up by someone who had run across it and then across the roof of the building next to it.

The tac officer was back from the bedroom and bathroom. "Nothing in there."

"No," Morrison said, "he took off across the roofs, climbed down to the back porch on the other side and probably out into the alley."

Sirens now pierced the Uptown night, growing louder as they converged from various directions.

Morrison got on the tac officer's radio. "Police officer shot at Nine-oh-eight Sunnyside. Prime suspect escaped on foot, should still be in the area bounded by Wilson Avenue, Montrose, Broadway and Lake Shore Drive. Prime suspect, name Thomas Bates, sheets on him at Area Six Violent Crimes. About six-foot-four, two hundred fifty pounds, mid-thirties, long brown hair to about the shoulders. No make on what he is wearing." He went back to Castor.

"Dumb, Joe," Norbert said. "How could I be so dumb?" His breathing was labored. "Stood right in front of the fucking door. Just out of the Academy you know better than that . . ."

"Don't talk, Norb." It appeared to Morrison that the scarf had at least stanched the flow of blood some. He knelt there now pressing it down tightly himself because Castor's arm had gone slack and slid to the floor.

"Plus I'm such a fucking big target," Castor said, and then closed his eyes.

Moments later the hall was full of police. The paramedics went to work on Castor step by step, at the same time talking over their radio to the trauma unit at Ravenswood Hospital. Downstairs it was a movie set, except too real—all the lights flashing from the squad cars and the ambulance, the static-ridden noise of the radios, the commotion as police shouted at each other before fanning out on foot into the neighborhood.

After being briefed by Morrison and his own two tac detectives, the tac lieutenant from Town Hall set the manhunt in motion. Morrison followed the ambulance to the Ravenswood Hospital emergency room, where everybody would soon be gathering. A cop gets hit in Chicago, it draws a crowd.

WHILE THEY worked on Norbert Castor, Morrison went to the waiting room just outside emergency and called Norbert's sister, a pleasant woman he had met a couple of times before and who he knew was the only relative Norbert was close to. She said she would come right away. Morrison told her he would send a squad car for her. He called to Communications at 11th and State and gave them her address, then sat down to wait.

It was scarcely minutes later when the waiting room began to fill with police brass. The chief of detectives, Tony Morano, Morrison's friend, was among the first to arrive. Lieutenant Roland came in a little after him. The commander from Town Hall arrived with a sergeant from the same district. A couple of detectives from Area Six were there now. The Deputy Superintendent of Investigational Services was on his way, his dinner at a Rush Street restaurant interrupted by his beeper and the news a cop had gone down. It would not be long until the crime beat reporters from the *Tribune* and the *Sun-Times* and the television and radio people with their microphones and wires and mini-cams would be poking around and bothering everybody. What a way to make the ten o'clock news, Morrison thought.

It was about a half-hour after Tony Morano had arrived that they wheeled Norbert Castor up to surgery. Morrison was still talking to Morano when one of the uniformed cops pointed the emergency room resident in their direction.

"You the ranking police officer here?" he asked Morano.

Morrison thought he looked awfully young standing there in his pale green operating room outfit, the white mask hung around his neck.

"So far," Morano said. "And this is Detective Morrison, Detective Castor's partner."

The doctor looked at Morrison. "Sorry about your partner." He sounded like he meant it. "He took two bullets in the lower abdomen. I understand he was shot through a door. That must have slowed them down because neither exited. One cracked into his hip pretty bad, bounced around in there but doesn't seem to have done any other serious damage. The other entered just above the pelvis and has definitely done some damage to the spinal cord. We won't know how much until after surgery, that's where he's headed. I would list him as critical but I believe he'll make it." He looked from Morano to Morrison. "He has no feeling from the waist down at the moment. That could mean paralysis, but we won't know for certain until after surgery. You have any questions?"

"I don't think so," Morano said. Morrison shook his head.

"Well, if you have any I'll be around. Surgery's on four. There's a nice waiting room up there, if you want."

Soon after the doctor left, the door to the emergency room burst open and Alton Williams, the city's first black police superintendent, came through it, followed by an entourage that included the first deputy superintendent, the young lieutenant from Public Relations, the department's spokesman, and assorted other State Street officers.

Williams went over to Morano and Morrison, and after Morano brought him up to date on the situation the superintendent left to phone the mayor, who had already been told of the shooting. The mayor would not be coming over to Ravenswood, Morrison figured, as soon as he heard it was not a fatality, and especially when he learned there were no grief-stricken wife or kids at the hospital on whom he could lavish his compassion before the cameras. He would also be pleased to learn the suspect was as white as the wounded police officer. Interracial shootings were a major headache, they always got him bad press along with condemnations from all those other vultures out there who coveted his office.

Morrison detached himself from Morano and the remainder of the entourage when he saw Norbert's sister, surprisingly slender compared to her brother, come in the emergency room entrance with her husband and a uniformed officer. She looked bewildered, upset, so did her husband. "He's going to be okay, I think," Morrison said before she could speak. And he told her what the doctor had told him. He introduced them to Tony Morano and the others and then suggested he take them upstairs to the surgery waiting room. Morano suggested he wait until the superintendent returned.

Superintendent Williams, when he came back from talking with the mayor, bestowed his deepest feelings on them, praised Norbert Castor as a dedicated police officer who was now in the hearts and prayers of police officers throughout the city, and then excused himself and hustled off with the PR lieutenant to meet with the press and the media who were getting anxious down the hall in the hospital conference room.

They would be let down, the newspeople, Morrison thought as he walked with the sister and her husband to the elevator, when they found out Norbert was alive and would probably pull through—it would take the bite out of the story. A cop killed, that was a story, even in Chicago; wounded, shrugs all around, maybe sometime between weather and sports at ten and probably buried on page nine or ten in the morning.

SHORTLY AFTER nine o'clock Tony Morano stuck his head into the surgery waiting room on the fourth floor. "Joe, I need to talk to you," he said, trying at the same time to affect a smile for Norbert Castor's sister and her husband.

Out in the corridor Morano said, "We got your boy, Bates."

"Alive?"

"Very. That's the thing. According to the way I hear it he was sitting in a tavern on Montrose, half in the bag. Two patrolmen working that sector spotted him and called for backups. The tac dicks went in and took him."

"The gun?"

"No gun. And he's got two witnesses who swear he was in the saloon there from five o'clock until they grabbed him—the girl he was with and the bartender."

"The girl. You got a name on her?"

"Yeah." Morano pulled a sheet of paper from his inside coat pocket. "Faith Shipton. The bartender's Warren Oatford."

"You sure about the girl?" Morrison said, wondering if somehow Jo Kane had patched things up.

"That's the name they got. And she's not really a girl, like fortyish. She's a check-out clerk at the Walgreen's on Broadway." Morrison showed his disappointment. "They looked for a gun. The Tip Top Tap, it's called. Searched down everybody in it, including the broad. All told they came up with a couple of knives, a little grass on one guy—no gun. By the way, your unemployed redneck, Bates, had more than a thousand dollars on him."

"Where is he now?"

"In the lockup down at 11th and State. Took him down there to avoid problems. Superintendent insisted, safety first, you know. But it doesn't look like we're going to be able to keep him very long. We don't have anything. And by the way, there weren't any fingerprints on the window, just a pair of inconclusive hand-heel prints on the upper frame, smudges at best. That's apparently how he opened the window." Morano held his hands out in front of him, palms up, to demonstrate pushing up a window from the top frame.

Morrison's beeper went off. They both ignored it.

Morano said, "They're giving this Bates the good guy–bad guy routine downtown, got some heavyweights lined up to work on him, but like I said, we don't have anything other than we know he was staying in that apartment. You want to go down and have a crack at him?"

Morrison thought about it for a moment. "I think if I were in the same room with him tonight I'd kill him."

"Better you stick around here." Morano clapped him on the arm and went back downstairs.

30

WHEN MORRISON walked back into the waiting room, the surgeon was there talking to Norbert Castor's sister. "This is his partner," she said to the doctor by way of introduction, "Detective Morrison."

The surgeon nodded. "I was telling Mrs. Polanski and her husband that the surgery is over and Officer Castor is being taken to Post-op and then to Intensive Care where he'll be for at least the next twenty-four hours." He focused on Morrison. "Unfortunately one of the bullets severed Officer Castor's spine in the region of the fifth lumbar disc. There is nothing we can do to repair it. I'm afraid he will be paralyzed from the waist down." Morrison felt sick to his stomach. "We had to remove a portion of his large intestine. And we performed a colostomy. Other than that Officer Castor should make a full recovery."

Other than that, Morrison said to himself. *Other than that.* He pictured Norbert Castor in a wheelchair, a plastic bag attached to his side to collect his evacuations, a catheter up his flaccid penis to draw off urine.

"When can we see him?" the sister asked.

"You can see him after he's transferred to Intensive Care. But he won't be able to talk to you until probably tomorrow morning."

"I'll stay with him," the sister said, "so someone's here when he comes out of the anesthetic."

Morrison suddenly remembered that Castor's sister was a nurse. "How long will that be?" he asked the doctor.

"I'd say four or five hours."

"I'll be back around then," Morrison said to the sister. Then to the doctor: "The bullets?"

"We retrieved both of them. They've been tagged and sent downstairs to be held for whomever is going to take them to your crime lab."

FROM THE pay telephone in the hospital lobby Morrison called in to 11th and State in response to his beeper. There was a message for him. "Call Vinny." And a telephone number.

"J.J.'s." a harsh voice said after Morrison dialed the number.

"Vinny Salerno there?"

The voice called out "Vinny," a moment later Morrison heard the familiar voice, "Salerno here."

"You called, Vinny."

"Oh, Morrison, you got my message."

"Can you talk from there?"

"Yeah. Might have to jumble it up a little if Mason comes down to this end of the bar. I heard what happened, jeez. At first I thought it was you mighta got hit. Knowin' what I know and all."

"It was my partner."

"Is he . . ."

"Bad, but it looks like he'll live."

"There were coppers all over the neighborhood. Two of 'em came in here, that's how I heard about it. I almost fell off the fuckin' barstool when I heard they were lookin' for Tommy about shootin' a cop. I asked who the cop was and one of 'em gave me a name and it wasn't yours." A pause. "You find Tommy yet?"

"They got him."

"Hey, terrific." Vinny's joy was not some sudden appreciation for effective policework, it was the thought that Tommy was off the street, way the hell off it.

"You heard anything more at all on that girl, Jo Kane?" Nothing, Vinny told him. "You know a place called the Tip Top Tap, Vinny?"

"Sure, I know the joint, on Montrose."

"That's where they found Bates."

"Jeez, what a moron. He shoots a cop and then goes and sits in a bar a couple blocks away."

"He's got an alibi."

"Whaddya mean? I heard it went down in that apartment he was staying in over on Sunnyside."

"It did. He shot Castor through the door, closed door. He got out the window. Nobody got a look at him. You know a woman named Faith Shipton, about forty, works in Walgreen's on Broadway?"

"Nope, never heard the name."

"How about Warren Oatford?"

"Sure, he's the bartender at the Tip Top."

"They both swear Tommy was in there from five o'clock on. Never left the place."

"You know, Oatford's pretty palsy with Tommy, the only pal the redneck's got."

"You think he might lie for him?"

"Who knows? You want me to schmooze around a little for you?"

"That would be good, Vinny."

"I'll take a hike over to the Tip Top. See if I hear anything. I'm tired of this joint anyway."

AFTER HE hung up, Morrison started to walk away but then hesitated, looked at his watch. It was almost ten o'clock. He felt frustrated, there was nothing more he could do, short of going down to 11th and State and shooting Tommy

Bates in the balls. He needed to calm down, a cleansing. He walked back to the telephone and dug out his notebook to find the number.

"You busy?" he asked Linda Tate when she answered the phone.

"Not really."

"You into works of mercy?"

"What do you mean?"

"I feel the need to talk to someone."

"Where are you?" He sounded strange, she thought.

"At the hospital."

"The hospital?"

"Ravenswood. My partner was shot. He just came out of surgery. Going to be crippled for the rest of his life."

"Oh, my God. Were you with him?"

"Sort of."

"Are you *in* the hospital?"

"No, just at it."

"Are you all right?"

"Sort of."

"You want to come over here?"

"I want to come over there."

LINDA TATE had the ten o'clock news on when Morrison got there, it was just ending. "They had it on about your partner," she said after taking his coat. "Said they had a man in custody."

"For a while anyway. He's got an alibi. Don't know if it'll stand up, but if we can't break it he'll walk out of there tomorrow." Morrison took his sport coat off and draped it over a chair. "You got any of that Jack Daniels left?"

She walked to the bar and he followed. She found it a little unsettling looking at the gun holstered on his hip. "They said the man was a suspect in another murder case but not which one. Was it the one with the druggist?" Morrison nodded. He looked tired, drained, Linda thought.

He poured about three ounces of the Jack Daniels over the ice in the glass she handed him. "Incidentally, I had a little chat with your former friend this morning. You know where I talked with him? The detox unit out at Lutheran General."

He told her Dennis Courtland's story, and when he finished she told him she was not surprised. Then he told her about the shooting, about Tommy Alvin Bates and his alibi, about the guilt that he was beginning to feel for involving Castor in the first place, about the anger he felt. It happened then, as they both must have known it would. It started on the couch, naturally, effortlessly, like the other evening in the car when Linda Tate went back to high school and so did Morrison. Only this time the blouse came off, and the bra, and they went into a bedroom to a bed with a quilted comforter and sheets that had a faint aroma of flowers.

It was quicker than she would have liked. She preferred a gradual journey—caressing, fondling, stroking, mouths exploring, bodies in gentle motion against each other, but all the while the heat and longing steadily accelerating, intensifying, until every desire inside her cried out for him to enter her, ride with her. But she sensed in him the need to be quickly devoured, to replace the horror and sadness of the earlier evening with the passion and pleasure of the night, and she complied.

She lay there on the bed, her leg casually draped over his. "I think we graduated," she said.

"What?"

"From high school."

He gave a short laugh and gathered her close to him. "It was like I had to be torn away from things," Morrison said. "I don't think I ever felt that way before. I had to be ripped out of it. And I was." He patted her rump in appreciation.

"Good."

"I wasn't very considerate of you."

"That's okay." She patted him on the rump. "We'll go slower next time."

IT WAS nearly one-thirty when Morrison walked into the Intensive Care Unit at Ravenswood. Norbert Castor was in a private room, illuminated only by a night-light and the dials and digital readings on the equipment that was providing him the intensive care and monitoring his condition. His sister, a shadow, sat in a chair next to the bed.

"How's he doing?" Morrison said to her.

"He came out of it about a half-hour ago. Seemed lost at first. Then he seemed to get with it. He recognized me but couldn't talk." She nodded toward the two tubes that went down Norbert Castor's throat. "They come out first thing in the morning, I'm told. Then he dropped off to sleep so I turned out the light."

The light came back on, the switch flipped by a nurse, a young woman who had learned to smile despite the human misery she dealt with five nights a week, carrying the tools of her trade: blood-pressure kit, digital thermometer, syringe and a couple of towels. She told them Norbert was doing "just fine." All his vital signs were good. And then she asked them to wait outside. When she came out about ten minutes later she said he was awake.

Castor raised his hand in recognition when Morrison stepped back into the room, almost dislodging the tube that was stuck in his arm. He said something that sounded like "ohhh," which Morrison took to be Joe. Morrison walked over and stood beside the bed, putting his hand on Castor's burly arm. "You're going to be okay, Norbie," he said. "Doctor said it takes more than two bullets to bring down a grizzly bear."

Castor tried to smile, pointed at the tubes going into his mouth and said something unintelligible. "He's not happy about those," the nurse standing at the foot of the bed said.

"Just take it easy, Norb. Don't try to talk. They're

going to have those things out of your mouth in a couple hours."

"That's right," the nurse added. Castor started to nod off again. "He's still pretty heavily sedated," she said to Morrison and the sister, "but he'll be much better in the morning. I think we should let him rest for now."

The three of them walked out into the corridor leaving a dozing Norbert Castor perhaps to scrambled clips from *Casablanca* or *Twelve Angry Men*, or whatever was on the channel his mind was now tuned to. Morrison told the sister he would be back in the morning, maybe around nine or ten. "Tell Norb when he wakes up, by that time we hope to have Tommy Bates's balls nailed to a cellblock wall."

Before he left the hospital Morrison checked with 11th and State. Nothing new. Tommy was holding to his story, which did not surprise Morrison. They were going to keep at him throughout the night, one of the detectives handling the interrogation told him. Wear him down, he said. They would not succeed, Morrison thought, not downtown; probably not even in a district stationhouse where a cop shooter was in a far more precarious position, where the shooter sometimes got so desperate to escape he jumped out a second-story window, or so nervous that he fell down a long flight of stairs, or, well, they just seemed to have a lot higher accident rate in the stationhouses.

The detective said they had looked all over the roofs of the two four-flats for the gun as well as along several routes Tommy might have taken to the tavern, but it was dark and so far they had come up with nothing. They would search again in daylight. The Assistant State's Attorney was already talking about releasing Tommy first thing in the morning, the detective said, unless they came up with something, anything. Morrison said he wanted to talk to the ASA, but learned he was gone and would not be back until morning. Morrison left a message for him, and went home to get a few hours' sleep.

31

WITH THE kid not having a telephone, Morrison woke Vinny up in person.

Not a morning kind of guy, Morrison thought as he looked at Vinny's puffy face, watery eyes, and tousled hair, standing there still sleep-dazed in his jockey shorts and T-shirt; staring back, trying to clear the cobwebs.

All Vinny could think was that two seconds ago it was two-thirty in the morning, his boozy head hitting the pillow, and then out of nowhere somebody's trying to break down the door, and he almost shatters a shin bumping it on the end of the bed frame, stumbling into it, the shit scared out of him, until he finds out it's Morrison, and Morrison is standing there all dressed up like he's going to a wedding—overcoat, tie, little gold bar holding the collar underneath it, shiny shoes—looking serious, walking right in, asking questions. More than two seconds had passed, though, nearer twenty thousand. It was just past eight in the morning.

Vinny, shivering, went back to the bed and grabbed the blanket and wrapped it around himself, then proceeded to tell Morrison he had not found anything to refute the story that Tommy had spent the entire evening in the Tip Top. Nobody was talking about it over there, situations like that in Uptown were commonly ignored, conveniently forgotten, Vinny pointed out. He did, however, find out who the woman Faith Shipton was—an old friend of Warren the bartender. She had been hanging with Tommy for close to a week now, he heard last night. She had been unhappily married to Warren's brother, Malcolm, who Warren hated and almost killed in a drunken rage one night about a year ago, leaving him just alive enough to stagger out of Uptown forever, endearing Warren to Faith for life.

Another thing. There was something about Tommy and Warren being in business together, too, something like warehouse heists. Tommy would scout around during the day and mark a place, then they'd hit it late at night using Warren's van. Once or twice a week, they'd work. A guy who was alleged to fence certain stolen property and happened to be in the Tip Top told him that, Vinny said. Neither of which he approved of, Vinny assured Morrison, heisting warehouses or fencing.

Vinny debated telling Morrison the last thing, then decided what the hell, he didn't use that stuff anyway. "Heard also if you wanted some horse you could talk to Warren or Tommy about it. Not bags, now. One-shot deal, maybe a half-K. Quick clean sale's what they want. That's the scoop, Morrison."

Go back to sleep, Morrison said, and dropped a twenty-dollar bill on the card table and left.

Morrison wondered as he stepped out onto Broadway in front of the Army Surplus Store, across the street from the Covenant Thrift Shop and the World Outlet Shoes store, under the roar of an el as it clattered and screeched into the Wilson Avenue station, just what kind of dreams Vinny must have.

NORBERT CASTOR was awake, looking pretty damn alert under the circumstances, Morrison thought as he walked into the Intensive Care room. The tubes were gone from his mouth, though the ones in his arms were still in place.

And the machines were still pumping, monitoring, blinking, sending their signals out to the nurse's station.

"Well, my partner's awake," Morrison said. "More than I can say he'd normally be at this hour down on State Street."

"You asshole," Castor said weakly but with the trace of a smile.

"So how you doin', pal?" Morrison reached down and held Castor at the wrist. "You look a lot better than the last time I saw you."

"Betty left. Helluva sister, huh? She stayed here all night. Went home to get a little sleep. You were here last night, too, or else that was just part of the nightmare."

Morrison smiled, thinking it really would take more than a pair of bullets to drop a grizzly. "I was here, and you were grouchy . . . just like any ordinary day. Anybody else been in?"

"Yeah, the doctor, he took the tubes out of my throat, then we had a wonderful conversation, gave me all the wonderful details. Two seconds after he's out of here the Chief's got two guys in here. I told 'em"—his raspy voice began to crack but he cleared his throat as best he could—"this is all I could tell them. I heard noise inside, a window opening, I figured, and I went to kick in the door, then I heard World War Two and then I saw the ceiling and then I saw you, and that was it. Big help, huh?"

"Well, you were right about the window."

"He went out it, I heard."

"He did."

"They got the ape, the guys from Morano's office told me."

"Bates is in the lockup, eleventh floor of our home office. Only thing is, it's going to be tough." Morrison then told him the story, the alibi, all that he knew about it at the moment, much the same way he had told Linda Tate—only difference being when he was done he did not slip into bed with Norbert Castor. He could see Castor was very tired, struggling to stay with it. He decided not to tell him that he had talked with the ASA on the telephone a little earlier and was barely able to persuade him to keep Tommy Alvin Bates in custody until Morrison got down there to interrogate him. At noon Bates would walk, the ASA said, if they did not come up with something reasonably substantial. And Morrison felt sure that Tommy now would not only walk out of 11th and State but he would keep on walking out of Chicago and Illinois as well and lose himself in the bowels of some other city.

The nurse came in, Morrison left. Waited in the hall. The nurse came out, he went back in. "Where were we?" Morrison asked.

"We were somewhere between the fiftieth and fifty-fifth time she has stuck a needle in me. I hate needles."

"I really feel bad about this, Norb." Morrison shook his head.

"So do I. You know what I feel worst about? What I don't feel!" Castor started coughing.

"Take it easy, Norb."

"Did they tell you?"

"Yeah, they did."

"How the fuck am I gonna get a wheelchair around in the sand in Florida, Joe?"

"Slowly," Morrison said. "But maybe we can get you one with treads, like the kind on tanks."

"Hey, yeah, I could be the Rommel of Fort Lauderdale." He paused. "Norbert the Desert Fox."

"Norbert, if anybody's going to make it, it's you."

"I'll give it a shot. But it's not what I had in mind."

Morrison patted Castor on the shoulder. "I've got to get downtown. I've got a guy I want to get." He started for the door, then turned back. "Look at it this way, Norb, you're going to get all the good parking places now." Castor managed a weak laugh, then started to cough again.

Morrison thought that that doctor out at Lutheran General was right, cops do have a peculiar sense of humor. "Anything you need?" Morrison asked from the doorway. "I'll stop back probably around the end of the day."

"No. But be careful out there. It's more dangerous than I thought."

THERE WAS a note on Morrison's spindle when he got to OC. From Terry Sawyer, it said the beat patrols who had snooped around Uptown had not found any spare body parts. That prompted Morrison to phone the Medical Examiner's office—he liked it better when they used to call it the morgue, morgue sounded more honest—only to find out that they had not gotten around to examining the legs with the painted toenails. They promised to get to them as soon as they could after Morrison explained there might be a link between the person who detached them and the person who shot a police officer the night before.

TOMMY WAS standing there, slouched against the wall in the interrogation room, arms handcuffed to a steel railing that was bolted to the wall, ankles in eighteen-inch shackles, waiting. Morrison's first thought as he stepped into the room was that he was entering the ring with one of those grotesques that made their living pretending to wrestle on some obscure cable-television channel. But Tommy was not going to come raging out of his corner for a flying dropkick, not unless he could take a major chunk of the south wall of police headquarters with him.

There were two other detectives behind Morrison, orders of Chief of Detectives Tony Morano, who took no chances.

Tommy Bates glared across the room at him. "You the one that's causin' me all this shit," he announced. "I shoulda figured that."

"You the one that's causing yourself all the shit. You

wouldn't be in it if you didn't take potshots at police officers, asshole.''

Tommy stared at him for a moment, then broke into laughter. ''I got to thank you, officer, you and your buddies did me a fine service last night, you all breakin' up a robbery in progress in my place of residence. Scared that dumb dude of a burglar off and saved my valuable property. Have I properly thanked you?''

In the room there was only a desk and a chair on either side of it. Morrison put his foot to one chair and sent it skidding across the floor toward Tommy. ''Have a seat if you want,'' he said as it bounced off Tommy's leg.

''You know, I don't even remember your name,'' Tommy said. ''Only thing I remember is I got a real hate for you.''

Morrison ignored the remark. ''You got a lawyer? You want him in here with you?''

''Like I told 'em last night, I don't need no lawyer. Don't need no snively-ass kid standin' up for me. You got nothin'. I got two witnesses to where I was when your asshole buddy got shot.''

Morrison sat on the edge of the desk. ''Suppose I got a witness that places you elsewhere, places you at the apartment?''

''You can't.''

''Why not?''

''Cause I weren't there. Not since four-thirty or so.''

''You know that Detective Castor is alive?''

''Don't know, don't care.''

''You crippled him, put him in a wheelchair for life.''

Tommy shrugged. ''You mean some no-good burglar did.''

''I was with him this morning at the hospital.'' Tommy just stared at Morrison. ''What if I told you he saw the man who shot him as the man ran out of the apartment, gave me a description of him?''

"Then that's the guy you should be lookin' for instead of hasslin' me."

"The description fits you."

"Lotta handsome guys like me around." He fixed Morrison with a dreamy gaze. "I know he didn't see me there, I know it for fact. Nice try."

"How do you know it?"

"You *know* how I know it." There was electricity in the silence. "But just to keep the record straight, let me repeat, it's like I told you, I weren't there. Got my witnesses."

"We both know why he couldn't ID you. And it's not because you weren't there."

"You so smart, you cops, you know everything. Your buddy, he was real smart, fuckhead goes and gets himself shot." Tommy shook his head. "Real genius."

Morrison was off the desk and beside Tommy before the other two detectives knew what was happening. All they saw was a kind of blur and then Morrison's hand slamming into Tommy's crotch, staying there, grasping tightly.

It got Tommy's attention.

As he squeezed, Morrison said, "You shut the fuck up about my partner or these balls I got in my hand are going to be raspberry jam."

One of the detectives standing behind the desk looked at the other. "You think he should be doing that?"

The other said, "I don't know, is there anything specific in the manual about squeezing a suspect's balls?"

"I think for minor offenses there is, you know, traffic violations, things like that. But I'm not sure about a major, like shooting a police officer."

"I'm not either. Maybe we should go look it up."

Even Tommy, who was doubled over now and emitting gasping sounds, had his soft spots. Morrison squeezed harder. "Am I making myself clear?"

Tommy grunted, tried to twist away but there was no place to go.

The first detective called out, "Joe, we're wondering if this, uh, falls under what you would call the proper line of questioning. We're not sure now it isn't. We're probably gonna have to go look it up so as to be sure. But in the meantime we thought maybe we should go on record as voicing our concerns."

Morrison looked over at them, then back to Tommy. "I want an answer."

"Okay, okay," Tommy said rather breathlessly.

"Now, lest you want to sing soprano in the Uptown Boys Choir I want you to say 'I'm sorry.'"

Tommy uttered an agonized moan as Morrison increased the pressure.

"Well?"

"Ah'm sorrah," is the way it came out.

"You're *real* sorry." A little additional squeeze. "Say it."

After the sudden shout of pain, Tommy said, "Rawl sorrah."

Morrison let go and walked back to the desk. "Now let's see, where were we? Oh yeah, your whereabouts last night."

Tommy remained slightly bent over, waves of pain still engulfing his testicles and rolling upward into his stomach. His eyes seemed about to pop out of his head, but that was from the firestorm building inside rather than the pain.

"We're going to break one or both of your so-called witnesses," Morrison said, hoping to sound convincing because, judging from what he knew of the two, it was unlikely, "and when we do your ass is ours." Tommy just stared at him. "And when we find the girl, your pal who set up the druggist, we're going to turn her and you'll be facing murder one." Morrison searched for any kind of reaction, anything that would tell him what might be going on inside Tommy's mind. But Tommy was as impassive as if Morrison had told him nothing more than that there was a front of warm air headed for the Chicago area.

"You got nothin'. You ain't goin' to get nothin'."

"We've got you placed with her and the black guy in a car across the street from the drugstore the night of the murder. We've got the three of you placed in a saloon there as well." Morrison hoped the next one would invoke something. "We got her in the drugstore that day looking for the man, asking for him the day that he was killed. We're going to turn her. Count on it."

Nothing. The wall-eyes did not even lose focus. "When do I walk out of here?" was all he said.

"One second before the time the Assistant State's Attorney tells us we can't keep you any longer."

"Mebbe I ought to talk to that man."

Morrison turned to the other two detectives. "Get him out of here."

They got a guard to uncuff Tommy from the railing. Morrison walked with them from the interrogation room down the corridor to the entrance area of the lockup. There were some people sitting there in the plastic, armless chairs, the ones that looked like flattened pears, the ones they had for the relatives or friends waiting for their loved ones to be released or to learn their loved ones are not going to walk unless the relative can come up with, say, ten or twenty thousand to cover the hundred- or two-hundred-thousand-dollar bail necessary to get the loved one back on the street. No wonder they looked morose. All of them gazed vacantly at Tommy as he shuffled along in the shackles, forced into mincing steps so out of character, his hands cuffed behind him, with his coterie of three detectives and a uniformed guard. There were several other police officers standing around talking quietly. It was like a wake without a corpse laid out.

Tommy took it all in as the guard behind the desk

logged him back into the lockup, saw all the people there—witnesses—then turned to Morrison, grinning, and said, "You know, as I probably won't be seein' you again, I thought I ought to tell ya I'm as happy as a fly in shit your buddy got shot last night. Only thing that'd make me more happy be if it were you instead."

Morrison lunged but the other two detectives grabbed him before he could get a hand on him, one of them saying, "Jesus, Joe, cool it." Tommy just kept grinning back over his shoulder at Morrison as the guard led him through the now open gate into the cell block, the cold corridor picking up his last words resoundingly. "He'll be ridin', your buddy, in a buggy, wheelin' himself along but I'll be walkin', maybe hoppin' and skippin' right out of here."

32

MORRISON SAW Terry Sawyer sitting at the other desk in his cubicle when he strode in looking like a man who had just confronted the molester of his daughter.

"How's Castor doing?"

"I'd say he's doing surprisingly well for a guy with a severed spinal cord and a hip that's a pile of splinters. He even called me an asshole this morning, so we know he's alert. What brings you downtown?"

"I was at the lab. Just thought I'd stop by and see how the resurrected homicide cop was doing. They told me you were upstairs chatting with the animal."

"Animal is too nice a name. You combine a psychopath and a rabid gorilla and you're closer."

"I took the liberty of answering your phone. Ballistics said to tell you the bullets they took out of Castor and the three they took out of the wall in the hall were fired from a nine-millimeter gun, from the markings probably a Beretta—fourteen-shot automatic."

"I heard it was an automatic Bates was waving around."

"Also said to tell you they were remarkably similar to one of the bullets that had passed through the head of a known heroin dealer the night before and was dug out of the roof of his car, a silver Lincoln Continental."

Which set off a siren in Morrison's mind. Sawyer then proceeded to tell him what else he knew, which was rather skeletal and secondhand, this being an Area-Four homicide. The dealer, one Emilio Rodriguez, was shot inside his car next to a vacant lot almost under the Stevenson Expressway near Damen Avenue at about three in the morning. Rodriguez was in the driver's seat, and the bullet entered just under the chin, point-blank, taking off most of the top of Emilio's head and repainting the roof of his car. The EV tech, always alert for details and trying to spice up his report with a little graphic imagery, noted there were suction-cup-based statues of Our Lady of Guadelupe on one side of the dashboard and a brown-robed Franciscan friar on the other, in between a sponge-rubber replica of a nude couple embracing or copulating, depending on your imagination, that dangled from the rearview mirror. He also said that the overall interior looked like a turn-of-the-century whorehouse, what with the fringed and brocaded upholstery with matching pillows.

One witness who lived about a block away, another Mexican, said he heard the shots and looked out the window. He saw two men running to another car, jump in and take off, but it was too dark and too far away to get a make on the car or the two. The men looked big, according to the Mexican, which Sawyer shrugged off, saying everybody looked big to a Mexican.

Morrison clapped his hands together and held them that way in front of him. "That's it," he said. "Now it makes sense." Sawyer looked at him for an explanation. "The one thing I couldn't figure about last night. What was the goon doing in there that he'd shoot at a cop rather than be caught doing it?" Morrison unclasped his hands, tapped them on the desk in front of him. "My snitch, Vinny, he told me this morning he heard the slimeball upstairs and his alibi, the bartender, were trying to move some heroin. I bet my ass Tommy Bates didn't get around to ditching the gun and was sitting in there with it and probably a shitload of heroin too. No wonder he didn't want us popping in on him."

"Incidentally, I checked with Town Hall a few minutes ago. They been back over there looking down every sewer hole, in every garbage can, everywhere, since seven this morning but they haven't found a gun."

"Bates may be a psycho but he's street-smart." Morrison shook his head. "He knew as soon as we knocked on that door he had to get rid of the gun now that it had been used, and especially after shooting at Norb. You can bet he's been creative about dumping it."

"Well, they're still at it. They're also going door-to-door, see if anybody saw the ape on the street between the time he says he got to the tavern and the time the tacs took him."

"Oh, what I'd give to have a gun with the psycho's fingerprints on it. But even if we find the goddamn gun, I'm sure it'll be clean. I got one potshot, though. My snitch saw him waving it around. If he could identify it, then I got a tie between Bates and the gun. Don't know whether that'll be enough but it'd be more than we have now. I think I'll bring Vinny down here, let him look at our collection, see what he can come up with."

"Well, I gotta get back to Six, Joe. You need anything, give me a holler, I'll be inside all day."

THE TELEPHONE rang just as Morrison was on his way out to see the Assistant State's Attorney, his mind preoccupied with how he was going to try to talk the ASA into holding Bates another day or so—like selling icicles to an Eskimo, he thought. But worth a try.

The voice on the other end belonged to an authoritative black man, the deputy chief of police of East St. Louis, Illinois, a town Morrison had once passed through and one that by comparison, would give a leper colony resort status. He wanted to talk to Detective Castor.

"He can't come to the phone right now," Morrison said.

"When can he?" The voice was not only authoritative, it had a clear hostility.

"Not for a while. He was shot last night. Twice, in fact."

There was silence at the other end. Hostility fading maybe. Then: "Sorry to hear that."

"He's getting along. Maybe I can help you, I'm his partner." Morrison listened as the voice told him that he was responding to Detective Castor's inquiries about Johnny Jonnell, who indeed had returned home.

"This Johnny Jonnell you're looking for up there is now in detention down here," the deputy said. "Deep shit, too."

Who said you can't go home again, Morrison thought.

"Johnny and his buddy tried to stick up a liquor store last night," the deputy said. "Wrong place. The owner's son heard what was goin' on, came out of the back room like Wyatt Earp. Shot the other guy, name of Duane Harper. He's history. Jonnell shot back, nicked the kid, wounded the owner, not bad, just in the leg. Got out but we grabbed him a block and a half away, the gun still on him. Not too bright."

Morrison agreed that, no, Johnny Jonnell was not too bright at all. "Harper," Morrison said, "a white guy, used to be Jonnell's roommate at Pontiac?"

"You got it. This Jonnell goin' to do heavy time on this one, which happens to be his third major."

"I'll pass the word on to my partner. He'll be happy to hear the news."

"You wantin' somethin' up there with this Jonnell?"

"I think you got enough," Morrison said, thinking the last place in the USA he wanted to visit was East St. Louis.

Johnny Jonnell off the street, his buddy off the face of the earth, that should do it, no more rapes from that duet. Maybe in a few days he would update Norbert's sheets on Jonnell and his buddy and drop them on Roland's desk, depending on how he felt about Jonnell at the time . . . maybe not. He'd talk to Norbert about it. "If we want anything more we'll be in touch. But one thing, even though we haven't got anybody pressing any charges, he did rape somebody up here, he and his late buddy. So don't do him any favors."

"We don't intend to."

MORRISON INVOKED every art of persuasion at his disposal in talking with the young Assistant State's Attorney. Listen to me, he said, trying to sound imploring, one thing he was not very good at but making the effort anyway. He was certain Thomas Alvin Bates was the man who shot Detective Norbert Castor. It occurred in the apartment where he was staying. They had a tip he was carrying a gun. There was an all-out search going on that very moment for the gun. The same gun might be the one that was used to dispatch a heroin dealer on the west side the night before. An informant had told them Bates might be trying to move some heroin. Bates had played games with Morrison during the interrogation earlier that morning, implying he might have done it. There was so much they were trying to pull together at the moment. Getting close.

And, by the way, he was a goddamn psychopath.

Point two. There was a very good chance he was the person who murdered Theo Warner or at least was there when the murder took place—the fingerprint check had not yet been completed, in fact, Morrison pointed out—grasping at the old straw game he so often talked about but not letting the ASA know that. The girl in the case, *his* former girlfriend, had not yet been found, and he was convinced they could turn her if they could just get their hands on her and then they would have Bates, Murder One.

He was a goddamn psychopath . . . who almost killed my partner . . . who probably killed the only close friend my father ever had in life. Morrison looked at him, the intensity apparent.

The ASA looked back across the table, snapped open his briefcase—they always do that, Morrison thought, can't talk without a prop—and took out a sheaf of papers, held them up, shook them a little. "You got nothing," he said. "We got nothing. We don't have anything by five o'clock, he's out of here." He put the papers he had been waving back in the briefcase, snapped it shut. "Case closed."

"He walks, he's walking way far away, things being what they are now," Morrison said. "He knows it. He's guttter-smart. You corner him, he'll lash out at you, bite the shit out of you. You threaten him and he senses the consequences, and he does now, and you give him the chance, he's gone. And it'll be a cold day in hell before we find him. Give me seventy-two hours more. You can come up with something, you guys always can if you want."

The ASA looked at him, adjusted his tie to make sure the knot was not slipping down. "You people just don't understand. This is not a game, good guys beat up bad guys. The law's the law. That's why we have it."

"Don't give me that bullshit. The law bends . . . if you guys want it to. Seventy-two hours, all I ask."

"Police academy is not law school," the ASA said, then stood up, briefcase in hand. "Five o'clock. You come up with something, we can talk again. If not . . ." He shrugged and walked out.

Morrison just glared after him. He looked at his watch, it was ten after twelve.

THE CONVERSATION was bizarre from the outset when Morrison, after going back to his cubicle on the third floor, returned the call to the Medical Examiner's office. Who he got was the liaison officer over there, IQ in the range of Arnie Palmer's score for eighteen at Pebble Beach, who spent his day relaying messages from the pathologists who did not care to talk to anyone below the rank of deputy superintendent.

"Those legs you were concerned about, the ones with the toenails painted red, Medical Examiner says here they belonged to a Caucasian, approximately thirty-five years old, approximately five feet ten inches tall."

That was not Jo Kane, Morrison thought.

"And you're gonna love this. They matched up with a torso we got in spare parts. Torso came in three, four days ago wrapped in a plastic garbage bag. No head, no arms, though. Some guy found it in his garbage can in the Lincoln Park area. Torso still had on a pair of panties and a bra. But funny thing, inside the bra there weren't no tits. And inside the panties, guess what, there was a dick and a pair of balls—attached, I might add. How about that?"

That surely was not Jo Kane, Morrison thought.

33

THE TECHNICIAN from the crime lab was excited when he stuck his head in Morrison's cubicle. "Sorry we're a little late with this," he said regarding the report he dropped on Morrison's desk, "but you're going to like it."

Morrison looked like he had a desperate need for something to like.

"We got prints from the belt, clean as can be. It was vinyl, picks 'em up like a magnet. And we got another and a palm print from one of the shoes. And none of them are the victim's."

Morrison opened the top drawer of his desk and took out the file marked Theo Warner. "Run them by the three in here: Thomas Alvin Bates, Jo Kane, Manford White. How soon can you get back to me on those three?"

"How soon you want?"

"As quick as you can."

"Half-hour, say?"

"Terrific. Oh, and if you don't get a match from one of those three, see if you can come up with some prints on Dennis Courtland. There's sheets in here on him. See if the Bureau of Identification came up with anything on him yet. If not, send somebody out to Lutheran General and take his prints. Try not to upset the detox unit.'' He handed the Theo Warner file to the technician.

''Will do. Now on the other thing. We found no trace of drugs on any of his clothes. What we did find, though, were some beige carpet fibers on his overcoat and the front of his suitcoat and trousers, wool and flannel, real gatherers. The only way he'd pick those up in that quantity is if he took a dive on a carpet or, more likely, if somebody threw him or knocked him down.''

Morrison was thinking about the broken nose and the welts on Theo Warner's face.

''Well, there's no carpet in that drugstore. So this morning we went over to his apartment and sure enough he has this beige carpet in his living room. We took some samples and they match. And you asked about eyeglasses. Well, none were inventoried but when we were checking the carpet we found a couple of shards of glass and they check out to be from prescription eyeglasses, if that means anything.''

''It means that whoever whacked Theo Warner grabbed him at his apartment first. All along we were thinking he was hit at the store first, then whoever it was took his house keys and went over and ransacked his apartment. And you said he had the fibers on his overcoat, so that means whoever it was either was waiting for him at the apartment or followed him from the store. They apparently didn't get all they wanted so they took him back to the store.''

''Sounds logical to me,'' the technician said. He held the Theo Warner file in front of him. ''I better get hustling if you want a read on these three in a half-hour.''

Morrison sat there trying to figure if there was any significance to the reversal of the sequence of events. He could see the Uptown trio leaving the tavern and following Theo home, but why. Why not rob him right there instead of following him home and then bringing him back? He also wondered if Dennis Courtland really had spent all that time in the Belmont Hotel bar.

Didn't seem to change much, where Theo was hit on first, he thought. What mattered was somebody killed him.

TRUE TO his word, the technician got back to Morrison in a half-hour. "The prints do not match any of the three of your suspects," he said. "I'll get to work on this Courtland character. We're also running the prints through AFIS," AFIS being the acronym for Automated Fingerprint Identification System, the Chicago PD's own identification system. Should get a read on that by the end of the day."

The news did not make Morrison's day.

MORRISON PICKED up the phone and called the Town Hall district and got the tac squad lieutenant. He asked for somebody to pick up Vinny Salerno and bring him down to Morrison at 11th and State. No problem when he explained it had to do with the shooting of Detective Norbert Castor in their district the night before. He gave the lieutenant Vinny's address and said to check out the saloons in the immediate neighborhood if Vinny wasn't home. He was not a suspect, just a snitch, and therefore did not need to be handcuffed, Morrison added.

IT WAS nearly two-thirty when the tac detective ushered Vinny into OC.

"What the hell's this all about, Morrison?" Vinny said.

"I woke him up," the tac detective said.

"Yeah, second time today. What's with you guys?"

"Shut up and sit down, Vinny," Morrison said. He thanked the tac detective who nodded and left. Then back to Vinny: "I got something I want you to do."

"Like what?"

"You said you saw the gun that Bates was carrying."

Vinny's eyes were darting now from Morrison to other objects around the room, like he was cornered, looking for some place to run. "Yeah, I said that."

"Did you get a good look at it?"

"A glimpse." Vinny thought he knew where this was going and he did not want to go there.

"You think you could identify it if you saw one like it?"

Vinny shook his head. "Doubt it. I don't know much about guns. I told you that, Morrison. They're not part of my act."

"Vinny, I know you're not a toter, at least I never thought you were. But in the world where you dwell, Vinny, I'm sure you're not totally unfamiliar with them either. You said you thought it was an automatic. I want to take you upstairs to the gun room, show you some guns, and I want you to tell me the kind Tommy Bates was flashing."

Vinny thought, Jeez, what am I getting into. He wants me to mark the gun. Tie it to Tommy. Testify, maybe? Holy Christ. He saw Tommy, eyes bulging, then with that weird grin. "Sure, I'll take a look, but you gotta remember, Morrison, I wasn't that close when he started waving it around."

In the gun room up on the seventh floor Morrison had a variety of different handguns laid out on a table: .38 Smith&Wesson; .44; .45; .22 Rohn better known as a Saturday Night Special; .9-millimeter Beretta, pieces like that. "Any of these look like the one Tommy was carrying?"

Vinny looked at them for a few moments. "Naw, don't think so."

Morrison brought out a thick looseleaf binder, maybe a hundred plastic-covered pages in it, each with a black-and-white photo of a different handgun. "Sit down and look through these and see if you can pick one out."

When Vinny turned the last page, he shrugged. "Nothin', sorry."

"Vinny, why do I get the feeling you're not being straight with me?"

"I told ya, Morrison, I'd take a look. I don't see nothin' I could say for sure was the one Tommy had."

"Vinny, on the phone when you tipped me, you said you thought it was maybe an automatic."

"I didn't say it *was* one. I mean I haven't seen a whole helluva lot of guns. I saw a forty-five once, I see the kinda guns you coppers carry, that's all. I said it sorta looked like one. Maybe it was, maybe it wasn't."

"You see a forty-five on the table here?"

Vinny looked at the guns, then at Morrison. He pointed at the .45 automatic. "I think that's a forty-five, but I'm not sure." Then added quickly, "But that wasn't the one I saw."

Morrison, the frustration showing, grabbed the .9-millimeter Beretta. "Was this the gun, Vinny?" he said, almost shouting.

How the fuck did he know that? Vinny said to himself. "No, don't think so," he said, trying not to show the shock he felt. "Why? Is that the one he used to shoot your partner? You find the gun?"

"The bullets were shot from this type of gun, we believe. But we haven't found the gun . . . yet."

MORRISON LEFT Vinny sitting in the OC cubicle, then went to Tony Morano's office. "I need a bad guy," he said as he dropped into the chair in front of Morano's desk. "I've got this kid downstairs, snitch I've used before. Lives in Uptown. Knows Bates, the guy we feel sure shot Norbert. Knows the girl we're looking for in the Warner homicide. I think he knows her a lot more than he's letting on. I think he might even be protecting her, maybe in fact knows where she is. I also think he knows what kind of gun Bates was flashing in that saloon but isn't about to identify it for us because he's scared to death of getting involved. I've been the good guy with him. Hasn't done me any good. Maybe you got somebody around here could scare him about *not* getting involved."

Morano didn't hesitate. "Khatisian, works Vice out of the First downstairs, and his partner, Booker Bonds. They don't get any badder than them, this side of the Albanian secret police anyway.'' He reached for the telephone. ''Let me see if they're downstairs, they're on days this month.''

They were. Morrison's first impression of Petros Khatisian—better known as Pete-meat around One, a hulking Armenian with eight-ball eyes and unkempt bushy black hair—was that his first duty probably should have been to arrest himself. Booker Bonds, on the other hand, shorter, athletically slender with a hairless mahogany face, looked like he could still legitimately be playing guard for Marshall High School's basketball team. Lean and mean was the way he described himself.

Morrison explained the situation in detail, suggested they come down hard on Vinny Salerno. He mentioned that Vinny perhaps needed to be reminded what the penitentiary was like these days for young white boys. They said they would be happy to oblige. Morrison left to fetch Vinny.

When he brought him into the austere interrogation room down in One he said, ''Vinny, I'd like you to meet Officers Khatisian and Bonds. They would like to have a few words with you.''

BACK IN OC Morrison called Terry Sawyer to tell him that over at the Medical Examiner's office they had partially put together a jigsaw puzzle and it did not turn out to be Jo Kane, and to learn that in Six they had come up with nothing new. Nor had they at Town Hall district, he heard in his next call.

Sitting there, gazing absently out the window across State Street, Morrison thought about Norbert Castor lying over there alone in Ravenswood Hospital, trying to handle it. The dismal reality of the rest of his life had not sunk in yet, Morrison thought. But it would. He decided he would take one more crack at Tommy Bates.

TOMMY WAS sitting on the edge of the cot in the first of the six-by-eight-foot holding cells, lost in a morass of thought. Tommy did not even look over at Morrison standing there now looking into the cell at him. The lockup guard stood back, leaning up against the door, bored.

"Let me guess," Morrison said. "You're thinking about billowy clouds, orange-red sunsets, a house with a white picket fence, Aunt Emma's apple pie . . ."

Tommy turned slowly, coming out of his reverie. "Oh, fuck, it's you again."

"It is." Morrison grabbed the bars to the cell, looking between two of them.

Tommy grinned up at him. "You come mebbe to tell me your stupid shitass buddy done died of his wounds. That we all gonna have to go into mournin' for a cop who is dumb, dumb, dumb." Tommy's grin widened, waiting for an answer.

"He didn't die. And he isn't going to."

"Too bad. They tell you I'm walkin' outa here at five? They told me."

"Don't be too sure of that, asshole."

Tommy got up from the cot, stretched, then turned toward Morrison and grasped the bars just above the ones Morrison was holding, their faces about a foot apart now. "Be so nice it was just the two of us without these bars between us. One on one."

"You'd lose," Morrison said, looking up at those walleyes, knowing he would shoot him, the only way.

Tommy laughed.

It was such an insulting laugh. "I do believe you shot my partner," Morrison said.

"But you cain't prove it." The grin was back.

"And I do believe you robbed the Warner drugstore and killed the man who owned it."

"But you cain't prove it, and you ain't gonna ever." His expression didn't change.

"We're closing on you," Morrison said, eye-to-eye, but not believing a word of it. "Just so you know. The gun you flashed in the Tip Top Tap. We match it with the bullets we've got. We've got you."

"You don't got no gun you can put with me." Tommy laughed again. "You try all the tricks." But there was concern on his face, wondering where Morrison got a tie to the gun and the Tip Top, remembering, and worrying a little more. "What time is it anyway, gotta be near five o'clock?"

Morrison ignored the question. "Beretta, nine-millimeter," he said.

"That what your buddy took? Them suckers can do a lot of damage." He was grinning again. "Bounce around inside, tear the shit out of you. Bet he felt it. Bet he felt it *bad*."

Morrison threw the punch before he even knew what he was doing. Tommy just danced back, seeing it coming, giggled when he saw it glance off one of the bars and Morrison wince in pain.

The lockup guard, suddenly awakened from whatever daydream he had drifted into, rushed over to pull Morrison away from the cell. "Cheez, come on. You want all our asses in a bag?"

Morrison shook him off, stepped back to the cell, holding his painful knuckled right hand in the other. He was about to say something but before he could Tommy, standing a few feet back, said stone-cold, "You know, Joe Morrison, that's what they told me you had for a name, these ain't good times." He let the pause linger, settle, before dropping it. "They just don't make doors like they used to." Shook his head. "Used to be they made 'em thick, strong, oak. But these ones today. *Lordy*, they don't stop *nothin'*."

That was the trip-cord.

DOWNSTAIRS IN OC, Morrison called Town Hall. Still nothing. He called Terry Sawyer. Nothing there either. He got the ASA, told him about the conversation:

That the animal all but admitted he shot Norbert Castor. That he let on he knew about Norbert being shot through the door. The only way he could possibly know it was by being on the other side of it.

Pleading now, which evoked from the ASA: Get something. You've still got nothing. Five o'clock. Still stands.

It was now three-thirty.

Morrison knew what time it was. Knew that the system, as good as it could be, was not going to work for him . . . in this one. Thought again about Norbert Castor . . . Theo Warner.

Saw in his mind's eye a snarling, salivating Doberman pinscher. Then he picked up the telephone.

"Terry," he said to Sawyer when he got through to him over at Six, "you get anything at all this afternoon be sure to call me. The animal walks out of here at five if we don't come up with something before. And I want you to do me a favor."

"Name it. Unless it's kinky."

"If you don't hear different from me again this afternoon, I want you to call me here at four-thirty. Just call and when I answer hang up."

"Mind if I ask why?"

"You don't want to know."

IN THE hallway outside the District One interrogation room, Petros Khatisian told Morrison what the bad guys had gotten from Vinny. No more than the good guy.

"He doesn't know where she is, I'm pretty sure," Khatisian said. "We worked him over best we could without beatin' the crap out of him. We could still do that, you want, but I don't think he got anything to give us. My gut feeling."

Morrison shook his head. "Threaten the crap out of him, no more than that."

"We already done that. I even told him I was thinking of puttin' him in the lockup on the eleventh floor in the cell next to his buddy. Let his buddy figure out why he was down here. Could tell that really got to him but we still got nothin' from him." Khatisian shrugged. "Sorry."

"Okay, but keep him down here till about four-twenty. Then bring him back to me in OC."

So much for the Albanian secret police, Morrison thought as he rode the elevator back up to three, OC.

AT PRECISELY 4:20 P.M. Khatisian appeared in the doorway to Morrison's cubicle, Vinny in tow, now handcuffed, his expression a combination of fright and Italian outrage. "Here's your boy," Khatisian said, and pushed Vinny into the room. Behind Vinny, he just threw his arms out, palms turned upward, signaling he had nothing.

Vinny looked back at the menacing bear of a man who had worked on him downstairs and manhandled him all the way upstairs, then over at Morrison. "What is this," he said, but there was a meekness in his voice. "Cuffed. Hey, and downstairs, the shit . . ."

"Relax, Vinny," Morrison said.

Khatisian uncuffed him. "He's all yours," he said before leaving.

Vinny sat cornerwise at the desk from Morrison, his hands free now but far from steady.

"Vinny, I want you to understand my feelings in this whole thing," Morrison said quietly, the good guy coming back. "The guy upstairs—your buddy, Tommy Bates—I'm sure is the one who shot my partner, crippled him for life. I'm reasonably sure he was involved in the robbery and murder at Warner's drugstore. And I know he's involved in several other major crimes. We just don't have enough to keep him. He's out of here at five today we don't come up with something. The something I need is that girl."

"Jeez, Morrison, I told you a hundred times, I told those goons downstairs, I honest to Christ do not know where she is. I think she's probably dead and ground up into a glop in some garbage dump."

"If she isn't, we could probably turn her, give her a deal if she gives us Bates."

"What can I tell you?"

"You can tell me if you've got anything I can use to keep him locked up. Anything."

"I would if I could, Morrison."

"You positive?" Morrison's eyes bored into Vinny's.

"Sorry."

Morrison kept staring at him in the silence, finally decided he believed him. When the phone rang, Morrison let it ring, his eyes still focused on Vinny.

"You ain't gonna answer your phone?" Vinny finally said.

Morrison looked away from him and picked up the receiver. "Morrison," he said, and heard the click at the other end, waited, then said, "No, we haven't got anything more. Look, give us some more time. You're the State's Attorney's office, you're the only ones who can. We can't let that guy walk out of here. If he does he's gone for good." Morrison paused, listening to the silence at the other end, looking frustrated, aggravated. "Listen, I admit I don't know if we'll ever find the girl or the gun he used to shoot Castor, but maybe on the other thing, the Facia rape case, maybe . . ." Morrison suddenly cupped his hand over the mouthpiece, looked over at Vinny and said to him, "Wait outside there until I'm done."

Vinny got up and stepped outside the cubicle where he could hear Morrison almost as plainly as when he was sitting inside it.

"Give me another twenty-four hours," Morrison said. "Maybe I can talk Rudy Facia into letting his daughter press charges. I mean, for God's sake, we *know* him and that dope dealer White, the one that got himself killed, raped the girl. Jesus, we found her wallet on Bates. C'mon just another twenty-four hours." Morrison paused again. "I know it's not likely, but give me one more shot at Facia." Another pause. "So he walks out of here at five." Then angrily, "Thanks a helluva lot," and slammed the receiver down.

Morrison stepped out into the squadroom to find a wide-eyed Vinny standing there next to the door. He thought he could even hear Vinny's heart thumping away. He's all yours, Vinny, Morrison said to himself as he took Vinny by the arm and started walking him toward the elevator bank. "Well, your buddy'll be back on the street tonight," shaking his head in disgust. In front of the elevators now: "You hear anything at all on that girl, you call me, right?"

"I hear a word, you got it, Morrison."

"Be careful out there, Vinny," Morrison said as Vinny stepped into the elevator.

Morrison walked back to the OC cubicle and over to the window and gazed out. It was still daylight but the moon was up already, almost full, a mottled, whitish ball against the gray sky. It looked like it might snow again. Morrison looked down on State Street just in time to see Vinny dodging through the traffic, running to the telephone booth outside the entrance to the subway station. He watched as Vinny fumbled in his pocket for a quarter. He watched as Vinny talked animatedly on the phone, his free hand moving like he was conducting an orchestra. He watched Vinny hang up and vanish into the subway.

34

MORRISON, FEELING the emptiness in his stomach from a variety of things, one of which happened to be that he had not stopped for lunch that day, decided to go over to Dottie's and get a sandwich.

Sitting at the counter there, eating his hot pastrami on rye, he could not help but think of Norbert Castor and how many meals the man must have had here over the last ten years. Probably should own the place with the amount he slapped across the counter all those years. He thought about whether to tell Norbert about Tommy Bates, but realized he could not. There were some things a cop cannot share, not even with his partner, not even if he did it for his partner.

ABOUT NINE miles west and maybe three north of Dottie's, Rudy Facia was also in a restaurant, in his corner booth at Allegorio's, talking with three of his compatriots, an expensive bottle of Barolo on the table next to a platter of antipasto and a bowl of peeled shrimp. Snacktime. They seemed to be having a good time telling stories, bullshitting. No business talk, though. Allegorio's was his club, not his office. His office was anywhere that he was certain his business could not be overheard. He knew only too well how the G had managed to get into Pete Fish's restaurant downtown some years back and bug the entire private room on the third floor where no one ate unless he was a made guy. Five guys went to Leavenworth, the result of that one. He knew you never conducted business in a place you were known to frequent.

Facia was telling a story about one of their buddies who was having some trouble with his girlfriend when Moretti, one of his soldiers, walked in and approached the booth, standing off a bit, knowing you didn't interrupt. "Complainin' he's not givin' her enough dough," Facia said. "He's got her set up in an apartment, gives her whatever she wants, can you imagine. Freddie hasn't got enough problems with a wife and four kids, two in Cat'lic schools. But she calls him up, says she needs more. She says she worries about the dough so much she can't sleep at night. He tells her, *Madre mia,* that's terrible. He'll take care of her the next day. So he goes over there the next day, screws the socks off her all afternoon and when he leaves gives her cheek a little tweak and hands her a thick envelope. She's gushin' all over him. After he leaves, she opens it and inside's four sleeping pills wrapped in toilet paper."

When the laughter subsided, Moretti stepped up, nodded to Facia, then to the others, and said softly, "Rudy, I got something for you."

Facia took a gulp of the ruby-colored wine, held the glass in front of him. "Important enough to take me away from this?"

Moretti just nodded.

" 'Scuse me," Facia said to the others, one of whom slid out of the booth so Facia could get out. When he stood, he waved at the heavy-set, olive-skinned young man sitting across the way at the bar with a Coke in front of him, who got up instantly and disappeared into the coatroom. A moment later he was back with Rudy Facia's overcoat and his own.

The bodyguard went outside first, about ten seconds

later reopened the door and held it for Facia and his soldier. The two walked about halfway down the block, the bodyguard a few steps behind. To get out of the cold, Facia stepped into the doorway of a flower shop whose windows were totally steamed over from the humidity in the store but he did not go inside. The bodyguard stayed out on the sidewalk. "So what you got?" Rudy said.

"I got a make on one of the guys hurt your daughter."

Facia's eyes flashed.

"I got a name. I got a description. An address where he's livin' and the joint he hangs out in."

"Where'd you get this?"

"A so-so source, you don't know him. But he got it from downtown, 11th and State. He says the guy had your daughter's wallet on him. They got him down there for something else, but he's walkin' "—Moretti looked at his wristwatch—"in about ten minutes, the way I hear it."

They walked quickly back to Allegorio's. Facia strode to the booth, gestured with his head and the three scrambled out of it and went for their coats.

MORRISON WENT back to OC, checked to see if Thomas Alvin Bates had been released. He had. The formal fingerprint report—in a manila envelope with just the CPD return address in the corner and Morrison's name scrawled across the front—was sitting on top of the thick Theo Warner file in the middle of his desk. He sat down to read it. When he had finished he felt sick to his stomach. He opened the Warner file, started at page one.

By the time he was done reading, digesting, it was nearly eight o'clock. Too late to go visit Norbert. He thought about calling Linda Tate, those sculptured legs, those special hazel eyes, maybe go over there, remember to go slower this time, but he didn't really feel like it, not now.

So he drove over to Flannery's, sat at the bar with a

noisy group of colleagues, ordered a schnapps, listened to the stories going back and forth, sex and mayhem, what somebody did, what somebody didn't do. His mind trailed to Sally Spermatozoa, to Timmy Blake, the hole in his foot. Some things never change, he thought to himself.

WARREN LOOKED surprised when Tommy walked in the Tip Top at about six o'clock. It was surely not Happy Hour. Quiet Time, maybe. There were only three people at the bar and a couple at one of the tables up front. Cocktail hour as such was not big in Uptown. Ten to two in the morning, that was a different story.

Tommy said hello to Warren and then walked to the far end of the bar, sat down on the last stool, the television perched in a corner above blaring out a rerun of "Night Court" that no one at the other end of the bar was watching. Warren followed him.

"Got yourself out, huh?" Warren said.

"They ain't got nothin' to keep me. Gimme a double Early."

Warren poured it into a shot glass that looked like a paperweight. "Thought they might keep ya longer."

Tommy shrugged. "Assholes. Another." He pushed the shot glass back across the bar. "And somethin' to wash it with."

Warren refilled it and drew a glass of beer from the tap. "They been here three times today," Warren said, his tone hushed. "Twice upstairs and once since I came on here at three." Tommy just looked at him. Warren broke into a big smile. "Told 'em the same thing each time. They been botherin' Faith too, but she's true-blue, Tommy. No worry there."

"They got me with the piece in here. Any idea how they got that?"

"Sure as hell don't. They was how many people in here when you showed the damn thing, besides the little guy?

Fifteen, twenty? Could be any one-a 'em. But no matter. It's gone."

"It's the one thing could gimme some trouble."

Warren's face blossomed again. "Won't, my buddy. Warren took good care of that for you." Then, leaning across the bar, quietly said, "Buried. Nobody's ever goin' to see that bugger again." Warren straightened up. "And you're welcome."

"And the other?"

"Stashed." Warren was leaning across the bar again. "We gotta let that sit for a while, Tommy. Too much heat right now to try to move anythin' like that."

Tommy nodded. "Too much heat for a lot of things."

"I don't wanna go shoppin' that with Mr. Blue becomin' a reg'lar customer, not that I'd be shoppin' it around here, but still . . ."

"Ah'm outa here tomorrow, Warren. Gonna have a few more here tonight, go over catch a couple a winks, and dis-a-peer." He drained the shot and slid it toward Warren. "Leastways for a while, till things get a little less uptight round this place."

"Good thinkin', Tommy."

"But I'll be comin' back for my half. Don't know when, but I will."

"It'll be here." Warren was beaming again. "Money or horse, your half."

"It better be."

Warren felt it was time to go tend to his few other customers at the other end of the bar.

The Tip Top began to fill up around seven-thirty. When Tommy decided to leave about an hour later there were some twenty people at the bar and the little tables up near the door. He got a pint of Early Times from Warren to take with him back to the apartment, put on his Eddie Bauer jacket and, brown paper bag in hand, headed out into the cold. He paused outside under the light that illuminated the sign Tip Top Tap hanging above the entrance to zip up his jacket. He hated the cold. It was never like this in Georgia, he thought as, hunched over, he walked east on Montrose.

Tommy had not noticed the two men sitting at one of the little tables up front who got up as he passed through the door. They left too, walking east. One of them raised his arm, looking across Montrose, and a car's headlights came on before it slowly pulled out into traffic.

Tommy turned north on Hazel Street for the two-block walk to Sunnyside and the warmth of the Tudor Arms. The car passed him, then turned left, disappearing into the alley down the street. Head down, Tommy didn't notice it, more concerned about the cold wind that was blasting into his face, into the faces of the two other men from the Tip Top who had also turned north on Hazel.

IT WAS close to midnight when Morrison let himself into the bungalow that he was soon to abandon. No light was left on for him. He made his way to the kitchen, turning on light after light in his wake, not lurching but not walking the rail either. He looked in the refrigerator, took out a carton of orange juice and poured himself a large glass, thinking the vitamin C would help him in the morning, that and three Extra Strength Tylenol, which he was gulping down when his wife appeared in the doorway.

"What're you doing up at this hour?" he said.

"It's hard to sleep when your friends keep calling every hour. Terry Sawyer wants you. He said it was important, to call him no matter the time. I told him I'd give you the message but you were rarely around here these days."

"Do you know my partner Norb got shot?"

She seemed a little unnerved. "No."

"Last night. You don't watch the news anymore?"

"Are you drunk?"

"Half-drunk. You even care he got shot?"

"I'm sorry," she said, and turned and walked out of the kitchen.

A moment later she was back, an envelope in her hand. "You want to know if he's dead, or what?"

"I hope he's not."

"He's not."

She handed him the envelope. "Here's the papers. See you in court next week." She turned and walked back out.

He threw the envelope on the kitchen table. Goddamn, he thought, I bet I blew that apartment in Rogers Park. Then he got up and grabbed the wall phone and dialed Terry Sawyer's home number.

"Where you been?" a groggy Sawyer said.

"Out trying to rid this city of schnapps and beer."

"Sounds like you maybe succeeded."

"Almost."

"I been trying to get you since about nine. We got the girl. Jo Kane." Morrison began sobering fast. "Picked her up in the Greyhound bus station about eight o'clock. Undercover, a decoy there, thought she looked like the girl in the *Daily Bulletin*, followed her into the women's can. When Kane lit up a joint in one of the stalls she busted her. Had a one-way ticket to St. Louis in her purse and a bunch of bottles of pills in her suitcase from, you guessed it, Warner's Discount Drugs. They called me at home here once they got a positive ident on her."

Morrison let out an audible sigh. "She talking?"

"Yep. Only problem is she was pretty high. They were going to let her come down a little before taking a full statement."

"Where is she now?"

"Down at the First District. She said it was the three of them, Bates, White, and her. She's scared Bates is going to kill her, she said."

She's perceptive, Morrison thought.

"We got an APB out on Bates, and a stake-out of that

apartment over in Uptown. As of about an hour ago he hadn't shown up. All his stuff's there though. So he should be showing up sometime soon."

I wouldn't count on it, Morrison said to himself.

"You want any more on it you can get hold of Jim Panelli, VC at the First, he's the one I been talking to."

"I'll wait till morning. I want to talk to her myself."

After he hung up Morrison felt suddenly drained, exhausted. He turned out the lights, went to bed, but as tired as he felt he could not go to sleep, simply lay there thinking about the day that had just passed, the night, what he did for a living, Norbert Castor and his wheelchair mired in the sand in Florida, Rudy Facia's dim daughter, Rudy Facia himself in his tasteless resplendence, Theo Warner gulping water instead of air and wondering why his life was coming to an end in such a bizarre ill-deserved way . . . He tried to think of Linda Tate but couldn't focus. He waited it out in the darkness and the loneliness of his room. Finally, mercifully, he dropped off into a deep, dreamless sleep.

IN THE morning, early, driving under a cement sky, listening to the beater make strange noises, knowing spring was nowhere near, Morrison kept seeing the sign in Dennis Courtland's room: One Day at a Time.

He stopped by Ravenswood Hospital on his way to 11th and State. It was busy there at eight in the morning. Castor had been moved to a private room. He was still pretty well doped up, quieter, things beginning to come into awful perspective. But he was glad to see Morrison.

Morrison told him about Johnny Jonnell and his pal named Harper. Norbert told him where he could find the sheets on Jonnell and Rose Shaman. Left it in Morrison's hands. They did not discuss the details. Norbert was not up to it, and he told Morrison he knew he would do the right thing. Morrison wasn't so sure.

Morrison told him they had a wrap on the Theo Warner case, gave him most of the details.

Norbert said a lot of things seemed to have come down since he got blown out of the picture, that was the way he put it.

Morrison did not bring up Thomas Alvin Bates. Begged off, had to get downtown. He told Castor to hang in there, told him he'd stop back later, had a few things to do that morning, and was gone.

MORRISON TALKED with Jo Kane in the interrogation room in the First District. She was down now, withdrawal would probably come next. The girl looked pretty much the way Morrison thought she would: street-worn, no trust in those eyes. Tommy Bates, still missing in action, was on her mind. She was resigned now, even cooperative, told Morrison what he wanted to know. She was on her way to the Women's Correctional Facility in Dwight, Illinois, for a relatively lengthy stay, Morrison thought as he walked out of 11th and State.

35

DRIVING SOUTH on Halsted, Morrison reached the stoplight at Belmont, which had just turned red, and wheeled a U-turn across the intersection. It would have been a tire-squealer if the street had not become a linoleum of impacted snow and ice. He did it to the accompaniment of a blaring horn and some unintelligible cursing from the driver of a BMW under the impression he had the right of way crossing Halsted Street on a green light. The shouting, which couldn't be heard through the closed windows of the car anyway, and the horn-blasting stopped when he saw Morrison peel into the No Parking space in front of Warner's Discount Drugs, facing the wrong way, the driver now figuring the only one to pull off a maneuver like that was either a cop or else somebody he definitely would be better off not calling an asshole.

Morrison walked into the store, said hello to Miss Weisenhurst, who smiled in return but was not in the least distracted from raking product after product across the computer screener on the counter and dropping each item into a plastic bag as some cartoon voice squawked the name of the product and the price from somewhere inside the cash register.

''Bruce in?'' he asked the young pharmacist at the back counter, who recognized Morrison immediately.

"In there, sergeant," gesturing with his head toward the backroom.

Bruce, at the aluminum worktable mixing some white powder with some chunkier beige powder, looked up when he heard Morrison step into the room. "Oh, Joseph, how are you?" He stood up. "Here let me take your coat," which Morrison was unbuttoning.

"No, that's okay. I'm not going to be here that long."

"A trench coat, Joseph. In this weather?"

"It's got a lining, Bruce."

"Well, I hope so. This is about the worst winter I can remember."

Morrison nodded. "Can't disagree with that," and sat down in an empty chair at the table, crossing his legs.

Bruce sat down across from him and pushed the powder mixture to the side and rested his elbows on the table. "Anything new on the case?"

"A lot. We picked up one of them last night, the girl."

"Wonderful."

"She still had some of the drugs she took from here." Morrison paused, then added, almost as an aside, "She told us what happened."

Bruce leaned closer across the table, his eyeglasses sliding a little down his nose. "She confessed?"

"She admitted it. She and her two boyfriends pulled it off. Bates and White. White's dead, of course. And we've got an APB out on the animal." For all that was worth, Morrison thought.

"Well, that's great. Theo always said you were a good cop, Joseph. You did it."

"I didn't bring her in. They caught her in the bus station trying to leave town. I just talked to her this morning, got some details I wanted, that's all." Morrison's fingers drummed a little staccato on the table. He shook his head. "Said they followed Theo home, ripped off the apartment and when they didn't find enough money there brought him back here—about eight-thirty or nine, must have been." Morrison paused. "We thought all along they grabbed him here, then just took the keys and went to the apartment. Sure would've been smarter that way rather than parading him through the streets. Shows you just never know."

"Why did they kill him?"

Morrison shook his head. "She claims *she* didn't. She stayed in the car. Bates and White took him into the store."

"I can see why she doesn't want to own up to it. Murder, after all."

"I believe her." Morrison started the staccato again with his fingers on the table but did not say anything, just shrugged and let the silence carry on. Then, he asked, "Why'd you do it, Bruce?"

"What?" Bruce Warner suddenly sat upright, his elbows jerking back, leaving his fingertips on the edge of the table as if he were playing a piano. His expression one of mystification mixed with hurt. "What're you talking about, Joseph?"

"Why did you do it, Bruce?" Morrison moved his head slowly, not so much in disbelief, as in disgust.

"Joseph!"

"Stow it, Bruce." Morrison reached inside his suitcoat pocket and pulled out an 8–by–10 manila envelope folded in half. Morrison squeezed the metal wings and opened it, drawing out three stapled pages. He placed them in front of Bruce Warner. "It's a match, Bruce. A perfect match."

Bruce started to say something but Morrison waved him off. "We found three full fingerprints and a partial on the back of Theo's belt." Morrison flipped the first page over, the one with Identification's analysis typed on it. The second sheet was a Xerox of those fingerprints and a palm print. "And another fingerprint was on the shoe and a clear palm print, heel of the palm, was on the sole of the same shoe. They weren't Theo's prints, Bruce." Then he flipped to the last sheet, a full set of finger and palm prints. "They match these.'' Morrison pointed to the prints on the third page.

''When they didn't match the girl's and her two pals', we ran them through AFIS—AFIS had the elimination prints we took. Elimination prints, remember when they took them? You and everybody who worked in the store, so that they could eliminate any of those prints they found back here. Well, that's what these are,'' pointing again at the third page, ''one of the sets of the elimination prints. Yours, Bruce.''

''Now wait a minute, Joseph.'' Bruce Warner's eyes were nervous and darting, like a chipmunk just out of his hole taking in a hostile world.

''Bruce, you want to know how I read it?'' He did not wait for Bruce to answer. ''I know you and Theo had this little thing going here. Speedballs for special customers, or at least one.'' Bruce looked as if he was going to protest, but Morrison went on. ''Dennis Courtland, for example. He's in a rehab program out at Lutheran General, detoxing. He told me all about it. Your logs tallied, but you deal in a good amount of morphine and pharmaceutical coke because you supply clinics and nursing homes in the neighborhood here. I know the deal. You short them—the prescription calls for a gram of morphine, it gets half that, you keep the other half; it adds up. You get enough to make some high-quality speedballs and your logs tally in case anybody looks at them. Not a big operation, but enough to provide a nice little tax-free side income. Courtland told us he's been getting them here for four, five years now.''

Bruce was nodding his head sadly. ''We did, Joseph, provide some of that to him. We certainly shouldn't have, but we did. But killing Theo? Joseph. No. *No*.''

Morrison ignored him. ''Last night I went back through all our reports, looking at them from a different angle now that I knew your prints were on the belt and shoe. And then I saw it. Among the drugs they found in Manford White's apartment, along with those immediately traceable to here, was some high-quality morphine and pharmaceutical coke. He wouldn't have gotten them on the street or from his ordinary channels, I realized. He would have gotten them here. But on the inventory of missing drugs there wasn't any coke or morphine, they never even got into your pantry back there. So where did they get it?"

Morrison pointed at the aluminum table. "They got it from right here, Bruce. You came over here to make up the speedballs for Courtland. Got interrupted when they brought Theo back. You managed to hide but didn't have time to scoop up the stuff. The girl told me this morning her pals told her the stuff was just sitting out there on a table."

Bruce's look of persecution was fading. "The way I see it, when they left, you came out of wherever you were hiding . . ." Morrison stood up, bent over and pretended with his right hand to be gripping a body by the back of the belt, his left hand going out as if grasping the invisible body at the back of the collar. "You grabbed him like this. Oomph, over and in," he said as he mimed dumping a body over the lip of the barrel.

Now Bruce winced.

Morrison walked back to the table, leaned over it, his hands on either side, gripping it, staring down Bruce. "Probably gave him a little extra push, how you got your prints on his shoe." Morrison took a deep breath. "How could you do it, Bruce, your own brother, for chrissake?"

"We were only half-brothers . . ."

"Still, Jesus, you grew up together, were in business here, how long? Thirty years?"

"We were never very close . . ."

"I've got you, Bruce. You understand that, don't you?" Bruce said nothing. "But I still don't know why."

"The store," Bruce finally said. "He was selling his half. We had a deal. If one of us died, the other got his half. In our wills. When those terrible people left, he was half-dead anyway. The store's worth a lot of money. My life. What more can I tell you, Joseph . . . ?''

Morrison stood up. "Let's just say I read you your rights, Bruce, okay? They'll read them to you again over at Six. Stand up.'' Morrison pulled the handcuffs from the back of his pants.

"Oh, no, Joseph. You don't have to do that. Don't take me out of here like that, in front of everybody.''

Morrison handed Bruce his overcoat and waited as he put it on, then he turned him around and flipped a cuff over one wrist.

"Joseph. Let me just walk out of here. I'll go quietly with you. Please don't embarrass me.''

"I have to.''

"How long have I known you, Joseph? Practically all your life.''

"How long did you know your brother . . . half-brother?''

They walked out into the store, down the long center aisle past dozens of customers, only a few of whom noticed Morrison with his hand on Bruce's arm leading him, his hands cuffed behind him. A suddenly wide-eyed Miss Weisenhurst gathered in the scene and a small gasp escaped from her as they passed. Bruce Warner averted his eyes from hers and Morrison ignored her.

Outside it had begun to snow again, shards of sleety snow this time driven by the wind. Morrison opened the back door of the unmarked squad car and guided Bruce in, closing the door and walking around to the driver's side.

The icy snow was adding a veneer of white to the grimy snow and slush that had been on the ground for several weeks now. As he opened the car door, Morrison became aware of the grate of snowshovels against the sidewalk as merchants tried to clear the walks in front of their stores, the rasp of steel against concrete blending into the shrill, discordant symphony of the street.

Can't do much about it, the snow, Morrison thought as he lowered himself into the driver's seat. Keep up with it, maybe, that's about all you can do.

ABOUT THE AUTHOR

RICHARD WHITTINGHAM, a native Chicagoan, is also an established sports writer and the author of *Joe D.: On the Street with a Chicago Homicide Cop*. *State Street* is his first novel. He currently makes his home in Wilmette, Illinois.